Her Greatest Fantasy

Mustering her courage, she stepped to rap on the door just as it flung open. A man bolted out and knocked right into her. His hands grabbed her upper arms to steady her. She met his eyes, and the breath was stolen from her lungs.

He was tall, broad, tanned. And as dangerously handsome as any rogue she'd conjured for herself in the past twenty-four hours. His features were masculine, with a strong nose, full mouth, and an unruly thatch of dark brown hair. She stared at his pale blue eyes, willing them to twinkle.

Aidan? She opened her mouth to ask, but all that came out was a squeak.

Straightening his arms, he placed her away from him. "Who are you?" His voice was gruff and as rich as island rum.

She hiccuped in a breath. "I . . . I . . . I'm—"

He gave her a brusque nod and stormed from the castle and out of view.

She swallowed hard, her arms tingling where he'd touched her.

Praise fo

Dev

"You will not forget Cormac and Marjorie, two valiant, passionate lovers who belong together for all time."
—Catherine Coulter

"Their passion flames off the page and delivers the best first-kiss scene I've read in years." —*The Season* (Top Pick)

"Cormac is one lusty Scotsman . . . The sexual tension is hot and very sexy." —*Romance Reviews Today*

continued . . .

Lord of the Highlands

"Wolff delivers a humorous and sexy love story that pits a very modern heroine against a macho Scotsman in a delightful game of cat and mouse. Wolff charms with her characters and her personal take on the time-space continuum."
—*Romantic Times* (4 stars)

Warrior of the Highlands

"Passionate and magical." —*Publishers Weekly*

"A rich, beautifully written love story that will haunt your heart long after you turn the last page."
—Penelope Williamson

Sword of the Highlands

"Entrancing, luminous, and powerful . . . Heroes you never want to let go."
—Monica McCarty, national bestselling author

"A passionate tale . . . Very entertaining."
—*Night Owl Romance*

"A delightful time travel . . . refreshing and intriguing."
—*The Romance Readers Connection*

Master of the Highlands

Berkley Sensation titles by Veronica Wolff

MASTER OF THE HIGHLANDS
SWORD OF THE HIGHLANDS
WARRIOR OF THE HIGHLANDS
LORD OF THE HIGHLANDS
DEVIL'S HIGHLANDER
DEVIL'S OWN

DEVIL'S OWN

Veronica Wolff

BERKLEY SENSATION, NEW YORK

THE BERKLEY PUBLISHING GROUP
Published by the Penguin Group
Penguin Group (USA) Inc.
375 Hudson Street, New York, New York 10014, USA

Penguin Group (Canada), 90 Eglinton Avenue East, Suite 700, Toronto, Ontario M4P 2Y3, Canada
(a division of Pearson Penguin Canada Inc.)
Penguin Books Ltd., 80 Strand, London WC2R 0RL, England
Penguin Group Ireland, 25 St. Stephen's Green, Dublin 2, Ireland (a division of Penguin Books Ltd.)
Penguin Group (Australia), 250 Camberwell Road, Camberwell, Victoria 3124, Australia
(a division of Pearson Australia Group Pty. Ltd.)
Penguin Books India Pvt. Ltd., 11 Community Centre, Panchsheel Park, New Delhi—110 017, India
Penguin Group (NZ), 67 Apollo Drive, Rosedale, North Shore 0632, New Zealand
(a division of Pearson New Zealand Ltd.)
Penguin Books (South Africa) (Pty.) Ltd., 24 Sturdee Avenue, Rosebank, Johannesburg 2196,
South Africa

Penguin Books Ltd., Registered Offices: 80 Strand, London WC2R 0RL, England

This is a work of fiction. Names, characters, places, and incidents either are the product of the author's imagination or are used fictitiously, and any resemblance to actual persons, living or dead, business establishments, events, or locales is entirely coincidental. The publisher does not have any control over and does not assume any responsibility for author or third-party websites or their content.

DEVIL'S OWN

A Berkley Sensation Book / published by arrangement with the author

PRINTING HISTORY
Berkley Sensation mass-market paperback edition / March 2011

Copyright © 2011 by Veronica Wolff.
Cover design by George Long.
Cover illustration by Phil Heffernan.
Cover photograph of Celtic cross-sword tattoo © Shutterstock.
Handlettering by Ron Zinn.
Interior text design by Laura K. Corless.

ISBN: 978-0-425-24018-2

BERKLEY® SENSATION
Berkley Sensation Books are published by The Berkley Publishing Group,
a division of Penguin Group (USA) Inc.,
375 Hudson Street, New York, New York 10014.
BERKLEY® SENSATION and the "B" design are trademarks of Penguin Group (USA) Inc.

PRINTED IN THE UNITED STATES OF AMERICA

10 9 8 7 6 5 4 3 2 1

For my dear friend, Amalia,
who is a more patient teacher than even
the most bookish of heroines.

That all masterful and strong beggars found . . . may be taken by any man, and, being brought to any sheriff, bailie of regality or burgh, and getting them declared masterful beggars, may set his burning iron upon them and retain them as slaves; and, if any of them thereafter escape, the owner may have restitution of them as of other goods.

—ACTS OF CONVENTION, JUNE 7, 1605, EDINBURGH

Prologue

Aberdeen, Spring 1647

Ten-year-old Aidan glared from his twin brother to their playmate, Marjorie. The two of them were ganging up on him. Again. "Not the fire," he said.

"Aye, the fire." Cormac linked arms with Marjorie, glaring defiantly. "Marjorie wants to."

"But we always play the Ogilvy fire."

"I'll have your head," his twin shouted, ignoring him. "I will claim my revenge!"

Aidan narrowed his eyes. Lately, when Marjorie was around, Cormac dove heart and soul into their playacting. And somehow Aidan always ended up cast as the bad guy. "Why do I have to be Campbell again?"

Marjorie stepped forward to peer at his face. "Because your nose is bigger than Cormac's."

Aidan wanted to punch that nose. "But we're twins."

Cormac shrugged. "It's not my fault we don't look alike."

"I always play the cursed Campbell."

Cormac paid no attention. Instead, he spun and grabbed Marjorie's hand. "Revenge shall be mine, I say! Fear not, Lady Ogilvy, I'll save you from the blaze!"

Aidan threw his wooden sword to the ground. The two of them were annoying him more than usual, and he refused to play along. "Why do *you* always get to save Marjorie?"

Marjorie picked up his sword, thrusting it back to him hilt first. "That's just how we play it, Aidan."

Marjorie and Cormac looked at each other, all treacly-eyed. It made Aidan want to sick up.

She sauntered to the window, swaying her hips as though she were a real woman. Cormac followed right behind, like a starved pup. She stared out, while Cormac just stared at her shoulders. "You boys should climb the chimney," she said, "like the sweeps."

Aidan scowled at her. Fancy girls like Marj always thought they'd the right to boss menfolk around. And at ten, he and Cormac were definitely almost men. "You mean up *in* the chimney? I'm not climbing your uncle's stinking chimney."

His brother swung around, aiming his sword at Aidan's chest. "You'll not speak so to the lady."

Cormac was so much more fun when Marjorie wasn't around. Aidan wanted to stick out his tongue, but knew it wasn't something an almost-man would do.

"Those boys do it," she said, pointing out the window.

Aidan shook his head. "*You* climb the chimney."

"I'll do no such thing." She pulled her shoulders back, making like she was the Queen of England. "I shall wait here for my rescue."

"Aidan." Cormac gave him a pleading look. "Mum will be back soon. And soon we'll be gone from Aberdeen, and then it's back to home. Don't be so contrary."

Wretched. His brother was in love, and it was wretched.

He strode to the window. A cartload of chimney boys were filing into the neighboring town house. They were a ragtag bunch, younger than he, covered in soot and tar. It occurred to him how to get Marjie back. "She's afraid. I should've known a lass would be afraid."

"Och, she's not afraid, Aidan. As I recall, she climbed higher than you last time."

Aidan crossed his arms. Of *course* Cormac would leap to her aid. "That was a tree, not up into some stinkin' chimney."

"And I could've gone higher if I'd wanted."

Sure she could have. He crossed his arms, looking skeptical.

"It's just that I tore my dress last time." She and Cormac flashed looks at each other.

Aidan thought he might gag. Rich girls like her always got whatever they wanted, no matter the price. "Your family has enough money to buy you twenty new dresses. Your mum is with our mum right now, buying you even more."

"Leave it," Cormac said. "Her family has money, but not so much that she can go about mussing her gowns."

Aidan stared at his brother. *Gowns?* He'd never heard him talk like that before. It was like Cormac had been taken by a spell.

"All right, then. We shall *all* climb the stinking chimney." Marjorie tilted her chin up, like they were her unruly servants. Girls like her always thought they were better than everyone. "I dare you. Whoever climbs fastest wins. Unless it's you *boys* who are afraid."

His fool of a brother bristled. "I'm not afraid." Cormac went to peer up into the chimney. "I fear nothing."

Aidan sneered. Marjie might be able to make Cormac do her bidding, but *he'd* have no part. "*You* climb it, then, if you're so keen to."

His brother climbed onto the grate and stood up. His head and shoulders disappeared from view.

"Cormac!" Marjorie gasped like a maiden in a fairy tale. "You're truly going to climb it?"

One would think Cormac had agreed to slay a dragon. The whole business was foolish. "*I'm* not climbing it," Aidan said to nobody in particular.

"Hurry now. We've not much time before the sweeps come to Uncle's house." Marjorie raced to the hearth. "What's it like in there?"

"Sticky!"

Aidan knew a flash of curiosity. He wished he could go and feel for himself, but his pride prevented him. He balled his fists instead.

"Here goes." Cormac jumped, clambering up into the small space.

Aidan laughed. His brother's feet were scrabbling in the air, and it made him look like an upended crab.

"Shut your trap, Aid!" Cormac shouted, then he was quiet for a time.

Aidan stole a glance at Marjorie. She gaped at the chimney like Cormac was off fighting the heathen masses, instead of simply climbing up the godforsaken flue.

He had to look away. No girl ever looked at *him* like that. Treacly-eyed stares seemed reserved for his brothers alone. But never for Aidan.

He shouldered past Marjorie, and went to stare blindly up into the chimney. "You still in there?"

"Move it, stink-breath. I can't see." Cormac scuffed his toes along the sides, sending mortar flying into Aidan's eyes.

He scrubbed at his face, and then laughed as an idea struck him. "When the chimney boys stop their climbing, the master sweep lights a fire to get them going again."

Marjorie pinched him, hard. "You'll do no such thing!"

Aidan stumbled backward. "Ow! Criminy, Marj, I was only joking."

"It's *Marjorie*, you beast."

"That's the way, Ree," his brother said. Why did Cormac get to call her stupid nicknames, but Aidan never could?

"Now stop breathing my air. I think it's getting smaller up here." Cormac's voice was growly, like he was trying to sound the man.

"You getting scared?" Aidan taunted.

"No, I'm not getting—oh!" There was a loud scuffling inside the chimney.

Marjorie shrieked. "That's enough, Cormac. You win! Now just come back down."

"I best get a good prize for this, Ree," Cormac said, and Aidan wondered what *that* meant. "I'm getting the way of it now. Like a wee monkey I am."

Cormac's laughter stopped abruptly, and he muttered, "Och, hell."

"Och, hell, *what*?" Marjorie sounded nervous.

Aidan eyed her. That'd teach her to tease and taunt boys.

"You answer me right now, Cormac MacAlpin," she said sternly. *"Och, hell, what?"*

"I . . . I think I'm stuck."

Aidan laughed. His twin wasn't the conquering hero after all. "You've ate too many pasties from the Aberdeen baker!"

"It's not funny," Marjorie snapped.

"I'm stuck," Cormac said, and Aidan knew his twin was trying to tell him something. Cormac was much loved, but it was Aidan who seemed always to pry his brother out of jams.

"Aye, I hear you." He propped the grate onto its side like an impromptu ladder, then stepped back to study it. A thick layer of ash blanketed the fireplace. He'd get filthy, and it'd be *his* hide tanned for Cormac's folly. He always pried his twin from jams, but did anyone ever appreciate it? *No.* "Och, Mar-*jorie*, could your uncle no' sweep the bloody hearth?"

He shook his head, resigned. There was nothing for it. His brother was stuck, and of course he'd help him. Aidan climbed onto the grate, using hands and feet to scale it like a ladder. He teetered at the top for a moment, then the whole thing toppled sideways. The metal jabbed into his ribs, and it hurt bad, but he'd never show that to Cormac and Marjorie.

Instead, he got right back up, propping the grate on its side and climbing again. This time he found his balance. The chimney above was pitch-black, but with the ambient light from below, he could make out the silhouette of Cormac's dangling feet. "You get to save Marjorie, but it seems you need me to save *you*."

"Thanks, Aid," Cormac said, his voice tight.

Aidan realized how scared his brother really was, and it softened him. Because when all was said and done, he loved Cormac more than anything. More than anyone. "Eh, don't fash yourself over it. Though it does mean you lose the dare."

Aidan jumped, swiping at his twin's foot. He fell again, harder this time. The grate clipped him on his chin, and a cloud of ash exploded into his face.

"Mind the grate!" Marjorie shouted.

Girls. Aidan shot her a look. "Thanks. I hadn't considered that."

What did Cormac see in her anyway? His twin was smitten, and it was making him a fool. And now he was a fool stuck in a chimney. "Losh, Cor, how'd you get up that high?" He coughed, slapping at his clothes. "My breeches are a wreck. Mum will have my hide."

Nobody spoke. Everyone was waiting for *him* to save the conquering hero. Sighing, he climbed the grate and jumped, and then again. His fingertips grazed Cormac's feet each time, but he didn't manage to get purchase.

Aidan stared up. It was impossible. Cormac was wedged up too high. He could try to climb it, but then he'd have his brother's feet jammed in his face and likely *he'd* get stuck too.

He needed something higher to stand on. A chair, mayhap. "Marjorie, what say we bring one of your uncle's chairs to—"

Hands grabbed him hard from behind. Thoughts tumbled into his head. *Why'd Marj grab me? Losh, the girl is strong.*

But then the smell hit him. A foul, man smell. *Man's hands. Her uncle Humphrey home? We're in for it now.*

"Still yerself," a gruff voice whispered in his ear.

A servant of Humphrey's? He held still, waiting for his mother's voice to chime out in a scold.

Aidan caught a glimpse of burly, hairy arms. Definitely not a servant.

A sack was shoved over his head. His heart exploded, and with it his limbs, kicking and flailing.

Someone was dragging him backward. He heard his brother calling out useless, clueless things, and Aidan tried to yell for him, but the bag only got in his mouth. He spit it from his lips. The air inside was hot and smelled of sour cheese, and it turned his stomach.

He hammered his heels against the floorboards, but the man was too strong. Aidan had thought himself almost a man, and this proof of his weakness shamed him, terrified him.

Marjorie screamed. Were they taking her too? Like her or no, what kind of man would he be if he let that happen?

He struggled wildly, imagining a miracle, willing it to happen. For once, he wanted *Cormac* to be the one to save *him*. Aidan cried out to him, and Cormac shouted back.

Hearing the panic in his brother's voice made the

moment real. This was really happening. Someone was hauling him away. A quivering sensation jittered through his body. He trembled, his every instinct to act, but he was held powerless in the man's iron grip.

Cormac cried out, but his voice was growing faint as Aidan was hoisted from the room. The knowledge that he was in real, dire trouble broke him. No longer did he think of manhood bravado. Aidan screamed for Cormac, over and over, tears flooding his cheeks.

Marjorie's shriek pealed from the other room, and as much as she'd annoyed him, a bolt of fear for the girl cut him through. He kicked his foot back, clipping his attacker on the knee, and was answered by a satisfying grunt. He bent his knees to kick again. "Take your hands—"

Something clouted him hard on the back of the head and stars exploded inside the black bag. He heard his own whimpers as though from a distance, and then Aidan blacked out.

It wasn't until hours later that he awoke. There'd been a cold splash of water to his head that left the taste of salt in his mouth. Another splash, and the rocking and creaking of a ship cut him through, his body knowing at once he was far from land.

The bag was peeled from his face, revealing a man staring at him, smiling. "Fancy a sail, boy?"

Aidan blinked at the sudden brightness. His eyes adjusted, and then all he saw was the glare of gray sea all around, and the glimmer of a black pearl earring in a pirate's ear.

Chapter 1

Stonehaven, Aberdeenshire, 1660

She wasn't chilled. Her back didn't ache. She wasn't in a barn, nor was she seated upon a three-legged stool. She wasn't in the milking room, and her cheek was most certainly not nestled deep in the thick, musty wool of a sheep's haunch.

No, Elspeth Josephina Farquharson was at a country dance.

Well, not truly. But she shut her eyes, dreaming what one might be like. There would be laughter, big jugs of ale, and girls with broad smiles walking arm in arm. The pipes would set into a lively reel. She swayed in time.

The door creaked open. The room stilled. Footsteps sounded. The heavy step was confident, masculine.

It was him. He approached from across the room, his eyes only for her. He swept her into his arms.

The reel began again, and he pulled her, steady as the tides, into the middle of the dance floor.

His breacan feile wrapped about her legs as he swung her. She gazed up, easy laughter on her lips, staring into his . . .

Elspeth's hands froze on the sheep's teat.

Brown? Emerald green? Gray as a storm-choked sky? Nay, blue.

She sighed, smiling.

She gazed up, laughter on her lips, at his blue eyes. He had a smile just for her. It was wicked.

"Elspeth, I say. Are you deaf, girl? That sheep's wrung dry."

She sighed again, heavily this time. Her eyes fluttered open. It was her father who stood there, not the dream man.

"Fool girl," he said, shaking his head, "always in your head. Now come up to the house and put that brain to better use. It's accounting time, and you know you're the one with the mind for books."

Elspeth scooted back from the sheep, clapping her hands clean. "Aye, Father."

Even though the family farm was small, she the only child, and her mother long dead, her father needed her. And when he needed her, she always went. How he'd managed before her was a marvel.

"You know I don't have a mind for reckoning." He gave a loving poke to her temple. "Not like my wee Elspeth."

She smiled weakly. The day was coming when she'd need to sit her father down and have a serious talk. He'd sold five head of perfectly good cattle to start a woolen business, without consulting her. And now she was the one left to milk the sheep *and* mind the accounting.

But the books told a grim story, and it grew grimmer by the day.

She worried there might not be enough left to buy back even one cow, if it came to that.

They returned to their two-room cottage, and Elspeth pulled her chair close to the fire. Candles were dear, and the hearth was the only spot bright enough for reading.

"You're no lad, but still, how would I survive without you?"

She looked up, and despite the cut in her father's words, she found a rare smile on his face. Tenderness seized her heart. Her parents had been long married before they'd been blessed with their only child. When her mother died in childbirth, she'd left her newborn babe with a man old enough to be a grandfather. A man who'd wished for a son but gotten Elspeth instead.

Her father waited expectantly for a reply. His frizz of gray hair erupted from his head like a halo, or a misshapen bird's nest.

No, he couldn't survive without her. Nor would she want him to.

"Good thing it shan't come to that," she said. The words pricked her, and she forced a smile. She'd spoken the truth: living without her would never be in question. Any dowry there'd been in linens and woolen goods had been sold off long ago. And what coin there'd been for making Elspeth's plain features more attractive to a prospective husband had gone to the beasts instead.

"Here's your things, then." He pulled her wee worktable by the fire. It bore a sheaf of papers and her precious quill, and the sight of it automatically switched her mind to the business at hand.

"Thank you," she said, already engrossed in her work. She fished out that month's tally, squinting to focus.

With a *tsk*, he rose to stoke the fire higher. "Stubborn lass. I wish you'd allow yourself a reading glass. I've heard talk of a man in Aberdeen who fashions spectacles. They even have a wee ribbon that holds them to the head."

She tilted her chin to bring the numbers into focus, skimming her eyes over the lines. They'd had this argument before. "You know we haven't the money."

"But we've spent less this month. Or it should read so in that book of yours." He came and hovered over her, and she shifted so as not to lose the light.

"How is that possible?" She scanned the rows, and one number caught her eye. Growing stern, she put her finger to mark her place. "Da, how is it we have more left over this month, and yet we're making less than ever?"

She craned her neck to stare a challenge at him. He'd sold personal items off before, and Elspeth wouldn't put it past him to do something foolish like sell off her mother's wedding band. She frowned, for it wasn't as though she'd ever have call to wear anyone's ring.

"I've begun to trade. With *Angus.*" He paused, letting the farmer's name hang.

"Angus." Shaking her head, she looked back down. Her father dreamed of marrying her off to the man. "Not that again."

Though Angus Gunn was kind enough, and his neighboring farm profitable, he didn't make her swoon like all the great heroines swooned. And if Elspeth couldn't have a great love like those she read about in her novels, then she'd rather skip the whole enterprise entirely.

Besides, she knew of another woman who'd stolen Angus's heart long ago.

Elspeth shut her eyes, pinching the bridge of her nose. "What, pray, have we to trade with Angus?"

"Our sheep's milk for his oats."

Her eyes flew open. "Raw oats? However will we mill them?"

"They're to feed the sheep."

She bit her lips to halt the first words that came to

her tongue. She'd simply have to talk to Angus herself. Perhaps arrange to trade for *milled* oats so they could fill *their* bellies instead of just the sheep's. "Very well, Father."

There was a knock at the door, and he bolted up, a wide grin on his face. *"Talk of him, and he doth appear."*

Elspeth rolled her eyes. When would her father get it through his thick skull that she neither wanted Angus nor he her?

The farmer stood in the doorway and gave her father a stoic nod. He was so tall and so broad, he had to hunch to fit. "I put the oats by the barn."

He shooed Angus in. "Come in, come in. Say hello to Elspeth." He swept an arm in her direction. "Doesn't she look lovely by the firelight?"

"Oh, Da," she muttered under her breath. Little did he know that what men likely saw was a shy spinster, with plain features adorning a too-thin frame.

Spotting her, Angus slipped his bonnet from his head, crumpling it in his hands. "Good day, Miss Elspeth."

She put her papers down and gave him a warm smile. She didn't have feelings for the farmer—he'd been besotted with her best friend, after all. But that didn't mean she didn't think him a kind and dependable soul. "Good day, Angus."

An awkward silence filled the room.

"Very good, very good," her father said, looking from one to the other.

"If that's all, then." Angus turned as if to leave.

Her father shot her a meaningful, wide-eyed look, nodding encouragement.

Elspeth shrugged. She'd never been good at idle chatter. "Do bide a wee, Angus. We . . . we've just stoked the fire, and I'm afraid I've had enough of numbers this day."

"Very well." Angus went to the corner to retrieve another stool.

"What's the word from town?" her father asked jovially. "I hear the oldest MacAlpin girl has returned a widow. Lost her husband to a war wound, or some such." He looked to Elspeth. "You two were mates. What was the lassie's name?"

"Anya?" Was it possible her dearest friend had returned? How strange to hear such tidings, as though Anya had been beckoned by Elspeth's thoughts alone. Though sadness for Anya's loss pierced her, she couldn't help but beam. "Anya MacAlpin is back?"

She cut her eyes to Angus, feeling instantly guilty. He'd not weather the news so well. Long ago, Anya's sudden marriage had struck him hard.

Sure enough, he still faced the corner, stool in hand, standing frozen. She was certain Anya was the reason Angus had never married.

Her smile faded. Would that a man felt half for Elspeth what that farmer must've held in his heart for the oldest MacAlpin sister.

Anya hadn't wanted to marry a stranger, but her father had given her no choice. The day she watched Anya carted away in tears, Elspeth decided she'd either marry for love, or not at all. And now to think her friend was already a widow, while Elspeth seemed destined to remain forever a maiden.

Her father seemed baffled by the tense silence, and filled it with mindless chatter. "Quite a year for that family. Cormac—and what a strange, dour fellow he is, aye?—he up and marries the prettiest girl. From Aberdeen proper, she is." He shook his head, marveling. "And now there's a rumor the brother's back too. The twin. You remember the lad who was stolen? Aidan?"

"None would soon forget that name," Angus replied, his features once again a stoic mask. He settled his stool before the fire.

Elspeth put her hand to her heart. "Young Aidan lives?"

She hadn't known the MacAlpins when the lad was taken. But like every other villager on the outskirts of Aberdeen, she'd heard about the kidnap. Folk said he'd been mistaken for a poor climbing boy. Everyone had presumed him dead or worse, indentured to a faraway plantation.

Angus shook his head. "Not so young anymore."

The mysterious Aidan popped into her head, a shadowy, featureless silhouette. What came of a man after such an ordeal? And what would he look like? If he'd turned out half as handsome as his twin Cormac, he'd be handsome indeed.

"Aye, he's returned. But the family is keeping a tight lip about it." Her father leaned in. "He was a slave in the tropics, I heard. They say he was branded."

"Branded," she gasped. Owned like a common slave. And yet he'd escaped. Bearing secrets, no doubt.

She shivered, letting her mind wander. How on earth had he made his way back to Scotland, sailing all the way from Jamaica, or Barbados, or Hispaniola? Battling pirates, almost certainly.

Aidan MacAlpin would be dangerous, swaggering. Just like one of the heroes in her books. Would he speak a foreign tongue? Months on the open seas, his skin would be as smooth and brown as a cowry shell.

The sun beat down overhead. The timber planks were hot beneath her bare feet. She stood, gazing across the endless sea. The afternoon was sultry. It loosened her muscles. She felt heavy with the heat. Wanton.

She sensed him, and turned. He was climbing up the ladder, his virile form rising from the cabin below. His sun-kissed skin glowed with the fine sheen

*of exertion, accentuating his rippling muscles. He
called to his sailors, his voice commanding.*

*But then he saw her. Their eyes met, and the rest
of the ship fell away. He stalked to her, his very being
intent on one thing and one thing alone. Her.*

Elspeth's breath caught. She put her hands in her lap,
wringing her skirts. She hoped the men blamed the flush
in her cheeks on the heat of the fire.

She pretended to listen to her father, all the while
enjoying the wicked pattering of her heart, as she let herself imagine.

Chapter 2

Aidan sat, folded into a too-small chair, situated as close as he could to the door without appearing like he wanted to run. Which he did.

Home. It was a foreign notion. And Dunnottar Castle, no less. How this cavernous pile of rubble would ever be his home, he had no idea.

He hadn't intended to return, at least not until he'd found and avenged himself on the mysterious man who'd stolen him so long ago. But chance had reunited him with his twin brother on a dock in Aberdeen. And just as when they were children, Aidan had found himself enmeshed in one of Cormac's dramas, but this time of a very dire, very adult sort. In the end, he'd decided to remain with his family, hunting for his enemy from the unlikely hide-out that was Dunnottar.

"First you, now Anya," his sister Bridget said.

He forced himself into the moment and found her peering at him with a frank stare. It'd do no good to rouse his family's suspicion, and so he cracked his mouth into what he hoped was a smile.

Bridget swelled. "Oh, Aidan, it's so wonderful to have you back where you belong. The family together again."

A bolt of grief sheared him through. *Not the whole family.* Just the siblings. Their father had died in the Civil Wars, but that wasn't the loss he felt keenly. It was their mother whom Aidan mourned.

Apparently, she'd died the year he'd been kidnapped, and though everyone's grief appeared to have blunted through the years—indeed, Bridget didn't even have memories of her—Aidan felt the loss as keenly as if it'd just happened.

Because, to him, it had. He'd endured his captivity by forcing himself to hold on to memories, even though they cut him sharp as any blade, and thoughts of his mother had been especially acute. He'd while away long nights, recalling her trilling laugh, or how she always smelled of rose water. The way she'd tuck his blanket about his shoulders when she thought he was asleep. He'd dreamed of the day he could sweep her into an embrace. She'd have been shocked at how he'd grown. She'd have been wild with joy.

But it wasn't to be. Yet another dashed dream for Aidan, his beautiful mother lying cold in her grave, thirteen years past.

Anya came in, and he scrubbed a hand over his face to clear his thoughts. She crumpled into a chair, looking bled dry. "The lad's asleep."

Their brother Gregor reached over and gave her hand a squeeze. "Are you certain you want to share a room with the boy? I assure you, we can clear out another room for him that'd suit."

"No, I'm happy to share. Duncan is my son, after all."

Anya mustered a smile for Gregor, and it was the first he'd seen on her face since her arrival.

It was such a small interaction, but it made him feel more of an outsider than ever. Gregor's charm had always come naturally—it'd been the same when they were young. It was impossible for Aidan to imagine offering such blithe comfort to any woman, even one of his sisters.

He scanned the room. All of them, they sat with such ease, huddled close to the fire. It was all he could do not to resent the lot of them. But of course he didn't. And yet, he couldn't rise above the pained feeling in his chest when he was in their midst.

"What a fine boy you've raised," Marjorie said. She was nestled close by Cormac's side.

"You'll have your own chance to raise one soon enough." Smiling, Anya nodded to Marjorie's belly. It was still flat, even though she was already with child.

Cormac beamed, and Aidan had to look away. Though Aidan couldn't begrudge his twin's happiness, it was a gulf between them. It always had been.

Only now, after his indenture, it was worse. He couldn't fathom finding such easy joy with a woman. The only women *he'd* known had been either pretentious plantation wives, or their hard-used servants. Aidan had found physical release with both. But love? Never that. Never had he been the object of anyone's care or concern. All he'd ever known was the hard heart, cold eye, and sweaty brow to which the Indies reduced a person.

Bridget shifted, getting a better view of Anya in the firelight, studying her features. "Duncan's got your eyes, but that's it. He must've been the very likeness of your husband. It's a shame you could never visit when he was alive."

Aidan watched, mesmerized, as Bridget got up and plopped next to Anya, grabbing her hand and stroking it. "It seems he was a fine man. You must've felt the luckiest

of all women to have married such a nobly born gentleman. And a fine soldier, no less."

Their older sister only nodded. The amber light accen-
tuated the furrow in her brow. Aidan wondered at the
look that flickered in her eyes.

His eyes went from oldest sister to youngest, as different in appearance as they were in attitude. Anya was thin
as a willow and quiet as the breeze, with the lighter coloring of their mother. But Bridget's eyes were almost as
dark as her black hair, and they danced with wickedness.

Despite himself, Aidan felt a kinship with his older
sister. Bridget had been just a babe when he'd been taken,
and he found himself discomfited with her bold and
buoyant ways.

"There's so much to catch up on," Bridget said. "As it
is, it's nearly impossible to pull stories from *Aidan*." She
shot him a scolding glance. "So, Anya, it falls on you. *You*
must tell us your story in full. You must be so proud. Your
husband died a war hero!"

Anya's mouth was tight. "Not a hero, precisely. Donald died a full ten years after battle."

Aidan would wager there was more of a story there
that she wasn't telling. He knew how to read people.
Being attuned to the secret wants of others had been key
to surviving his long years in captivity.

Bridget tucked her feet beneath her, settling in for a
grand tale. "But from wounds suffered on the field. 'Tis
no less heroic. Come, tell us the story."

There was a moment of stilted quiet.

Marjorie spoke up. "Bridget, love, I fear I'm too tired
for tales of war. Cormac, do find the Chaucer for us." She
gave her husband a meaningful glance.

Cormac rose dutifully, perusing a small stack of books
on the side table. It appeared his twin was still doing
Marjorie's bidding, after all these years.

Anya shot Marjorie a relieved look. It'd been meant

for nobody else's eyes. But Aidan prided himself on seeing what he wasn't meant to see.

Bridget slumped. "Not the Chaucer again. Come now, Anya. Don't you wish to tell us a story? Just one?"

"I'm just very tired is all," Anya said. She was a widow at twenty-seven, with a nine-year-old son in her care, who'd recently made the long journey all the way from Argyll, across the length and breadth of Scotland. Aidan imagined she must be tired indeed.

Gregor spoke up, chiding the youngest sibling with his signature easy smile. "She said no, Bridget. So stop your badgering. And besides, you forget I was a cavalryman." He shot Anya a wink. "I'm in no mood to hear captains' tales."

Aidan gave his older brother a thoughtful look. So Gregor had also noted their sister's exhaustion. For all that easy charm, Gregor saw what others didn't expect him to see.

Declan stumbled in, a book in hand. It seemed his younger brother's nose was always to be found between the pages.

"Perhaps Deck can read to us," Gregor said. "What've you got today?"

Declan pointed the cover toward him, even though it'd be impossible to read from that distance. "Peloponnesians."

Aidan kept his features smooth. Declan had been too young to fight in the Wars, and he longed for battle. Longed to read about it, talk about it, study it. It was all that he'd talked about in the weeks since Aidan's return. The boy was clearly touched in the head. If he had any real notion of what it was to face his own death, he'd not carry on so about the whole bloody business.

"Oh no, Declan. No." Bridget flopped backward with a dramatic flourish. "Not the Greeks again. Cormac, get *Sir Gawain* down. We haven't heard that in some time."

"Here it is." Cormac pulled a yellowed sheaf of papers bound with a leather thong. He tried to hand it to Bridget.

She shook her head, her face alight with excitement. "Oh, no, not me. I've just the idea." She craned her head, catching Aidan's eye. "You read it, Aidan! You do have the best voice of any man in the family."

She bestowed regally apologetic nods upon the other brothers. Gregor laughed, Cormac rolled his eyes, and Declan didn't even seem to notice.

He stiffened. "No. I'm not in the mood for reading tonight. Someone else."

"Truly, Aidan. Your voice is so gruff, and so manly. With your tanned skin, you're just like a pirate. So dashing! I want to hear *you* read the part of Sir Gawain."

"I'm not inclined to read just now." *Not able*, more like. He forced the stern line of his mouth into a smile. He'd not let his siblings know his shame.

"Are you shy? You battled, what, smugglers, pirates, privateers . . . marauders! And you won't read us a wee story?"

"I've no time for this." Aidan stood, and with a stiff nod to his brothers and sisters, he left the room.

He didn't have time for foolishness like reading. He had one goal. One thing alone drove him. He would hunt down the man who'd ruined his life. He was going to find and kill the man with the pearl earring.

He sat on the bed he'd set up for himself in the old guardhouse, staring at his papers. He'd stolen them from a slaver, from a smuggler he'd helped Cormac take down. He knew in his heart that somewhere in that stack of parchment, there was some clue as to his enemy's identity. But the letters and numbers swam before his eyes, all meaningless loops and lines and dots.

The door opened, and he startled. He quickly shoved the papers under his pillow.

Anya stood there, hovering like a shadow, her pale

skin making her seem a ghost of the girl his sister had been. "You can't read, can you?"

"Must you ask me that?" He bristled, bracing for a fight. He wouldn't admit to anything. Since his return, his family had clothed him, fed him, tended him as though he were a child. "Haven't I already suffered enough shame?"

"Easy, brother. There's no shame in it." She came and sat beside him on the bed, the heather-stuffed mattress crackling with the added weight.

He barked out a laugh. "No shame in a grown man not being able to write his own name?"

"I'm your older sister. Don't forget it was I who sang you songs, I who kissed your scratched knees. Listen to me when I tell you, it's not your fault. Your childhood was stolen from you, and your education with it."

He couldn't bring his eyes to meet hers, but he sensed her stare, until he felt his face burn.

"Aidan, do you want to learn?"

He thought about the sheaf of papers hidden under his pillow. How would he ever find his enemy if he couldn't decipher a simple shipping manifest?

She sighed, realizing he had no reply. "Well, there's no reason you shan't learn. Think on it."

She rose, silent as a wraith, but paused at the door. "Tell me, Aidan. The sweetest wee horse, carved of wood, mysteriously appeared in my Duncan's things. It brought a smile to his face, and trust me, there've not been many smiles of late. Do you know how it might have appeared? Where it might have come from?"

He kept his head down, raking his fingers through his hair. "What do I know of toys?"

She was quiet for a moment, then said only, "I thought as much."

He didn't look up until he heard her whispered footsteps leave. He stood and closed the door, leaning his forehead against the cool wood. *Learn to read?*

Could he suffer further humiliation before his family? Would he confess his ignorance, doing lessons and exercises more suitable for young Duncan? But he knew, if it meant catching the man with the black pearl, he'd stake his very soul.

Thoughtful, Aidan dropped onto his bed, kicking back. He pulled a small bundle from his sporran, unsheathed his *sgian dubh* from where he'd tucked it at his calf. And he began to whittle.

A bit of wood, taking the shape of a knight.

Chapter 3

Elspeth stood before the scarred slab of wood that served as the front door to Dunnottar's living quarters. A featureless silhouette of the mysterious Aidan MacAlpin had kept her up all night. Would he be wandering the grounds wearing sailors slops for trousers, topped by a half-opened shirt with sleeves like great bells? Had his hair been lightened by the sun? Would he have a roguish twinkle in his eyes? Would they twinkle for her?

She'd simply *had* to come see for herself.

She smoothed her skirts, chiding her silly notions. But then, raising her fist to knock, she made the mistake of sweeping her eyes upward, taking in the cavernous ruins the MacAlpins called home, and she snapped her hand back down. Last time she'd visited, her family had had more money. Her dress hadn't been quite so threadbare. She, not quite so desperate.

But it was Anya, she assured herself. Anya wouldn't care about last year's dress.

Mustering her courage, she stepped forward to rap on the door just as it flung open. A man bolted out and knocked right into her. His hands grabbed her upper arms to steady her. She met his eyes, and the breath was stolen from her lungs.

He was tall, broad, tanned. And as dangerously handsome as any rogue she'd conjured for herself in the past twenty-four hours. His features were masculine, with a strong nose, full mouth, and an unruly thatch of dark brown hair. She stared at his blue eyes, willing them to twinkle.

Aidan? She opened her mouth to ask, but all that came out was a squeak.

Straightening his arms, he placed her away from him. "Who are you?" His voice was gruff and as rich as island rum.

His eyes never strayed from her. "Who are you to enchant me so? I've been waiting. For you."

She gave a seductive laugh. "You wicked, wicked man. You know I've been here all along."

She hiccuped in a breath. "I . . . I . . . I'm—"

He gave her a puzzled look, then turned, and leaning back inside, shouted, "Bridget! Someone's here for you." He gave her a brusque nod and stormed from the castle and out of view.

She swallowed hard, her arms tingling where he'd touched her.

"I must run." He reached out, the backs of his fingers trailing down her cheek. "But I shall return for you. Our ship sails at dawn."

"Hello?" Bridget stood in the doorway. Her perplexed expression said Elspeth had been standing there, staring into space, for a few seconds longer than was customary. "Oh, it's just you."

Anya appeared behind her sister, her eyes going wide. "Elspeth!" She turned and held a bucket out to Bridget. "Be a dear, will you? I was off to fill this, but . . ."

Bridget let the implication hang for a moment, and then with a grand huff, took the bucket and edged past both of them out the door.

Anya stood in the doorway, smiling. But Elspeth saw through the surface cheer to her friend's exhaustion—in the strain of Anya's posture, in the faint purplish circles beneath her eyes. And yet, despite it all, Anya was even more ethereally pretty than she'd ever been.

"Anya," she said, joining her in an embrace, "you're as lovely as you ever were."

Anya pulled back, taking in Elspeth's face. "And you."

She returned Anya's smile, accepting the lie for what it was. She knew *lovely* was a word that would never be used to describe her. But she'd long ago told herself that though she might be plain, she wasn't decidedly ugly, and that was something indeed.

Elspeth held out her arm. "I heard you were back. I thought perhaps you wanted to go on one of our sojourns."

As girls, they'd whiled away countless hours on their walks, during which Elspeth would spin tales about ships in the distance, or imagine secret tragedies suffered by passersby. Sometimes she'd pretend they were on a dangerous trek across faraway lands.

"It's been some time since our last expedition," Anya said, linking elbows. "Where shall we venture today?"

They fell into step easily. Despite the playfulness of Anya's words, Elspeth heard the strain in her voice.

"Mmm." Elspeth tapped a finger on her chin, eager to

do what she could to see a true smile on her friend's face. "Exotic *Afrique*? Perhaps a journey to ancient Carthage? Mayhap," she added in a wicked whisper, "we'll espy a Roman soldier on the road."

The errant image of Aidan flashed in her mind. Might they run into him on their walk? And how might *he* look in Roman helmet and breastplate? With that height and resonant voice, his bearing was decidedly gladiatorial.

There was a moment of quiet, in which their grins faded to contented smiles.

Anya patted her arm. "How I've longed to see you." There was a distinct note of melancholy in her voice.

"But you've been the one journeying, in truth. Living all the way in Argyll?" Elspeth squeezed her arm in excitement. "The trip alone must've been a grand adventure."

Anya shrugged. "Would that life turned out as we'd imagined as girls."

"What's happened to make you feel so decrepit?" Elspeth cocked her head, as though if she looked hard enough, she could read Anya's story on her face. "I see that you're tired. I can guess that you're sad. But the rest . . ." She shook her head thoughtfully. "The rest is a mystery." Her eyes grew playfully sharp. "Perhaps I'd know if you'd written me more faithfully. Your last letter was over a year ago. Uncommunicativeness is an unforgivable defect in any best friend."

"Uncommuni . . ." Anya patted her arm. "Truly, Elspeth. Where do you come up with these words?"

Elspeth steered them onto a path leading down to the shoreline. It was a clear day, and she hoped breathing the salt air might be invigorating for her friend. She might even spare a moment to contemplate swashbuckling, seafaring sorts of men. "You shan't change the topic," she said, as much to Anya as to herself. "And don't tell me it's because young Duncan—who, by the way, I'm desperate

to meet—took too much of your time. Tell me truly how
you are."

Anya sighed. "You had the right of it. I am tired. And
relieved to be home. My husband was . . . a difficult
patient."

"It must be a hardship, though." Elspeth stopped in her
tracks, staring back up at the ruins of Dunnottar Castle,
looming high on the mammoth seaside cliff top known as
Dunnottar Rock. It'd been ravaged during the Civil Wars
and then abandoned. The MacAlpin siblings had claimed
it as their own, and thanks to three—now four—strapping
sons, the townsfolk hadn't the heart to challenge them.
"You always loved finery, Anya. But now, to squat with
your family in such a place, not knowing from day to day
if someone might come and claim the castle from under
you?" She sighed. "While your husband's Stewart estates
must've been grand indeed. It was always your dream to
be a lady of such fortunes."

"Donald was merely a very distant cousin. But yes,
our home was grand. Though, I confess, I find myself
preferring it here." Anya paused, studying the jagged
coastline. Veins of rich, green grass fanned down the
cliffs toward the beach, a reminder of the tenacious farmland that clung to the eastern coast, refusing to be denied.
Something in her eyes cleared. "Don't you know, dear
Elspeth, oak wainscoting and one's own privy don't make
a home. And besides, Dunnottar has . . ."

"A peculiar charm?"

Brightening, Anya pulled them back into a walk. "Aye.
Just that." Loosening her arisaid, she led them to a large
flat rock, where she spread the wool out like a blanket.
"Come bide a wee. All I've done since arriving home is
answer questions about my son, and my husband, and
my husband's infirmities, and his military career, and
his land holdings." She sat, growing stoic. "And *my* prospects." Anya set her shoulders, as though those prospects

were something to be borne physically. "I'd hear instead how my bosom friend is faring. So tell me, Elspeth. How fare *you*?"

"I'm well." She shrugged, not much interested in talking about her own exceptionally mundane life. To do so would only be an exercise in fabricating some interesting tale where there was none to be found. It was enough of a strain to maintain a pleasant countenance among acquaintances; she had no wish to create such a charade around her oldest friend.

Anya pursed her lips. "That's all you've to tell me? You're *well*? We've known each other since we were girls hoisting our skirts and climbing to steal apples. I know when you're not telling me something. Begin with your father. How is he?"

Elspeth settled onto the rock with a sigh. "I fear Da's head is still in the clouds."

Anya's eyes narrowed. "You're holding something back, I think. Tell me you're no longer living your life completely in service to him."

The words cut to her heart, though she feared the truth of them. "My life's not so dire as all that." She forced a smile. "Father began a woolen business."

Anya sat next to her. "Well that's a good thing."

"Not when he had to sell off everything in order to do it."

"Everything?"

Elspeth knew her friend really meant, *Even your dowry?* "Everything. Cattle, linens. All of it. For twenty head of sheep."

"I hope you fancy mutton."

It was such a serene rendering of such a preposterous situation, Elspeth had to let free a long, hard laugh. It felt good to find humor in the face of her despair. Dabbing tears from her eyes, she said, "Would that we *could* enjoy a spot of mutton. My father hasn't yet grasped the concept

of 'give us this day our daily bread.' Do you realize he's
trading Angus Gunn for raw oats?"

Anya froze at mention of the farmer.

Elspeth's smile vanished. She grabbed Anya's hand.
"I'm sorry. I . . . I didn't think—"

Anya gave her hand a squeeze. "Don't fash yourself
over it. Now that I'm back, I'll be hearing his name, and I
best get used to it. Go on. Finish your story."

She hesitated. She knew there was much Anya wasn't
telling her. She wanted to probe and plumb and speculate—
it was what friends did. But they both had a lifelong habit of
avoiding talk of their private pains.

Elspeth wrung her hands in her skirts. Anya was a
widow and a mother. Elspeth's woes were silly nothings
compared to what her friend had endured. She shrugged,
and putting a fine point on it, said, "What more is there
to say? My maddening, stubborn, doddering codger of a
father is reducing us to paupers."

Anya's spine bolted straight, her face taking on a look
Elspeth didn't recognize.

Elspeth stiffened. "What is it?"

"You need money," Anya said, her eyes bright.

"No." Elspeth shook her head vehemently, thinking she
knew what was coming. She wouldn't stoop to charity,
even if it was from her best friend. "I will not accept—"

"No, no, goose. I'm not trying to give you money. Well,
you'll make money, but . . . you'll see." Anya sprang from
the rock, looking more animated than she had all morning. "I have an idea."

Elspeth laughed weakly, not budging. "You're frightening me. You're not going to propose I sell the sheep in
favor of a goat-breeding enterprise?"

"Nothing so coarse as that. You're a smart woman.
The smartest I know. The most well read in and around
all Aberdeen, I daresay." Anya waved her hand for
Elspeth to take it.

Elspeth slid from the rock, taking her friend's arm. "Which enables me to what? Write novels? Become an essayist? I'd have a better chance of wedding a mysterious foreign duke and ruling with a velvet glove over . . . over the Grand Duchy of Luxembourg."

They made their way back to the path, Anya steering them back toward home. "No, no. Not a writer. You'll be a teacher."

Elspeth pondered for a moment. She supposed Anya's son would need some tutoring. "But I've not much experience with children."

"Not with *children*," Anya chided. "You shall tutor Aidan."

Chapter 4

"What are you thinking, coming to Dunnottar?" Aidan grabbed his hired man, dragging him by the scruff of his jacket away from the castle grounds. "I told you. Nobody can know what I'm about."

"But I assumed they was your family, sir."

He thought of his brothers. They'd just meddle, Gregor and Cormac especially. Finding and vanquishing the man with the black pearl was *his* secret alone to tend, *his* revenge to savor. "Particularly not my family. Now, what news have you?"

Aidan began to head down the steep path to the beach, but saw his sister Anya talking with the strange girl who'd appeared on their doorstep that morning. Turning, he led them north instead. He knew of a secluded cove up the coast where they could shelter from spying eyes.

Aidan walked quickly, and the hired man stumbled, a city man uneasy on such rugged terrain. "You were very wise, sir," the man said, clumsily recovering his step. "Wise indeed. It's just as you said it'd be."

Aidan clenched his fists, mustering patience. He slowed his stride. "Spare me the bootlicking and say it plain. What did you learn?"

"You and your brother done took down the smuggler."

"Yes," Aidan said, through gritted teeth. It was an episode he'd not soon forget. Cormac's sentimental folly had almost killed him. Again. "So I recall. I'm not paying you to restate the obvious."

"You cleared the way, you did. For your own slave trade." The man looked around, his dim face looking muddled. "But what do you need with slaves out here? Seems you'd rather put that boat of yours to better use. For fishing, like. Less risky." The man smiled amiably, revealing a mouthful of decaying teeth.

"You overstep." Aidan fought the urge to clout the fellow. Pretending to start his own slaving trade was a tenuous enough ruse; the last thing he required was the unsolicited counsel of hired dock men. "My business is precisely that. *Mine*. Now continue."

"Well, you nabbed the smuggler, but he weren't the boss, see. There's another, a fancy broker type. Him's who ordered the slaves. And there's another too—a freebooter like—and him's your man doing the physical work. Sailing the ship, seeing the bodies to and fro."

The bodies. Aidan had been just such a *body*. A ten-year-old one.

He channeled his rage toward the hired man. "So there are two men outstanding. I don't suppose it occurred to you to get their names? Or to come bearing any useful information beyond *him's this* and *him's that*?"

The man opened his mouth and snapped it shut again. He gave a tight shake to his head. "I tried, sir."

"I thought as much." Aidan dug in his sporran and

tossed him a shilling. "A bob for now. A full crown if you come back with names."

The hired man's face twitched.

Aidan stepped closer to the man in a show of dominance. "If you're disappointed with the pay, consider it motivation. To return with *actual* information. As it stands, this meeting was dangerously close to a waste of my time."

The man looked at his feet, dejected. "As you say."

"Then why do you still stand before me?"

With a nod, his hired man turned and jogged back the way they'd come.

If he wanted information, he'd just have to go back to Aberdeen himself to look for it. He suspected he held clues already, but damned if he was able to read well enough to find out. It was a complication he needed to remedy, and fast.

He couldn't fail now. He'd been fine-tuning his plan for years: he'd act the part of a wealthy businessman starting his own slave trade and hope he presented competition enough to rouse the man with the pearl earring from whatever rock he hid beneath.

Him, a slaver. The thought was absurd. But lies spilled easily enough from his lips. He wondered grimly, who was *Aidan* really? His true identity had been stolen from him thirteen years past. If anything, *Aidan* was the thing that felt foreign. He'd spent his childhood simply called "boy," and then, when his body far surpassed what one could reasonably consider a boy, that'd evolved into "Scot." He'd been pretending ever since, the past thirteen years naught but lies and half-truths.

The first of his many lies had been to his purported *master*. The man—Nash was his name—had been a simpleton. His was an old Barbadian family, what islanders referred to as "Bims." A few years older than Aidan,

Nash had been born into a plantation fortune. "Sweet money," he'd call it, his "sweet sugar money. White gold."

Amassed from the labors of stolen souls.

Aidan sneered, remembering. It'd been simple enough, ingratiating himself with the man. Nash had been eager to speak of Mother Country, and Aidan had dredged as many of his father's war stories from his memory as he could. His master had lapped up every word, like a starved and stupid pup.

And then he simply bided his time, slowly working out his plan, dreaming of escape. For years, he waited.

Until one day he realized how much his half-wit master had grown to trust him. When he learned Nash was planning a sail to Aberdeen, it didn't take long to convince him that Aidan could be trusted as part of the crew.

A few favors, some thrown fists, and several promises later, Aidan found himself captaining a pretty sloop and her three crewmen out of Bajan Harbor, with the imbecile Nash left hog-tied at the dock. As the idyllic crescent of white sand faded into gray sea, the swell of freedom in his chest had been sweeter than any sugarcane.

And then came Aidan's second lie, to his crew: that his sole purpose was to make his fortune in the slave trade.

He'd regretted the telling of it, but there was no other choice. He had one goal, and one goal only. Not friendship, nor camaraderie. It was to track, to find, and to kill the man who'd abducted him. To do so, he needed to infiltrate the smuggling network.

It would be an impossible task, tracking down the ghost who'd haunted him all these years. But revenge was all Aidan wanted, vengeance all he was.

He'd hide out in Dunnottar, using spies, coin, and his own wits and muscle to guide him. He had only two clues to his enemy's identity. Knowing the man had been in Aberdeen, thirteen long years ago. And a single black pearl.

The hunt was on.

The hunt was off—if every soul in Aberdeenshire knew what he was about.

"I told you, told all of you, to keep my identity close." Aidan shifted his glare from Anya to Elspeth. He was seated at the great slab of wood that was the dining table, simmering with rage. "And now you go and bring this stranger into our home?"

"Elspeth is no stranger." Anya kept her chin held high. "I trust her more than I trust my own . . . my own . . ."

"Your own sister?" Aidan rolled his eyes, his temper abating. "That girl Bridget has trilled about my homecoming to whoever might chance to look her way."

"*That girl Bridget* is your sister. And we've told her she needs to be more . . . circumspect. But I still don't understand why. Are you in trouble? Are you in hiding?"

"No." He tossed back the last of a tankard of ale. He wasn't hiding—he just didn't want folk to uncover the truth of his goals. He studied Anya's friend, doubtful this mouse of a girl would be able to help him. He glared at her, to make his meaning clear. "I don't wish every villager from here to Aberdeen to hear about my return."

"Elspeth will keep your secret," Anya told him in a calming voice. "The MacAlpins lost you once. We'll not lose you again. Until you decide to tell us why you insist on such secrecy, we shall all respect your wishes."

Elspeth nodded. Nobody knew better than she how to keep a secret. She had no doubt he had a good one too. She was certain Aidan was embroiled in some private scheme. A thrilling plot, involving mystery and intrigue.

Aidan was furious, and she secretly rejoiced. Because he wasn't angry at the thought of reading, or her, or of reading with her. It was simply that he wished to be discreet. Clearly, he only wanted to keep his identity a secret so as not to bring danger upon his family. Or to the *friends* of his family. That meant her. Ergo, he wanted to keep *her* safe too. She shivered.

He tore a hunk from a loaf of bread and pinned her with that blue gaze. "You'll keep your mouth shut, aye?"

Elspeth's voice was breathy when she replied, "I shall be the very picture of obsession." She blanched. "*Discretion.* I . . . I . . . I shall be the very picture of *discretion.*"

He gave her a peculiar look. Her heart pounded, and she was certain it was pumping twenty shades of red into her cheeks.

She assured herself it could've been worse. She might have accidentally misspoken something more embarrassing. *Possession,* for instance, or *affection.* Or, God forfend, *erection.*

The thought made her squeak.

Not taking his eyes from Elspeth, Aidan posed a question to his sister. "You're certain this chit has the wits to teach me?"

His tone broke her spell. "Indeed," both women said in unison.

Anya was bristling. "Elspeth is the smartest girl you'll ever meet. She knows Latin *and* French."

"I just need English," he said over a mouthful of bread.

Elspeth watched, hypnotized, as he swept crumbs from the table into his hand, and then popped them in his mouth.

"She's quite proficient in that as well," Anya said. "She even does her father's accounting."

"That's more a comment on her father than on her." He looked at her, speculating. "Tell me, girl."

"Her name is Elspeth." Anya's tone was steady and calm.

"Tell me, *Elspeth.* Are *you* to speak to me when you teach, or will my sister have to translate?" A smile, a true smile, cracked his face.

The sight of it made Elspeth's heart soar. She spoke

slowly and carefully in her response. Just in case. "Indeed, sir. I am perfectly capable of speaking for myself."

Aidan tilted his face, considering her. Never before had a man considered her like that. Never had one so handsome ever so much as looked her way.

Her chest tightened, and she forced it to rise and fall. No good came of fainting from lack of breath.

Anya cleared her throat. "It's settled, then?"

"It's settled." His eyes were hooded and intense, and Elspeth thought he might just be able to see through her clear into the next room. "She can begin our lessons tomorrow."

Chapter 5

Elspeth stood in the doorway on the following day, mustering her courage. Aidan was sitting alone at the dining table. He hadn't yet realized she was there, and she seized the opportunity to study him, letting her eyes roam his broad shoulders, that roguish tangle of hair.

Something held his attention. She angled her head to see. It was a scrap of paper.

Her heart fell. Was he *reading*? Her services wouldn't be needed after all.

But then she saw how his eyes flicked to and fro, rather than scanning as though reading lines on a page. A smile spread on her face, wide, like he'd just paid her a compliment rather than simply offer proof of his illiteracy.

She lifted a foot to walk, then put it back down again, wondering how to approach him, what to say. *Good day, Master MacAlpin. Good morning. Hello, Aidan.* Or perhaps she should simply clear her throat.

In the end, she blurted, "What's that?"

He startled, shoving the paper into his sporran. "*You.*
How long have you been standing there?"

"I . . . I . . . just a moment."

He touched a finger to his ear. "What? Girl, you're as
quiet as the grave." He looked around the room as though
there might be other spinsters hidden about. "What are
you doing anyway, lurking around? Come in here." He
scanned the length of her. "I daresay, you'd make a tidy
wee spy."

His tone and his gaze had been suspicious, but secretly
she rejoiced. Her. A *spy.* She *could* be one, she knew it.

But what did one say to such a statement? It wasn't
exactly a compliment. She walked to him, forcing one
foot in front of the other, willing herself not to trip. She
could be worldly. She could be mysterious. She formu-
lated a sophisticated reply in her head.

And then she tripped.

Quickly, she set her skirts to rights, glaring hard at the
ground as if it were to blame for her clumsiness. Maddening tears stung her eyes, and she blinked hard, refusing to
let embarrassment get the better of her.

This was about her father's debts, not mooning over
Aidan MacAlpin.

Stiffening her mouth, she risked a glance at her so-called
student. She'd borne men's scorn before and expected she'd
find no different with Aidan. But rather than a smothered
laugh on his lips, or disdain, he studied her from beneath
a furrowed brow.

"Come on, then," he said, with unexpected gentleness.
He scooted over on the bench, making room for her. "Sit
just here."

"Thank you," she managed. Other men might have
mocked her, but not him. Even if she never saw Aidan
again, she knew she'd be forever grateful for that single,
small kindness.

She settled next to him, pretending she didn't feel the heat of his body like an open flame along her side. With a sharp inhale, she focused, shuffling her papers, setting up quill and inkpot for their first lesson. "I thought we'd begin with a simple reading." Each word tripped over the other as she spoke.

There. That was simple enough. She could do this.

"As you say." He shifted closer, reaching for the small bound book she'd brought to use as a primer. He riffled through the pages. "Is this what you'll teach me to read?"

"Yes, it's common for"—she paused, wanting to choose her words carefully so as not to offend. *Students? Readers? Learners?*—"p-people to begin by reading *The Book of Common Prayer.*"

"I didn't sign on for sermons, luvvie."

She girded herself to look at him, but his relaxed smile told her he wasn't angry. "Nor I." She managed a smile, which seemed to broaden his. "It's the most . . . the best . . . it's a good book for this sort of endeavor."

She'd meant, it was *easy.* Simple, with repetitive words.

She'd actually fantasized about the other books she might bring, entertaining sinful thoughts of him reading aloud from her translation of Boccaccio's *Decameron.* Or, better yet, to hear his rich voice pitched low, reciting from her collection of sonnets.

He swung his leg to straddle the bench. Hitching his hips closer, he cupped the side of her face. He leaned close and whispered, " 'Shall I compare thee to a summer's day?' "

Her skin shivered to gooseflesh.

"Do you need the fire?"

She clicked to. "The fire?"

"Aye, you seem cold." He was giving her a quizzical look.

"Cold?"

Aidan inhaled deeply. "I don't ken much about tutoring, luvvie, but I do have enough sense to know this would get on more easily if you didn't repeat my every last word."

"Of course." She felt silly. Why could she not focus? She was the most focused person she knew.

He gave her an awkward pat on her shoulder. "Don't worry yourself over it."

He was trying to make her feel better. This piratical rogue of a man was trying to make *her* feel better, and it only made Elspeth feel more the fool.

Aidan took the prayer book from her hands. "I need letters and numbers enough to read, say, a simple ship's manifest. And you say this will help?"

It sounded as though he had some very specific reading materials in mind. It piqued her curiosity. "Was that what you were looking at? A ship's manifest?"

He considered her for a moment, then said, "Of sorts."

"Might I see it?"

His face was like stone staring at her.

She mustered her courage, her curiosity now exceeding any uneasiness. "That's the only way I can get an idea. Of what I need to teach you."

Another few seconds passed before he finally gave a sharp nod. Reaching into his sporran, he retrieved a small sheaf of papers. He flipped through, hesitating over what to show her.

She craned her neck, trying to get a peek. Were these his papers? Maybe he really *was* a pirate, with a grand ship docked in a hidden cove.

He caught her snooping. and looking annoyed, he selected one sheet and folded the rest. "I think mayhap you really are a spy."

She felt a blush spread to the roots of her hair.

"All right, then," he said, tilting it toward her. The

name of a ship was written at the top, followed by a list of crewmen. It didn't enlighten her one little bit.

"You want to read *that*?" she asked.

"Well . . . mayhap." He sounded uncertain. "It's just a list of names."

She wasn't sure if he'd spoken a question or a statement. Did he truly not read well enough to discern Christian names on a roster? She decided some early praise might go far. "Yes, very good. That's precisely what that is. A list of crew members. Let's begin today's work on letters and sounds, and that will help you work out the exact names."

Though she couldn't imagine why he'd need such a thing. Was he in trouble? Running from somebody?

She reached for the list, but he gave a shake to his head and returned it to his sporran. "Not yet. We'll start with all that." He nodded to the materials she'd brought.

He seemed so serious. She thought he might indeed be in some sort of danger.

"I . . . Of course. First we'll work on letters, and we can read later." She extracted a fresh sheet of paper and slid it toward him.

He gave her a blank look in response.

"Do you know any letters?" She cringed at how the question had come out. His mouth was set in a tight line, and she cursed her thoughtlessness. "Never mind that," she said quickly. "I think I should be the one to start."

She gasped a nervous laugh, riffling her papers with shaking hands. What would she mess up next? "You must forgive me, Master Aidan. I've never done this before, and I'm afraid you're the one forced to suffer my inexperience."

"Not 'Master Aidan.'" His voice was deep and commanding. A pirate's voice.

She froze. Curse her heart, fluttering away like the

wings of a bird, and for what reason? He'd said a simple phrase, and her body reacted as though girding herself for her theatrical debut. "I . . . I beg your pardon?"

"My name. It's Aidan. I've had a *master* in my life, and believe me, luvvie, I'll die before I'm referred to as one. Call me simply Aidan."

She looked blindly at her papers, unable to meet his eye. "Aidan, then."

Her voice was quiet, her pale cheeks flushed red, and Aidan marveled at what a peculiar bird she was. He'd never met her like.

He watched her quivering hands as she withdrew a blank sheet from her stack. Her discomfort was beginning to unsettle him, and he wondered if the tightness he felt in his chest was annoyance or concern. He fought the urge to capture that hand, pinning it till she stilled.

She began a neat row of letters, saying the name of each as she wrote, and even her voice seemed to quaver. Her every aspect was like a lone flower in the midst of a windstorm.

Why was she so nervous? He inspected her profile as though he could read the truth if only he searched hard enough.

Perhaps she *was* cold, but too shy to ask for a fire. He let his eyes roam her figure. She was certainly a willowy wisp of a creature, her trembling only making her seem all the more insubstantial. She hadn't an ounce of flesh to spare, and he wouldn't be surprised if she spent half her life chilled to the bone.

She remained focused on her work, and so he let his eyes linger. She raised an arm to her ink jar, and with a shock to his loins, he realized that perhaps this Elspeth did indeed have an ounce or two of flesh to spare. Her breasts were modest, but lovely and well formed, a pair of treasures hidden beneath her layers. He had to shift

in his seat to adjust himself, spying that, yes indeed, the
woman was cold. Her pert nipples formed two faint shadows along the front of her bodice.

Just who was she? She seemed so nervous, reciting
her letters. What might she be hiding that he wasn't seeing, and more importantly, what would he have to do to
find out? Because, oddly, he found he wanted to know.
There'd been many women in his life, and never had one
held any mystery for him.

Most importantly, he needed to discern if she could be
trusted as much as his sister had promised. He decided
he needed to test matters. See if he could get a rise out
of her. If she had deceitful intentions, he'd uncover them.

"There's no need to whisper on my account," he said,
pitching his voice and curling his mouth in a way that'd
gotten a perfect rise out of dozens of women before her.
"You have a *fine* voice."

Her hand hung in midair. Slowly she raised her head
to him, her eyes gaping wide as a fish's. He bit his cheek
not to laugh at the sight.

The girl was innocent as an angel, or he wasn't the
devil's own. She clearly hadn't an ounce of deceit in her.
It was as Anya had said—Elspeth would be discreet
about their meetings and his identity. So what, then, was
the source of her discomfort? And who was she to be so
book-learned?

At first sight, he'd assumed she was just another of
the mindless, entitled lassies as plentiful in Aberdeen
as cured fish. But now he suspected she wasn't so easily
pegged. She'd been reduced to tutoring for pay, after all.
And that was in addition to work she did for her father.
He'd gathered she didn't have siblings either. The girl
seemed to have even less support than she did prospects.

By reflex, he gave her one of his smiles, though his
mind was racing. "Go on. I didn't mean to interrupt."

Elspeth lowered her face back to the page, looking

rattled. It was almost as though she didn't realize how fine she was. Not that she was pretty. Not exactly.

He stared hard, taking the opportunity to graze every inch. She was, on the face of it, quite plain. Especially when compared to a rosy-cheeked spitfire like Bridget, or the walking grace that was their eldest sister, Anya.

But Elspeth was unassuming and gentle, and those were qualities he hadn't encountered in . . . perhaps ever.

He watched her mouth form each letter. When she concentrated on the page, she looked relaxed. Books appeared her element, putting her at her ease, and oddly that pleased him.

He studied her lips. They were neither thin nor thick. In fact, there was nothing about her that stood out. Nothing too grossly large, nothing too unusually small.

She wasn't unappealing, he decided, which made it surprising that she hadn't yet married, for she wasn't a young maid. Rather, she was Anya's age, and his widowed sister already had a half-grown son.

He wondered why Elspeth might *not* be considered pretty. What alchemy made one girl stand out from the rest?

Not that he cared for pretty. He knew the saying *handsome is that handsome does*, and he'd found it borne true in his own experience, time and again. How many plantation women had he seen, with skin like cream and eyes like jewels, wielding their whips so very prettily? It'd been up to the men to discipline the adults, but children had been the women's domain, and after a beating, a plantation wife's pretend remorse was very pretty indeed.

He knew because *he'd* been one of those children. He had the jagged scars on his back to prove it.

"And *zed*," Elspeth said, writing out a perfect Z. She'd finished the alphabet and now held the quill out to him. "Now it's your turn."

He swallowed hard. *Scythe, plow, shears, hoe, shovel,*

rake, sword, dagger . . . These were all tools he'd held in his life. But a quill? Last time he'd held a quill, he'd been a ten-year-old studying at the kirk schoolhouse with the other children.

But he had no choice. If he was going to present himself as a wealthy lord, he needed to know how to read. How to sign his cursed name. And so, like a child, he had to learn the basics.

But it didn't mean he didn't hate it, and hate himself for his ignorance.

"Fine," he said, grabbing the quill from her. It felt so tiny in his hand, his fingers so awkward and thick. It was *his* hand that trembled now, and he pressed it onto the table to anchor himself. He slammed his other hand onto a blank page and slid it under the tip of the pen.

She nudged the inkpot toward him. "Don't forget, you must dip it first."

Of course. He'd known that. With a tight nod, he dipped his quill then brought it to the paper. He pressed too hard, and ink bled from the tip, forming a sloppy puddle.

"Hang it," he muttered. His life was black luck, a black soul, and now worthless black blots of ink. He moved to crumple the ruined page.

"Don't." She touched his hand, and they both grew still.

He tilted his head to catch her eye. She looked nervous. He wanted her to stop looking so damnably nervous. He wasn't *that* terrifying. She hadn't even seen his scars yet. He raised his brows impatiently, waiting for instruction.

"You mustn't stab it. Hold it sideways."

Her voice was gentle, and it calmed him. *Not a wee spy*, he thought, *perhaps a trainer of wild creatures*. He did as she'd told him, and tilted his hand.

"Yes. That's the way." He heard the smile in her voice, and a foreign feeling of warmth flickered deep in his icy heart. "Now write your first letter. *A*, for 'Aidan.'"

He began the letter, but pressed too hard, and the quill squeaked along the parchment. His muscles flinched, ready to crumple the sheet and quit this nonsense. He couldn't form a simple, childish letter, and it shamed him. But then he felt the barest touch on his forearm.

"Lightly," she urged. "You're too strong."

Too strong. Like a brute was too strong, or an ox. He looked up, a quip ready on his lips, but saw she'd turned nearly purple with embarrassment. Something about her words had made *her* self-conscious. Such a fascinating, peculiar bird of a girl.

His own shame vanished, and he brought his attention back to the paper. "Like this?" he asked, wanting to put *her* at *her* ease.

"Yes, but don't press down. Just touch it lightly. A gentle touch for each stroke is what you need."

His mind went to a place decidedly more sexual than this bit of book learning warranted, and he suppressed a smile, keeping himself intent on the paper before him.

Elspeth mistook his silence for confusion. "Perhaps if you held it thusly." She brought her hand to his to adjust his fingers on the quill, her movements as tentative as a frightened cat.

He'd have thought her hands would be clammy, but they were warm, their touch soft and light. He felt a bolt of lightning shoot up his spine. A gentle touch from an innocent was something far outside the realm of his experience. He relaxed his hand, letting her mold his grip, savoring the feel of those delicate fingers on his.

As she positioned his hand, he attuned himself to her utterly. Her breaths came evenly, and he imagined he felt each brush against his skin. The barest scent wafted up to him. Nothing like his mother's rose water, nor the cloying ambergris of elegant plantation wives. Elspeth smelled sweet and fresh, like freshly turned earth and grass.

Her long, thin fingers mesmerized him, so pale against

his tanned and callused skin. He dared not look higher than her wrist, a peek of it visible at the cuff of her sleeve. She was so fragile, with bones like a graceful seabird.

He imagined she'd never touched a man so. Perhaps it meant she was no longer nervous. Perhaps *he* had put her at her ease.

He needed to say something to fill the quiet, but he found he was speechless. He, whose blithe words had seduced some of the most exotic women in the world, found himself at a loss.

She sat so close to him, and yet he couldn't picture her eyes. What color were they? He thought they were blue, but what else would he see there? Flecks of green? Of violet? He needed to find out. He risked a glance, caught her gaze.

And saw terror there.

Anger swamped him, sudden and blinding. This Elspeth was as skittish as a calf surrounded by a pack of wolves.

He knew he was different from other men. He knew he didn't belong. But was he so coarse? Was he such a threat?

Aidan snatched his hand away. "We're done here."

He stormed from the room and didn't look back.

Chapter 6

Wrenching her body upright, Elspeth arched back to ease the knot at the base of her spine. She'd hauled bucket after bucket of Angus's raw oats to feed the sheep, and the labor was beginning to take its toll.

She let herself take a moment. Despite the frustration over her father's lack of business sense, despite the dirt that seemed forever to cling at her skirts and beneath her nails, she found tending the sheep to be a more pleasant chore than she'd have believed. At least as pleasant as minding their few cattle had been, and some bit easier too. They were serene creatures, and more social than the cows, butting their heads against her legs for attention, vying for handfuls of grain.

She dusted off then grew thoughtful, contemplating her hands, rubbing them, wiping the dirt from her palms. And remembering.

She'd touched *him* with those fingers.

Never had she touched a man's hand before. Never had she touched a man, period. At least one who wasn't her father.

It had only taken a moment to adjust Aidan's fingers on the quill, but still she'd lingered, lost to thoughts of what those hands might have seen. They'd likely harvested sugarcane, and climbed ship's rigging. But had they also punched men? Touched women? Touched himself?

A sultry warmth bloomed in her belly, and she glanced side to side, to ensure that nobody was there to witness such wicked musings.

Sure enough, Anya was at the top of the hill, walking down to the glen where they kept the sheep penned.

Elspeth shook out her skirts, gathering herself. With one last rub of her hands, she cleared her mind of these stolen dreams as surely as the dust from her fingers. Then she smiled, happy with any interruption if it meant seeing her friend. Especially now. Even though Anya bore no resemblance to Aidan, Elspeth felt somehow closer to him for sight of his sister.

"What brings you—oh!" Elspeth chirped at the sight of the young boy who raced from behind Anya. She'd brought Duncan. "It's your boy!"

"Aye," Anya said, returning her smile. "If he'd be still for but a moment, I'd introduce you."

But apparently nine-year-olds didn't stand on ceremony, because Duncan simply raced up to Elspeth and, skidding to a halt, asked, "What are you doing?"

Elspeth couldn't help but laugh at his intensity. With freckled cheeks panting for breath and bangs that'd turned reddish brown with sweat, the boy looked nothing like Anya.

"Why, I'm feeding the sheep, naturally."

"What are their names?"

"Their names." She put her hands on her hips, considering. "Let's see. Why there's Juliet, and Imogen, and Miranda is just there . . ."

Elspeth conjured a name for every last one, Duncan hanging on her every word. He frowned when she'd finished. "Don't you have no boy sheeps?"

"Don't we have any male sheep?" she repeated, gently correcting his grammar. She sighed. Didn't they indeed. Her father hadn't thought so far as to purchase them a godforsaken ram, so set he'd been on the prospect of milk, cheese, and wool. "Why no. They're spinsters, every last one."

"Like you?"

"Duncan, *a bhobain*!" Anya cried in a breathless gasp.

But Elspeth only laughed. Nobody knew better than she about her marital status. "Oh, it's fine, Anya, really."

Duncan put his hands on his hips, looking defiant. "Well, that's what Auntie Bridge called her."

"Well your aunt Bridget best mind her tongue."

One of the sheep bleated, calling Duncan's attention back to the flock. He tore a handful of grass and tried to feed it. "Will they never marry?"

"The sheep?" Elspeth tilted her head, considering. "Why, I think not, actually. Particularly not the one you're feeding. That one's Artemis. She's very wise, and brave too. And she's chosen not to marry just any silly old ram who ambles into her pasture."

"Won't she get lonely?"

She tapped her finger on her mouth in exaggerated contemplation. "I suppose she does. Sometimes. But she has her oats to occupy her. And she enjoys meeting new people, like you." The sheep nudged Duncan's hip, smelling the remnants of what she imagined were probably crumbs from a bit of food he'd hidden in his pocket. "But this way, Artemis has the freedom to graze where she likes. Wander where she likes."

"Does she wander? What if she doesn't come back?"

"That's a risk, isn't it? She's not wandered off yet. Though I suppose one never knows." Elspeth smiled widely, and looked at her friend to share in the moment.

Her smile froze. Anya's gaze was restless, scanning the horizon from beneath a furrowed brow.

"Duncan, would you please do me a favor and get one last bucket of oats from the feed shed?" Elspeth pointed across the glen. "It's just over there, near the cottage. Don't you know, if you feed a sheep from your very own hand, you'll have a friend for life."

He grinned. "Oh, aye, straightaway," he said, and raced off.

Anya was looking uneasily at the trough, now empty of oats. "Were those from . . ."

Elspeth knew her friend was nervous at the prospect of running into the neighboring farmer. "Aye, we get our feed from Angus's farm. But don't fret." Stepping closer, she put a soothing hand on Anya's sleeve. "He's nowhere about. The man works harder than a plow horse. Rare is the sight of him setting foot off his own lands."

Though Anya sighed and nodded, she still appeared upset.

"But whatever is the matter?" Elspeth asked. "You mustn't hold back. I can see the trouble on your face."

"Oh, Elspeth. I have horrible news." Anya wrung her hands in front of her.

Elspeth's stomach heaved. Had Aidan left? Had he said something terrible about her? He'd stormed off after their lesson. Did he say he never wished to see her again? She waited mutely for Anya to explain.

"We haven't the money to pay you," Anya confessed. "Aidan, when he arrived . . . I found . . . please don't believe me to be rifling through my brother's effects, but I saw he had a pouch full of gold coins. I'd just assumed . . . all that time sailing about . . . perhaps I've spent too much time with you!" She gave a dismissive, self-deprecating laugh. "I suppose I'd assumed that, on his flight from the Indies, he'd absconded with a chest of treasure. But he tells me that single pouch is all he owns in this world, and so it turns out we haven't the money to pay you after all."

Anya put a fretful hand to her temple, continuing, "I get the impression Gregor has some funds tucked away, but my maddening brother is being uncharacteristically miserly. I suspect he's waiting to see what Aidan's truly about, to see if he decides to stay on with the family. So there you have it," she finished in a rush. "We require your services and yet find ourselves unable to pay."

Elspeth's shoulders sagged with relief. But a queasy anxiety was quick on its heels. She and her father needed the money. Very much so. And yet, foolishly, she couldn't bring herself to mind. The only thing she could think was that she *must* continue to see Aidan, and she'd just have to figure out another way to fill her father's and her belly, even if it meant opening her own schoolhouse. "Don't fret over the money. I know your family needs me, and I'll not quit you." *I'll not quit him.*

"But I can't allow you to do so much for us, when we have nothing to offer in return"—Anya put up a hand to stop Elspeth's interruption—"but there is a possible solution."

Her friend looked distressed, but Elspeth gave her an encouraging look. "Yes?"

"We could barter. Aidan has much experience. You could trade labor for reading."

Elspeth paled. He'd spent life as a slave, how could she ruin his newfound freedom by making him do labor? And for *her*? "I wouldn't. I couldn't."

"He needs to learn, and you are the most bookish of all of us."

"Your brother Declan is quite learned."

Anya shook her head, looking beleaguered. "He insists

on you. Don't argue." She glanced at the ring of muck at Elspeth's skirts. "It seems you need the assistance."

"But this place . . ." Elspeth looked at the meager pasture around her, at the mucky hooves and empty trough. He'd sailed the seven seas, and their paltry situation mortified her. "He'll hate it here."

Anya waved a hand at the thought. "My brother will accustom himself to the idea."

She didn't want to be something this heroic man had to *accustom* himself to. She found an excuse to turn her back, scraping a bit of mud from the trough. Chagrin twined deep in her belly, nauseating her. The thought of making Aidan labor on her family's farm was too much to bear.

But she needed to keep seeing him. Which meant she needed to keep up their lessons. She felt Anya's gentle hand on her shoulder and turned to face her friend.

"The fact is," Anya said, "he has no choice."

"But what will he think when he hears the idea?"

Anya smiled. "Elspeth, it *was* his idea."

Chapter 7

Aidan lay sprawled on his tiny cot, whittling a wee dragon for his nephew. He'd stalled on his plans to set himself up as a slaver, deciding he'd best improve his reading first. It was just too dangerous for him to blunder into this so ignorant. He had to be careful—everything had to be perfect. Now that he was back on Scottish soil and reminded of all he'd lost, he was desperate to find the man with the black pearl.

He studied his wee carving. Too bad dragons weren't as easy to slay as they were to whittle.

Paring a bit of wood from the dragon's belly, he let his thoughts turn to family. Young Duncan was almost as new to the household as he, but even so, Aidan thought the lad had guessed him to be the source of his mysterious gifts. Perhaps the boy sensed his uncle's aversion to attention, but he'd kept his mouth shut, and so Aidan kept the figures coming.

During the long years he'd lived as the property of another man, it'd become a habit not to call attention to himself. Even the quarters he'd chosen at Dunnottar kept him outside the domestic fray of his MacAlpin siblings. The old guardhouse lay apart from the main tower house, and he loved opening his door to the sound and smell of the waves. Long had he lived in—and been choked by—the sweltering heat of the tropics, and he couldn't get enough of the brisk air off the North Sea.

"Hard at work?"

The breezy tone told Aidan exactly whom he'd find standing in his doorway. Twilight was upon them, and though the shadows cast Gregor's light brown hair a darker shade, his brother still bore the unmistakable coloring of their mother. Aidan's chest clenched.

"Gregor." He quickly slid the bit of wood he'd been working under his mattress. He was still becoming accustomed to the company of his family. They were a solid unit, complete with their own dramas and woes, harboring conceptions of him that were in utter disharmony from the man he'd become. Aidan found the lot of them made his mood bristle and his head ache. "What brings you this far afield?"

"Cormac insists I give this to you." Gregor bowed his head, touching a sword to his brow.

Aidan recognized the simple, unadorned steel basket at once. Though he remained sprawled on his cot, his muscles tensed. "Don't be put out on my account. You should've just had Cormac deliver it, if you're so loath to."

"So prickly, brother." Gregor tossed him the sword, and Aidan bolted upright, snatching it from the air. His brother laughed. "And nimble too."

Aidan had no taste for blithe chatter and ignored the attempt. Instead, he slid his hand into the basket hilt, tilting the broadsword to catch the light of the window.

"Father's blade. Why are you bringing this to me? I was never the man's favorite."

"No, you weren't his chosen son, were you?" Gregor's lip curled into a sardonic smile. He strolled into the room, eyeing what few objects Aidan claimed as his own. "That was me, and more's the pity."

"You'd have *me* pity *you*?" Aidan tried to view the room through Gregor's eyes. Candle, table, knife, washbowl, and the plaid Anya had given him that he'd yet to wear. He must seem quite the piteous creature to one like his dashing elder brother. "How do you figure?"

Gregor leaned back against the stone wall, arms crossed over his chest. "While you had playmates and outings, I was being trained to follow in our father's illustrious military footsteps."

"Are you completely lacking in sense?" Anger was a continual roil in Aidan's belly, and it erupted now, the bilious taste familiar and—God spare him—reassuring. "You'll recall it was on just such an *outing* when I was stolen from the lot of you."

"Aye. But you're home now, and like it or not, we want you here." Gregor considered him for a moment. "I find I trust you, despite myself."

It was Aidan's turn to laugh. He was certain the thought had crossed Gregor's mind that he was secretly a hardened pirate come to loot the family and be off again. "Why should I care whether you trust me or not?"

Gregor seemed amused. "Try to have faith in us, because I'm trying to have faith in *you*."

Assuming his place in the purportedly loving arms of his family was a more awkward mantle to bear than he ever would've imagined. "Why bother?"

"Because, prodigal brother, if I didn't, Cormac would beat, Anya harry, Declan battle, and Bridget badger me until I did." Gregor wandered back to the door, an easy smile softening his words. "Now put on that plaid"—he gestured to the pile of wool dropped haphazardly in the corner—"and act the MacAlpin."

Aidan stared at that stretch of tartan long after Gregor had gone. He'd not worn a plaid since he was taken—they didn't wear such things in the Indies, of course. And since his return, that simple, foreign scrap of cloth had struck him as so rife with meaning and import, he hadn't the heart.

He donned it, finally, and was reluctant to admit just how moving it was to wear a Scotsman's *breacan feile* again.

It took Aidan an hour to walk to the Farquharson farm. He would've loved to ride Gregor's chestnut gelding, but something about his older brother's manner spoke to a lingering distrust, despite what he might claim otherwise.

Aidan had been the one kidnapped so many years ago—why the burden would fall on *him* to prove his loyalty, he couldn't fathom. But he'd noticed the MacAlpin men postured like roosters at a cockfight, each one angling for dominance, particularly Gregor. So, it seemed until Aidan proved he wasn't really some criminally minded blackguard come from the tropics to swindle the family, he'd be held in suspicion.

And now he was to suffer the humiliation of once again laboring for another man's bread. His dread grew with every step.

But he needed to act the aspiring businessman, and businessmen knew how to read simple words on a page. He'd rather indenture himself again before confessing the shame of his illiteracy to his brothers. Anya was the only one who knew, and with her son, she had no time for tutoring.

He crested a low hill and spotted the humble Farquharson cottage. Modest pastureland spread before him like a knotty green blanket.

His eyes found Elspeth at once, tripping over her skirts in a mucky paddock, dragging a heavy bucket behind her. Reaching the trough, she hoisted it up to dump the contents, but even leaning it against the edge, she couldn't get the bucket high enough, and it kept sliding down.

The scene was preposterous. He jogged down the hill. What was a bookish girl like this doing as a farmhand?

Aidan watched the bucket slip from her hands, fall, and land on her toe, the contents spilling along the muddy ground. She doubled over to lean on the fence, breathing heavily, her hands fisted.

He noted her entirely inappropriate footwear. She'd be lucky if she hadn't broken a toe.

Last time he'd seen her, she'd thought he was a brute. He might as well be a brute in truth.

"Easy, luvvie." With a hand on the fence, Aidan vaulted into the paddock. He plucked the bucket from the dirt, scooping as much of the oats back in as he could.

She looked up, stricken. Her blond hair looked yellow in the sunlight, and he wondered if it was his imagination that put matching yellow flecks in her light blue eyes. "Thank you."

He bit his tongue, wanting instead to snap, *Don't fret, I'll not sully you with my boorish hands.* Instead, he asked, "Is it breeding time?"

Seeing the girl's blush, he swallowed a swear. She'd best be a good teacher, because it seemed he was going to have to work hard for these lessons.

"Breeding?" she asked weakly.

He spoke through gritted teeth. "Yes. I asked, are the sheep currently breeding?"

"Oh, *breeding.*" Her shoulders relaxed. "No, we're not breeding. My father didn't . . ." She turned from him and shrugged. "We don't own a ram."

He ran his hand through the oats in the trough. "But if you're not breeding, why do they eat this?"

"It's their feed."

He cursed under his breath. What sort of daftie was this girl's father? "They get grain this time of year?"

Though she wasn't facing him, he could tell she gave a cursory nod.

He studied her back. She was a wisp of a thing, her shoulder blades sharp against the linen of her dress. Anger flared, hot and quick. "And what have *you* eaten today?"

She turned to look at him, and he saw he'd hit close to the mark. But instead of seeing her usual fear of him glimmer in her eyes, Aidan read despair.

His tone softened. "What I mean to say is, unless the beasts are breeding—which, without a ram, they obviously are not—grass is enough for them."

He eyed the fence. Why they'd penned the sheep in a muddy paddock rather than put them out to pasture was beyond him. "But it seems your father didn't take the time to learn this properly."

That kindled a fire in her. "You'll not speak so of my father."

He felt a grin pop onto his face. The girl had unexpected mettle. She was loyal to her family. He liked that.

"Fair enough." The flock had come to feed at the trough, and Aidan waded among them, prodding at bellies, peeking in ears. "He's started a wool business, you say?"

"Aye, we have."

We. He grinned at that. If her father captained a sinking ship, Aidan imagined she'd set herself up as first mate. "And who will shear them? Come spring?"

"I will, I suppose."

His grin faded as renegade anger surged anew. "Luvvie, shearing is hard work. It's *man's* work. Do you even have the proper tools?"

A muscle in her cheek twitched. "I do."

He knew she was lying, but he saw right through it. The woman was guileless, and it was foreign to him.

Aidan stepped closer, and this time when she shifted away from him, it stoked an entirely different emotion. There was anger, yes, always anger. But at the sight of the flush on her cheeks and her breathlessly parted lips, that anger mingled with something he didn't recognize. An unfamiliar, wanting spark of a feeling that he found he wanted to stoke to life.

He stepped even closer, backing her into the fence, close enough to discern the scent of oats that clung to her. On the most preposterous impulse, he raised his hand to brush some dirt from her cheek, then quickly lowered it again. "Shearing happens but once per year," he said, his voice huskier than he'd intended. "How will you manage between times?"

"H-how do you know all this?" She glanced away, avoiding his gaze as nervously as she'd avoided his question. "I thought you worked sugarcane."

Aidan felt the emotion bleed from his face. *The cane.* He took a long step back. Was that why she couldn't look at him? Because she saw him as an indentured servant? Whenever he looked at his scars, at his detested brand, he saw a body that was forfeit. His had been a body owned by another. If he couldn't see beyond the marks of his slavery, how could he expect *her* to?

He turned away, anxious that this perplexing woman not see his temper flare yet again. He took a deep breath before speaking again. "It was a sugar plantation, yes. One with many hands to feed. We ... *they* ... they raised sheep. Barbados Blackbellies. For meat."

Eager to busy himself and calm his mind, he began to walk along the spindly fence, inspecting as he went. The rails had been poorly cut, and already hung broken in a number of spots. They needed a stone perimeter, not this makeshift thing. He jiggled the gate to test it and then opened it wide.

"Wait." She jogged up behind him. "What are you doing?"

"Letting these beasts roam. The sheep need to graze. And you need to save the oats for your own belly."

He scanned the surrounding countryside. "You'll want to parcel this off into two pastures. How do you currently herd the beasts to and fro?"

"I . . . I do that."

A laugh burst from him. "*You* chase them about? By your lonesome?"

She looked abashed, and he cursed himself. Talking to the woman was like walking on eggshells. "Well, we'll have to amend that. Can't have you racing around the countryside like a sheepdog."

Her brows knit into a frown. "I don't race about like a dog."

"Then how do you herd them?" he asked, trying his damndest to look serious.

She wrung her hands. Poor chit appeared to be summoning all her dignity, which was a tall order considering the ring of muck about her skirts. "I . . . whistle."

He couldn't help it any longer. He let free a broad smile. "You whistle?"

"Aye. I whistle."

"Luvvie, I'd pay my last bob to hear you whistle."

Her answering shrug was meek, but the smile in her eyes wasn't, and it brightened her, transforming those delicate features into something luminous and deep. She shuttered herself just as quickly, but not before Aidan had spotted it: like him, this Elspeth was more than she pretended to be.

———

Days later she found them: a pair of shears, sharp, shining, and new, nestled atop the paddock gate, with only a blue ribbon tied in a neat bow to tell Elspeth they were a gift meant for her.

Chapter 8

They'd had nearly a dozen lessons, and each had meant a visit from Aidan to her family farm. Elspeth treasured each one, waking early on days she expected him, getting well on top of her chores so that she could spend more time watching him by the sheep pasture.

And watch was all she could do, for he truly was doing a man's work, cordoning off proper pastureland and building a low stone wall to fence it in.

Their old paddock, originally built for a pair of ponies now long gone, had been a good way to keep their few cattle penned and safe from reivers. But Aidan claimed it wasn't large enough to accommodate twenty head of sheep. He said if the beasts could roam, they'd give better milk.

Elspeth didn't care a whit either way. All she knew was it meant Aidan showed up to haul fence stones, and that she got to watch him.

Not that his magnificent physical presence was all she appreciated about him, though his taut, sweaty maleness was a shock indeed to her body. But more than that, more than his roguish appeal, and even more than what she liked to think of as his unexpected moments of thoughtfulness, she'd been taken aback by just how bright Aidan was.

And it wasn't just that he knew about farms and could speak with authority on the tending of sheep—though how reassuring it *was* to have a man speak with confidence on things about which she felt so at sea. It was that he was not merely world-wise, but quick too, with a sharp wit and ready understanding. It was clear in his words, in the way he expressed his thoughts.

He was a torch that burned brightly, but crudely yet, like a great, unruly blast of flame, his mind ablaze with opinions and questions that, though he didn't always give them voice, she could read in his eyes.

She'd spent the past hour dithering about what excuse she could devise that'd bring her out of the house to see him down at the pasture. As she dabbed a fine sheen of sweat from her brow, it hit her. It was an unusually warm day, with no wind to cool the bright sun, and the man would be thirsty.

The shade of their tiny cottage had cooled the morning's milk, and before she could change her mind, she filled their best pewter cup and set out to find him.

The sight of him stole her breath, as it always did. Stole her breath, and broke her heart. He hauled the heavy rocks with such ease, placing them with the skill of experience, and the overly masculine display set her heart tripping. But it was heartbreaking too, to think how he'd come by that experience, how he'd earned the thick cut of those muscles on his arms and torso.

He must've sensed her there, standing across the glen,

because he looked up. Shading his eyes, he gave her a mute nod. Even from the distance, she saw the exertion writ plain on his body.

The day was uncharacteristically clear, with no clouds to shield the sun. Aidan wore his plaid, which must've felt like a blanket around him, and his linen shirt was soaked through with sweat.

He nestled a stone into place, and using a sleeve to wipe his brow, he came and met her halfway. She watched his stride, so powerful and sure. Was this how he'd looked aboard ship? She imagined his mouth curling into a cocky grin. He'd call out to his men, and with a nimble leap, would race up the rigging as graceful as a cat.

She blinked hard to clear the image from her head.

As he got closer, she saw he really was soaked through with sweat. Even so, he refused to take his shirt off like other farmhands she'd seen.

The tropics had turned him a burnished brown. She'd tried and not been able to find any end to that tanned skin through the V of his collar. Did that mean he'd shucked his shirt while he worked?

And yet here he was, the fringe of his brown hair slicked black with sweat, and he hadn't even pushed up his sleeves. Why would he choose to stay covered in such heat?

Was it because he was branded? She'd heard rumors he had been, and fretted over where the mark might be and what it might look like. Were they initials? An image? Was it on his buttocks, or chest, or back? The thought of him undergoing such suffering chilled her.

The cup was warming in her hand, and she cursed her foolishness. She'd brought him milk when what he really needed was water, and an entire bucketful at that.

"I'm glad you've come," he said, reaching her.

"You are?" Her heart swooned.

*He greeted her with a kiss. "I can't make it through
the day without you . . . the sight of you, like a cool
stream, refreshes me."*

*She twined bold fingers through his hair. "And
yet, you enflame me. You, a fire which cannot be
doused."*

"I've been mucking through sheep shit all day. The
beasts need to spread out more. How far does your pasture reach?" He pointed away from their cottage into the
distance. "Does your father own just the glen, or does he
have rights to that hillside beyond?"

"Oh . . ." She followed his line of sight. "He . . . I . . .
we maintain the house, down across the glen, just to the
base of the hill."

He scowled. "It's narrow, your valley."

She needed no reminders of how little she claimed in
this world. "I know."

He turned to get back to work. Leaving too soon.

"I have milk," she blurted. She stepped up behind him,
and he almost knocked into her as he spun back around.

He stared at her cup as though she'd offered a mug of
hemlock tea. Her cheeks burned hot, realizing she was
a naive fool. A dangerous man like him—he was nearly
a pirate, after all—was surely only interested in harder
drink, like whiskey or rumbullion.

"It's just I thought you must be thirsty. In this heat."
Backing away from him, she stumbled on a clump of dirt,
spilling some of the milk onto her hand.

Elspeth recovered her footing and masked her clumsiness by spinning and heading straight for the old paddock. It had the side benefit of concealing her furiously
blushing face as she wiped spilled milk onto her skirts.

She felt him follow her, making her intensely conscious of her every move. They kept a barrel of rainwater

outside the gate, and she busily retrieved the dipper. "We also have water. Unless you don't drink water."

He reached beyond her, grabbing the dipper from her hand. "I drink water like any other man."

His voice had been brusque. Was he annoyed? Simply thirsty? She had no way to know.

She watched his throat work as he guzzled the water. It spilled from the corners of his mouth, dripping down his chin and onto his chest. Damp bloomed across his shirt, making it translucent. The fabric stuck to him, and she couldn't pull her eyes from the carved muscle of his torso and the dark halo of hair leading from his chest down the line of his belly.

When he came up for air, their gazes caught. He looked like a wild man, a true rogue, dirty and panting, his sweaty hair skewed every which way. She'd never seen a more handsome man. Remembering herself, she closed her mouth and swallowed hard.

"That's better," he said.

For a split second, she thought he referred to the way she'd been gaping like a fish, but then realized he was merely referring to the drink. "Yes. It's water. I mean, rainwater. It's fresh rainwater." She cringed.

Something softened on his face, and pointing at the cup in her hand, he asked, "Might I really try that?"

"Oh." Nodding eagerly, she held out her cup. "Aye."

"I don't remember the last time I tasted milk. As a boy, I didn't think of it. Until I couldn't have it." As he reached, his sleeve inched up to reveal a wide braid of skin, paler and smoother than the rest, wrapping around his wrist like a bracelet.

Or a shackle. She stifled her gasp with a fake cough.

Aidan was scarred. Of course he was. That was why he never pushed up his sleeves. What other atrocities did that thin layer of linen hide?

He brought the milk to his lips and, shutting his eyes, drank slowly, savoring it like he hadn't the water. Finishing, his eyes opened, and he met hers with a smile. "All those years, all those sheep, and never a cup of milk."

Elspeth's heart had been cracking since she'd first laid eyes on him, but those words marked the moment it broke for good. The sight of him relishing such a simple pleasure had her mourning the childhood he'd never known. One like hers, with ladlefuls of fresh milk, and innocently snatched apples, and rare sunny days in the glen, narrow though it may be.

She vowed to steal him an apple the first chance she got.

"Do they have apples?" she asked abruptly. "In the Indies, I mean. Did you eat apples?"

He gave her a puzzled look, but didn't seem annoyed, and that struck her as a small triumph. "No, no apples. Cornmeal boiled with sheep scraps, salt bread, salt meat . . . not an apple in sight."

She ached for the child he'd been, living on cured meats and scraps. Glimpsing his scar had made her blood run cold. Had he been shackled as a child? Had he been in and out of shackles his whole life?

She believed Aidan hid other scars, on both body and soul. And she now believed the hideous rumor must be true, that he concealed a brand somewhere on his body. Her eyes inadvertently skimmed his shirt. She knew she'd never be able to discern it through his clothing, but still she couldn't tear her eyes away, straining to see altered texture or color through the fabric, scanning his chest, down his arms, to the flat sheen of scar at his wrist.

She looked up and blanched.

Aidan had noticed her scrutiny and was staring at her through slitted eyes. Stiffening, he tugged his sleeve back over his wrist. "Enough of this," he snapped. "It's time to work."

He left her standing there, an empty cup in her hand and an ache in her soul.

———

Just when he'd been enjoying himself, enjoying the Scottish air in his lungs and home soil beneath his feet, living the fantasy of an honest day's work with an honest woman by his side, he'd looked up to find her staring at the cursed scar on his wrist. Staring at him as though he were a monkey in a cage.

Sitting shrouded in darkness at the edge of his bed, he studied his wrist, the guttering candle casting yellow light on the slick band of skin. *Shackles.* It was merely one of the many marks that others had carved upon him, like dogs pissing on their territory. He'd been mutilated, swaths of his skin buckled and gnarled into ribbons of scars. From shackles on wrists and ankles. The whip at his back. And the brand on his forearm that would forever announce him the property of *Wellcome Plantation.*

Elspeth's eyes had gone wide when she'd seen his wrist. If she flinched so at that, how would she react to his brand? How she'd pale. It would disgust her, terrify her. Shock her even more than she was already.

Tugging up his sleeve, he glared at the crudely shaped letters. *WP.*

His tutor seemed too good to be true. Meek and nervous, thoughtful and kind. Such a woman would probably be too frightened, too repulsed even to touch him.

She'd touched him once, with a light hand on his, guiding his quill. But what would it feel like to have her hands on his *body*? His chest ached to imagine it.

He'd only ever been with hardened women, who perceived sex as currency, or pursued it for their self-flattering pleasure alone. But Elspeth was gentle, and innocent still.

In her darkest, most passionate heart, who was she really? If he touched her, would he find the meek girl she showed to the world, or the woman with the spark in her eyes? Because such a woman would be a wondrous thing—over, under, and beside a man.

Which was the true Elspeth? He ran his finger over the brand, thinking he had a mind to shock the real woman right out of her.

Chapter 9

Elspeth nearly fainted as she led Imogen back into the paddock after milking. Aidan had showed up shirtless, wearing naught but his plaid, and was galloping down the hillside to the pasture. To *her* pasture.

> He crested the hill. Hiking her skirts, she ran to meet him halfway.
> Naked chest heaving, he swept her into his arms. "I raced the whole way. I couldn't stay away."
> She laughed as he spun her. "Are you come to kiss me?"

A sheep butted her hip, and she looked down to find a lean black face looking up at her. The creature was a scraggly thing, with a star of white on her forehead. "Aye, Athena, and so you're right. A girl needs to remember what she's about." She stole a glance at Aidan setting to work in the distance. "And it's not dashing rogues who don't care a nit whether or not we're alive."

Digging a handful of oats from her pocket, she lured Athena back inside the gate. "I'm just a tutor, and we best remember that. Aidan only helps us because he owes a debt. I'm not a pirate bride—just a farmer's daughter, and a decidedly poor one at that."

She realized her palm was empty and dusted her hands, seeing the sheep had wandered off again. It happened to be in the direction of Aidan's fence. Elspeth scurried to follow. "Going to steal a closer look, are you? Naughty lass."

Aidan continued to work, but he ignored them utterly, and so she let her eyes linger. "Can you fancy that? The man is half naked. I'll bet you thought you were dreaming the sight. He's magnificent, like an Adonis." She butted the sheep with her hip. "You're a wanton to be staring so. What say you? Has the sun and sweat finally gotten to him? Is that why he's come only in his plaid?"

Aidan's head popped up as though summoned, his eyes landing directly on hers.

Cheeks burning, she gave a weak wave, and turned her attention back to the sheep. "Now look how you've embarrassed yourself. We need to concentrate—there's work to be done. Shall we take you to the far hill for a graze?"

She let the other animals out of the paddock, stealing another look at Aidan as she held open the gate. "Losh, but his body is the same color as his arms. You mark me, ladies: this isn't the first time the man has labored shirtless and bootless. They say he has a brand, but blast if my cursed eyes can make it out."

She squinted. The sun shimmered on his skin, and there seemed to be an uneven glint of light and shadow. A scar? She couldn't be sure.

He picked up a stone and hauled it into place.

"Look how he moves, lifting those rocks as though

they were nothing." The last of her flock had exited, and dragging the gate shut, she stepped closer to him. "I'm afraid we need to walk right by him, so mind your manners. None of you make fools of yourselves." Herding the animals, she peered his way, and he came into focus as she neared.

"Losh," she whispered, "he's powerful indeed." His was a broad expanse of flesh, and though she'd seen through his shirt how strong he was, it was nothing compared to how he appeared without it. He had muscles in places she'd never before seen—at the slope between neck and shoulder, on the backs of his arms. "Like a Greek marble."

He angled toward them. Catching a glimpse of his chiseled chest, Elspeth cut her eyes away with a gasp. Her eyes went to her flock, and she spotted a few sheep toddling off. She scolded herself as she ran to herd them back into place. She dug her hands into her skirts to tempt the sheep with handfuls of grain. "Please come, girls. I'd sooner eat my bonnet than whistle like a fishwife in front of our pirate hero. So please just follow me, like the docile wee lambs I know you are."

She shooed them along, adding, "And we must all of us stop spying."

But she felt Aidan's presence. He was like a grand ship on the horizon, inevitably drawing her gaze once more. He was settling a particularly large stone into place. As he braced it against his thighs, the rock snagged the wool of his *breacan feile*, hiking it up to reveal a glimpse of carved thigh.

"Oh!" She glanced away, then back, then away again, her cheeks burning with awareness. But she spotted more of her beasts making a break for it, and her exclamations grew more heated. "Oh, pish!"

She jogged to catch them, circling them back into place. "Stay put, you," she said, digging in her pockets, and was surrounded at once by dull eyes and butting heads. "Crud.

I'm afraid that's it for the oats. We must all stay where we belong." She sighed, knowing *her* place. It was alone, with only a flock of dull-eyed sheep for company. "*All* of us."

Reaching the base of the hill, Elspeth did a quick head count and frowned. She was off by one. And so she counted again. "Nineteen. Fool chit of a fool lovesick girl," she grumbled to herself. "Who's missing?"

As the sheep began to graze, she scanned them. A runty, wee thing with a jet-black face and white patch at the forehead was notably absent. "Wee Athena has given us the slip."

Her eyes went from the sheep, all busily eating, to Aidan, hard at work in the middle of the valley. "What say you, girls? Do you think our mysterious hero has seen her?" Standing tall, she beat the dust from her skirts. "No time like the present to ask. And none of you budge," she ordered, though amid ankle-high grass, she knew none would.

She walked toward him, imagining confidence, practicing in her head what she might say, but she frowned at the results. *Do you know where my sheep is? Has a sheep wandered by?* It all sounded ridiculous.

"Have you seen my sheep?"
　　He threw the heavy rock from his hands as though it weighed nothing. "Forget the sheep."
　　Stepping close, he wrapped his hand about her neck for a deep kiss. He smelled of earth and sweat.
　　Breathless, she parted from him. "What sheep?"

Elspeth clenched her fists, forcing herself not to clap a hand to her mouth. She saw Aidan clearly now, as well as the thick scars that crisscrossed his back, gruesome testament to whippings past.

She hovered behind him, waiting in silence, but he

didn't look up from his work. No longer able to bear the sight of his back, she finally blurted, "Have you a sheep?"

He turned to face her, his expression flat. "No, luvvie.. But haven't you twenty already?"

She cringed. "I mean . . . have you *seen* my sheep?"

"Aye, and I've smelled them too." He bent, returning to his work.

"No . . . that is to say . . . one went missing. Have you seen her?"

He gave a brusque shake to his head, this time not even sparing her a glance.

Elspeth's gaze lingered on him a moment more. Shirtless and gleaming with sweat, the man truly did look a pirate from the seven seas. Or a boxer. Or a gladiator. She imagined him conquering a bloodthirsty lion with naught but a splintered pike, the wind ruffling his hair. Of course such a man wouldn't spare a glance for a woman like her. "Oh, then," she said to that scarred back, "well . . . thank you."

She was a fool *and* a ninny.

She smoothed her skirts, wishing it were as easy to smooth her pride. Looking down, she noticed a bit of sheep muck smeared along her hip. She frowned. What a plain homely-dowdy she was, in last year's frock of threadbare tan linen, speckled with the ghosts of stains too stubborn to wash out.

She trudged back to the flock, deep in her despairing thoughts. If only Aidan could see the *true* Elspeth. If only he could see into her heart, he'd realize what a passionate and deeply feeling soul she was.

Driving the dull-witted beasts back into the paddock gave her too much time to think. If only she could have more in life. Not more money—though she could certainly do with some of that—but more of things like love, or adventure. It was why her books called to her. They transported her to a life greater than her own.

But when she put her books down, she was always reminded of her real and dreadfully boring life. Sometimes she wished she were as dim-witted as her livestock, and maybe then her days might be easier to tolerate.

She thought of Aidan's world, so mysterious and dangerous and tragic. How he'd managed to escape indentured servitude was surely something worthy of epic poetry.

If only he could see that she too would never shy from adventure. Never would she turn from his pain. She'd trace her fingers along his scars, and ease his haunted memories.

They could sail the seven seas together, avenging his stolen youth. She'd wear loose trousers and a scarf tied about her head. There'd be thick ropes of gold looped around her neck, to match the hoops in her ears.

But she was no pirate bride. Instead she was a supposed sheep farmer, and doing quite the mediocre job at that. And Elspeth knew for a fact that poets weren't exactly inclined to sing the virtues of shepherdesses in their romantic sonnets.

She shooed the last of her flock back into the paddock and then turned a circle, scanning the surrounding hills, but it was no good. Athena was long gone.

They couldn't afford to lose a single one of those blasted animals. Her eyes snagged on the old dule tree at the top of the hill. She'd climbed it a thousand times and would just have to climb it once more. It afforded a panoramic view of the glen, and if she couldn't spot Athena from that vantage, then Athena wasn't to be spotted.

Dules were good for hanging, and apparently this particular one had seen its share. It was ancient and gnarled, and folk had called it the hanging tree for as long as she could remember. Though she'd never been allowed to witness, Elspeth knew for a fact it'd served as a Covenanter gallows in her own lifetime.

Hiking up her skirts, she strode up the hill, humming an old folk tune.

Come follow, follow, follow, follow, follow, follow me.
Whither shall I follow follow follow,
Whither shall I follow follow thee.
To the Gallows
To the Gallows
To the Gallows, Gallows Tree.

Her voice grew louder as she went, and she fancied *she* was as bold as her voice. She could climb ships' rigging and sing pirate songs too, if but given the chance.

She didn't pause when she got to the base, didn't need to think, simply placed hands and feet in the same spots she'd been using her whole life, and so clambered quickly up. Reaching a spot she thought was high enough, she straightened and edged along a branch, steadying her hands on a branch before her. Chewing her lip, she sang to the same tune:

Athena, Athena, come to me,
I'm climbing like an ass up the Gallows Tree.

No sheep to be seen, but *he* was right in her line of sight. She flicked her eyes away, fearing the merest glimpse of Aidan might call his attention to her. She'd cling to every scrap of dignity she could get, and climbing like a lad up the hanging tree wasn't the most elegant of pastimes.

Oh, Aidan, Aidan, Aidan, let me be,
I can see your broad back from the Gallows Tree,
I'd be your pirate bride if you'd agree,
You could call me luvvie and your wild sweet pea—

Needing to scan over the far hill, she scampered higher, humming as she went. The greenery grew denser as she climbed, and no longer did she need to watch her step to find decent footing. Focusing only on the branches under her hands, she lost track of how high she went.

Until her foot slipped. She clamped her lips around a squeal, cursing herself. Pirate brides most definitely neither squealed nor yelped.

Glancing up, she realized just how dense the leaves had become, and shimmied out along the branch for a clearer look. Again, she purposely avoided looking in Aidan's direction; she had more pride than to somehow call his eyes to her. Instead, she squinted, scanning past the hilltop to a ridge in the distance. Her vision wasn't perfect, but she could spy green from white, and thought there might be a woolly body in the distance, though she couldn't be sure.

> *Athena, Athena, Athena, appear to me,*
> *Appear this instant, or my wrath you'll see,*
> *I'll bet you taste so good and muttony . . .*

Jutting her chin out, Elspeth peered as hard as she could, willing the distance to resolve into focus. If only the angle were just a wee bit better.

"You beast!" She knew it. It *was* a little white beast, she was almost sure of it. She stepped higher, and the movement was answered with a loud creak. This time she did yelp, gripping tight to the branch in front of her. Another crack swiftly followed, and the bough dropped six inches.

Heart galloping in her throat, Elspeth wrapped both arms around the branches at her chest. "Oh, sweet Jesu Domine, fool lass," she whispered. "What've you done now?"

She scanned at her feet. She'd edged too far out from the trunk, teetering on wispy thin branches high above the ground. Too high to survive a fall. As though on cue, there was a groan and a snap, louder than before, and the branch simply dropped away from her feet.

Elspeth clung tight to the boughs at her chest, feet scrabbling like a beetle on its back. She regained footing, and quickly began her descent, hugging her body close to *all* the branches, hoping if she spread out elbows and hands and feet, the thinner branches would hold her.

She grew calmer as she neared the ground, but she grew more cavalier too, and made the mistake of grabbing something too thin to support her weight. As she reached her leg down, searching for her next step, there was a loud, splintering crack, and she toppled forward into the other branches, arms splayed before her, one leg dangling in the air, the other crooked awkwardly high behind her. The branch she held was still attached to the tree, but not for long, and not strongly enough to support her weight. She was paralyzed, feeling absurd, like the statue of some great, ungainly bird, frozen in flight.

"What on earth are you doing?"

Oh damn, damn, blasted . . . Every curse she could muster tripped silently through her lips. *He'd* come. She peered down through the leaves to see him standing beneath her, greenery casting dappled light on his sweat-sheened body. *Cripes.*

Of all the people to come witness her folly, it had to be Aidan. Why couldn't it have been someone else? Her father? Angus even?

She reached her free leg out, bobbing her ankle, in a blind attempt to find purchase that wasn't there for the finding. *Criminy.*

Clearing her throat, she assumed what she hoped was calm and ladylike composure. "I . . . I seem to be . . ."

"Stuck in a tree? I can see that, luvvie." Amusement threatened to curl his mouth into a smile, and Elspeth wished the sight elicited anger rather than this hideous mortification she currently felt. "Might I be of some assistance?"

"No, thank you," she said primly. "I can manage."

"Clearly." Humor tinged his voice, and she pretended not to hear it. He strolled a circle beneath her, and she flushed red and hot to realize he must have a perfect line of sight straight up her skirts. "But," he added, "before I leave you to your . . . aerie, I must ask what you're doing up there in the first place? You are a wise and wide-eyed girl . . . perhaps you are playing at being an owl?"

She set her chin, mustering as much dignity as one could when one was stuck in a tree. "Athena scampered off, and I was merely trying to find her." She stretched her leg all around, and though she finally found a branch on which to rest, she could tell by the give at her foot that it wasn't strong enough to bear her weight.

"Athena?"

She caught his eye, informing him in all seriousness, "My sheep."

"Your sheep." That budding smile bloomed full force. "Your sheep has a name?"

"She does."

"And that name is Athena."

"Yes, that's right." She adjusted her hands. The bark was beginning to cut into her palms, sweating now with her efforts. "It's the Greek goddess of wisdom."

He nodded sagely. "Wisdom . . . like climbing onto a too-thin branch?"

"She is the patron of Athens," she explained. Her voice was even, but inside she was crowing, *Go away, turn around, leave me be.*

A fine plume of panic was unfurling in her belly. If she had to fall—and she feared she might—she'd just as soon fall in private.

"Oh, well that does change it, doesn't it? Does this goddess of a sheep come when called?"

"Don't mock." Her humiliation gave a snap to her voice. He chuckled. "Oh, luvvie, I'd not think of it."

She'd pretend he was being serious, hoping the equanimity in her voice would show him how blind to fear she was. "As you can see, she most decidedly does not come when called."

"Or whistled, as the case may be?" He cocked his head. "Because you told me you whistle to herd them. So I think you meant that this Athena does not come when *whistled*."

"I think you *are* mocking me." She clamped her teeth against the quivering of her chin.

Aidan gave her an earnest half bow. "There are many things in this world that I mock, and to my surprise I am finding that you, Elspeth, are not among them."

The sound of her name on his lips sent a quivering through her limbs. She studied him intently, wondering if this was fresh mockery of a sort.

"So then." Shading his eyes, he scanned the horizon. "Any sight of the missing mutton?"

The branch creaked again, and she squeaked. Lips pursed, she gave a quick shake of her head. So much for her display of passion, bravery, and spontaneity.

"You're stuck, aren't you?"

She shrugged as well as one could whilst dangling from a tree, but realized it was no good hiding her current situation. She was clearly as stuck as a thief on the gallows. "Mayhap."

He strolled around the trunk. "*Mayhap* I think you are." He returned to his original spot, and crossing his hands at his chest, asked, "When were you intending on asking for help?"

"I'm not—"

There was a horrible, shuddering groan as the branch listed dangerously lower. Aidan leaped to beneath where she hung. "Jump to me, luvvie. I think this sheep hunt is at an end."

She shook her head, avoiding his gaze. Surely she'd squash him. Or break his bones. Or land with her skirts up over her head. No, she would find her way out of this. Without *him* to bear witness. "I'm fine here. Please get on about your work."

He laughed outright. "Get on about my work? What if I propose this *is* my work? A farmer's daughter in possession of an unbroken neck strikes me as the linchpin of a smoothly running enterprise."

"No, truly, I can manage."

There was the sound of splintering wood. She reached to a neighboring branch and held firm just as the other finally cracked. Aidan jumped out of its path as the bough slammed through layers of green, coming to rest at a sharp angle, its tip digging into the ground.

She dangled there, arms wide, feet hanging limply beneath her. She could let go, but she'd follow the same path, slamming through sharp branches on her way to the ground.

"Come now, Elspeth." His tone was somber now, standing beneath her, beckoning with open arms. "Drop down to me."

She gave a tight shake to her head.

"Dammit, girl. If you herded as other farmers do, you wouldn't find yourself caught up a tree." He disappeared from her view, but she heard him rustling at her back.

His hands grasped her waist from behind, and she choked. Chagrin screwed her face, her eyes shut tight. He must be at eye level with her thighs, or God forfend, her bottom.

"Come, then." His voice was tight, and she wondered if he was affected too. "I've got you. Just let go."

Aidan's voice was gentle, and it gave her the courage to look back, dragging her eyes from the strong hands at her waist, along a chiseled arm, to the man standing below her. He stood on a thick branch jutting off the base of the trunk.

She was fooling herself to think she heard something in his voice. Why would a man like him be affected by *her* meager bottom? A dashing rogue like Aidan would desire someone more exotic. And more curvaceous, surely.

She'd heard the stories from Cormac's wife, Marjorie. How wealthy plantation wives engaged in scandalous liaisons with their fieldworkers. One look at Aidan's rippling muscles and Elspeth knew: *he'd* have been irresistible to each and every one of them. He'd be accustomed to grand ladies, flamboyant and worldly, who'd be the pinnacle of fashion.

Her eyes went to her ugly old skirts, and she grimaced.

"Are you afraid I'll muss you?" he asked, his voice gone steely.

Was he angry? "What? No, of course not. I . . ."

His fingers curled more tightly into her waist. "Or perhaps it's that the dirty farmhand isn't good enough even to help."

"Oh, no." She shook her head frantically. "You misunderstand."

"Do I? It appears you'd rather fall and break your neck than let me—"

Elspeth let go.

Chapter 10

She dropped, and he caught her hard about the waist, steadying himself at once, his legs braced wide on the thick branch beneath him. They were in an awkward position, both facing forward. He gave her a quick toss and a spin, and Elspeth found herself cradled in his arms.

She gazed up into his blue eyes, and they were hard on her, wary and suspicious.

"You misunderstood," she repeated, more quietly this time. Feeling like an unwieldy bundle in his arms, she tentatively wrapped her arms around his neck.

To her shock, he let her.

His naked skin was hot, even through the fabric of her dress. She longed to stroke a finger down what she knew was a glistening expanse of chest, but she dared not even look down, much less touch him. She waited for him to drop her, or shove her aside, but he merely held her, their eyes locked in this strange and wonderful moment.

Branches creaked and leaves rustled, but those were the only sounds. Feeling emboldened, she shifted and turned into him, twining her fingers snugly together. She hoped he'd mistake it as her holding on for dear life, but really Elspeth just wanted to be as close as possible. She tightened her grip even more.

"Easy, luvvie. Suddenly *now* you're afraid of heights?" He chuckled, but rather than pull her loose, he hugged her closer, cradling her with one arm while he used the other to ease them back to the ground. Ducking, he wended his way between branches and out from under the tree.

She didn't let go at first, and neither did he. They simply remained silent, until a quizzical expression wrinkled his brow. "You're a peculiar wee thing, aren't you?" Her face fell, and he added quickly, "Not peculiar bad, mind. Simply . . . peculiar."

Time had suspended for her. He stared, and it felt as though he were searching for something, plumbing her depths for some sign, or signal, or meaning.

She didn't know what a man like Aidan might seek. All she knew was that despite his dreadful past, in spite of his enigmatic ways and suspicious motives, she trusted him. He could look in her eyes and see what he would, and she'd let him.

He spoke again, his voice a tentative rasp. "I've not met your like before."

"Nor I yours," she managed.

Aidan eased his grip, and she slowly straightened, sliding down his body, savoring the feel of his hard muscle against her soft flesh, of his heat against her quivering limbs, until her feet touched the ground.

Rather than pull away, she roved purposeful hands down his arms. Though she sensed knots of scarred flesh at her fingertips, she didn't dare look. Instead, she closed her eyes, slowing her touch, trying to picture those scars in her mind. Such pain had been carved onto his body, a crude and vivid map of his suffering.

"I'm to go away for a time," she heard him say, and she opened her eyes, realizing she'd stopped moving. He was looking down at her, that intense gaze appearing more intrigued than skeptical now.

She swallowed. "Away?"

He smiled, stating simply, "Yes. But I'll be back."

She wanted to ask him where he was going, when he'd be back, but she knew such crass, overeager phrases would never cross the lips of a great heroine. A truly bold heroine would ask her man for a kiss, but Elspeth could barely manage to ask him about sheep, much less attempt saucy banter. Instead, what popped from her mouth was "When?"

Aidan's eyes glinted, watching her.

Oh Lord. That lone word had sounded desperate—she couldn't imagine what he must think.

"I mean . . . when shall we schedule our next lesson?" The question tumbled nervously from her mouth.

Shrugging, he began to pull away. She wanted to cling to him, to say *don't go.* But then he leaned down, and though his voice was playful, the timbre was a low rasp. "You're looking forward to teaching me?"

Heat flamed from her toes to her cheeks. Had she imagined his tone? Had she instilled her own innuendo into a perfectly innocent question? And had he really been looking at her mouth as he asked it? "I . . . oh . . . yes, of course."

He *was* staring at her mouth. He looked intense, some unspoken battle waging in his expression.

Oh God, would he kiss her? She wanted to wrap her fingers around his arms, to lean into him and say something coy or sultry, but all she could do was stand stiff and frozen, wishing, hoping, wanting above all things that he'd kiss her.

The silence was unbearable, and Elspeth turned, needing to look anywhere but at him. "The sheep. I must go fetch the sheep."

Hiking her skirts, she bolted down the hill. If she were a heroine from a novel, she'd have parted her lips. She'd have *made* him want to kiss her. He wouldn't be able to think on anything but kissing her.

But she wasn't a heroine from a novel. She knew naught of kisses and seduction. She was a poor sheep farmer's daughter, running from her hero, wishing for all the world that he'd tutor *her*.

———

Aidan strode to the docks, trying not to dwell on how good Elspeth felt in his arms. He'd mistaken her for a wisp of a thing, but she was substantial, her limbs strong and sure from toiling on the land.

He'd wanted to leave her farm earlier, but damned if she hadn't gotten herself caught in a tree. Even after he'd helped her down, he'd found himself staying, all thoughts of slavers and subterfuge fallen away. Working with Elspeth was far more satisfying than his intrigues, and he'd wanted to remain as long as he could in her company.

He'd never felt tied to the land, to Scottish soil—he'd been too young when he was taken, and such thoughts didn't enter the minds of lads—yet he was finding it oddly invigorating to be working that land, the master of his own day's labor. To be consulted, to share the work as an equal. And to be sharing it with a woman.

She'd looked so forlorn at the mention of his departure, her guileless expression so unlike anything any other woman had ever shown him. It'd flooded him with sensations—yearning, comfort, desire, belonging—each feeling so novel, but familiar too, as though he bore the heart of a regular man, as susceptible as any other, his sentiments merely rusted from disuse.

For a moment, he'd forgotten his pain and his anger. For a moment, all he'd wanted was to kiss her.

Shaking the thoughts from his head, he boarded his ship, climbing straight up the rigging. It wasn't good to be back in Aberdeen—the place held too many memories—but it *was* good to be back aboard the *Journeyman*.

A few months had passed since he'd commandeered the boat and made his escape, yet he still found it hard to view himself as a free man. But back on the water like this, with one shoulder to the endless horizon, he didn't feel so hemmed in. The rocking waves promised freedom. Feeling the sea's lurch and roll, Aidan could actually believe he was his own man, unchained and unfettered.

He'd fallen in love with the boat the moment he'd laid eyes on her. Aidan was no cheat, but he'd felt no qualms about liberating her from Nash, his fool of a master. Caribbean sailors favored one-mast Jamaican sloops, and this craft was no different. Constructed of cedar not oak, Jamaican sloops rode famously faster and lighter in the water.

When he'd taken her over, the tub had sailed under the name *Providential*, and as there'd been naught about his life thus far that he considered particularly blessed, he'd changed it at once. Besides, he couldn't risk being recognized. Even though Nash had run a tin-pot enterprise, new Caribbean money tended to have deep familial roots in unexpected places, and Aidan couldn't risk questions upon docking back in Scotland.

He swung his legs over the edge of the crow's nest, grateful that he'd worn simple breeches in lieu of the Scots *breacan feile* that still felt foreign on his body. Opening his coat, he fingered the coin pouch tied at his belt. He hoped it'd be enough for his ruse, for it marked all he owned in the world. A sack of gold jealously saved through the years thanks to the largesse of grateful plantation wives.

Largesse. He scowled and buttoned back up. Its only cost had been his soul.

He leaned his head back and thought of Elspeth. *Hers* was a soul miraculously untouched by the world's vanity and greed.

What a strange creature his tutor was, but refreshing too. Sincere and artless, like no other woman he'd ever met. Her gentleness was an unexpected balm to his befouled spirit.

And though she wasn't what the world would call beautiful, he couldn't erase the memory of her eyes. He found he woke thinking about that pale blue gaze, flecked with a yellow to match her long, pin-straight hair. The uncommon combination made her resemble one of the fey, somehow both wary and all-knowing.

She'd felt so lean in his arms, but with a tensile strength too, like the last of some dying breed of bird, fluttering alone through the world. He wondered if her spirit was as fragile as her body looked—he suspected not.

There was a distant commotion on the quay below, and scrubbing a hand over his face, Aidan remembered himself. He was in Aberdeen for one purpose alone, and it wasn't to ponder some peculiarly bookish farm girl.

The yeoman. He needed to find the man with the pearl earring, and with no clues to hand, he'd start at the bottom, and at the bottom lurked the yeoman.

Logically, he knew that it wouldn't be the same strongarm who'd nabbed him from Humphrey Keith's home so many years past, but even so, he stifled a shudder when he finally tracked the man down in a seedy tavern off Justice Port.

Bluebeard's Ghost was a hole like any other, with all manner of foulness littering the floor, a smoking chimney, and the reek of ale and bodies within. He'd been told

merely that the yeoman was "the bald one," and he knew
the man at once, beefy arms, fat neck, and a pate as shining as a cue ball.

"I have a boat," Aidan said, diving straight to the heart
of the matter.

The yeoman put his tankard down and looked up
slowly. "Bully for you, laddie. Now you'll be wanting to
move along. This here's a table for men only. Or are you
the new alewife?" His table erupted in laughter.

Aidan had expected just that sort of a response, and
smiled wide. "A merry andrew, I see. I look forward to
passing your jest along to your boss." He put an easy hand
on his hip, crooking his thumb in his jacket just enough
to reveal the sack of coin at his belt. He wasn't so foolish as to bring his entire savings, but with the help of a
bit of sand and some well-situated coin, the bag was full
and clinked enough to catch the attention of any criminal
worth his salt. "Or should I tell him instead that you stood
in the way of new business?"

The yeoman's laughing eyes hardened. "You're a braw
one, coming in here, flashing your wee purse about. What
if I've a mind just to take it from you?"

A dagger appeared in Aidan's hand and he plunged it
hard and fast, stabbing the yeoman's sleeve to the table
before the man realized what was happening. "And what
if I've a mind just to take your *hand* from *you*?"

The yeoman tugged at his arm, but the knife was
planted too deeply in the wood. He rested his hands back
on the table as though being affixed to pub furniture were
an everyday occurrence. "Leave us," he snapped to his
companions.

The other men scattered. Retrieving his blade, Aidan
plopped onto a stool, kicking his feet out in front of him.
"As I was saying before you so unwisely interrupted, I've
a ship, and I've a mind to fill her hold with able-bodied
men and have a sail to the Indies."

The yeoman fingered the hole in his sleeve, scowling. "And what's this ship to me?"

"Don't play dim with me." Aidan's patience was flagging. He knew in his heart the man with the pearl earring was out there somewhere. Plantations in the Indies and Americas were booming, which meant the slave trade was too, and his enemy wouldn't walk away from such potential profits.

Assuming he was still alive. But Aidan had spent thirteen long years living for this moment—he refused to entertain the notion that his enemy had up and died on him.

No, he'd tease the man out of hiding, and how better to do so than by applying pressure where his enemy would feel it most: on his purse.

"I know you're the muscle who gathers the slaves. But I'm not a patient man. I want a fast start out of the gate, and will raise the stakes if it fills my hold the sooner." It was a game of economics. He'd pose as a big spender, eager for slaves and ready to pay double the current rate.

The yeoman sucked on his teeth, looking thoughtful. "If you want to set up a collection, you'll need to talk to the boss. He's our benefactor, like. No business happens without his saying so."

"What's his name?"

The man shrugged. "Our man's a respectable fellow, see, who don't like to give his name. By the docks, we just call him the Bishop."

"And this Bishop, he's in charge of the whole business?" Though Aidan knew it wasn't the man he sought, it was one step closer to the man he did.

"He's in charge of the money, and that's all I need to know." The yeoman pulled a greasy wad of papers from his breast pocket and riffled through till he found what he was looking for. "Here," he said, pinning a scribbled address with his beefy finger. "You can find him here."

Aidan felt the yeoman's eyes on him as he considered the meaningless scrawl he pretended to read.

"You *can* find it, aye?" the yeoman asked, a hint of insolent humor in his tone.

Aidan peeled his lips into a snarl and simply grabbed the paper out of the man's hand. "I can now."

Chapter 11

Elspeth sat alone in the cavernous Dunnottar dining hall with naught to do but fidget. She knew she should've waited for Aidan to come to her, but when Anya casually mentioned that her brother had returned from his trip, she couldn't wait. She had to seek him out.

I've not met your like before. The words had been a constant hum in her head since he'd left a week past. Her body, a constant hum, as she remembered the look in his eyes as they'd lingered on her mouth.

He'd had a sort of serious aspect, gazing at her with purpose, like he'd wanted to kiss her. Could such a thing be true? Never had a man studied her in such a manner, but then again, she'd never been kissed. What sort of expression did a man get before kissing a woman?

She nervously adjusted her quill and ink again, shuffling her pile of papers, again. What would he think of her appearing like this on his doorstep? What madness

had overtaken her? It was time for another lesson, certainly, but to show up so shamelessly unsolicited?

Elspeth replayed their moment once more. *I've not met
your like.*

Why had memory infused such simple words with
such pretty meaning? Of course he'd never met her like—
she was the awkward and bookish daughter of a poor
farmer. He was used to exotic women, who'd wear richly
brocaded gowns, draping ropes of gold along their sun-
kissed skin, with giant gems nestled in lush décolletage.

When she walked away from that silly hanging tree,
she'd felt so close to him, like they were connected. But it
wasn't as though he'd *really* touched her, like a man touched
a woman, so why did it feel as though he must have? Truly,
she was the only one who'd been doing the touching, roving her hands down his arms like some Jezebel.

She looked nervously around the dining hall, feeling
like a bird who'd had its wings clipped. She could simply
leave, though if Aidan's siblings found him, then they'd
surely embark on a search for *her.*

Elspeth heard disembodied voices coming down the
hallway.

She needed to fashion some pretext for coming. Fisting
her hands in her skirts, she racked her mind for possible
excuses.

*"Did I misunderstand?" She smiled coyly. "Did you
not say we should meet today?"*

*"If I didn't make such a suggestion, then more fool
I." Aidan took the room in three great strides, grasp-
ing her hands in his. "It is lovely to see you again,
Elspeth. I've thought of little else but this moment."*

"I don't know where that girl has got to. Hiding like a
church mouse. Such a strange creature! Who's to understand the ways of . . . Ah!" Bridget leaned against the

doorjamb, sticking her head through the door. She called back over her shoulder, "Here she is."

Elspeth sat tall, imagining refinement, poise. She'd be cool and collected.

Aidan appeared in the doorway, his magnetic presence eclipsing all else around him. Despite her preparations, she knew a dizzying rush. It was so good—and so terrifying—to see him again.

She'd begun to wonder if she'd imagined his virtues, if Aidan wasn't really some boor, shorter or stouter than the man in her fantasies. But he wasn't. He was *better* than she'd remembered.

He was tall and strong, and though the tan of his skin had faded, the sun had left behind fine lines at his eyes and mouth. His eyes narrowed on her, looking much like a dashing buccaneer.

She opened her mouth to speak, but feared she resembled a gasping fish more than a genteel lady, which had been the effect she'd hoped for. She forced words out. "I'm afraid . . . it seems . . ."

Aidan swooped past his sister, his expression dark and dour, storming in like a Viking set on plunder. "Just the woman I'd been wishing to see."

"Did I misunderst—" Elspeth froze. "*Me?* You'd been wishing to see . . . *me?*"

He held a rolled blanket and adjusted the awkward bundle in his arms. "There's no lassies hiding under the table, are there?" Kicking a chair away from the table, he sat next to her. "I feel you at my back, girl. You can leave us now."

As Bridget scurried from the doorway, Aidan grumbled, "If Gregor were ever here, he'd realize the only course is to marry that brat off and make her some other man's virago."

Elspeth half gasped, half laughed. She'd always envied Bridget her beauty and bold sass, and it was a pleasure to hear her criticized, even if had come from her brother.

"I've something to show you," he said, looking stern. She prepared herself for the worst.

His bundle began to wriggle, and Elspeth straightened in her chair.

"Don't be afraid," he ordered.

"No, it's not . . ." She hated how he always assumed she was a shrinking miss of a thing. "I'm not scared."

"Good." He opened the blanket and a tiny puppy burst out, clambering onto the floor.

Elspeth yelped in surprise. The creature was a blur of bushy black fur, with white and brown spots, and a long narrow nose. It was the most darling sight she'd ever seen, but Aidan mistook her reaction and snatched the pup back off the floor. "He's a bit of a mongrel," he apologized.

"No, no! He's a wonder!" She leaned forward in her chair, dying to stretch a hand to where Aidan held the dog in his arms, but too shy to.

"Truly, you think so?" he asked, betraying an unexpected vulnerability.

"I do." The notion that *she'd* been the one called upon to offer reassurance warmed her. "But why on earth do you need a dog?"

"Not *why*," he said, sounding gruff once more. "The question is *who*. *Who* on earth needs such a dog." He nearly threw the pup into her lap. "You do."

"I do?" The animal exploded into movement, skittering tiny paws and claws over her skirts, and she nestled his chest in one hand, petting and soothing him with the other. "He's for me?"

He tossed off her comment. "And who else? *I* certainly don't need a sheepdog."

"But . . . me?" Something in her chest clenched. Aidan had thought to give *her* a gift. Then she remembered the shears, recalling this wasn't the first present from him. Though why he was so gruff and grudging about it, she couldn't understand. "You got him for me?"

His eyes lit on her for a moment, looking quizzical. "Yes. For you. We can't have you managing your flock from the treetops. This beggar will help you drive them to and fro."

He'd thought of her enough to bring her such a gift. So many emotions filled her, she thought she might burst. How long had it been since anyone else had given her anything? "What's his name?"

He shrugged, looking like he could care less. "You tell me, luvvie." The pup had grown calm, and Aidan reached over and scruffed him roughly on the head. "Just please, as someone who spent a lifetime being called 'boy,' I beg you not call him 'dog.'"

"I'd never think it." She rubbed her hand, burning from where his fingers had brushed hers. "He's a grand animal in need of a grand name." She'd have treasured the dog even if he hadn't been a gift—though the fact that he'd been from Aidan made him all the more precious. "But where did you find him?"

"I have my sources. It's a long enough road from here to Aberdeen." He leaned back in his chair, looking satisfied. "The pup's mother was of superlative breeding—a sheep-dog all the way from Shetland. Until she had the grave misfortune of having her virtue compromised by a terrier."

Elspeth laughed. "A terrier?"

He nodded, mock gravity setting his features. "A terrier."

His gruffness was fading, and she loosened in response. Picturing a regal Shetland bitch in coitus with a wee terrier, she laughed again. "Oh my. That must've been a sight indeed."

"My thoughts precisely. The rest of the litter was claimed, but as this fellow was the runt, the owner had no use for him."

She clutched the dozing pup to her breast. "Well, I do."

This woke the dog, restoring his energy at once, and he leaped from her lap onto the floor. Elspeth patted her leg. "Come back! We must name you." She patted again, but the dog ignored her, too engrossed in sniffing every inch of the dining hall.

"Oh, bother." Forgetting her shyness, she simply put two fingers in her mouth and blew. The dog's ears perked up and he ran straight for her. She scooped him back off the floor, and looked up to find Aidan gaping at her. "What?"

"Your infamous whistle. I'd been hoping to hear it, you know."

She blushed to her very toes. Ignoring his comment, she held up her new pet to gaze into his eyes. "I shall call him . . . Achilles."

A laugh burst from Aidan. "Achilles?"

"Oh yes." She placed the pup in her lap, but he wriggled madly, and finally Elspeth just shooed him free. "Achilles was famously heroic, you know. And peripatetic, just like this fellow."

"Peripa . . . ?"

"He enjoys moving about."

He gave her a skeptical look. "Achilles seems a long name to shout about the glen. How about something simpler?"

"Like?"

"I don't know. A real name. Like Duncan."

She bit back a disbelieving smile. "Duncan is the name of your *nephew*."

"Fine, then," he said with a dismissive wave of his hand. "Why not Fergal, or Alasdair, or . . ."

The dog sniffed his way to the corner, and finding a patch of weeds that'd broken through the masonry, squatted and availed himself.

Aidan laughed again. "Pissing in the bloody dining hall. Bridget will be livid."

"You see? He *is* Achilles." Elspeth turned to face him, and this time she was the one to speak with mock stoicism. "He's a warrior."

"A warrior? Seems to me pissing in corners is something more suited to drunkards in public houses." He looked back at the puppy, who was enthusiastically flicking bits of rock and weed over where he'd just let his bladder. "No, this fellow's a sheepherder, plain and simple."

"A sheepherder with *a white paw*." She pointed to the white hind paw amid three black ones. "Just like Achilles, with his vulnerable heel. You see?"

"No, luvvie, I do not see."

She turned to face Aidan, realizing he didn't get the connection. And of course he didn't. When would he have had the chance ever even to hear about the Greek myths? She knew a flare of regret, but seeing the open curiosity in his expression, she relaxed.

"Well, there was this man . . ."

As she began to recount her story, Aidan marveled at how she seemed to forget herself, rapt in her own tale. He tried to listen to her words—it was a rousing story, after all—but he found he kept watching her instead, how those pale eyes lit with emotion, how her delicate hands fluttered with expression.

But the true revelation was her pretty smile. He realized he'd never seen it, not like this. She'd given him polite ones, nervous ones, self-deprecating ones, but never this broad, easy grin telling him that, for just a moment, she'd forgotten herself.

It was only a squirming, wee mongrel, but the way Elspeth had looked at Aidan, one would've thought she'd never before received such a gift. And who knew? Perhaps she hadn't.

She finally seemed comfortable with him. His coarse ways had cowed her at first. That he'd finally put her at her ease was nearly as great a triumph as escaping Barbados.

The dog came sniffing back to them. Aidan saw how Elspeth longed to hold the creature, but as he bent to get the pup for her, she practically jumped out of his way, and her elbow knocked aside the inkpot she'd put out for the day's lessons.

"Oh." She clapped a hand to her mouth, and chagrin bled her face of the joy he'd seen just a moment before. "I'm so sorry."

"You've naught to be sorry for," he said, dropping to the floor to grab the rolling inkpot.

Unfortunately, she'd knelt at the same time, and they knocked heads. "Oh," she said again, with a hand to her temple. "Sorry. I am so sorry."

Anxiety and embarrassment were seeping into her features, and Aidan would have nothing of it. He refused to surrender the contented rapport they'd attained. He snatched up the inkpot and said, "It's all my doing, luvvie. I'll fetch a rag."

He raced from the room, and Elspeth was convinced it was to flee the likes of her.

She plopped onto her bottom. Her hair had come loose, and she brushed a lock from her eyes. Too late, she noticed the black ink smudged along the side of her hand. "Fool," she said, scrubbing at it, but her efforts only served to spread the blot along her fingertips. She was certain she must have ink spread all over her face, too. "You're a fool."

She sat in silent shame for a moment, then realized there was an odd stillness in the room. She glanced around. "Achilles?"

Hearing a muffled whimper, she hopped to her feet, pacing the room, calling gently for the dog. She tamped down a surge of panic. Though Dunnottar Castle was clearly inhabitable, there were areas that'd fallen to ruin, piles of rubble in which a tiny pup could get lost or crushed. A high-pitched whine came from the corner.

"Achilles? Come on, boy. Where are you?" She heard the sound of settling rocks, and this time when the panic flared, Elspeth let it flood her. She ran to the noise, dropping and scrabbling on hands and knees. "Achilles?"

Spotting a small hole, she squatted low, putting her cheek to the ground just as a tiny black nose sniffed into view. She began to clear rocks away from the hole, but her dog was either too startled or too curious, and he disappeared from view.

"Where have you gotten to?" She worked quickly, plucking rocks away, revealing a narrow burrow, low and dark.

She thought about the layout of the castle. Such a place would likely feature a pit off the dining area—ogling prisoners had once been considered grand entertainment between courses. Was this a passage to a long-forgotten dungeon? The thought didn't give her comfort—if the pup fell, they'd never be able to pull him out. "Get back here this instant," she said, her tone distinctly alarmed.

Elspeth heaved aside a few of the larger rocks and, sweeping away loose bits of masonry, uncovered a hole large enough to crawl through. She didn't hesitate, just dove in after him. The tunnel soon shrank around her, and she sank onto her belly, slinking forward on her elbows.

A mass of fur barreled into her. She yelped, and he scampered away again.

"Blasted pup." He thought they were playing at some game. "Get here, you rascal." She patted the ground, reaching an arm before her in the darkness, and seized a fistful of soft puppy. "Gotcha."

She crept backward, doing her best to hold on to the dog, alternately nipping and licking her. "I should've named you Pan, not Achilles, you wee troublemaker. Don't you know you could get crushed in here? Or you could've dropped down the pit, and then where would you be?"

"One could say the same for you," a decidedly masculine voice replied.

Aidan. Elspeth dropped her forehead in defeat. He'd seen her embarrassed, helpless, and stuttering . . . he might as well see her covered in dust, engulfed to her waist by a hole in the wall.

Her heart gave a hot, shamed pounding in her chest as she realized her skirts were surely up around her knees. She held her breath, and sure enough, felt a cool breeze dancing above the cuff of her half boots.

"It appears I find you stuck again." Restrained laughter vibrated in his voice. "I must know: how did you manage before we met?"

"I am not stuck. I am merely . . . retrieving Achilles." But she found she couldn't continue to worm her way back out while keeping hold of the dog.

"You appear to have stopped moving." His voice was closer now; probably he was squatting down next to her. "Might I be of assistance?"

"I . . ." She blinked her eyes tight. Yet another instance of dashed dignity. "Yes, please," she said, deflating.

He grasped her calves, and a bolt of lightning shot straight from his palms, crackling up through her body. His hands seemed to linger overlong on the skin just above her boots, and she wondered distantly if he might not have accomplished the same thing by simply grabbing her booted feet.

He tugged as gently as the situation permitted, but her knee scraped along the slate floor, and she flinched. "Damn," he whispered. "A moment."

She sensed him move closer. He loomed there, hesitating, and then a hand slid beneath her knees.

A foreign sensation exploded to life, buzzing through her body, settling to a hot pulse between her legs. A cry escaped her, and she lost hold of Achilles. "I . . . the . . ." Elspeth cleared her throat. "I've let go the dog."

"Relax." He gave her knee a squeeze, and her stomach flip-flopped. "He'll get hungry and come out. Let's attend to you first," Aidan said, freeing her the rest of the way.

She cringed at how she must look—surely she was covered in dirt and crumbled mortar—and dismay alternated with this new yearning she felt in her breast. She tried to blow the dust and hair from her face.

He rolled her carefully onto her back and brushed the hair from her brow. "Hush," he murmured, even though she hadn't said anything.

Their gazes met, and her mind went blank, silly concerns like dust falling away. His eyes were a crisp blue— not a pale, washed-out shade, but blue like a summer sky.

Faint lines were etched around them, from where he'd squinted in the sun. Her eyes traced a path down to the matching lines bracketing his mouth. He'd labored in the sun, but her roguish hero had smiled too.

He licked his lips, and she couldn't help but stare at that mouth. Would his kiss be firm or soft? A gentle peck, or deeper? Because she guessed kisses could go deeper.

She desperately wanted him to kiss her, wanted to find out for herself what he'd feel like, breathing in the very breath from his lungs. But she hadn't the slightest idea how to go about making a man kiss her. Surely one didn't just ask. Great heroines communicated their desires with a glance or a gesture.

Elspeth looked back up at Aidan with widened eyes, imagining illicit things like kisses and touches, but his expression remained an unreadable mask.

He wasn't getting her message.

And so she blinked, then opened her eyes even wider.

He tilted his head, studying her. "Did you hurt yourself?"

She cut her eyes down, shaking her head mutely. *Only my pride.*

"What's the matter, then?" Touching her chin with his finger, he tilted her face so that she couldn't help but look at him. His hands and fingers handled her so deftly. He was nothing short of a pirate king—of course he wouldn't be swayed by a farm girl's clumsy attempts at seduction.

But the expression that met hers was so somber, so gentle, Elspeth found herself confessing, "I feel such a fool sometimes."

"A fool?" He smoothed hair from her brow. "Silly Beth. Not a fool. Never a fool."

Beth. He'd called her *Beth*.

Nobody had ever called her by that name, or by any other name aside from Elspeth, for that matter. But with Aidan, she'd been "luvvie," and now she was "Beth." Such a simple little syllable, and yet, in that instant, it'd become the most precious she'd ever known.

"Aye, you're a fool for books." He added with a chuckle, "I daresay, you already seem a fool for that ridiculous scrap of a mutt." He leaned gradually closer as he spoke, voice slowing, eyes growing hooded. "A fool for that flock of idiot sheep, mayhap."

She held her breath, wondering what was happening. Her body was in chaos, her every sense attuned to this man, so close she could smell the scent of his person, near enough to see the texture of his skin.

He paused for a moment, and when he spoke again, there was a hard edge to his voice. "A fool, certainly, to put up with a father who doesn't appear to recognize your worth."

But then, with a sharp inhale, he softened just as quickly. "But a fool, plain and simple? Not that. Not you."

His movements slowed—time slowed—as he leaned even closer. She felt his breath warm on her face. Her lips parted on a gasp. Could this be what she thought it might be? Would he finally kiss her? She'd sacrifice everything just for one kiss from Aidan.

She shut her eyes, ready, hoping, desperate to be swept away.

But instead of his touch, there came a loud scrabbling

sound, followed quickly by the rollick of paws of an eager and dusty puppy. Aidan rolled away with an amused curse.

Elspeth fended off the dog's enthusiastic licks. "Achilles, you beast," she scolded, thinking ruefully that it was far from the kiss she'd been hoping for.

Chapter 12

"Are you certain?" Aidan asked, standing at the threshold of her cottage. When Elspeth proposed that they meet so late in the afternoon, the idea had seemed a fine one. But something had happened the day he gave her that damned puppy, and suddenly this meeting felt entirely improper. He looked back over his shoulder. "Dusk will be here soon."

"I'm certain." Stepping aside from the door, she invited him in. When Achilles galloped to fill her place, Elspeth laughed, and it speared him. It was the same bright, feminine giggle that'd erupted from her when he'd given her the dog, and he realized he'd been longing to hear it again. It was an open and joyful sound, especially sweet since she was so often such a still and quiet creature.

His eyes went to her lips, still curved in a careless, artless smile. She was staring at Achilles, and Aidan had the absurd thought that someday she might stare at *him* with just such a smile.

Her eyes met his, and they shone with happiness. An impulse seized him, to pull her close into his arms and kiss those gentle lips until her laughter made him forget himself. Until he found himself laughing with her.

"You see, I've my new dog to protect me."

The moment ended as he thought of another of her self-appointed protectors. "What of your father?" He stepped inside, looking to the right and left. Aidan had only met him a handful of times, and the man had eyed him with varying degrees of distrust and distaste. Not that it mattered—he'd been predisposed to dislike the old cadger once he got wind of how the man handled his farm, his business, and his daughter.

"He's not here tonight," she said.

It seemed Farquharson spent more time enjoying the taverns of Aberdeenshire than he did the company of his only daughter.

Elspeth was watching him carefully, and he realized he must've been scowling. Not wanting to offend, he smoothed his face. Her father was away—again—but he supposed it was just as well. From now on, they'd do their tutoring when Aidan's workday was through, and it'd be best not to have the old man lurking about all the time anyway. "There's no other time," he said, thinking out loud.

Her face fell, looking puzzled. "You don't have the time?"

"No . . . I mean, yes . . . I do have the time." He raked a hand through his hair, starting over. She seemed so nervous all of a sudden, it was making him agitated, too. "What I mean to say is, there aren't enough hours in the day, so doing our lessons after work is a good plan."

"Oh, good, yes." Her shoulders seemed to slacken in relief. "We'll be done long before the sun sets."

She said nothing after that, and instead bustled about, fetching him a cup of milk, and so he pulled a stool to their usual spot by the fire. "Tell me, teacher," he said, trying to put her at ease, "what's on the docket?"

It was a simple question, but the woman seemed to have been struck dumb. For a moment, she stared at him, and his world hung suspended, with only the incessant bleating of the sheep filling the still air. "The docket?" she asked uncertainly.

"Please don't tell me you've decided I'm beyond hope, and you're of a mind to send me away." He'd tossed off his words playfully, but deep down he feared perhaps she *might* consider him a hopeless case. It was a strangely disquieting thought.

"No, no," she said quickly. "You've gotten quite good, actually. I was thinking to have *you* do the reading tonight." For some reason, this pronouncement had pink blooming in her cheeks.

"If you think I have it in me," he said.

"Oh, you *do* have it in you." The pink in her cheeks turned to red. "To read. You have it in you to read."

He studied her, feeling his lips part in a smile. He'd give anything to know the thoughts that danced through her mind to make the woman blush so. "What am I to read, then?"

"Poetry."

"Poetry?" He wondered if their somewhat indecorous interlude on the floor of the Dunnottar dining hall might not just have her feeling a bit daring. "How . . . *audacious*."

Elspeth dropped her jaw, looking short of breath, and a realization floored him. He'd been on the mark: the woman *was* feeling bold. Why else would she look like a cat caught in the cream?

Usually, such a revelation would have an easy laugh rolling from him. This time, though, he found himself mute, feeling as uncertain as a lad in leading strings.

"Do you not like poetry?" she asked, sounding fretful.

"I like poetry just fine." He forced a jaunty smile.

"Though, generally, the verses one hears aboard ship or in the fields aren't suitable for a lady."

"I'd be curious to hear those." A strange tremor energized her voice, but she turned her back to him so quickly, for an instant, he doubted he'd heard correctly.

Heat shot into his groin, and he adjusted himself, leaning forward, elbows on knees. It seemed this Elspeth might indeed enjoy having a bit of wickedness whispered in her ears. "What a strange girl you are."

She stilled. "Did I do something wrong?"

He studied the line of her back, the long neck, straight shoulders, and slender torso that tapered down to a small waist. He'd thought she was a scrawny bird, but given this opportunity to stare unabashedly, he discerned curves hidden under her layers of linen. She was simply taut from her labors, leaner than the plush bodies he'd known in the Indies. "No, luvvie, I find you do things very right."

He watched, mesmerized, as she began to drag a stool beneath a high shelf. Realizing what she was about, he hopped up to assist her.

"Have a care." He came up from behind, catching her around the waist just as she scrambled atop the rickety stool. "It appears I must remember your penchant for climbing."

"Oh, I do this all the time." She held still a moment, waiting for the stool's three legs to steady.

He shook his head. "If ever I get you on board ship, I'll have to remain on my guard."

She looked down at him, wide-eyed. "Why?"

"I fear you'd catch sight of the crow's nest, and be up the mast in a jiff." He laughed, partly because of her innocence, and partly because her waist felt so good in his hands. Standing so close, the scent of her filled him, like grass and soap and bread. Like home.

"How I'd adore climbing high into the sails," she said with a sigh.

"I believe you would." He'd give his last coin to see such a thing.

She stared dreamily into space, a look of bliss on her face. Was that how she'd look after a kiss?

His own thought startled him, but then he let himself sit with the notion. His eyes lingered on her mouth. There was a gentle curve to her lips that struck him as eminently kissable. She was so gentle, would she rouse to a man's touch? Would her awkwardness dissolve in passion?

She was lean in his hands, but not angular, and there was something pleasant in the feel of her—her figure speaking to work and vitality, rather than the artful layers of skirts and adornment of the plantation women. Surely he wasn't the only man in Aberdeenshire to see her charms.

Had Elspeth ever been courted? But she was such a shy piece, and even if she weren't, what man was in her life even to provide an opportunity? Angus, the neighboring farmer, came to mind.

At the picture of the brawny, silent bachelor, Aidan bristled. He told himself it wasn't jealousy that made his chest clench so.

He cleared his throat, in an effort to clear his mind, and nodded to the shelves. "Are you meaning to fetch something, or shall we do our lessons from here?" Giving her waist a squeeze, he added, "Because I find I'm enjoying this particular vantage."

Her cheeks went pink, and he sidled unnecessarily closer. He was becoming quite fond of those blushes.

Reaching high, she plucked a tin from the top shelf. Her body shifted in his hands, and the slide of fabric over firm flesh roused him.

He swallowed a curse. What kind of base rogue was he that he grew excited over a woman reaching for a tin of flour?

He guided her as she stepped down from the stool, her tin in hand. "Wait," he said, coming back to himself. "Flour? I thought we were reading."

"It's where I keep my book." Something wicked glimmered in her eyes, making him wonder again what sort of thoughts might be dancing through her mind.

There were, it seemed, many mysteries surrounding the quiet Elspeth. He glanced at the lump of cloth in her hand. "You store your books in flour?"

"No, just my sonnets." She patted the fabric, sending a cloud of flour in the air. "It'd do no good for my father to find them."

"You provocative little thing," he said, raising a brow. "Poems that you keep secret from your father? That's not a book of sailors' verse, is it?"

"Shakespeare." She unfolded the cloth, revealing a tiny leather-bound book, trying—and failing—to subdue a proud grin.

They went to sit in their usual spots, and she opened the book at once, flipping through to a particular spot. "I thought . . . this sonnet . . . Sonnet 29 . . . put me in mind of you."

"Of me?" He gave her a wink. "Is it a love poem?"

"No!" She turned red as a beet, as he knew she would. Teasing color into her cheeks was becoming a most diverting pastime. "They aren't love poems. Well, some are love poems, yes. Many. Many are love poems." She flipped through the pages, looking agitated. "They're varied."

"Be easy, Beth." He put out his hand. "I'm curious to read it."

He began eagerly, but it was slow going, this sonnet, and by its midpoint, his voice had grown cold, his recitation suspicious. *This* was the poem that reminded her of him? It seemed a cursed ode to misfortune and envy.

When in disgrace with fortune and men's eyes,
I all alone beweep my outcast state,
And trouble deaf Heaven with my bootless cries,
And look upon myself, and curse my fate . . .

He glanced up to challenge her choice, but when he did, he saw that she was listening to him with her eyes shut. She held her head canted at a slight angle, as though attuned to some whispering angel only she could hear.

The picture of her held his stare. Though her skin was luminous and pale as porcelain, that wasn't what appealed to him. She was always so serene, and now she was doubly so, sitting and savoring her sonnet. After his long years of barbaric captivity, he longed to be near such gentleness, such quiet reserve. It was like entering a warm and tranquil pool after spending an eternity pummeled by hostile tides.

With Elspeth near, his rage abated, leaving him calm to his very soul. He'd always been restless—even as a young lad—but she was so peaceful, her presence was a balm, soothing him, melting his agitation and resentment, leaving peace in its wake.

What contentment a man might find, coming home every night to such a woman. What a loving wife she'd make someone, someday. Would she raise her children with such equanimity, such patience?

She opened her eyes. "I'm sorry . . . do you need help? Shall I sound a word?"

He tensed. He'd almost forgotten—he was the illiterate outsider. Loving wives and contented homes weren't in the stars for men like him.

He didn't answer her, and so she pressed, "Aidan, why did you stop?"

He stopped because it was a damned cruel poem that hit too close to the mark. He stopped because Elspeth had the knack for seeing clear to his blackened heart, when all he'd wanted to do was keep it hidden away forever.

He skimmed ahead, taking in such lyrical nonsense as larks, and daybreak, and love. Sweet poetry wasn't for one like him. Sweet girls either. He snapped the book shut. "This is foolishness. I'm not sentimental."

She sat for a time, contemplating him. Just as his discomfort was becoming unbearable, she told him quietly, "On the contrary. I have the feeling you're quite sentimental."

Her kindness threw him. He shoved the book at her. "*Beweep?* Good Lord, woman, is *this* how you understand me?"

"Please don't misunderstand." She opened the book, flipping back to the page. "May I?" she asked gently.

He gave her a brusque shrug.

She reread the sonnet from the beginning, and he heard with chagrin the poet's wish that he were like other men, with as much hope, as many friends. As much freedom.

Only this time, Elspeth read to the end, in which the poet finds somebody to think on, someone to lift him from melancholy. The final line lingered loudly in the stillness of her cottage. *"That then I scorn to change my state with kings."*

They sat there in the glaring silence, and he watched her, but she stared only at the page before her, as if she dared not glance elsewhere.

Elspeth. He felt the muscles in his jaw loosen, and knew an ease in his chest. Ever guileless was this Elspeth. He'd misread her skittish nature. Because, in her heart, she was unafraid. And unafraid of *him*.

For the first time in his life, he could almost imagine how indeed a man might come to forsake a kingdom for love of another.

Chapter 13

A knock on the door startled her. Elspeth blew wisps of hair from her brow, frowning at her rolled-up sleeves and her apron covered in a fine dusting of flour. Visitors were rare, and she glanced from the bread she was kneading to the door, as if that could tell her who stood on the other side.

Because, though it was early yet, she had a wild hope it might be Aidan.

"Come in?" she announced, though it came out sounding more like a question than an invitation.

The door opened, and it *was* him.

"Aidan," she said, instantly regretting the oddly chirping sound to her voice. She pasted what she hoped resembled a composed smile on her face.

He stepped inside, filling the cottage as was his wont, making it seem so small in comparison with his powerful frame. He touched a hand to his brow as if tipping an imaginary hat. "Morning."

Nerves seized her. Aidan never came to see her during the day. Had he decided he was done with their arrangement? Had her father found him and said something horrible? "Is there a problem?"

He scanned the room, and she had the odd thought that he might not know why he was there either. But then he said, "No problem at all, luvvie. I simply find myself . . ." He got a peculiar look in his eye. Tilting his head, he walked toward her.

She held her breath.

"I find myself . . . in need of a kiss. I find myself . . . unable to work a moment longer without seeing you, my dearest darling."

"I find myself parched, and came to see if you might spare a poor laborer one of those cups of milk you seem always to have at hand. But first—" He stopped just in front of her, a warm smile quirking his lips. "You have a bit of flour on your . . ."

"Oh!" Her apron was a frightful mess, so her hair and face must've been so too. Horrified, she clapped a hand to her cheek. Unfortunately, the cloud of flour told her she'd just mussed herself up even more.

"On your nose," he finished, with a low chuckle. "Here, I'll—" He raised a hand just as she did, and they knocked into each other.

She flinched back. "I'm sorry—"

"I've got it," he said definitively, wrapping one firm, warm hand over hers while he used the other to smudge her nose and cheek.

"Th-thank you." She stared up at him, and her mind went blank. His skin was weathered from the sun, and it made him seem so masculine. So unlike the pale Aberdeen fops in their velvet waistcoats and polished boots. Aidan might not have been a nobleman, but he was a *man*.

He pinched her chin. "The milk, luvvie? Hauling stone builds a powerful thirst."

"Yes! Milk! Of course." She clapped the last of the flour from her hands and went to the small pitcher they kept in a shadowy corner. "It's fresh, just a couple hours old," she told him, pouring him a small glass. Doubt froze her. "Unless you might like it warmed?"

"Never you worry," he said easily, taking it from her. "Cool is best for a working man."

He gulped it down and wiped his mouth with the back of his hand. "I came this morning, thinking to check on Achilles, but he found me instead. The pup's spent the past hour nipping my heels. He'll be more tired than I by the end of the day."

"It's because we're fond of you." She smiled, but it froze on her face. What had she just said? "*He*. I meant, *he's* fond of you."

"Are you not fond of me too?" He handed the cup back to her with a wink.

He'd only been playing, but still, her heart stopped in her chest. Was this what it was to flirt with a man? She floundered for words, fretting about what secrets her blush might be betraying.

Aidan gave her a peculiar smile, then, to her everlasting gratitude, changed the subject. "Weeks at sea, I'd forgotten how it is to have a dog trailing about."

He seemed so comfortable working her farm, she'd forgotten he'd be just as at home on a ship. She'd never been able to muster insipid chat like other women, and found an unusual question spring to her tongue. "Was it grand, the sea?"

He considered her with an inscrutable look on his face, and she worried she might have offended him somehow. Was it possible that nobody had yet asked him—truly asked him—about his experiences? But considering the other MacAlpins, she saw how that might've been the case.

Bridget wouldn't have thought of it, Anya wouldn't have dared, Gregor would've been too busy, Declan too preoccupied, and Cormac too caught up in Marjorie's pregnancy to have thought of much beyond himself and his new wife.

Aidan surprised her when, his features softening, he pulled up a stool and sat. "Aye, Beth," he said, a faraway look in his eyes. "The sea was grand indeed. It scares some men. But confinement has always struck me as more frightful than any death."

She sucked in a sharp breath. "Your days in captivity must've been horrible for you. More than horrible," she amended, cursing the impotence of her words.

"Aye, horrible." The word rolled on his tongue, as though he were testing it. The expression on his face said he found it wanting. Even though he shrugged, she could see the ghost of his pain in his tight brow and clenched teeth.

"For years I felt trapped—*was* trapped." Putting his elbows on the butcher-block table, he leaned closer, as though anxious for her to understand. "But it wasn't just that I couldn't escape. I was . . . hemmed in. By day, it was the other workers, and the cane, and the heat, closing in around me till I felt I couldn't breathe. But nights were the worst. Once my body stopped moving, the thoughts took over . . ."

Anguish swept his features, and he checked it just as quickly, with just a single twitch of his lip speaking to his pain.

"What thoughts you must've had," she said somberly. "You must've been so terribly heartbroken, thinking of your family. And terrified—you were just a boy. How you must have longed for home. And for revenge."

His eyes brightened. "Aye. All those things. I'd spend my nights in such dark reveries, too exhausted to sleep, surrounded by men who chattered on and on. On through the night, till I believed never would I know silence, never stillness."

"To have been plunged into such a nightmare as a mere boy. It's unthinkable." She imagined how it would be, to spend one's days laboring, surrounded by men—and among such as those who'd find themselves indentured on a faraway island. Aidan was intelligent and thoughtful. He'd not have found a like-minded soul among them.

She sighed. Despite the weight of his memories, she'd willingly share every one. "My own days are spent alone. Well," she amended with a rueful laugh, "alone but for the sheep. And I can't imagine it differently."

"Aye, sheep would've been preferable." He caught her eye, and it seemed to her that his brow had smoothed a fraction. "So you see, I longed for peace . . . until I first climbed to the top of my ship's rigging. There I found naught but the sea for miles all around, the only sound the creak of the lines and the slap of the waves. And me, my own man."

"How exhilarating." She gave him a wistful smile, wishing she might one day have her own adventure, knowing at the same time she'd only find it in the pages of a book.

"Aye, Beth." He looked blindly in the distance, savoring the memory, and then snapped back, with a rakish wink. "The only thing grander was the escape itself."

"Will you tell me of it?" She was desperate to hear how he'd broken free. Desperate to hear all his tales . . . were there pirates, and sea monsters, and storms? She snatched at the first detail that flitted across her imagination. "Do men really sing on the open sea?"

He gave her a startled smile. "Do they sing?"

"I mean," she said, feeling her cheeks color, "is it like the books? With pirates singing sea-shanties, and men crying the oars?"

He stared at her, an unreadable look in his eyes. "A bit, I suppose."

"I do so long for a sail someday." She drifted for a

moment, thinking how she'd stand at the railing, shading her eyes from the sun. Aidan would come stand beside her. He'd wrap his strong arm around her shoulders. The heat of him would warm her, shielding her from the chill winds whipping off the sea.

"It would be dangerous for a woman."

"No," she protested at once, enthusiastically quoting the old proverb "Danger and delight grow on one stalk!"

Chuckling, he kicked his legs out and relaxed against the table. "I've told you before, Beth, you're an odd one. But I daresay, I like it."

She thought she might burst from the joy in her chest. Never would she have thought being called odd would be so distinctly wonderful.

She wanted to hear more—she could listen all night to that resonant voice, telling swashbuckling tales. "Would you tell me a sea story?"

"A story of the sea?" Spying Elspeth's intense attention, he gave a low laugh. "If you're longing for tales of serpents, or Arabian pirates bearing silks and scimitars, you're to be sorely disappointed. Truly, once we got under way, I mostly spent my days wondering what I might find when I arrived."

"It'd been many years since you'd been home," she murmured, speaking her thoughts aloud. Acquainted with the MacAlpins, she'd thought of Aidan as a Scotsman. But really, his country and his family would've been strange to him. It must've been unsettling to sail for home, not knowing what or whom he'd find. "You must've wondered what'd come of your family, of Scotland. I've always wished for siblings, but I imagine it must've been daunting indeed to return to a castle full of them."

"Aye," he said, his voice tight.

The sound of it tugged at her heart. Aidan was surely concealing a riot of emotion in that strapping chest of his.

"Were you afraid what you might find?"

He seemed amused by the question. "Afraid? I can't think of a thing I've not yet seen, nor yet endured, that might frighten me."

She leaned her hip against her worktable, completely enthralled. "Well, surely you were *excited*."

He gave it some thought. "Not excited, precisely. More like there was a fire in my blood. A hunger."

"A hunger for what?" she asked quietly, risking the question foremost on her mind. "What had you missed most?"

Again, she spied that pained expression. It flickered quickly and then disappeared, replaced by Aidan's dismissive good humor.

"You ask of hunger. I daresay, *that's* what I missed most." He shot a lighthearted glance toward the ball of dough on the butcher-block table.

"Bread?"

"Well, yes, I suppose that. But I mean . . ." He gave a boyish shrug. "I missed food. Real food, good food, the kind my mother would make."

She froze, holding utterly still, despite having one hand knuckle-deep in bread dough. Her rogue had been young and happy once. Vulnerable, needful, and joyous. Was that person still to be found somewhere in his heart?

She didn't want anything to make him think twice about continuing with this amazing confession, and her voice came out a near whisper. "What would she make you?"

"Well, I remember one thing." He chuckled, his gaze looking to someplace faraway. "She'd call it her Whim-Wham Pudding. I adored it. Lord, how sweet it was, made with sugar and wee currants. But 'twas filling too—thick, like a meal."

The sound of her father's shouts brought them back to the moment. Her heart thudded to the floor. All she wanted was to sit there forever, listening to Aidan, knowing him.

He must've read something in her expression, because when their eyes connected, she fantasized that his carried a message. She read an apology, for her situation, and a question too.

Aidan's real question, when voiced, was unexpected. "What does he do all day?"

She stood upright, resuming her kneading. "Who? Da?"

"I'm here, and I see you doing woman's work," he said, with a nod to her bread dough. "Yet I see you doing man's work too, minding the accounts, tending the animals."

She wiped a sleeve across her brow, then continued with the bread. "I'm cannier with numbers. And he's too old to be mucking about in the pasture."

"So?"

She could no longer meet his eyes. "So?"

"So, what does he do?" He reached across the table and stilled her with a gentle hand on her wrist. "Much more of that kneading, luvvie, and you'll be serving hard-tack not biscuits for dinner."

She pulled her hands free, smudging the excess dough from her fingers. "There are just the two of us," she said, bristling. But even as she said it, she wondered why she defended her father so unquestioningly. Trying to convince herself as much as Aidan, she explained, "I've had to be responsible for things a woman generally isn't. But he does things a woman could never do."

"Like?"

"Like traveling to Aberdeen. He does a fair bit of that, setting up the new business. He visits neighboring farms, arranging trade."

But the seeds of doubt had been planted. Did he really need to spend that much time on these so-called business relationships? It wasn't as though his efforts bore great fruit.

"I've fashed you," Aidan said, misunderstanding her frown. "And I'm sorry for it."

She tuned into her father's voice, growing closer and louder, singing in the way he did after a good mug or three of ale. It'd been just the two of them for so long, it wasn't until she'd seen their relationship through Aidan's eyes that she felt there was anything wanting.

And though she knew her da loved her, she'd never felt truly taken care of. *She'd* been the one who always cared for *him*. She'd done all the fretting and the tending, as though their roles were reversed and she were the parent and he the child.

"Your mind is elsewhere, and I've overstayed." Aidan stood. He hesitated for a moment, and then giving her a gentle smile, he reached across the table to sweep his thumb across her cheekbone. "Next time, put more flour in your bread, and less on your pretty self, aye?"

She watched his back as he walked to her door, feeling as though her heart had been skewered through. Because somehow, since she'd met Aidan, she'd begun to feel worthy of someone else's tending. With a single smudge of his thumb on her cheek, she felt cared for.

Aidan left as her father entered, and the two men exchanged polite but chilly nods.

Her father strode to the fire, stoking it to life. Glancing at the dough, he asked, "Are we finally to have bread with dinner?"

"No, Da." Elspeth smiled to herself, making a decision. Wiping off her hands, she walked to the cupboard, retrieving a small packet of dried currants. "Bread pudding."

She held the spoon, and he took it into his mouth, shutting his eyes with a moan. "How did you know I longed for pudding?"

It was a perfect mouth, his full lips framed by a strong jaw. Putting the spoon down, she used her fingertip to dab a bit of pudding from the corner. "I just

*knew," she said, her sultry tone implying so much
more.*

*His eyes met hers, energy snapping between them.
And then, turning his face into her hand, he sucked
her finger between those perfect lips.*

"Oh dear," she murmured, her hip collapsing against
the table.

"What?" Her father came over to peer at her work-
space. "Don't tell me you used all the flour again."

"No, Da, not that." She bit her lip, feeling wicked. "It's
simply gotten warm here by the fire."

Uninterested in domestic activities, her father found
an excuse to leave, and Elspeth welcomed the opportunity to work the rest of the day by herself. By late afternoon, she had a supper plate set for him, and was out the
door and on her way to Dunnottar, carrying a bowl of
pudding, still warm from the oven.

By the time she arrived at the old guardhouse Aidan
called home, the sky was slate gray with coming twilight.
A faint halo of golden light shone in his window, speaking
to a lone candle flickering inside. Her arms were tired from
holding the awkward delivery during so long a walk, and
Elspeth carefully balanced the bowl on her hip to knock.

The door opened abruptly, and Aidan studied her for
a moment, looking baffled. As he fully registered her
appearance, his puzzlement turned to concern. "Are you
all right?" Stiffening, he asked in a louder voice, "Did he
do something to you?"

"He?" She shifted the bowl to her other hand, giving
a quick shake to her arm. "Oh, Da? *Losh*, no. He'd never
hurt me." Smiling, she proffered the bowl. "I made you
something."

"You made me something?" His anxiety flashed into
anger. Placing a hand on the doorjamb, he leaned out
over her shoulder, scanning the grounds behind her as

though she might have been followed by a mob of angry criminals.

His eyes flew back to her. "What are you thinking, coming here alone? And for this?" He gave her bowl a disparaging glance. "It's growing dark. You could've fallen on the road. Or worse."

She felt a queer churning in her belly as her heart fell and her gorge rose. Summoning a pride she didn't feel, she said, "I am my own person, Aidan MacAlpin. I went where I would before I met you, and shall go where I will long after you're gone."

He stared at her, his expression hard. He still didn't move to take the pudding, so she bent and put it on the ground outside his door.

Swallowing against the ache in her throat, she turned to go. "It's bread pudding," she said from over her shoulder.

"Wait," he called, after she'd gone a few paces.

Though she stopped, she felt a tear running hot down her cheek, and the shame of it prevented her from turning back to face him.

"I'm not going anywhere," he said.

What could he have possibly meant by that? There might've been an apology in the words, but she was uncertain. She risked a quick scrub of her cheeks with her hand, dreading the thought he might realize she'd let a few tears spill.

She heard him step closer. "And though it may be true that you once gadded about the countryside with no one to say otherwise, the fact is, *I* am here now, and I'd ask that you cease your gadding, particularly after dark." She sensed movement at her back, then felt a warm hand on her shoulder. "Puts a man on edge," he added, with humor in his voice.

She sniffled, protesting with a weak laugh, "It's not dark."

"But it soon will be. I'll put on my boots and walk you home."

Her shoulders slumped. He was going to send her home. "Oh," she said, in a small voice.

"No need to fret. I promise you'll be safe from me in the dark."

She raised her head, meeting his gaze to tell him he'd misunderstood, but his eyes held a playful gleam. Her inner heroine wanted to respond, *Not too safe, I hope.*

He snatched up the bowl, casting a longing look at its contents. "I've not had pudding in . . . as long as I can remember."

"I know." She remembered her last fantasy of him and nearly choked. Clearing her throat, she said, "Are you certain you won't . . ."

"Have a bite?" He stirred it with the spoon she'd brought. "I suppose there's no harm in having just a bite before we leave."

Relaxing at last, she gave him a warm smile.

He pinched her chin. "Wee Beth. Always with a thought for others before yourself, aren't you?"

"I just thought you might like it."

"You thought correctly." He went back inside and plopped onto the room's only stool. When she glanced around nervously, he gestured to the edge of the bed. "No need to cling to manners here. Sit yourself down." His anger was gone now, and he nodded enthusiastically at the bowl in his hands. "I can tell by the feel, this will take me but a moment to dispatch."

She frowned. "Should I have brought more?"

"Aye, you should have." He dug in for his first bite and sighed. "Delicious," he said, swallowing a mouthful. "A man can never have enough pudding." He grew silent then, polishing the bowl off as quickly as he'd promised.

She watched his lips, mesmerized, as he savored each

bite. He seemed to revel in it, offering an occasional nod or moan, his reaction better than anything she could've conjured in her own mind.

She was more certain than ever that she wanted to kiss that mouth.

He was at home in his room, paying attention to nothing but that bowl of pudding, and she drank in his every detail. How he casually leaned against the wall, and the way the stones at his back tugged his shirt tight against his body.

She'd stroke her fingers along his neck, down to the triangle of skin that peeked through the V of his collar. It would be smooth and tanned.

She'd slip off his shirt. Her arms would wrap around him in an embrace. He'd tense when her fingers touched the scars on his back, but she'd tell him she loved him, and kiss him, and blot those scars from his memory.

He liked her food, a simple fact that gave her a delight she'd never known before. She'd cook for him all the time. And as she watched him now, it seemed he might let her. More than that, it seemed he might *enjoy* it. Just the notion had her feeling more confident, and less the stammering, whey-faced ninny she'd thought herself when first they'd met.

She was more confident, maybe. But was she desirable?

She studied Aidan's mouth as he licked the last of the pudding from his spoon. Would he relish her kisses as much as he relished a simple spoonful of pudding? Would his lips and tongue be slow and deliberate, luxuriating in every taste? She shivered.

"You're cold." He shook his head, scraping the last of the bowl. "And look at me, taking my time."

"I'm not cold." She realized she'd licked her bottom lip suggestively, and she bit it, wondering when she'd become so wicked. "Not cold at all, I assure you."

"But it's late, and you've been too kind." He put down

the bowl and stood to fetch his boots. "Come, then, luvvie. I'll walk you home."

"Thank you, Aidan," she said, her voice clear and bright. She rose, standing tall, her chin lifted. She would be resolute, acting more the heroine than ever.

Because she had questions about his kisses, and she was determined to get answers.

Chapter 14

"I still don't understand why that boy is working on our farm." Elspeth's father stoked the fire with a vengeance.

Elspeth prayed he wasn't imagining Aidan on the other end of the poker. "He's not a boy. Aidan's a man." The words sent a shiver along her skin.

Her father grunted in response. "Humph. Man, boy . . . whatever he is, why does he have to come *here*?"

Refusing to face her father in anger, she squinted at her balance sheet instead. "You're blocking my light, Da," she said, shooing him aside with the sort of distracted patience born of living with someone so vociferously opinionated.

He paced to stare out the window. "And he's still here. It's night, Elspeth."

"It's barely evening yet. Aidan's been working hard fencing off pastureland for *us*, and this is the only time left available for our lessons. Unless you want that I should somehow spirit myself back and forth to Dunnottar before dawn each day?"

"Lessons." Her father raked a hand through his wild white hair. "Why do you insist on this daft business anyway?"

Her stomach growled as though it would answer the question for her. Putting a hand to her belly, she said, "We need the money."

"But he's not paying."

"I need the help, Da," she said in a weary voice.

"You have me."

Putting the papers down in her lap, she met his eye. "And you're truly going to haul rock back and forth to build me a new fence? This so-called woolen business was your idea. I am merely the innocent and earnest executor of your wishes."

His fuzzy white brows twitched. "What will folk think? I'm having a hard enough time of it finding a suitable match for you, without some knave coming about to sully your reputation."

"Aidan is no knave." She was tired—beleaguered really—and turned her attention back to her papers, idly shuffling through the month's accounts. Anything was better than thinking on the third-rate widowers her father had entertained as possible spouses for her. "He's simply a good man who's had the misfortune of a lifetime of bad luck."

"I don't understand why he needs to bandy his bad luck around *our* farm."

"I told you." She peered over the top of her papers. "Aidan and I are bartering my tutelage—"

"What kind of man can't read?"

She dropped her hands in her lap. "What have you against him, anyway? It's not as though we're to marry." A thrill shivered through her. Did Aidan want what other men had? Would he eventually find a wife, raise a son?

"Against him? What *haven't* I against him? Angus will never ask for your hand with that gudgeon lurking about."

She thought her head might explode from frustration. "Father, would you please listen when I tell you there's nothing between Angus and me, nor will there ever be."

He gave her a pinched look. "Well, there *might* be others, and I don't want them getting scared off by that pirate."

"Is that so? After *all these years*, we're to have an influx of bachelors in want of a bride? And their only requirement, that she's short on coin and long on books." She jabbed a triumphant finger in the air. "Ah! Not to mention tooth, as in long of."

Her father scowled. "It's not just finding you a husband. That boy's spent his life working among heathens, in a heathen land. Who knows what manner of woman he's bred with? What poisons mayhap course through his blood, what seeds of evil planted in his brain?"

"Seeds of evil, Father? *Really.* You're being an insular old cadger. Barbados is a British possession."

"Not till recently it weren't."

"Well, it is now, and I'm certain it's perfectly civilized." She loved her father dearly, but when he was in a mood, there was no talking sense. Making a conscious effort to calm her breathing, she tilted the month's tally toward the fire. A change of subject was in order. "The farm did well this month." *Thanks to Aidan*, she thought, with a little flush of satisfaction.

He walked back to the fire, touching a long match to the flames. "It's because I arranged to trade with Angus," he said, sucking his pipe to life.

"No, Da." She narrowed her eyes on him. "It's because *Aidan* arranged with Angus to trade for *milled* oats instead of raw."

He shrugged and spat into the fire. "Just means less oats."

"It means we have something substantial with which

to fill our bellies." Her mood snapped back to life. Rarely did she talk back to her father, and her tone elicited a slit-eyed stare.

"I told you, I don't want that slave boy scaring off Angus." He stormed back to the window, peering in the direction of Angus's place, even though surrounding hills obstructed the view. "Angus Gunn is a good man, with a profitable farm."

She sighed, dropping her papers onto her lap. "Either way, we've turned a profit for the first time in months. And you must trust me when I tell you, Aidan has been instrumental."

"Here comes the devil now." Her father ducked his head back in and slammed the shutters shut.

Elspeth's pulse jumped. "Aidan?"

"Why does that man need to come here? Folk do call them devils, you know. Those MacAlpin children."

"They're far from children. And they seem to have managed well enough, through the years." She smoothed her skirts, trying to still the trembling of her hands.

Her father went to the window on the other side of the door and gripped the shutter edge. He looked like he wished he could slam it right on Aidan's face. "It's not right that he comes here in the evening. It's bad enough I have to see him at daybreak, shirtless as a pirate, flaunting those shameful scars."

"Hush, Father." Her cheeks burned with rage. "It's not his fault he was kidnapped."

He shook his head, tsking. "MacAlpin blood is sour, girl."

She saw Aidan's silhouette, approaching their doorstep. She frantically put a finger to her lips, trying to silence him. "Hush! You hush now, Da."

But he only crossed his arms at his chest, no sign of stopping. "They've *always* run about like a pack of demons."

"Hush," she hissed, feeling the agony of it. Why did her father persist in being so dreadfully opinionated?

"It mightn't have been his fault he was taken," he continued, "but it *was* his mother's fault, letting those children run about so."

"That's a horrible thing to say." She wished he'd close the shutters. Aidan's shadow was at the door now. "Please, Da. He's a good man. It's a good family. You just stop now."

"Don't shush me, lass. Someone needs to spare my only daughter from blackguards like that MacAlpin."

"I *will* shush you, so long as you persist with these ridiculous assertions." Her whispers had turned venomous, shocking for a girl who'd always prided herself on being tractable, obedient, and respectful. "You're being prejudiced and narrow-minded."

There was a knock at the door, and she froze. Neither of them moved to answer it.

Her father scowled at her, visibly taken aback. "You can use all the fancy words in the world, lass, but mark this: if Aidan MacAlpin hadn't been as filthy and classless as an urchin, he'd never have been mistaken for one."

The door opened as her father had spoken the words, revealing Aidan standing there, rigid as a statue. He glared unabashedly at her father and said, "The urchin has arrived for his lesson."

Chapter 15

Achilles ran to the door, wagging madly, and Aidan bent to give him a distracted pat on his head. Satisfied, the dog went to the fire, turned a few circles, and plopped down, dropping into a sound and instant sleep.

Aidan looked at Elspeth, his face softening. "Sorry to burst in, luvvie. I heard raised voices and was concerned for you."

Relief washed over her like a cool wave. He wasn't scared off by her father's words. She could handle her father's parochial ways, so long as she and Aidan were on the same side.

Her father sneered. "I'd never lay a hand on my daughter."

"Then it seems we've something in common after all." Aidan strode nonchalantly to the fire, making as though to warm his hands, though she could see by the sweat at his neck and arms that he was already warmed through.

Her father followed, standing behind him at the hearth. "You're spending too much time 'helping' my daughter."

Aidan turned to face him, towering over the much older man. "And you're not spending *enough* time helping her."

"Oh, hush, both of you." Elspeth sprang from her chair and went to the sideboard, fetching a cup of milk. "Here," she said, handing it to Aidan. "I've been cooling it in the shade."

"So *he* drinks our milk now?" her father asked. "All you do is harp about money, money, money, and you're giving him the milk for free?" He glared at Aidan. "That best be the only thing she's giving away."

"Da!" Elspeth was mortified. She knew her father was overprotective, and that he clung to set ideas and old ways, but this was too much. "It's time for our lesson. Now, if you'll please leave us."

"I'll be doing no such thing." He kicked a bench against the back wall and sat down defiantly.

She sighed. "You may stay, Da, but please be polite."

He only glared in reply, sucking thoughtfully at his pipe. The smoke drifted lazily out the open window.

She went to retrieve her small worktable from the corner, her face burning. Her father had the habit of putting the lion's share of responsibility on her shoulders, until it didn't please him, and then he'd treat her like a girl who didn't know better.

Why did he insist on watching them? He was acting as though Aidan might steal something. And what had they to steal anyway? A cup of milk? Some oats?

Her virtue?

She shivered. *As if* his paternal presence could curb her improper thoughts. Sinful thoughts of Aidan danced in her head every day, throughout the day, no matter the place, no matter the company.

Discomfited, she tossed out the first rational words that popped into her head. "You'll recall, Da, it was *you* who taught me the importance of being a gracious host."

Her father only grunted, but Aidan was at her back in an instant. He brushed a surreptitious hand at her elbow, telling her quietly, "Don't worry yourself on my account. Your father is welcome to stay. It's his home after all." Though he gave her one of his jaunty smiles, it wasn't in his eyes. Reaching from behind her, he snatched the table and stool from her hands. "I'll just stoke the fire before we begin. I've noticed you see better by the firelight."

The heat of him at her back made her skin pull taut. "I . . . yes . . . that'd be lovely, thank you."

"Well, aren't you two just a couple of maids in the hen-house?" Her father tapped his pipe against the window-sill, then began to refill it from a pouch in his sporran. "Is this a lesson or a tea party?"

"Da, I told you, you're welcome to stay, but please hold your tongue." She stole a glance at Aidan as he tended the fire. She longed to gauge his mood, but it was impossible to read him from just the set of that strong back.

Her father was being a horrible curmudgeon, and she was terrified he might frighten Aidan off. She didn't have much in her life, and getting to spend time with her rogu-ish hero was a precious gift—one that she knew wouldn't last forever.

But then Aidan turned, and she read calm on those chis-eled features. There was no cowing him, she realized. The man had faced God knew what in his life; a cold shoulder and some harsh words from a country farmer would roll off him like rain from wool.

Elspeth admired him. She knew the MacAlpins were frustrated by what they thought were his secretive ways, but she knew Aidan was simply his own man, who kept his own counsel.

He was persistent—learning to read was no easy trick for a man grown—and brave, too, for it was only a cou-rageous man who admitted his weaknesses. In fact, it seemed he'd returned from his last trip to Aberdeen with his passion for learning redoubled. And though it baffled her, she didn't question it.

So long as he kept coming.

"Do your worst," he said, dropping onto the stool next to hers.

His knee jostled hers as he sat, and she burned with awareness of his body, his proximity. She attempted a breezy smile, hoping to be as charmingly casual as he.

"What's this? Miss Beth with a smile?" Aidan leaned aside to let the firelight hit her full on her face. "I fear I am to be the victim of your cruel intent."

The flirtatious banter brought a flush to her cheeks. She worried she might begin at any moment to grin like a baboon with her pleasure, and her lips trembled with the effort to look dignified at all costs. "Not so dire as all that," she said, pulling a prized manuscript from her lap.

"A fine thing." Her father's voice boomed from the corner, where he sat glowering at both of them. "Having the lass read at night. Don't you know it hurts her eyes?"

"I'm fine," she protested, not lifting her eyes from the page. Cutting off the comment she knew might be coming, she quickly added, "A translation of Homer's *Iliad*. It's a bit rough going, but I thought we could both have a try reading from it."

"Ah," he said, taking it from her hands. "This is the one you told me about?"

"Yes, with Achilles."

"Mary, Mother of God, preserve me," her father erupted. "You're not with that heathen nonsense again, are ye?" He tapped his pipe hard on the windowsill and then glared regretfully at the empty bowl.

Elspeth bit back a smile, realizing what would liberate them from her father. "Angus keeps a pipe. I imagine he can refill you."

Her father's eyes flickered bright, but then worries of propriety drooped his shoulders. He looked for all the world like he wanted to flee, his tastes running more toward tales of Cromwell and songs made for singing in the fields.

"It's truly fine for you to leave," she pressed. "I'm alone with men all the time, with Angus and with other merchants too, sorting our accounts."

He shot a measuring glare at Aidan.

"We've coin to spare this month." She nodded toward the door. "Now go refill that wee pouch of yours."

That decided it for him. With a brusque nod and dire admonitions for his daughter's safety, Elspeth's father left.

"I apologize for his rudeness," she said quietly.

Aidan waved it off. "To the contrary. I'm glad to see he has a care with you. I'd wondered, you know."

"You did?" she asked, brightening. She'd be sure to replay those words in her head later, mulling every possible implication.

Rather than answer, Aidan turned his attention to the book. Even though he'd grown gruff, he was leafing through the pages gingerly, and she appreciated his care. "Where do you keep this one? In the sugar?"

"Your brother Declan lent it to me." When he looked up at her with raised brows, she nodded. "Dunnottar has a library, you know. Well, it's mostly in ruins, but a tidy collection of classics seems to have survived the devastation."

A peculiar look furrowed his brow. "You even talk like a book, you know it?"

Frowning, she looked down.

With a fingertip to her chin, he tilted her face back up. "It's a good thing."

"Well, what of you?" she asked defensively. "You speak very well yourself, despite the . . . for a . . ."

"For a man who's spent much time in shackles?" He gave her a careless shrug, seeming to sense how she regretted her words. "Don't worry, you can speak of it. It's not as though it ever slips my mind."

She tried to keep her face a blank, though she wanted to cringe. How would Aidan ever forget his past, how could he ever forget the outcast he'd become, when men like her father were quick with their suspicions to remind him?

"Yes," she said. "You speak well, especially for one who's led a life of such privation and cruelty."

But even as she said it, she knew. She'd seen for herself just how smart Aidan was. Unlike most men, who postured arrogance and pretended to know it all, he was ever ready with another question on his tongue, as if he could make up for his lost years of refinement and education in their evening lessons alone.

"I'll tell you where I got all my pretty turns of phrase, luvvie. Though you may not like to hear it. You see, early on, I learned the true currency of the Indies. Husbands are never about, and that leaves the wives, and they've a taste for parlor talk around rough-looking men with gently bred voices." He sneered. "I spent my mornings chest-high in the cane, and my evenings serving rumbullion and fruit to rooms full of rich plantation women, bored of the heat and their entitlement."

Her mind spun with the hideous image. What else might bored plantation wives have wanted of their indentured servants? She opened her mouth to speak, but no words came to her.

Aidan's laugh was self-deprecating. He shoved *The Iliad* back in her hands. "I'm certain Achilles makes a better story."

He leaned forward, resting elbows on knees, watching her. He tried to look casual, but Elspeth saw his shoulders were flexed taut. "So you and Declan, is it?"

"Declan?" The odd question threw her, making her forget her earlier discomfort.

He nodded slowly. "Aye, Declan. Do you have a fancy for my brother or don't you? He'd be able to talk bookish things with you."

"Declan?" she repeated. Was she misunderstanding the implication? Aidan had sounded wary—was he just a little vulnerable too? "No, not Declan," she said, more slowly this time, and smiled at the relief she thought she saw along his brow. "He's merely the self-proclaimed guardian of your family library."

He barked a quick laugh. "Self-proclaimed? *Uncontested*, more like. Can you truly imagine someone else caring two whits about a library? Bridget? Gregor, mayhap?"

She allowed herself a giggle. "No, I suppose not."

He nodded to the book forgotten in her hands. "Well, shall we get on with Sir Achilles? You say he was a warrior."

"Indeed." She smiled, thinking the man next to her no less heroic than any of the Greek gods. "He was away for many years. So the story went, he could have either homecoming, or glory, but not both."

Aidan curled his lip. "I feel a kinship already."

She paused, realizing she needed to tread carefully. Her intent hadn't been to draw any parallels between the real man and the literary one.

But then he told her, "Go on." When she raised questioning eyes to his, he added with a wink, "I like when you read."

That single wink had a catastrophic effect on her composure. Deciding the best course would be simply to let Homer speak for her, Elspeth went to the first page, and tilting it toward the fire, squinted to make out the words. It was growing dark, and it was always harder to read at night. She began, " 'Sing, Goddess, of the rage of Peleus' son Achilles, murderous, doomed—' "

Aidan startled her with a loud laugh. "Such drama already."

She smiled back, and their gazes caught again, sending a ripple of pleasure across her skin. This time she let herself enjoy the connection for a breathtaking moment.

"I suppose you could say the Greeks had their histrionic proclivities, yes. Our Achilles was no different."

He gave her one of those peculiar looks she was beginning to recognize, looking something between warm and baffled. "*Rage*, eh?"

"Oh yes, he was a gloomy fellow. Consumed by anger, wanting only vengeance against those who'd wronged him."

"I told you I sensed a kinship." Aidan's words were light, but his eyes were grave.

Chagrin choked her. She'd been right—though they talked of Achilles, they were somehow speaking of Aidan, too. "But he was so much more than just his anger," she insisted. "He was tremendously brave too. A true hero."

"Indeed?" Aidan glanced at the dog asleep by the fire. "Such a complicated name with which to saddle a poor, innocent pup."

"Well . . ." Her mind raced, this banter more than she could handle. Night was falling, and the firelight cast one side of Aidan's face in shadow. He was so handsome, her dark rogue, and she was struggling to put two thoughts together. "It was an arrow. That killed him. Achilles, I mean. He was killed by an arrow to his heel, and *that* Achilles," she said, pointing to her dog, "has a white heel, and so you see . . ."

Her voice tapered off, but Aidan was quick to pick up the thread. "I do see, clearly." He pinned his gaze back on her, so intense it was as though he'd touched her. "You say he was away from home for many years. What happened when he returned? Did he have his vengeance?"

Were they just speaking of Achilles, or was there some deeper meaning at work again? She fluttered through the pages, as though she might be able to flip to the answer.

"Did he return a hero?" he pressed. "Does he die a hero?"

With a nervous laugh, she quipped, "Some say he died because of his ill-advised marriage to a Trojan princess."

She'd hoped to change the topic to more swimmable waters, but that bit of trivia kindled something sinful to life in his gaze. "An ill-advised affair, was it? Was there nobody to counsel our hero against such an ill-fated love?" He leaned closer, his voice growing huskier. "Or was it simply lust that felled our great Achilles?"

"I . . . I'm uncertain . . ." *Lust.* He spoke to her of lust. Liquid heat flooded her body, making her cheeks hot, her chest tight, her nothing more than a creature of acute desire. She rubbed her forehead—between the evening's reading and repartee, she was becoming undone. "We'll simply have to read till the end," she finally managed, her tone overly bright.

"Shame on me." He leaned away, and the moment ended, leaving her wondering if there even *had* been a moment. "I'm making you read, and it clearly pains you." He reached out his hand. "I daresay it's time for me to give it a go."

"Take me." Her eyes widened, and she foisted the book at him. "*It!* Take *it*. Perhaps . . . I think it's your turn. To read."

As Aidan grasped it, their fingers brushed. He stilled, and for a moment, both of their hands held the book, fingertips touching.

The door swung open, and Elspeth flinched away, mentally flaying her father with every curse she'd ever read. Why did he have to choose just then to return?

The man stood in the doorway, glowering at the pair of them. Seeming to find everything to his satisfaction, he strode to the fire to stoke it. "That fool farmer's not around. And now I've spent legs *and* a spent pipe."

Elspeth glanced from her father to Aidan. Should they continue? Surely he wouldn't want to read in front of anyone else. Tentatively, she reached out her hand. "Sh-shall I?"

Her father was restless, strolling about the cottage, seemingly everywhere at once, making her feel hemmed in. "The boy's not reading for himself yet?"

She felt Aidan tense, and shame choked her. She knew her father didn't like Aidan, but couldn't see why he had to be so rude. "He's a *man*, father."

Aidan raised the book in the air. "A man about to read for himself." His smile was jaunty, but his eyes were cold flint.

"Remember," she told him quietly, hating that her father was watching, "scan the words before you begin. I think it helps to have a picture of the page in your head before you dive in."

He did as she instructed, shaking his head. " 'Death . . . bodies . . . feasts for dogs and birds . . . ' " He glanced up, warmth in his eyes. "You've truly read this? Seems unsuitable for a gentle lady."

Gentle lady. She swelled. Not farmer's daughter, nor rustic, nor unrefined. He'd called her "gentle," and a "lady."

"Oh, I am. I mean, I *have*." She took a breath and tried again. "I have read it. I adore tales of battle. Swashbuckling tales. Adventure." Would that Aidan would tell her more of *his* tales. Would that she were brave enough to ask.

He began to read, and though he was slow, his pace was steady. "You're a quick study," she told him between sentences. "I daresay, whatever you knew as a child has mostly come back to you."

"It's the quick wit of my teacher I'm to thank," he said, and she gave him a blushing smile in response.

Her father's voice boomed from behind them. "Are you learning or courting, lad?"

She tensed, but refused to grace her father with a response. "Go ahead," she told Aidan. "Please continue."

He did, until he reached a word that stumped him. "Ag . . . Agam . . . Agamem . . ."

Her father laughed. "Just sound it out, boy."

"That's just fine coming from someone who's not read a book in his life," she muttered. Then, in as quiet a voice, she whispered the correct pronunciation.

Aidan was the only one to hear, and he met Elspeth's eyes over the book. His quick nod and smile made her feel like his co-conspirator.

He read on, eventually stumbling once more. " 'Dish . . . dish—' "

Brows raised, he pointed out the passage, but the cottage had grown too dark. As she adjusted the page for a better look, their hands touched. Wildfire razed her senses. She thought he drew in a sharp breath, but she refused to look, fearful she'd just imagined it.

She thought she saw him glance to her mouth. The most peculiar light was in his eyes, and he looked at her with purpose, as he had before, and as before, she wondered if he might kiss her someday.

What would it feel like? Would he open his mouth to nibble her like a sweet? Would she taste him on her tongue? Perhaps, someday, before he sailed away again, called by distant shores, she might ask if he would kiss her. Just one, just once.

She'd ask as a favor. For surely she wasn't Aidan's type. Aidan's type of woman would be dark and voluptuous, not pale and reed thin. His type would have full, red lips. She'd know when a kiss was imminent, and she'd lick those lips, sending her man a telling, lingering gaze.

Something overcame Elspeth—a bolt of courage, of desperation—and she flicked her tongue out ever so slightly, to graze her bottom lip.

Aidan sucked in a breath, and this time she saw it to be true. This time she saw that gaze alight on her mouth. She felt suddenly too hot by the fire, too trapped by her own skin pulling taut over her breasts, at her belly.

She heard her father's footsteps shuffle across the room, and it was a splash of cold water. He was watching, and she refused to give him any more reason to mistrust. She cleared her throat. "It's *dis—dishonoured.*"

"As in, what a man feels when forced to pay his debts in labor not coin," her father grumbled, oblivious to the moment occurring by the fire. He'd been puttering about the cottage, in and out, fetching wood, stoking the fire, rifling through the cupboard. "You best get supper on soon, or we'll be up till midnight."

She felt Aidan tense again, and knew a surge of anger. The last thing she wanted was for him to storm off, disgruntled, or worse, discouraged. She whispered, "It's not as though *he* has a coin to spare."

Aidan's laugh was a low rumble in his chest. Though she was too nervous to do anything but swallow her own laugh, she hoped her smile told him how much she was on his side.

"It's dark, Elspeth," her father said sternly. He spoke from over their shoulders, and she startled. "And though I don't know the man who'd choose *you* for his seduction, it's improper. You'd not be alone with the parson himself after dark."

She knew her anger could have no vent, and it tightened her lungs and set her pulse throbbing in her temples. When she answered, her voice was tight. "Aye, Da."

Aidan shut the book and shifted in his seat, and she wondered if she only imagined the feel of him bristling beside her. His knee touched hers for a pregnant moment. "The fence is almost done."

She felt the blood drain from her cheeks. If he was almost done with her fence, did it mean he was almost done with her too?

"So, I was thinking," he began slowly, watching her

father begin his puttering again, until finally the man stormed out the door, water bucket in hand. "Perhaps we should have our next meeting in daylight."

"Oh!" A little gasp escaped her lips. Aidan wasn't done with her, after all. One more meeting—and perhaps she could devise a way to ensure one more after that. "Yes, that sounds lovely."

"Oh." He mimicked her, with a rakish grin. "You see, I've a . . . document I can't quite puzzle out."

She kept a smile on her face, even as the fire in her heart dimmed just a little. He wanted to meet with her, not because he wanted to see her, but because he needed her to read something for him. She told herself it was just as well—so long as it meant she'd get to see him. "But of course."

Did he mean those mysterious papers she'd glimpsed once before? He'd guarded them jealously.

Her mood spiked as she considered the possibilities. He was likely involved in some sort of swashbuckling pirate business—a treasure hunt, perhaps. "I'd love to read your documents," she said with enthusiasm.

A veil dropped over his face, making him seem grim and shuttered. "No, no, luvvie. You won't be reading all of them."

Elspeth pursed her lips. He'd be thinking those thoughts again—that she was too weak, or too frightened. Or perhaps it was worse than that. Perhaps he simply didn't trust her.

Whatever his reasoning, whatever his business, she had to find out what he was about. "Where shall we meet, then?" she asked, even as her mind raced with possible ways she could uncover his secrets, perhaps help him.

"Come see us at Dunnottar. Tomorrow." His grave expression vanished, and her handsome rogue appeared once more. He gave her a wink. "You can show me the library."

═══════════

Aidan knew he should keep his distance from her. Elspeth was too smart by half, and she'd figure out his business in a trice.

And he was growing impatient besides. He'd taken too long with his studies, and had begun to fear the man with the pearl earring might slip through his grasp. Though he'd never breathe a word of concern to Elspeth—never would he want her to think herself a failure.

He knew he should stay away from her, should keep his mind on his goal, but he found he couldn't stop from visiting, couldn't help but invite her to Dunnottar. Each time he told himself would be the last time.

The thing of it was, he *liked* her. He liked being by her side. He found he relished an honest day's work, tied to the land, and with a woman by his side. Days when he saw Elspeth were good ones, even if they did often mean he had to endure her father in the bargain.

He liked how she carried herself—she was reserved, but she stood tall. She seemed a good person, a person who knew herself, knew what she was about. He liked the little things about her too, like the way she held her books, and her look of wide-eyed appreciation as she read them, the way she bit her lower lip in concentration. She'd finish and look up at him, meeting him with a face of open pleasure, lacking artifice, or judgment, or pity.

It was as though Elspeth saw him simply as a man whose company she enjoyed. With Beth, he was neither servant nor victim. He was only Aidan. And he found he'd begun to crave the feeling.

He realized with a shock that he'd begun to crave *her* too, in ways that made him wish their collaboration lasted longer than dawn till dusk. Because Aidan had decided he might like to keep her close the whole night through.

Chapter 16

Elspeth set out that morning, using her walk as an opportunity to replay Aidan's each and every wink in her mind. She relived every brush of his hand, every twinkle in his eye, thinking if she could only but inure herself to his charms, she'd be able to face him with more composure.

However, she refused to be distracted by that charm. Surely Aidan knew how much his rakish ways devastated women, and she suspected that husky voice and those sparks in his eyes had only been tools with which to distract her from documents he wished to keep secret. But she wouldn't be dissuaded. She was too curious.

Not to mention too concerned for his safety.

She arrived at Dunnottar earlier than the agreed-upon time, her heart set on a little snooping. There was risk in her plan, but she was sure Aidan wasn't the sort to linger about the house. She knocked repeatedly on the tower house door, and was relieved to find nobody around. She promptly turned and strode straight for the old guard-house that he'd taken for his lodgings.

Elspeth listened at the door. *Silence.* Then, not allow-ing herself a chance to doubt, she darted inside, quickly shutting the door behind her. Bracing the door at her back, she gave her eyes a moment to adjust. Though light filtered in through a row of musket holes and the lone window, the room was dim.

Her heart pounded from the thrill. She was sneaking around as though *she* were the one on a secret and dan-gerous mission. Like a pirate bride helping her man. Or some mysteriously seductive lady spy.

As Elspeth's sight adjusted and his few belongings came into view, she began to tremble for an entirely dif-ferent reason. This was *his* room, and though she'd been in it before, it was a different experience getting to study everything so unabashedly.

She stepped farther inside, taking in every sight, every scent. She sat on his narrow cot. It was neatly made, and the crunch of dried heather was so loud in the silence she promptly stood again, careful to smooth the wool blanket back into place.

There was a small side table, upon which stood a child's toy knight, whittled from a bit of wood. She picked it up, marveling at the detail. Marveling at the strange, unknown layers to his personality that Aidan kept hidden. Carefully, she set the knight back in its place by the washbowl, then dipped her fingers in the water and smiled—he'd probably used this to wash, just this morning.

"Fool," she whispered to herself. Smiling and shaking her head, she dried her hand on her skirts. "Silly fool."

She'd come to find his secret papers. So where were they? She paced the tiny room, nudging the slate flooring with the toes of her boots—she'd read that wee cracks and chinks made excellent hiding places—but no luck.

Aidan appeared to live a spartan life. No desk, no drawers, no wardrobe . . . no possible hiding places. There was just an extra blanket and a few items of clothing, folded and stacked in a tidy pile under the table. She carefully sifted through all of it, but again, no luck.

She sat again on the bed, this time heedless of the groan of the frame and the crunch of the mattress. She smoothed her fingers over the blanket and, not really expecting to find anything, slid her hand under his pillow. And that's where she felt it: the crisp give of paper at her fingertips. "Here you are."

She dared not risk any rumpling or ripping, and moved the pillow aside to read his papers where they lay. Riffling through, she paused at a peculiar-looking receipt of sorts. Squinting, she made sense of the words.

WARRANT OF ENTRY
BRIDGETOWN PORT, BARBADOS
CAPTAIN WM. DERBY-PHIPPS
THE ENDEAVOR (ORIG. LEÓN DE ORO)
TYPE: XEBEC, 160 TONNES BURTHEN, 18 GUNS
CREW: 95
GUARANTOR: DOUGAL FRASER, KING'S QUAY, ABERDEEN

It appeared to be a Barbadian port-of-entry clearance. But whose? She recognized Aidan's handwriting by now, and these elegant loops looked nothing like his cramped scrawl. Who was Captain Derby-Phipps? And why would this hold such seemingly great importance to Aidan?

She lay on her stomach, propped up on her elbows. She adored a mystery—particularly a swashbuckling one—and scanned the document for clues.

She began to hum, distractedly at first, not even realizing that something had tripped a tune in the back of her mind. It was an old war song her father sang around the farm. Soon her humming became a low whisper of lyrics.

I sailed a great frigate by the name Nonesuch,
But I'd turn my coat for a four-bit groat,
And so I turned against the Dutch.
Yes, I turned against the Dutch, the Dutch,
I turned against the Dutch.

And what was a *xebec*? The name alone sent a shiver of excitement up her spine—it sounded so exotic, like something that might have a great, painted lady carved at its bow, or an army of swarthy men working its oars. It looked like the original name had been *León de Oro*, so maybe it was a sort of Spanish galleon, so laden with chests of gold and silver bullion, it rode low in the water. *León de Oro*, she mused with a smile, and sang another snippet.

But from Spain I stole their Lion of Gold,
And became the King's man again, again.
Became the King's man again.

William Derby-Phipps—why did the name sound so familiar? *Captain William Derby-Phipps*. The beginning of the song popped into her head, and her excitement turned to dread.

My name is Captain Will, oh Will,
I turned pirate when I killed good men,
Their worthy blood did spill.
Their worthy blood did spill, did spill,
Their worthy blood did spill.

Could this paper have belonged to *the* Captain Will? She racked her memory—was Derby-Phipps the name of the notorious traitor, or was her imagination running away with her yet again?

The Captain Will she knew had sailed in a small

British fleet against Spain in the Thirty Years War. Facing resounding defeat, he'd infamously convinced his crew to go pirate, slaughtering what British sailors wouldn't turn, and splitting from their Dutch allies.

But he'd reappeared weeks later, having repossessed a ship bursting with purloined gold from the Spaniards. Captain Will comported himself quite prettily, delivering a vast bounty to the Crown's coffers. King Charles saw only a fine line between pirate and privateer—particularly when the privateer in question had such a knack for acquiring riches—and so with a slap for one cheek and a kiss for the other, he sent the captain off with a pardon and the gift of a strange, sleek Spanish ship.

A chill shot to her bones.

Was it possible this Captain Derby-Phipps was *the* pirate? Was the man even alive still? And if it was possible, and if he was indeed the pirate, what would Aidan have to do with such a man?

There was another name on the warrant, one Dougal Fraser, King's Quay, Aberdeen. Did that mean the pirate had business in Aberdeen?

Surely her imagination was running amok. But she reread it, and the evidence was there, written clearly in front of her.

What sort of dangerous business was Aidan dealing in? Was he in trouble? He didn't seem to value himself overmuch; she was frightened he might blithely place himself in harm's way.

She'd read such things in stories. Men like him embraced danger, thrived on it. He was so secretive—did it mean he was involved in some sort of high-risk plot?

"You wicked chit."

Elspeth yelped in surprise and looked up.

Aidan glowered at her, his broad shoulders filling the doorway, looking like he was deciding between ravishing her or delivering a sound thrashing. He glanced at his papers, and then back to her, lying prostrate on his bed.

His gaze raked a slow path down her body, inflaming her as it dragged along her back, over her rump, down her legs, and back up again. "I knew there'd be perils lurking beneath still waters."

His words implied perils beyond her wildest imaginings. She fumbled to respond. "I—I—I came early, and you weren't—"

"*Three hours* early?"

Painfully aware of the papers under her fingertips, she gave them a quick shuffle, but there was no hiding them completely. She could only explain them away. "I wanted to help you . . . you said you needed help deciphering."

He slammed the door. The room had felt small before, but now that his presence filled it, the sense of large, vibrant male closed in all around. "A lesser man might think you're spying."

"Oh, no, it's not like that." She turned to get up, but he loomed so close over the bed, and her skirts were in such a tangle, that her movements were awkward. She spotted the flicker of his eyes over the front her body, and she froze, half on her side, half on her back, the breath caught in her chest. She felt exposed, splayed in such a vulnerable position, keenly aware that she was lying on *his* bed.

Again, he swept his eyes over her body, and when he spoke again, his voice was a husky rasp. "Then how's it like, luvvie?"

Sensation flooded her. Every rumple on the bedding was an agony beneath her, her skin too hot, too tight. Her bottom, her breasts, the backs of her legs—all a mass of nerves too sensitive to bear. "I only want to help."

Muttering a curse, he turned his back on her.

She smoothed the papers into a neat stack. It took every ounce of her spirit to keep her voice composed. She was determined to show Aidan how helpful she could be, how intrepid. "Where did you get these? What's the meaning of them?"

He sat next to her on the bed, and his weight drew her close. "I stole them."

Rather than inching away, she shamelessly let herself roll toward him. Though it was merely a fraction of an inch, it was enough for her to sense his warmth, his scent. The heat of his hip and thigh transferred directly to her, becoming an inferno in her belly. She managed to ask, "From whom?"

"You're a determined wee spy." He glared at her, and just when she thought he'd ignore her question, he gave a defeated shake to his head and said, "From a smuggler. I found a stash of papers on his ship and stole the lot of them."

"Are you speaking of the smuggler you and Cormac took down?"

"The very one." He snatched the papers from her hands. "And though they may not be mine, they're not yours either."

"But why take them?"

"I'm tracking a man. A man I'm going to kill."

Gooseflesh crept along her skin. "I can help you," she said gravely.

Aidan burst into laughter. "You'll do no such thing."

Of course she was going to help him. He was right to think she couldn't help him kill a man, but she could be valuable in other ways. "I can help you decipher these. Who is it you're tracking?"

He gave her a long, raw stare, and she glimpsed some bleak thing haunting his soul. "A pirate with a black pearl earring. The man who kidnapped me as a child."

She shivered. She'd been right all along. He *was* her intrepid hero, tracking down evil pirates. She riffled through his papers, so full of danger and potential adventure. "Perhaps we can find a clue."

He snatched them away. "*Perhaps* you should go home where you belong."

"But I belong *here*." She reached for them again.

But he held them out of her reach, his expression shuttered once again behind his usual nonchalance. "In my bed, luvvie? How can I say no to that?"

Her breath caught, and she cursed her weakness for him. He'd tried to distract her with his rakish wink, and it'd almost worked.

Strengthening her resolve, she came up with the one excuse she knew would keep her there. "It's our day for lessons, remember? After all, if you won't let me read the complicated bits for you, you'll need to learn to read for yourself."

That gave him pause, and he relaxed his guard for a moment.

Because she had to try again, she darted a hand out for the papers.

Startled, he laughed, and this time there was warmth in it. He put a hand at her shoulder to restrain her. "You're a wily wee fox."

She wriggled. "And you're an exasperatingly large . . . bull."

Tossing all the papers aside, he gripped her other shoulder too. "A bull, is it?"

"Aye, and stubborn as one too." As she felt herself being eased back onto the bed, her mouth went dry. "But . . . but . . . what of our . . . lessons?"

"I'll teach you a lesson."

Excitement jolted her, and it made her feel as brazen as the pluckiest of heroines. "One I'll not soon forget?"

A true, hearty laugh erupted from him, and though it faded, the ghost of it lingered in his eyes. "You're a strange bird, Beth. Do you know that?"

Beth. That name again. She swallowed hard. "So you've informed me."

"I believe you truly do think you're helping me."

"I am," she said earnestly. "I do."

"What are you doing sparing a care for a man like me?" She was on her back now, his hand heavy and gentle at her shoulder. He gave her a squeeze. "Don't you know I'm beyond help?"

"Nobody is beyond help."

"You are. Just now, just here." He drew a tentative finger down her cheek, outlining her eyebrow, her cheekbone. "Look, for example, at how vulnerable you are right now. One could easily call *your* predicament beyond help."

Her pulse pounded, her face burning from his touch. "Mine is not a predicament. That . . . that would imply . . ."

"Imply what? That you won't come to harm at my hand?" He cupped her cheek, his movements bolder now. "How do you know that? After all, we've really only just met. My own family barely knows me." Keeping her cradled in his hand, he leaned close to brush his cheek along the other side of her face. "How are you to know I won't . . . take advantage?"

The rasp of his voice, the faint graze of stubble on her skin, the pure immediacy of him sent a shock of wanting between her legs.

"Or perhaps," he whispered in her ear, "you meant to imply that your current situation is a *desirable* one?" He brushed his lips over her skin. "Have I the right of it? Do you desire this situation?"

He was so close, the heat of his chest imprinted itself on her breasts. His hands were strong and sure, and their touch made her feel delicate and fine.

Was this how a seduction began? Was she supposed to give him a sign? Her mind was a tumult—she wanted to act, but had no idea how.

Someone shouted from far away, and Elspeth stiffened.

Aidan stilled, hovering at her cheek for what felt an eternity, his breath coming in warm, exhilarating puffs along her cheek. Dismissing the outside sounds as one of his brothers, she wondered if he'd kiss her when it grew quiet again, impatient to see how he might go about it.

But when he pulled away, his eyes had gone cold. "Perhaps not."

"Wait—" What happened? Had she done something wrong? Why had he not kissed her? *I do desire it*, she wanted to cry. She'd thought he had too, but he'd turned to stone.

Aidan bolted up from the bed, snatching his papers from where they'd drifted onto the floor. "I've business to attend to." He opened the door, and standing with his back to her, added, "I presume you'll see yourself out."

Chagrin, confusion, and embarrassment burned her from within. Like the greatest of heroines, she wouldn't be daunted. She *would* be resolved.

And then Elspeth sat up, secreting into her bodice the single, rumpled page that she'd managed to steal from Aidan's pile.

Chapter 17

Aidan stormed from his room, searching for someone to throttle. Preferably the half-wits who'd been making noise so near to his door. If his ears had the right of it, said half-wits had been Aidan's hired man and Gregor, who'd probably detained the stranger he'd found skulking about, likely with as much subtlety as a barn afire. He wanted to strangle both of them, even though their shouts had saved him from himself.

Or rather, it'd been Elspeth who'd been saved, from the likes of him. He'd almost kissed her. He'd wanted to, and badly. And if he ever kissed her, he didn't know if he'd be able to stop.

Aidan stopped in his tracks, scrubbing a hand roughly over his face, willing the cold sea wind to whip the memory away. But it was no good. The picture of her lounging so carelessly on his bed was etched in his mind.

He'd walked into his room, and for a joyful moment—
an exquisitely painful moment—he'd imagined himself a
man who might have a woman like her, sprawled there for
him, waiting to share her smiles, just for him. To come
home each night to such a sight would be heaven indeed.

But instead he'd entered, and panic had jolted her, and
the eyes that'd greeted him were guilty, not smiling. At
first he thought she'd been spying on him as though he
were a circus curiosity.

She was guileless, though. He always forgot just how
guileless she was. He still couldn't fathom that there were
people in the world decent enough to be motivated by
cares for folk other than themselves. But she was such a
person, and that innocence had lured him in, ever closer,
until he'd lain over her, wondering at the brief flickers of
lightness and happiness he'd begun to feel in his heart
when she was near.

God save him, but she'd seemed to want him. She'd
been a dream beneath him, responding to his every word,
his every touch, as though a woman starved.

He'd never met her like. He'd never touched a creature
so fine, so delicate, unsullied by guile, greed, or any of
the cheap tools of seduction with which he was familiar.
No fans, or perfumes, or coy laughter for Elspeth. She
was all that was right and true and good.

And he'd wanted to ravish her.

Until they'd heard a noise, and she'd stiffened beneath
him, and he was reminded who he was: coarse and unciv-
ilized, a dangerous man on dangerous business, with no
right to endanger an innocent like her.

He'd perched near the edge of Dunnottar Rock, hun-
dreds of feet above the roiling water. His hired man came
into view, and though the man was far from the ledge, he
shuffled toward Aidan, looking terrified he might somehow slip and tumble to his death.

Naturally, Gregor had to appear too, close on his heels. "Is everything all right here?"

Aidan knew his oldest brother couldn't resist throwing himself into the fray. The man had probably been lurking outside the guardhouse, waiting for Aidan to misstep. So much for familial trust. "Just because I got kidnapped once doesn't mean I can't take care of myself."

Gregor put his hands up in surrender. "No need to take umbrage. Simply trying to do the brotherly thing."

"Then go brother one of our other siblings."

Most men would bristle, but Gregor only laughed. "As you will, Aid."

He watched his brother head back the way he came, thinking it was time to remember himself. The farm he toiled on wasn't his own. The woman he toiled with not his wife. He needed to stop acting the morose and heartsick fool and get back to the business at hand. *Revenge.*

He turned to his hired hand. "You'd best have the names."

The man held a rumpled sheet of paper, and Aidan snatched it and began to read.

Dougal Fraser, Knitted Goodes
Aberdeen Burgess of Guild
sacke wool: 11
wool in cloth: 7

There was a signature and wax seal at the bottom of the page, with the words *Weighted and Approved, Dean and Assessors of Guild.*

It appeared to be a trade receipt, and though Aidan couldn't make sense of every single word, he managed most of it. He found himself once more pushing thoughts of Elspeth from his mind. That he could read anything at all was thanks to her skill and patience.

"What's this to me?" he asked, his voice gruff. "This isn't the man I asked you to find. This is some merchant."

"Aye," the man replied nervously, "but a merchant, I'm told, who sends his goods away on some verra peculiar ships."

There was a rustling in the bushes behind the man. He didn't notice it, but Aidan did and sighed. If he peered hard enough, he imagined he'd be able to make out a head of blond hair among the leaves. He folded the paper and shoved it into his sporran. "You can go."

"But you says if I bring back a name . . ." The man looked encouragingly at the sporran.

"So I did." Aidan plucked out half a crown and tossed it to him. "The name best have some merit, or I'll find you and take my coin back with interest."

The man nodded with gusto, and with an anxious survey of the rocks around him, he began to edge away.

"Ho," Aidan said, stopping him. "I'll throw in a tanner next time, if you can manage to get your daft head in and out of here without raising such a ruckus."

Once his hired man was out of sight, he said, "You can come out now." He waited in silence, then added, "I know you're there, so don't think to hide from me."

Elspeth's head popped up over a low rise.

"And so you should look abashed." He crossed his arms and tried to look stern, but it was difficult in the face of her endearing blush. "My business is just that, luvvie. *Mine*."

She clambered over the rocks she'd hidden behind. "Who was that man?" she asked, ignoring his order.

He reached up to hand her down to his side. "I hear something in that pretty voice of yours, and I don't like it. This isn't some countrified dance carouse I'm planning. It's business I'm about here. Business that has naught to do with you."

"But I can help." Her eyes went to his sporran. "I *want* to help."

He knew it was just his paper she was after, but when he felt her gaze rake the area of his groin, it was hard to keep his thoughts from wandering to a decidedly baser place. He settled the sporran low on his hips. "You can help by keeping your nose safely out of it."

"But I can help you decipher it."

He shook his head. The girl had more backbone than folk gave her credit for. "Your job is to help me decipher books, and your wee poems, and those hero tales you've such a fancy for."

"Please, Aidan," she begged sweetly. The wind gusted, whipping a bit of hair loose from her braid, and she tucked the fine, pale strands behind her ear. The movement pulled her bodice tight, its threadbare fabric molding to her modest curves.

She glanced again to a place between his legs. This focus of hers unsettled him. It'd been months since he'd had a woman. As for having a sweet innocent like Elspeth, *that* had happened only in his dreams. Add to that the fact that he'd not fully recovered from the sight of her sprawled on his bed, or the feel of her beneath him, and the cursed sporran had begun to chafe on his hardening cock.

She pointed to his groin. "Just let me relieve you of that."

"Mary and Joseph," he muttered. He loped ahead to adjust himself surreptitiously, leading them on a path away from Dunnottar. "Damned fiendish woman. You have *no* idea."

"I could have an idea," she said, completely misunderstanding. She jogged to catch up to him, slipping along the slick terrain.

He steadied her with a hand to her elbow. "Mind the mud, Beth. This bloody home of ours seems rarely to dry."

Though she nodded acknowledgment, her argument didn't pause a beat. "If you'd but hear me out."

"You spoke, I heard you, and now our wee chat is over." Aidan strode ahead once more, unsure how he'd found himself in this conversation. He'd *never* consider involving Elspeth. He was tracking the man who'd *kidnapped* him, for God's sake. It was far too dangerous. "You've had a peek at my papers, and it stops there."

"But I have a canny head for business," she protested.

"There is one thing I know on this earth, Beth, and it's that I'll not allow you to entangle yourself in this particular *business*."

"But I am very capable. I'm very clever with numbers and tallies, and I can help—"

"Help?" He spun to face her. She'd been at his heels, and he had to grab her by the shoulders to stop her from running into him. "You can barely take care of yourself, how do you propose to help me?"

"What?" The color on her cheeks was high, and her eyes were bright with defiance. "*Can't take care of myself?* What can you possibly mean? I run the farm!"

Aidan forced himself to keep his thoughts on track, but it was difficult. He'd sensed Elspeth's spirit, but to see it now so unfettered, to hear her words so uninhibited, made him want to grab her, pull her close, and see what other surprises she'd kept hidden.

Measuring his breath, he gathered his thoughts. "Yes," he said calmly, "you run the farm, but you don't have a care for yourself."

She opened her mouth to protest, but raising a hand, he cut her off. He'd thought long and hard about this particular topic, and he could tick off any number of examples. "Spectacles, for a start. You have trouble reading at night—don't tell me you don't—and you could use a pair of spectacles."

"Well, I just have our priorities in order. I put my *family* first."

"Family?" The word stung. Aidan was so alienated from the other MacAlpins, barely did he feel like he had any family at all. Someday this lovely woman would pledge herself to another, become some other man's family. "Don't speak to me of your *family* when your father ambles about as he pleases, in and out, leaving you to do work meant for him."

"He's an old man."

"Whom you spoil as though he were a child. Do you have him hide away his pipe? No. The man can smoke all he likes. He can have all the bread he likes, and all the meat he can eat, and all the ale he can drink. But you?"

"Don't be such a mule, Aidan. *I* eat, *I* drink. I take care of myself."

She was riled now. Forgetting her shyness, the woman she was in her heart blazed through like a glorious beacon. And damn his soul, all he could think was that she needed a thorough ravishing.

"A mule, am I?" The notion brought a wide grin to his face. But it faded quickly. Never could he take her. He couldn't—*wouldn't*—sully her.

Elspeth deserved some farmer, with a safely predictable life. Not that her father would ever let her go. He doubted the man would be able—or willing—to fend for himself. She'd spend her days caring for her father, then, upon his death, she'd marry herself and her land to someone like their neighbor Angus.

A hot brew of envy, anger, and frustration coursed through his veins. He could see *himself* as her farmer husband. He could envision himself as the man sharing her life, protecting her, buying her wee comforts. "A fine thing, this caretaking of yours. Your father has his wee luxuries, while you, Beth, you don't seem to have anything."

"Just because I don't have spectacles! I have, I have . . ." She huffed, putting hands on hips, looking like she was trying to come up with a list of belongings. "I have things."

"Aye, if you count chores to do and bills to pay." He took in the sight of her ratty shawl and her faded skirts.

"It's not just the spectacles. When was the last time you had yourself a new dress?"

Looking suddenly forlorn, she glanced down at her muddied hem. "What's the matter with my dress?"

"You should be in finest satin, but your father has you pinching every penny."

He regretted the dismay on her face—he was the last man to care about a silly frock—and altered course. "All I'm saying is, you seem always to put your father first. But you're not a child anymore. You're old enough to deserve the things that *you* want, that *you* need."

"*Old enough?* Are you calling me a spinster?"

Spinster indeed. With the sparks in her eyes and the blood in her cheeks, Elspeth was beautiful. Like a doe who'd stood frozen only to spring to glorious life. "*Spinster* is the *last* word I'd use to describe you, luvvie," he said with cold laughter in his voice.

"Don't you dare laugh." She swatted his arm, but slipped on the slick terrain. She had to grab his shirt-sleeves to steady herself, looking the angrier for it. "Folk have laughed, discounted, misunderstood, overlooked, and disregarded me quite enough." Clenching her fingers, she gave his arms a shove. "Quite enough."

"I've never discounted you, Beth." He nodded at one of her hands. "Your strength, however, leaves much to be desired."

"You maddening, maddening . . ." She shoved again, and this time when she slipped, he caught her about her waist.

He cocked a brow. "Mule?"

She held still, and when she spoke again, her voice was small. "I know you're used to well-to-do women. Women who wear rich silks and feathers in their hair. I know I'm not as fancy, or as well spoken—"

He gave her waist a squeeze. "You don't seem to be having any trouble speaking now. And trust me," he said, with an exaggerated shudder. "As for those other women, I've little use for fancy."

"But I can't believe you . . . you . . ." Her shoulders fell. "Aidan, you disparaged my clothing."

He laughed outright, teasing a reluctant smile from her.

She gave him one last good-natured shove. "I told you not to—oh!" She lost her footing and tumbled into him.

Aidan caught her in an embrace, but the weight of her body propelled against him was too much. He fell backward, landing on the mucky path with a dull splat, Elspeth lying atop him belly to belly.

His laughter was unchecked now, and he wiped drops of mud from her cheek while he gathered himself. "Are you happy, Beth? My clothes are now muddier than yours."

She tried to roll off. "Oh, good heavens. I am so sorry."

He only hugged her closer. "Nonsense. This serves my purposes quite nicely, because I'll not free you until I believe that you've listened. Elspeth Farquharson, you're more well spoken, more thoughtful, gentler, and lovelier by far than any of those *damned* plantation women. So please tell me I've heard the last of them from out of that mouth."

He glanced at her lips to underscore his point, but it was a mistake. Those lips were gently parted, looking long overdue for a kiss. Not to mention that the most charming mud spatter had graced her chin.

Aidan nestled her higher along his body, and the softness of her breasts on his chest was sweet torture. It was all he could do not to roll her and take her innocence there in the mud.

Not surprisingly, Elspeth remained unaware of her predicament. "I know you tire of it," she said, "but it's just . . ." Finally, his words seemed to register. Tilting her head, she gave Aidan a quizzical look. "Did you say lovelier?"

"I think I said 'lovelier by far.'" He could no longer fight it. The feel of her body on his held a promise too sweet to deny. Elspeth was guileless and pure, and the devil curse him, but he wanted a taste. He swept his hands down her back, resting just above the slope of her bottom. "Though I can think of one way in which you're deficient."

Eyes wide, she asked, "You can?"

"Aye, Beth. I daresay, you've never been kissed."

Chapter 18

Elspeth could only stare, not trusting her ears.

Aidan shifted, his fingers splaying over the uppermost curve of her rump. She felt them through the too-thin fabric of her skirts, and then felt an answering hum between her legs.

He studied her from beneath a furrowing brow. "Might I?"

She couldn't believe this was happening. She'd fallen on him like a clumsy oaf, but when she'd tried to get back up, he'd only hugged her closer. And now her heart was pounding too loudly in her chest to make sense of it all. "Might you what?"

She waited for him to toss it all off with a laugh and a wink. But instead his voice became a husky whisper. "Kiss you, Beth."

Longing burst through her with a wild intensity. She wanted only to hear that voice in her ear, whispering dark things, his secret wishes conveyed on hot breath along her skin. "Yes, I wish you woul—"

He touched his lips to hers. They were soft, barely pressed on her closed mouth.

She breathed Aidan in and held the scent of him in her lungs, wishing he might never separate from her. But he did. Too soon he pulled away.

She opened her eyes to find him staring at her with a look so tender it filled her with a rush of feelings, all strangely new. For the first time, she felt seen, and known, and safe, and wanted.

But most of all, Elspeth felt bold.

She let go her hand from where she'd gripped his shirt. He stiffened for a moment, but when she laid it back down on his face, cupping his cheek, she sensed the muscles in his neck and shoulders relax.

Did it mean he was as unsure as she? Aidan was so confident, such an exhilarating rogue of a man, she couldn't fathom that he might be as uncertain of her feelings as she was of his.

She stroked his jaw, savoring the strange, rough feel of beard stubble under her thumb, thinking of all the places she'd longed to touch him. And now here she was, over him, able to touch him where she would. His jaw, his brow, down his cheek, to the corner of his mouth.

He didn't stop her. He only watched with an avid attention that deepened her pulse until it became a dull throb throughout her body.

Looking at her as he did, Aidan made her feel precious. In his arms, she was a goddess, like Aphrodite. Or Hera, the queen of them all.

"Might I?" she asked, in the barest whisper.

His blue eyes were intent on her. "Might you what?"

"Might I take a turn kissing you?" She traced his lower lip with her finger, and his answering groan made her feel like a woman in a way she'd never known before.

They came together, hard this time, each leading the kiss as much as the other. His breath changed, quickening, and it stirred her to a hunger so profound she thought she might burst from it.

They kissed, lying in the mud, with hungry mouths and questing hands, and she felt the rightness of all the books, and all the poems, that claimed that anger and passion were two sides of the same coin. For he'd made her so angry, yet now she thought she might not rest until she could consume him utterly.

She'd thought she wanted just one kiss—had hoped that her first kiss might suffice as her last. But she knew differently now. Elspeth wanted Aidan, wanted more, wanted it all.

Eventually they separated, and cupping her face close, he stared. "Beth, I . . . you . . ." A laugh escaped him. "It appears now I'm the one left speechless." He traced a languorous finger down her throat to a spot just above her décolletage. "What other secrets do you keep tucked in that silent breast?"

Knowing she'd tell him everything, give him anything, she placed an earnest hand over his. "I wouldn't keep a secret from you."

"No, Elspeth." He gave her a quiet smile. "I don't imagine you would."

After a moment, he squeezed her hand then let go. Bringing his hand to her face, he dragged his thumb along her lips, all traces of amusement gone. "Definitely beautiful."

"What?" she asked, not understanding.

He searched her eyes. "Before, I couldn't decide what sort of pretty you were. But you're not merely pretty, you're beautiful. I see that now. How is it everyone doesn't see?"

Self-conscious, she tried to look away, but with a finger, he turned her face back to his. "I think it's because you stay so quiet, hiding yourself away." He gently traced a thumb over her brow. "But these eyes, they see everything. Did you know they're flecked with gold?"

She shook her head, mesmerized by his words. She'd never thought overmuch about her eyes.

"Well, they are," he said. "I've never seen the like. They're light but not pale, as though you've a fairy's eyes, able to see into the hearts of men."

It was almost too much, this attention. Her deepest fantasies come true, and yet nearly unbearable, a pleasure so piquant as to demand respite. She broke the moment with a smile. "*Now* will you let me read your papers?"

He chuckled, quick with his answer. "Now, especially, I won't."

She contemplated this man beneath her. He posed as a loner. Cold and detached, he kept himself a stranger to all, and yet she felt she knew his heart. "You don't scare me, you know."

"That's what I'm afraid of." His trademark light good humor replaced the gravity in his expression. Aidan's hands roved along her back, thumbs edging recklessly inward, until his palms cradled the sides of her torso. "Though hopefully there are other feelings I rouse."

Her breasts pulled taut at the daring touch, until Elspeth couldn't help but lean close to take a kiss that made her forget papers and pirates.

For now.

———

Not even hauling water for young Bridget could wipe the smile from Aidan's face. In fact, he'd *volunteered* for the duty, stunning his sister, but he couldn't help how expansive he'd felt since seeing Elspeth the day before.

Since kissing her.

Elspeth was sweet and untried, yet so very unabashed, with a passion that'd nearly undone him. Twice in the night he'd been forced to seek his own release, so vivid was the memory of her, lovely and pure.

Lovely, with fey, yellow-flecked eyes, and a mouth shaped like a delicate bud, equal parts tender and hungry. And yet it was Elspeth's spirit that'd redoubled his desire. She saw him for who he was, for who he wanted to be. Saw straight through his facade to his very heart, and rather than turn away, she'd embraced him, had made him feel all the more complete.

With Elspeth he felt like a man—*his own man*—more than any fight or fisticuffs or hard labor had ever made him feel. She was a gift, this strange tutor of his, and the bachelors of Aberdeenshire were fools not to have noticed before he.

"What'd the girl threaten you with?" a voice asked from behind him.

Aidan's smile flickered, but he'd not let his twin put a damper on his mood. He finished drawing the bucket from the massive well before he looked over his shoulder to face him. "Girl?"

"Bridge." Cormac nodded at the bucket. "What'd she say to get you on water duty?"

Bridget—not Elspeth. Aidan breathed a sigh he didn't realize he was holding. "Oh, her. The chit has enough on her plate, and this is easy enough for me." He stood, lifting the bucket from the ground as though it weighed nothing, proving his point.

Though his little sister's brash ways still irritated, watching Elspeth's struggles had made Aidan more sympathetic to the vast amounts of work required to run a home.

Cormac lifted a questioning brow. "Helping her like you're helping that Elspeth?"

Aidan bristled, wondering if that was a smirk he read on his brother's face. Choosing to ignore it, he walked past him, headed across the courtyard and back toward the kitchens. He was a proud man, particularly in front of his twin, and so had underplayed how much Elspeth was tutoring him. No surprise, then, that Cormac might misunderstand Aidan's work on the Farquharson farm.

He felt Cormac walk up behind him to ask, "What are your motives with that girl?"

"Why would you think I have motives?"

"I've seen you on the road to her farm. A lot." Cormac reached out, stopping him with a hand on his arm. "She's no doxy to be toyed with."

Aidan shook off his brother's grip. "I'd never think to toy with her."

"So why?" Cormac asked, but Aidan just stared blankly in reply, and so he repeated, "Why go to her so much?"

Aidan sensed his brother wasn't going to let it go, and so he put the bucket down. "Why not go to her? She's a good woman in need of help." When Cormac had something to say, he was as tenacious as a dog with a bone—best to give him the chance to say his piece and be done with it.

"I know it's been years since you've been around Scottish women," his brother said in an aggravatingly deliberate tone. "But Elspeth Farquharson is a homely sort of girl. A spinster who probably—"

Resentment, frustration, and envy drove his fist, and his right hook connected with his brother's face before he knew what he was about. It was something he'd wanted to do for some time.

Cormac reeled backward, and caught off guard, he tripped on the uneven turf, falling to the ground. He sat up at once, rubbing his jaw, the look in his eyes more disbelief than pain. "What the devil was that for?"

"Don't speak so of her," Aidan said, his voice flat and hard as steel.

Cormac studied him for a time, until finally he said, "I see."

Aidan watched his brother's brow soften in understanding, and it made his own furrow all the more. "You see nothing."

Cormac only rolled his shoulders, proffering his hand for a boost up, but Aidan didn't reach out to grab it.

"Give it a rest, Aid," Cormac said, his voice tired. "We may not know you, but we certainly remember how much we loved you. You've got to meet us in the middle sometime."

Aidan glared at Cormac. The brother whom he'd once loved more than anyone. More than anything. He tried to recall the boy who'd insisted on climbing the chimney. The boy who'd vexed him beyond measure. Who'd squabbled with him, and bugged him.

And who'd always stood by his side when nobody else did.

He'd seen the joy in Cormac's eyes when they'd met again, for the first time in more than a decade, on that grim Aberdeen dock. He'd pushed his brother away, and had been pushing them *all* away ever since.

Except for Elspeth. She'd penetrated his defenses, and he'd let her, and it'd felt so good. Like a breath of sea air after weeks in the ship's hold.

It would take all his pride, all his courage, to do the same with his family. Though he didn't know why it should. They'd grieved him, but Highland life was hard, and thirteen years were long, and life went on.

He'd take a chance. It was what Elspeth would advise him to do.

He reached down, clasping Cormac's hand, and pulled him to standing. Aidan stepped back quickly, though, putting space between them. He needed this reunion to happen one step at a time. And the next step was making sure Cormac understood one thing. "I have your word you'll not disparage Elspeth again?"

"I wouldn't think of it," he replied quickly. Cormac

bent to pick up the bucket, adding, "Truly, I wasn't disparaging Elspeth. I *like* the girl."

Aidan glowered daggers at him.

"Not like that, you half-wit." Cormac rolled his eyes.

As they set off for the kitchen, Aidan knocked his shoulder hard into his twin. "*Who's* the half-wit?"

They walked on, their pace slow, unanimously agreeing to prolong the moment, though neither would ever confess to it.

When Cormac spoke again, his tone was grave. "I knew, Aidan. I felt that you were out there. Alive, somewhere. We'd been inseparable for years. We bickered, yes, but always we were together. Always we were one. We were even born at the same time."

"Well, I *was* first, you'll recall." Aidan tossed off the jest, needing to break the intensity of his brother's words.

Cormac gave him a playful slug on the arm. "Then act it."

Aidan relented, saying in a low voice, "I knew too. I knew you lived." He smirked. "Just as I *knew* I'd someday come back to find you and Marj married."

Their laughter broke out at once. "Mar-*jorie*," they said in unison.

"*Crivvens*, man." Aidan shook his head, pretending exasperation. "You and that girl. From the start."

"My wife, you mean," Cormac said with mock severity.

"Your wife," he said drily. "Better you than me." He had to sidestep to avoid Cormac's thrown elbow. With a laugh, Aidan added, "So, what do you get from her anyway?"

"Well that's an easy one to answer," Cormac said with a wink and a nudge.

"I'm serious," he said, realizing it was true. The feelings growing in his heart for Elspeth were overpowering—sharp, and hot, and terrifying too. It was hard to imagine they weren't the rarest of all emotions. But perhaps the sensation was normal, perhaps it was what men felt for their wives. Perhaps *his* wife was precisely what Aidan wanted Elspeth to be.

They'd reached the castle, their sisters' voices echoing off the stone corridor. Cormac handed the bucket back to Aidan, nodding toward the sound. "Bridge'll be wanting her water. Five minutes ago, if I know our sister."

"Aye," Aidan replied with a knowing smile. It seemed he wasn't the only MacAlpin of the opinion that the girl could stand to be taken down a peg.

Cormac's expression grew serious. "Have a care, Aid."

"I do." The words came quickly, dismissively.

"No." Cormac put a hand on his shoulder. "Truly, Aidan. Have a care. It was my fault we lost you once, and I'll not see it happen again."

"It wasn't your—"

Cormac punched his shoulder. "Just shut up and promise if you need help you'll tell me."

"Aye," Aidan said. He met his twin's eyes with a smile. "I will. I promise."

Chapter 19

Elspeth lay in bed. The sun had yet to rise, but she couldn't sleep for thoughts of Aidan. And his kiss.

Restless, she rolled onto her side, thinking of his mouth. It had been gentle at first, and then harder, and hungrier. Blood thrummed through her body at the memory.

Nestling deep under her covers, she grazed a slow hand along her torso and cupped her breast. Her skin tingled at the memory of *his* hands on her sides, of *his* thumbs roving that perilous line where rib meets bosom. She thumbed her nipple, and it stiffened, she imagining what he might do with *his* fingers.

She played the scene over in her mind, and this time Aidan didn't end the kiss. He didn't insist on propriety, didn't act like the most seemly of gentlemen and lift her to her feet.

Instead, in her fantasy, he rolled her onto her back. The mud would've been warm, still holding the heat of his body. But the air on her legs would be cool, her skirts rucked high on her hips . . .

"You, in there!" Her father's voice shattered her reverie, calling to her from the other room.

Her eyes shot open, her heart leaped to her throat, and her hand flew from her breast. Even though her father was in the other room, even though he *never* entered hers, Elspeth's heart pounded.

"Coming," she said, even as she nestled deeper in the sheets. Dawn had finally come, sliding gray fingers through the shutters. Rolling onto her back, she came to terms with the reality of her day.

Though it was set in a corner in the main room, she heard the creak of her father's cot. Heard him shuffling along the stone floor, followed by the pop and crackle of a nascent fire. "Fool girl," he was grumbling to himself, "lays abed, and there's work to be done."

Elspeth sighed, baring linen-clad shoulders and then arms to the chill air. Like every other morning, she swung her legs out of bed, bracing for the shock of cold stone underneath sleep-warmed feet.

"Time to wake up and feed the sheep," he called.

"Aye, I'm coming, I'm coming," she called back. But, unlike every other morning, this time she'd awakened with a smile on her face. Because she'd finally realized how she could help Aidan. And today was the day she'd take action.

They'd kissed, which meant the responsibility she'd felt for his well-being was justified. He was a roguish sort, and danger followed such men. She sensed trouble, and knew she needed to see just what sort of people he was involved with. She'd stolen just a single sheet from his papers, but it bore the name of a man in Aberdeen, and a name was a start.

Dougal Fraser.

She had to do all she could to ensure Aidan's safety,

because she was fairly certain she loved him. Unfortunately, she was also fairly certain he'd likely never love her back the same way. But he was her romantic hero, and she'd give anything to be his heroine, even if it was just this once.

And what did the heroines do in all the great stories?

They intervened in the affairs of their men.

Dougal Fraser was nervous, but not such a fool as to show it. Few men clawed their way free of the Aberdeen gutters, but Dougal had, and he knew that more than hard work, he owed his success to a talent for bluffing. His hair had gone gray, and his knees had begun to ache, but still it was upon this skill alone that he most relied.

He leaned back in his chair, affecting calm confidence. "Tell me . . . *Francis* . . . your captain guarantees I'll receive my payment in raw cotton?"

The beefy man who sat across from him flinched. Urchins on the street knew the fellow only as "the yeoman," and use of his Christian name had the unsettling effect Dougal sought. "Aye," he said, shifting uncomfortably, "them's the terms of our agreement, like."

"Fine, let's talk of our *terms*. I've staked the ship, I've filled your bellies." Dougal pointed with distaste at the man's overlarge girth. "But now I want *guarantees*."

The yeoman bristled. "Every docksman in Aberdeen kens Captain Will is as good as his word. If the man says a thing, it's because he means it."

"Captain this, Captain that." Something about this infamous captain rankled him. The man's past was shrouded in mystery, and Dougal wondered what he might be hiding. "It's not what your captain says or does in Aberdeen that concerns me. It's what happens once he sets sail, with *my* goods." Referring to their cargo as "goods" felt so much more civilized than calling them bodies, or slaves, or servants, or hides, or whatever distasteful nomenclature people bandied about.

The yeoman worried the cap in his hands, thinking hard, looking as though steam might come out his ears from the effort. "If you'll be begging my pardon, it takes a lot to keep 'em souls alive. I don't ken why you just don't trade with money like other folk do."

"These far-flung plantations need labor, which surrounds *me* in abundance." Dougal's lingering glare said he included the yeoman in the distasteful category. "And here *I* am, in need of cotton. Which—in addition to savages and the putrid fever—it appears these godforsaken tropical locales are choking upon. Meanwhile, the Crown wants taxes, taxes, taxes when goods are bought and sold, yet you might imagine I am loath to pay a farthing of my hard-earned income." Resting his elbows on his desk, Dougal steepled his fingers, smiling triumphantly. He was as impressed with his scheme as he'd been on the day he hatched it.

But the man only stared dumbly, not getting the connection.

Dougal spelled it out in an insultingly slow pace. "I fund and fill a ship with able-bodied men. Your captain sails it away. But then he sails it back. Filled with cotton. *Voilà!* I've made a trade, but the Crown is none the wiser."

The man continued to gape, and Dougal was forced to ask after a moment, "Do you see what I'm about here?" He gestured impatiently behind him. "*Knit* goods. Cotton from the tropics expands my offerings. Cotton I get by trading for men, not money. No money means no taxes."

"Seems a terrible lot of confusion to my mind."

Not confusing, brilliant. And he was convinced the scheme was only slightly illegal. The slave trade was loosely sanctioned by Parliament, after all. And with this elusive captain as his go-between, Dougal remained unexposed, and his reputation unsullied.

"Then it's a good thing it's not up to you to wrap your mind around it." Dougal sat upright and began to shuffle papers on his desk. He had no patience for dimwits and was eager for this particular interview to reach an end. "Now stop flapping your jaw and tell me what you've come to tell me. Have you finished gathering our cargo?"

"Aye, the ship's full, but captain's coffers isn't. He wants that—"

They were interrupted by a faint knocking on his door.

The yeoman stiffened, instantly on alert, vicious intent lighting his face.

Dougal rolled his eyes. "Calm yourself. This is my place of business, not a Cornish wrestling hall."

He stood and went to the door, meaning to crack it open himself. It'd be well if whoever had come calling didn't see him with one such as "Francis the yeoman."

But instead the door opened on Dougal, nearly striking him in the face. He rubbed his nose at the near miss, but his outrage faded when he laid eyes on his visitor.

It was a girl. Though she wasn't precisely pretty, neither was she rough on the eyes. She was a pale creature, with a delicate nose, lips that were curved but not full, and a chest that was sadly meager.

"Dougal Fraser?" she asked.

Her voice was meek, and it made her seem all the more fragile. All in all, he doubted she'd be able to stand up in a strong gust of wind, for all that she'd nearly swung the door in his face.

But who in holy hell was she?

"At your service," he said, knowing the charming words didn't match the tightness of his tone.

He stepped in front of the doorway to block her view, but it was too late. She'd seen the yeoman and her eyes widened. Though she recovered quickly, he spied the mental machinations that'd begun in that eerily pale gaze.

Whoever the chit was, she was canny.

His only choice was to control the damage. Dougal gave the man a pointed look. "Take your leave now."

The yeoman's ruddy cheek twitched. Looking ill-pleased, he rose and sidled past them out the door. "Verra well then."

The dock riffraff momentarily dispensed with, Dougal took the girl's elbow and, feigning graciousness, led her to a seat. "Whom do I have the pleasure of entertaining here in my humble office?"

"Woolen goods . . ." she mused, craning her head to read the sign on his door. "Woolen goods. Woolen goods!"

Those strange eyes met his. They'd gone bright, and he saw up close the unusual yellow flecks that streaked from her pupils like sunbursts.

Daft or deft, that was the question. The girl was a conundrum, and conundrums put Dougal on his guard. Her quavering voice bespoke a ninny-headed lass. But she'd clearly been braw enough to venture into the heart of Aberdeen alone. Was hers the trembling confusion of an innocent, or an act?

"Yes, my business is woolen goods." He sat at his desk, across from her. "But what is your business, Miss . . . ?"

Something in her eyes snapped to attention. "Farquharson. Elspeth Farquharson."

Her name nagged him. "Farquharson . . . Ah," he said, recognition dawning. "Just so. A Farquharson contacted me not too long ago. Said he was in the sheep business. A bit old, but . . . your father perhaps?"

"Yes, that's so." She sat tall, looking guarded.

He remembered all of it now. The man had been a bit doddering, striking Dougal as an addle-brained but unthreatening sort of fellow. Feeling the daughter's unsettling gaze on him now, he wondered if he hadn't underestimated the situation. If the man's purpose was to do business, why had he sent this girl in his stead? "I recall, he said he'd just one child. A daughter. So you're she."

"Yes," Elspeth replied, looking distinctly uncomfortable. "I am she."

Was she surprised she'd been recognized? Had her father sent her to spy?

Dougal's mind raced. "Your father is new to the sheep business, as I recall. He brought some papers here, outlining his vast enterprise."

The lass looked shocked to hear it. He smirked, thinking he'd been right—the man Farquharson *was* simply a doddering old grump.

But his smile faded when another detail popped into memory. "I recall seeing the initials *EF* on those papers. Yet your father's name is Albert."

Perhaps he was being overly suspicious, but his new slaves-for-cotton venture was just taking off. He was on the brink of making a great fortune, and it was not the time for young misses to be nosing around.

She lifted her chin. "You read correctly."

Dougal registered her every movement, realizing he'd misjudged. A shy and plain-faced creature she may be, but the chit wasn't meek. "I suppose *EF* stands for 'Elspeth Farquharson'?"

She gave a tight nod.

So *she* was in charge of the accounts, not the father. "Good on you, girl. You're brighter than I took you for. I'll wager many folk underestimate your like." He narrowed his eyes. The only thing worse than a scheming woman was a scheming, impoverished woman. "Why are you here? And don't insist you were in the neighborhood."

The girl was silent, measuring. Was she at a loss, or was this part of her ruse?

"Your father has a peculiar way of broaching a potential business relationship," he said, filling the silence.

"My father doesn't know I'm here."

"Indeed?" He was genuinely taken aback at this latest wrinkle. He suspected she played a deep game, but he'd been swimming in deep waters long before she was born.

He found himself smiling. To his surprise, he was not unamused. It'd been years since he'd been in the company of a young female. Moreover, he loved a lively discussion, and intelligent debate was something sorely lacking in his dockside venture. He suspected if he plumbed deeper, this Elspeth would hold up admirably in a mental crossing of swords.

"Would you like to hear what I think?" he asked. "Your father told me about his business. I worry how profitable such a harebrained venture might be. I think you worry too."

He could see in her pursed lips just how on the mark he'd been.

But then she shocked him by snapping, "You should worry more about your own presumptions."

Dougal laughed outright. "What a singularly puzzling thing you are."

The lass might look green enough to be his granddaughter, but she was a clever one. And, he realized, not unpretty at all. Quite fair, in fact.

He wondered if the girl could be brought to heel. He'd never married—business had always taken precedence—but he saw now that a man might go far with a partner of pleasant countenance and bright mind by his side. Even better that her family was in the woolen business.

A sheep farm could be just the thing to explain away his new profits. Elspeth's father was in desperate financial straits. Time for Dougal to see just how desperate.

He reached across the table and patted her pretty little hand. "Perhaps we should settle on an alliance, you and I?"

Chapter 20

Elspeth studied Aidan's profile and felt a pang. She'd been working distractedly on her tallies when he arrived, and when he'd asked to see them, she'd been happy to oblige. But now he was poring over the account book in such earnest, doing his level best to help her.

As she was doing her best to help him.

"Twenty head isn't many of the cursed beasts," he was saying, pointing to a figure. He tilted the book toward the window to aid her, even though the day wasn't dark enough yet to hamper her vision. "But they'll account for more wool than this at shearing time."

She stared blindly at the number, wondering who Dougal Fraser really was. The strongman he'd been entertaining when she arrived had done nothing to put her mind at ease. He'd seemed a shadowy, criminal sort.

"You're not just shearing it into sacks. If you grade it"—he met her eyes, mistaking her silence for confusion—"grade

it . . . meaning . . . to open up the fleece, aye? Tear out the
hard bits, clean it up. It increases its worth in a higher pro-
portion to the labor it requires."

She nodded, not caring. Why would Dougal Fraser's
name appear on one of Aidan's papers? What would an
aging wool merchant have to do with the pirate who'd
kidnapped him?

And what was her father doing meeting with the likes
of Fraser, anyway? Surely it just had something to do
with wool, but Da was pitifully lacking in good sense,
and she hoped he wouldn't get both of them in trouble.

"This word, though . . . this is *shoulder*?"

She glanced to where Aidan pointed. "Yes. Very good.
Shoulder."

How on earth might a knit export business be connected to the man who'd kidnapped Aidan? Had it something to do with ships? She thought of the paper she'd
stolen. Was it a dead end? Or did it hold a pertinent clue?
She wondered if she shouldn't just sneak it back among
Aidan's papers.

"So then, regarding this figure here," he said, pointing to a number. "You should account for it differently.
Shoulder wool is finer."

"Yes." She glanced at the tally. "Finer."

When she went to Fraser's office, she didn't know
who he was or what she'd find. And she certainly hadn't
wanted to betray her identity. Her plan had been simply
to feign innocence, get a sense of what he was about, and
scuttle home again.

But he'd recognized her name, and now she seemed
to find herself in a fix she didn't quite understand. At the
end of their interview, he'd patted her hand, and his touch
had made her flesh creep. Its implication had made her
deeply uneasy. Not to mention, she hadn't uncovered any
clues as to Aidan's predicament, leaving her more confused than ever.

She realized Aidan hadn't spoken for a time, and she looked at him.

He raised a brow. "Are you paying attention?"

"Beg pardon?"

"You're distracted, Beth. I've just pointed out a way you can double your profits, yet you seem to be off gathering wool of a different sort."

She stared back at him, utterly baffled.

"*Woolgathering*. As in daydreaming." He put her account book down. He'd been so excited to see her, wondering how he might steal another kiss. Yet she seemed to be a thousand leagues away.

Had he frightened her with his kiss? Put her off? But he knew those fears were unfounded. She'd kissed him back with the enthusiasm of a wanton—just the memory of it drove him wild.

She was likely preoccupied with troubles of her own. He knew she had them in droves, and he was trying hard to help her. His reading had improved enough to double-check her tallies, but not so much that he could be the man he wanted to be. A learned man, who could handle *all* the accounting, all of the bills and correspondence required of a responsible gentleman.

He stole a look at her. She was deep in concentration, her lips pursed into the most unintentionally sexy little pout. It was all he could do not to toss her papers to the ground and simply claim that mouth with his.

No, he decided, feeling more determined than ever, he needed to be a learned man, an erudite man. A man able to read her sonnets as they lay beneath a tangle of sheets, their bodies entwined.

She looked to him, catching his stare. He gave her a smile, and for once it didn't smooth the furrow from her brow.

"Never you mind it," he said, shutting the book. He'd just have to work harder so he could shoulder more of her burdens. She thought the work was tedious, but he found himself dreaming of such duties. He'd enjoy things like minding the monthly accounts, would enjoy a farm to call his own, and a wife like her to share it with.

"I'm sorry. I suppose I *am* woolgathering." She gave an absentminded half smile. "It's just . . . do you think your pirate is in Aberdeen? If you'd let me read your papers, I could help you search for clues."

He stiffened. He'd known when he found her that day in his room that trouble lay on the horizon. "I've told you. My papers are private."

"Don't you trust me?"

Her delicate brow was furrowed, and he was sorry to have been the one to put the worry there. "On the contrary, I trust you more than I trust any other soul."

"Then what is this business you're about?"

"My business is to keep you safe," he answered without thinking.

"Truly, Aidan?" Light snapped to life in her eyes, dancing clear and bright. She smiled at him—*for* him—and he felt his heart swell. "Truly you want to keep me safe?"

He stared at her a moment, taking in those all-seeing eyes, her gentle countenance, and her face, fine as porcelain. She was kind and good, sweet thoughtfulness and artless honesty. She was all that had been taken from him so long ago—and all that he desired now. He realized how true his words had been. He *did* want to care for her.

And it unsettled him.

More than any revenge or intrigue, it was this genteel, bookish woman who'd managed to unnerve him. A mere few moments of her uncharacteristic lack of attention, and he'd fretted and frowned like a schoolboy. But then, when he'd shown the simplest consideration, she'd come to life, looking at him with such warmth, and not an ounce of artifice. He fantasized what it would be to let her in. To tell her his secrets, feeling that gaze focused only on him, her responses ever transparent and true. Truly to keep her safe.

To keep her.

"Want to? Aye, Beth. I find I do."

But even as he said it, he knew he couldn't share a bed with a treasure like her while his nights were spent dreaming of revenge. In a distant future, when he was a respectable man, a man of books and accomplished in a trade, he would court her in earnest. But first, he needed to exorcise his past.

He'd spent most of his life wanting one thing: to find and kill the man who'd kidnapped him so long ago. But now Aidan found he had a second dream, a fragile one, only now blooming to life in his chest.

To be worthy of Elspeth Farquharson.

But first, he'd need to settle his business. He'd track down and kill the man with the black pearl. He'd put his past forever behind him. Because, for the first time, he could envision a future.

"Someday," he said quietly, "someday I'll be worthy of it."

She bolted straight in her chair and grabbed his hands in hers, sending papers fluttering to the floor. "You're worthy now."

He'd been bought and sold. He knew his worth. It was six pounds two shillings sterling.

"No, not of you, of this." He turned her hand over in his. It was so small, the fingers delicately tapering to clean, finely rounded nails. He traced her palm and then ran a thumb along a thin line of callus. She worked hard on the farm—harder than she ought.

She snatched her hand back with a rueful frown that cracked his heart. "My hands aren't fine like a lady's hands should be."

Grabbing it back, he kissed her palm. "You're wrong."

Tenderly, he turned it over, kissing her knuckles like the most dashing of courtiers. "Yours are the finest of all. You, everything a lady aspires to be."

Not letting go, he met her eyes. Her look of dumbfounded wonderment was so endearing, a little laugh escaped him. "Sweet Beth. I would like to care for you someday. If you wished it."

The door swung open, and they sprang apart.

Her father scowled at him. "Time for you to leave."

Aidan gritted his teeth. One day he'd have his own cottage, and he'd sit with Elspeth by the fire for as long as he cared to.

"But he just got here," Elspeth said, and the plea in her voice firmed Aidan's resolve. "He's helping me with my accounts."

"We're off to see a businessman who knows accounts better even than you, girl." Farquharson grabbed her shawl from a peg and strode to her, gesturing impatiently. "Up, up you go. I've a message from the greatest knit merchant in all Aberdeen."

Aidan curled his fingers into his knees, determined not to leap from his seat to coerce a more respectful tone from the old man's mouth.

She stood warily. "What are you talking about?"

"I'm talking about none other than Dougal Fraser, and he's a fancy to meet *you*."

Aidan's feet shuffled abruptly beneath him, his body very nearly springing to throttle the man's throat before he could think better of it. He'd seen the name Dougal Fraser before, on a slip of paper given to him by an Aberdeen hired man.

The movement had drawn her father's eyes, and while he spoke to his daughter, he continued to glare at Aidan. "Fraser asked if you were promised to anyone. I'm happy to tell him you're not."

She flinched back. "But he's an old man."

Aidan shot her a look. What did *Elspeth* know of Fraser?

Her father stepped close, tossing the shawl haphazardly around her shoulders. "What do you know of Lord Fraser?"

"I . . . I've heard of him," she said, adjusting herself. "I simply assumed."

"Well, he said some things, put me in mind of an alliance of sorts. Our brains run along the same track. Both business-minded men, you know."

"What sort of alliance?" Aidan demanded in a hard voice. But he didn't need to hear her father spell it out to know: the man wanted to marry Elspeth. The need to protect her, to possess her, seethed in his belly.

Farquharson ignored him, his face splitting into a grin that mocked Aidan. "I'm assuming he wants to see you to ask for your hand, fool girl. He spoke of the potential of *this very farm*." He nudged her. "I told you sheep was a grand idea. Lord Fraser thinks our wool production—regular and high quality—would be just the thing for his business."

Aidan managed to calm himself enough to speak. "Fraser's business is thriving, and on a much grander scale. I don't believe he'd have an honest interest in a farm this size."

"A farm *this size*," her father mimicked, glaring at him. "And what have *you* got, boy? Nothing, that's what." He crossed his arms, puffing with pride. "If you must know, Fraser said he's been long without a woman. He heard my Elspeth was fine."

Long without a woman. Fury roiled hot in his belly. She was more than a mere commodity—she was precious.

"But I don't love him." She cast a quick and plaintive glance at Aidan. There was a message in her eyes that he dared not hope was true—that her affections might already be claimed, and by him.

"Love? Girl, you don't have two farthings to rub together. Why do you want love when you can be a lady?"

Aidan bolted to his feet. "Elspeth *is* a lady. She doesn't need a rich old husband to prove that to the world."

Her father scoffed. "Well, now she'll be set up like one. And for the rest of her days."

"Set *you* up is more like it," Aidan said, his voice dangerously low.

Sneering, her father looked him up and down like a piece of rubbish. "What business is it of yours?"

Aidan scowled silently back, thinking the man was right. It *wasn't* his business. Would that it were. Would that Elspeth were *his* responsibility—he'd care for her better than the wealthiest of merchants could.

"Aye, that's right," her father mumbled triumphantly.

Aidan stepped forward, and Elspeth stopped him with an outstretched arm. "But we're getting by, Da. The farm is starting to turn around. I don't need to marry when I'm happy and needed here."

"You need to make house, respectable-like. Have a place of your own, a few bairns." He walked to the door, gesturing for her to follow, as though she should start that very moment. "A man like Fraser will do much for our respectability."

Elspeth held her ground and didn't follow. "I'm perfectly respectable."

"Aye," her father said with a shrug, "that's as may be, but our coffers aren't so."

Aidan watched as her confusion turned to anger, and a matching fury blazed in his chest. If only he had hard proof, rather than a hunch and a crumpled receipt from his hired man. "Anyone but him," he said, trying to keep his voice level. "Think twice about this. This Fraser is a stranger. And . . . I think he's tied up in a dangerous game."

Elspeth gasped. "Who is he? I must know. I've been desperate to know."

Her eager response gave Aidan pause. The question wasn't what did he know, rather what did *she*?

Ignoring his daughter, the old man glared at Aidan, demanding, "How do *you* know aught about him?"

How to explain that it was just a hunch? "I simply . . . know."

Her father laughed. "You simply . . . know? His *dangerous games*? Here's a dangerous game," he said, growing serious. "You sitting unchaperoned with my daughter. I see how you look at her. You just don't want another man to have her."

"That might be true. But trust me when I tell you, Fraser isn't what he seems." Even a vague link between this merchant and the man with the black pearl was too much. "I have reason to believe he's tied to the pirate who kidnapped me as a child."

Elspeth drew in a sharp breath.

"Pish!" Her father scoffed. "What nonsense. You were just a child. An . . . an . . ."

Aidan felt Elspeth sidle close behind to give his arm a quick, convulsive squeeze. "An urchin?" he finished, his voice dangerously calm.

Her father only sneered. "Aye. Your accusation is tripe. All of it, tripe."

Elspeth stepped forward. "We have proof."

Aidan shot her a speaking look. She'd seen his papers that day. He didn't know what she'd read, but he'd rather she told him before getting her father involved. "I'll find proof," he said definitively, cutting her off.

Her father's placid expression spoke volumes about just whom he did and did not deem trustworthy. "You won't find any proof, because I ken a respectable man when I see one."

Aidan didn't care about the slight. He cared that

this daft old man, who equated a pricey waistcoat with respectability, was going to sacrifice his only child for financial gain.

He stepped into the older man's face. "So you're simply going to throw your daughter to a stranger?"

"Aidan," Elspeth whispered, "don't fash yourself. I'm sure Da and I will discuss this."

He heard the plea in her voice, but couldn't help it. A great weight was pressing upon his chest. Fury, frustration, disbelief all crushing down, making his lungs tight.

"You see? I'm not throwing her. All Elspeth has always wanted was to help out her family." Her father gave her a careless wink. "Isn't that right, girl?"

"Oh, and you know so well what she wants?" Aidan clenched his fists, wishing for an outlet for his rage.

"Aidan, please." Elspeth placed a gentle hand at his back, and his tensed muscles flinched at her touch.

He'd treasured those tender hands, and now they were being stolen from him. Like everything else in his life he'd ever cherished. "*You're* the only family she has," he said, stabbing a finger toward her father. His jaws were clenched, each breath a labor now. "And by now you should know better how to take care of your own self, old man."

"I care for myself *and* for her," her father said, indignant. "Have all these long years, and all by myself, too."

Disbelief and outrage roiled in Aidan's belly. "You call what you do taking care of her?"

"She's been well tended. She has what she needs. The lass even has her own room."

"Truly?" Aidan exploded. "And *that's* proof that you know her heart?"

"What do *you* know of her heart?" her father snapped. "What can you know of anything? You're naught but an indentured, fresh off the boat. Of course your head is turned by the first skirt you see," he said, waving a dismissive hand in Elspeth's direction.

Aidan's vision turned red and black. He sprang at the man, punching him squarely on the chin.

"No!" Elspeth shrieked as her da fell hard to the ground.

Her father rubbed his face, working his mouth open and closed. "Damn you. You'll pay for this."

Elspeth's eyes were wide with shock, and Aidan stared at her, wallowing in his own shame and frustration. Perhaps her father was right. Perhaps he was, and ever would be, nothing more than another man's servant. Perhaps he'd never be good enough for something—for some-*one*—so fine. "I'm sorry, Beth," he said, his voice hoarse with feeling. "But you deserve more than that. You *are* more than that."

Eyes narrowing, he turned to glare at her father. "You don't understand Elspeth. You may think you do. But really you're not worthy to call her your daughter."

Rubbing his hand, Aidan stormed from the cottage.

Chapter 21

He'd lost his head. He'd punched Elspeth's father.

Aidan scrubbed a hand over his face, trying to clear the memory, but it was no use. It'd hounded him all night. His mind brimmed with episodes he'd rather forget, and this was one more to add to the lot.

First he'd punched Cormac, and now *this*. Perhaps Farquharson's accusations had been right—he was naught but a common laborer, unschooled, violent, and not to be trusted.

He upped his pace, walking the docks as briskly as he could without breaking into an actual run. The wind whipped off Aberdeen harbor, chilling him to the bone, but he embraced it. Though the weather was turning, he'd fled Dunnottar without a cloak, happy to freeze to death if it meant his mind would finally know peace.

He stopped abruptly. He'd reached King's Quay, marking the general vicinity of the offices of Dougal Fraser and his much-lauded "Knitted Goodes" enterprise. He scowled, thinking how Elspeth's father had raved about the man's brilliance, his wealth.

But a fat purse didn't make someone a man. And it certainly didn't entitle this Fraser to Elspeth.

He stormed up one of the roads that spiked from the harbor, in search of Fraser's offices, but slowed his pace as a flicker of doubt seized him. Perhaps this knit merchant *was* worthy. Perhaps he'd love and care for Elspeth in a way that *Aidan* was unable to.

Aidan made much about a man's worth, but how could *he* rate when the mere blatherings of an old man had the capacity to plunge him into a rage?

He rubbed his knuckles, regretting for the thousandth time how he'd struck Elspeth's own flesh and blood. Aidan might have spent long years away from civilization, but even *he* knew that this was not precisely the way to endear himself to a family. Far from it. How her father had glared, as if Aidan were the devil come calling.

But Elspeth was so refined, so good. Before they'd been interrupted, he'd come close to imagining himself as someone deserving of such gentility. So close to thinking he *would* someday be that man.

Then her father had come in, and with a word, he'd stolen her from Aidan forever. The man wanted her to marry an old merchant, and Aidan could see it. It was the way of the world. Rich men chose their lives and their wives, while men like Aidan served them.

He'd had enough. This Dougal Fraser might be rich, but as far as Aidan was concerned, Elspeth wasn't for sale.

But she was a sweet and gentle creature who'd do as her father bid. So he'd simply do the fighting for her. He'd find some way to discredit the man in the eyes of her father.

Aidan might not deserve her, but he could ensure that no other unworthy man claimed her either. He'd certainly

not stand idly by as she sacrificed her innocence to someone he suspected was old enough to be her grandfather.

He couldn't get past the faint nagging suspicion that
this particular merchant wasn't who he pretended to be.
Why was he connected with smugglers? And why would
he choose Elspeth over a bevy of wealthy, young chits
eager to be married into new money? Aidan was determined to find proof of some ill-doing.

He looked up at the sign. *Dougal Fraser, Knitted
Goodes.* The building was modest, but it was clean, and
located in a relatively upscale area of Aberdeen harbor.
On the surface, it was perfectly respectable. But Aidan
knew better than most how things weren't always as they
appeared.

He strode in, determined to get to the bottom of his
suspicions. But he'd be discreet. There was no sense in
alerting Fraser that he was under suspicion. Aidan would
save Elspeth from this absurd alliance. And if he happened upon some clue about his enemy's whereabouts in
the process, all the better.

The door shut behind him, and he was taken aback by
the great rustle and click of sound that engulfed him. He
strode down the narrow corridor, peeking in the handful
of rooms that sprouted along one side like petals on a
half-torn flower. With the exception of a couple of young
men whom Aidan assumed were apprentices, the rooms
were filled with women and girls, all knitting.

"Is there something I can help you with?"

Aidan turned, guessing at once it was none other
than Dougal Fraser who'd greeted him. The man was
well dressed, with graying hair and a pinched expression. Aidan estimated that he was in his early fifties—
old enough that he should've been married already, yet
still young enough to be vital. Young enough to father
children.

Aidan clenched his fists. He wanted to snarl at the

man, but instead he forced himself to smile his easiest smile, bowing his most cavalier bow. "Aye, I suppose you can."

Elspeth had recognized this Fraser's name. She must've taken something when she'd riffled through his papers. The woman was clever and cunning, with far more daring than was betrayed by her innocent appearance.

Aidan put his mind back into the moment, realizing how to approach the answer to Fraser's question. Gesturing at all the workers, he said, "I see you've got labor at the ready. Where do you find it?" He strolled down the hall, trying to look thoughtful. "I'm eager for slaves, you see, and ready to double the current rate."

Though Fraser smiled politely, his eyes remained cold. "What business are you in?"

"None of yours," Aidan replied, and upon seeing Fraser's scowl, he affected a nonchalant laugh. "Look, my only concern is setting up a collection. Of workers," he added, reading the other man's confusion. "Or did you think I was eager to get into the stockings business?"

"Worsted stockings are my bread and butter. I'd not mock them." Fraser's lips pursed and his expression became chilly. "Pray tell, why on earth did you think *I* of all people might be able to help in your quest?"

"I saw this address written on a sheet of paper. Next to a name. It was an odd one. What was it?" Aidan snapped his fingers as if trying to summon the memory. "Ah yes. The Bishop."

"Come." Alarm lit Fraser's features, and he spun on his heel, striding straight for his office. He turned on Aidan the moment the door shut. "You expect me to help a man I don't even know?"

Aidan remained silent. He had no desire to have his name bandied about Aberdeen harbor.

Red splotches mottled Fraser's cheeks, betraying his frustration. "*Now* you become suddenly discreet? Who are you, anyway, and why should I trust you? How can I even know you're serious?"

"I'm serious enough." Aidan shook his sporran, and the clink of coin was so heavy it could be heard through the thick skin of the pouch. Though he jostled it offhandedly, it represented all he owned in the world. He'd hoped to use it to find his enemy, but wouldn't think twice to spend it helping Elspeth. If his suspicions were borne out, the two goals were one and the same. "Now tell me, where's this Bishop?"

The merchant didn't take his eyes from the pouch. "You don't waste time."

"Time isn't a luxury I have," Aidan retorted, feeling for the first time during their meeting that he spoke the truth. "Now, what I'd like to know is why all the secrecy?" He gestured to the four walls of Fraser's office. "Knowing where to find affordable . . . *help* . . . isn't merely sanctioned, it's encouraged. And yet, according to my man, you hold clandestine meetings here, under the auspices of dealing in knit goods. Makes a person wonder what you're really about."

Fraser narrowed his eyes, looking dangerously close to snapping.

Aidan forced himself to calm. It'd do no good to make an enemy of this man. Pasting a stiff smile on his face, he added, "Not I, of course. I prefer subtlety in all things."

He needed to help Elspeth by discrediting Fraser to her father, and that meant getting to the bottom of his business. He would *not* succumb to his temper.

The merchant considered him for a long while, and Aidan affected his trademark easy nonchalance. He jangled his sporran again for good measure.

Inhaling deeply, Fraser appeared to come to a decision. He took and dipped his quill, carefully writing something on a sheet of paper. "Let's say I know where to find laborers. And, say they were held in a ship in Aberdeen harbor.

You'll need"—he proffered the paper to Aidan—"word from me."

Aidan stared at the sheet. He made out the words *Justice Port* and a ship's name—the *Endeavor*.

Fraser scoffed. "You *can* read this, right?"

He stared for one furious moment at the merchant's hands. They were trembling—weak, spotted, and pale. Aidan would die before he let those hands touch Elspeth. He snatched the paper. "Aye, I can read your damned scrawl." He folded it and slipped it into his sporran, forcing a peremptory thank you from between his clenched teeth.

Fraser raised his brows. "And now I think you owe *me* something."

Aidan took his hand from his sporran. "You won't see coin until I see laborers."

The merchant surprised him by laughing. "A man after my own inclinations. Now go to the harbor. It's a new ship, with a new captain." He shook his head in disgust. "My last contact sank before he'd even left Aberdeen harbor. Man was naught but a careless pirate."

He could only be referring to one boat: the one he and Cormac had sunk. Aidan forced a cold smile. "Pirates might be skilled, but they're not always smart."

Fraser appeared to like that assessment, and he nodded amiably. "True, true. This one got caught up with a woman, and there's no good ever to come from such an arrangement."

"And yet I hear I'm to offer you felicitations on a recent engagement." The words were out of Aidan's mouth before he had a chance to think them through.

The merchant looked puzzled for a moment, and then pleased. "Heard the news already, eh?"

The self-satisfied prig made Aidan long to punch something. "An eligible bachelor like yourself taken off the market? It's no surprise word got around."

"Aye, it's true." Fraser leaned back in his chair. "I'm to be married. At first, I thought her a plain-faced creature. But something about her appealed."

"Plain?" Aidan fisted his hands. There was an unassuming simplicity to Elspeth's beauty, but she was hardly plain—Aidan just called it natural.

"Well, that was what I'd thought at first." He leaned on his desk, confiding, "I'd never marry an ugly girl, you see."

"I do see." Aidan nodded, barely seeing the man through the film of red that'd dropped before his eyes. He imagined the dozen different ways in which he could beat this swine to a pulp.

"But she struck me as a bright sort of girl," Fraser continued in an annoyingly musing sort of tone. "Though very quiet. I imagine it indicates a biddable nature."

Aidan gritted his teeth in a smile. *Biddable* was the last word he'd used to describe Elspeth. "Found yourself a tractable girl, did you?"

"Indeed. Or so she'll be, once I get her out from her father's thumb and under mine. The man's a doddering old fellow." Fraser tapped his head. "Bit dim in the upper works too, if you ask me."

"It's remarkable how dim-witted some folk can be." Aidan forced his voice to be light, adopting his blithe mask to conceal what felt like a giant fist crushing his chest.

"Just so!" Fraser smiled, looking at ease now, nodding jovially. "You seem a bright lad. A man after my own heart." He began to turn his attention to the papers on his desk. Shooing Aidan toward the door, he said, "Now get yourself to the docks." He paused, giving Aidan an avuncular wink. "Tell them the Bishop sent you."

The Bishop. Aggravation fueled Aidan's stride. Wealthy men and their ridiculous flights of fancy.

He smelled Aberdeen harbor before he saw it, the stench summoning a churn of emotions. The heavy scent of salt, oil casks, and decaying fish would forever remind him how it had felt to dock as a free man, returned to Scotland once more.

But it also recalled a darker, more distant time, when he'd been a young boy, torn from his homeland for what he thought would be forever. His captors had pulled the sack from his head, putting him face-to-face with the man he'd sworn as his enemy above all others.

As a lad, he'd heard stories of pirates, but never had he pictured them like *that* man. He'd always imagined they might be dashing, or handsome, or perhaps even grotesquely ugly. But the man who'd ordered his capture had been decidedly average, neither tall nor short, with only a black pearl in his ear to mark him as anything other than ordinary. And somehow it was his unremarkable looks that'd made him seem all the crueler.

Aidan turned onto one of the larger streets leading down to the harbor. He girded himself for the inevitable onslaught of memories. Forever, he'd carry a picture of the docks as they'd receded from his young view. Forever the sight of them would invoke the old heartbreak and terror as the spires of Aberdeen, and then the coast of Scotland itself, had faded into a vast gray nothing.

He'd girded himself, but there was nothing to prepare him for what he saw docked at King's Quay. A wave of horror crippled him.

It was the ship, the one captained by the man with the pearl earring.

He shook his head, scrubbing a hand roughly along his jaw. Not *the* ship. This one bore a different name— *Endeavor*, painted in a cheery red script—not *León de Oro*. He was staring at an exact replica of the boat that'd stolen him thirteen long years past.

Sailors rarely changed the names of their ships. Pirates were a particularly superstitious lot, and the man with the black pearl had been no different. Aidan recalled the rules: no whistling, no cutting of hair or nails. No pigs, nor rabbit, nor salmon. With ice in his belly, he recalled the chimney boy who'd been tossed overboard to drown, his crime that he'd been born with red hair.

Despite the resemblance, Aidan told himself he was jumping to conclusions, that the two ships weren't the same. *Endeavor* was a rare craft, an exotic Spanish beauty known as a *xebec*, and she was fast, her foremast raking forward as though the ship itself were eager to slice through the wind. She bore a sleekly pointing bow, a hefty stern, and a wide hull exactly like the one in which he'd been imprisoned, laboring for weeks in a grim darkness that'd reeked of mildew and tar. But it seemed more than a coincidence.

Recovering from his shock, he realized he was striding straight for it, his hand braced on the hilt of his sword. He tempered his impulses, forcing himself to halt. He'd need to bide his time—his ghost wasn't aboard *this* ship.

His mind raced. The *Endeavor* was well guarded, sailors swarming on the deck and in the ratlines like flies over a mound of dung. She may not have been *his* ship, but she was so very like it that a deep foreboding crept through his gut. Elspeth was being wed to a man involved with *this*.

He just needed to prove hers was a bad match to a bad man.

Seeing a shadow, he stiffened. Someone was approaching. The day was hazy and overcast, but still, he could make out a gray shadow wavering along the rotting timbers of the dock.

He put his hand on his hilt and canted his elbow out hard. There'd be no mistaking the threat in his posture.

The shadow made straight for him, its amorphous shape speaking to a short, cloaked figure. He peered out the corners of his eyes.

"What have you discovered?" asked a familiar voice. The sound aroused much ire, a goodly dose of anxiety, plus a maddening pleasure, all melding together into a blade that cut straight to his heart.

Elspeth.

Chapter 22

He grabbed her arm. "What are you doing here?"

She flinched away, startled at the rough grip. "I followed you."

"Sorry," he said, smoothing her arm where he'd grabbed her. He visibly tried to clear the anger from his face, which left him looking pinched. "What were you—?"

A commotion got their attention—a handful of sailors riled up for what was looking like a brawl—and he swept her away, heading down the harbor and up the first alleyway. It was a dead end, and he ducked them into a shadowy corner. "What were you thinking?" he repeated in a low hiss. "You could get hurt."

She ignored his concerns, her voice vibrating with excitement. "You saw him, didn't you? Dougal Fraser?" *Aidan* would help her, she knew. He would save her from this ridiculous marriage.

"I saw him," he answered in a tight voice. "And you're lucky he didn't see *you*, though I'd like to know how you even heard of the man." He paused, taking in her outfit, and made a face that was half amused, half exasperated. "What are you thinking, skulking about, and in this ridiculous old cloak?"

"What else am I to do? My father is unrelenting. He doesn't believe that Fraser is a bad man." She clutched at his shirtsleeves. "*Is* he? What do you know?"

"What do *I* know?" Aidan's narrowing eyes alarmed her a little. But the sight was exhilarating too. She'd glimpsed Aidan vulnerable, yet now, the way he was taking charge, she saw just how powerful he was.

"Yes," she said, a bit breathless. They stood hidden in a corner, and the darkness etched black shadows along his cheeks, under his jaw. His chest was solid, and his heat radiated to her, and she felt she might be lost, consumed by his burning energy. Aidan was a force—knowing he was intent on safeguarding *her* over all other women was a thrill beyond measure. "When Da told us about him, it seemed you knew something."

"What of you?" he demanded. "I think you're the one who knows something. And I think it has to do with a little something you stole from me."

"Stole . . . something?" Her voice sounded weak to her ears. Stolen something indeed. A sheet of paper that was currently chafing inside her bodice.

He took her chin and gently tipped it to the right and left, studying her. "Very pretty, Beth. But it won't work on me." He gave it a gentle pinch. "Now tell. Where is it? This Dougal Fraser is up to no good, and I need to find proof. I'll start by looking at whatever it is you took from my papers."

"*We'll* find proof." If Aidan thought to embark alone on an intrigue—one intended for her own good, no less—

he had another thing coming. "And your paper is safe with me."

"What if your father reads it?" He let go her chin and stepped closer. "It's not safe if he can find it in the house."

"It's not in the house."

He stepped closer still, and something in her belly sparked in response. "The paper is on your person?"

She imagined his intention had been to make a threatening impression, but his proximity was having quite the opposite effect. "Perhaps," she said, not budging her eyes from his. She felt something inside her smolder, and willed it to burn clear in her gaze.

"Perhaps," he mimicked. "You little fox, you're more than folk take you for, do you know that?"

She shrugged, her lip trembling in a coy smile.

He took one last step forward, till his stomach was pressed against hers. "Shall I frisk you, then?"

He was a solid wall of hot muscle pressed along her thighs, against her breasts, inflaming her till she thought she might come apart from her trembling. "If you must."

He raised a hand to stroke up the side of her torso, and she answered instinctively by lifting her arms to rest on his shoulders. His eyes grew dark, his voice ragged. "What's the matter with me? You're being wed to a criminal. I feel in my gut that the man whose face has haunted me for years is in reach. Yet all I can think is that I want to kiss you."

"Kiss me?" Her voice cracked as he began to nuzzle her neck.

His hand roved her torso eagerly now, drifting thrillingly close to the swell of her breast. "I'll stop, if you wish it," he said, his voice a low rasp.

She opened her mouth to speak, but nothing came out. His mouth slowed, hovering hot over her throat. Oh God, did he think she wanted him to stop? How to show him she wanted very much for him to kiss her once more? She did as she imagined any romantic heroine would do, and pulling apart from him, she tilted up her face and shut her eyes.

He stroked her cheek. "I want you, and you want me too, don't you? Sweet Beth. There's naught you seem to fear."

She risked a peek from beneath her lashes. "What I fear is that . . . that you might not kiss me again after all."

"Not that," he said in a hoarse whisper. "Never that." He swooped in, taking her mouth in a hot-blooded kiss.

Elspeth's world exploded. She opened herself to him, melting into him, welcoming him, exploring with mouth and teeth and tongue, like a woman starved. Like a wanton.

The thought that she might *be* a wanton aroused her all the more.

A dam broke deep inside her, letting free every passion she'd ever harbored. Twining her fingers in his hair, she crushed her body as close as she could against his. She felt his startled laugh turn to a groan in her mouth, and it inflamed her desire to a fever pitch.

He gradually began to slow the kiss, gradually and regretfully pulling away. "We shouldn't."

She opened her mouth to protest, and he laughed low, interrupting her by saying, "Rather, we *should*. Just not here."

"Oh," she said, relieved.

Leaning her weight into him, she gazed up, a smile in her eyes for this man who seemed to soften for none but her. One needed only to see his scars, testifying to a lifetime of beatings, or imagine his escape, or his adventures across the sea, to know Aidan was the most dangerous of rogues. And yet she felt protected in his arms.

She'd felt such dread when her father had first spoken the name Dougal Fraser. She knew she should summon that dread now. She should, even now, be jumping into action, searching for clues, fighting for her freedom. Yet she and Aidan both stood, mesmerized by this happy dream from which they dared not wake.

She reached to cup his cheek for a moment, and as she stroked back down, she felt a strange, hard ridge in his breast pocket. She canted her head, giving him a quizzical look. "What's this?"

His eyes had been hazy from the kiss, and she watched as they cleared. He gave her a lazy smile and kissed the tip of her nose. "I got you something."

"Me?" She became woozy with panicked self-consciousness. Aidan was the first man—the first person, really—to give her gifts so freely. The thought that he'd bought her something else had her feeling embarrassed. "Something?"

"Most women receive such news with some degree of pleasure." He stroked the side of her hotly blushing cheek. "Look at you, flying your colors. I can see your blush, even in the shadows."

"You didn't have to get me anything," she said stiffly.

"I know it. But surprise is the nature of the whole enterprise, isn't it?" With a finger he tipped her face to his. "Do you not generally get gifts?"

She shook her head. "Not generally, no."

"Well, we're a pair," he said, "because I don't generally give them." *Not publicly, at least.*

"You didn't have to get me anything," she repeated.

He stared at her a moment, dumbfounded. Why did the woman feel so blasted uncomfortable? It was such a simple damned gift he'd gotten her.

He looked over his shoulder, but there wasn't a soul to be seen in their alleyway, and so he turned his attention back to her. "Shut your eyes," he said.

"What?"

"You heard me." Her eyelids fluttered nervously shut,

and he pulled the thin, velvet-wrapped package from his pocket. Brushing wisps of hair from her face, he gently placed a pair of spectacles on her nose.

Gasping, her hands flew up to her face, fingering the frames. "What have you—?"

"Hush. And keep your eyes shut for the full effect." He reached around, tying the thin ribbon that secured them to her head. "There. You may open them."

He laughed, warmed by her look of wide-eyed amazement.

"Oh, Aidan." She studied him up and down, outlining with her finger the path of her gaze. "Oh," she said again, "Oh, Aidan!"

He'd given gifts before in his life, but he'd always been careful to remain anonymous. When he was enslaved, he'd always found a way to help the younger, more innocent lads. But such gestures could be misconstrued as weakness, and so his help had always come in secret. He'd never been there to see the moment of surprise, the realization of pleasure. "Do you like them?"

She fingered his shirt. "Did you know, there are the tiniest wee threads that make up the weave of this fabric? I see them, even in these shadows."

He laughed, gratified to see her so animated. His heart soared to think this happiness of hers had been *his* doing. "Aye, I knew it."

"Though I think they're just for reading," she said, looking beyond him, to the mouth of the alley. "They appear to"—she alternately peered up over, then through, the lenses—"distort things that are far away."

"Dear Beth." He took his index finger and gently pushed the spectacles all the way up the bridge of her nose. "I asked if you like them."

"Oh, I do," she said, meeting his gaze in utter earnest. He noted the telltale uncertainty that generally preceded one of her blushes. "But I'm afraid"—she touched a finger to one edge of the spectacles—"I'm afraid I must look a sight."

He studied her, a smile broad on his face. Her eyes *were* a bit magnified, those mysterious yellow flecks enhanced, leaving her looking more than ever as though she could see all, understand all. "You do look a bit owlish," he added with a laugh. "But a very pretty owl indeed."

She smiled back at him, and he was pleased to see her self-consciousness beginning to ebb. "I'm tempted to give you a gift every day of the week," he told her. "Just to get you in the habit."

"Oh, no, Aidan." She shook her head vehemently. "These are too much as it is."

"Silly woman." Reaching around, he gently untied the ribbon. "It was long past time you got a decent pair of spectacles. I see you, straining to do your tallies by firelight."

"They are a wonder." Taking them from his hand, she held them out of the shadows, catching the light, tilting them this way and that. "This . . . this is more than I ever could have imagined."

Her sweet smile had him fantasizing that the *this* she referred to wasn't the pair of spectacles, but rather the two of them.

"But promise you won't buy me anything more," she said, earnestness drawing a faint line between her brows. "I don't need anything more."

"Hmm." He'd spotted a dress in Aberdeen with pretty blue and yellow stitching about the neck that he thought might bring out the color of her eyes. "On the contrary. I think there's much indeed that you need."

She raised a saucy brow, and a laugh exploded from him, surprised by the flash of heat in her eyes. "You wicked, wee minx," he muttered, placing a kiss on the top of her head. "Clear that look from your face, or you'll find me kissing you again."

She laughed with him, and the carefree sound of it loosened something in his chest.

"I need to hear more of that." At her inquisitive look, he said, "Your laughter. I don't hear enough of it."

The joy drained from her face, and he regretted his words. It appeared he'd only reminded Elspeth of her current worries.

"Aye, you nearly made me forget my troubles. What did you find out about Fraser?" She gave him a hard look. "But you've got troubles too. Why won't you tell me of them? I can help you find your man. And where, pray tell, did you ever find the money to buy me such a lavish gift?"

He stiffened. "Not lavish." But she spoke the truth: the money he'd spared for her gift would've been better spent tracking his enemy.

Money. It seemed always to come down to money. She was being married off to some aging blackguard, because of money.

"My finances are not your concern, Beth." As if he had any *finances* to speak of. All he had to show for his life was a jealously guarded pouch, filled with hard-earned coin intended to create the illusion that he was a man of worth.

Again, it came down to worth, to worthiness.

He needed to remember what he was about, and that was tracking the man with the black pearl. Until he found and bested the man who'd stolen him, his life wouldn't be truly restored.

But once he destroyed his enemy, he could get on with the rest of it, starting over, making a real life as a real man would. He'd start by saving Elspeth from this suspicious match. Then he'd make his own money, set himself up with a good living so he could care for his woman.

And none of that would happen with him mooning like a love-struck idiot. She'd distracted him, but it was time to get down to business. He narrowed his eyes.

"Now there's a little matter of something I think you're hiding on *your* person."

She looked like a startled doe, and he forced himself to keep a straight face. It'd do no good to scare her. Though, he thought with a grin, he might enjoy a little fun.

The hard years had honed his instincts, and those instincts told him the papers she'd stolen were hidden somewhere on her person. "You're wicked," he told her. "And do you know why?"

"No." He'd expected her to look shocked, but mostly she looked amazed.

It spurred him on. Staring at her parted lips, he said, "You distracted me."

"I did?"

"You did," he said, chuckling at the disbelief in her voice. He couldn't help it, he had to touch her again. Had to kiss her, and smell her, and taste her. He leaned in to nuzzle her, and pointing his fingertip onto the side of her throat, he whispered along her skin, "You had me looking here."

She made a gratifying little gasping sound, and he swept his hands down to clutch her firmly about her waist, tugging her closer. His cock stiffened at once, and he pressed into her, his flesh chafing against the wool of his plaid, straining to press through the layers of her skirts, to the soft, innocent flesh hidden beneath.

"And here," he said, kissing along her collarbone.

He had the distant thought that he should have a care. They stood in the open, in a seedy alley off Aberdeen harbor, him pressing her into a darkened corner, his desire precipitous, quickly spinning to a point of no return.

But he couldn't summon a care. All he knew was her precious body, yielding against his. It took the full force of his will not to succumb to the lust that pounded through him and simply ruck her skirts up above her waist and take her there, hidden in the shadows.

He stroked a hand up her torso, running his thumb along the soft flesh of her breast. "And here."

She drew in a sharp breath, but didn't stop him, and so he kept tracing his thumb up and down, his pressure growing just a bit firmer, his touch approaching just a bit closer to the tip of her breast.

"You . . . you were looking there too?" she asked, her voice breathy and shallow.

"Oh, most definitely."

She gave a little self-conscious wriggle. "B-but, there's not . . . I'm not . . . I'm so . . ."

"Ah," he said, guessing her fears. He brought his other hand up to caress her other side, calming her nervous body. Kissing up her throat to her ear, he whispered, "Is it you think you're too thin?"

He heard her breathing change, felt her reluctant nod.

"Silly, perfect, foolish woman." He kissed his way along her jaw to her mouth, where he hovered over her lips. "You see, Beth, you aren't the only wicked one. I've been looking here"—he cupped one breast—"and here"—then the other—"since first we met."

He touched his lips to hers just as he gave a gentle squeeze to her breasts. They nestled in his palms as though they'd been made just for him. "Perfect, I told you."

He could feel her hardened nipples through the fabric of her bodice, and rubbed his open palms over them, then closed his hands to squeeze again.

There was a faint answering crinkle. His stolen paper. And regretfully, he remembered his purpose. It was perhaps the only excuse strong enough to bring him to his senses, recalling where they were, pulling him from this lusty haze.

Aidan chuckled. "Perfect for my hands, but not perfect enough to conceal my papers."

She pulled away, and her face was an endearing tangle

of emotions: humor on her lips, embarrassment in her cheeks, and lust in her eyes. "You cheated."

"I wanted my paper back." His gaze was heavy on her as she reached in her bodice to pull it out. He vowed, someday *he'd* have the right to reach his hand under that bodice. To strip it off himself, if that was his desire. He knew Beth would have him—he saw it in those all-knowing eyes, felt it in her kisses. He just needed to finish what he'd set out to do, and then he would make her his. "I've gone long years without getting what I want. But no longer."

Chapter 23

Elspeth shivered. He'd spoken such dark, such rousing, such thrillingly sinful words. Had he meant he wanted her? Might he want more than just stolen kisses?

Putting a hand on Aidan's arm, she peeked past him. There were distant shouts and the faraway clopping of the occasional horse, but otherwise they were unseen in their dark corner.

Looking up at him, she slowly hooked a finger in the front of her bodice. She felt apart from her body, as though she were watching the actions of another woman. This other, sensual Elspeth moved lazily, her eyelids heavy, her wanting smoldering in her gaze.

She tugged at her bodice, pulling it a little away from her skin, freeing her naked breasts from their tight cocoon of linen. She wasn't bared to the world, yet cool air kissed her flesh, and a ripple of pleasure skimmed her body, leaving her skin buzzing and hot.

This sultry Elspeth reached in and grasped the edge of Aidan's paper. She'd hidden it tucked against her bare flesh, and as she slowly pulled it free, it brushed along her nipple, until every inch of her skin became hotter, tighter, the ache for his touch unbearable.

Aidan swallowed hard. He adjusted his plaid, and though she was desperate to steal a peek at what she'd felt pressed against her body, she found she wasn't yet *that* daring.

He cleared his throat, asking in a gratifyingly disconcerted voice, "Which of your books taught you how to do *that*?"

"That's from my own imagination." She gave him a slow sinner's smile that would've made the sauciest of literary heroines proud.

They froze, the sound of approaching chatter a splash of cold water on them both. Aidan cursed under his breath as a group of men—fresh from the tavern, by the smell of them—wandered into their alley.

She clamped the paper to her breast, but not before one of them spotted it.

"Oi, lads! The pretty lady's goin' tae read to us." Drunken laughter echoed in the cramped space.

Aidan spun, concealing her neatly behind his back, and like a mythical beast from a folktale, he transformed into something larger and infinitely more powerful. He pitched his voice loud and low, and it echoed off the dank stone, shrinking the alleyway into something smaller and more perilous. "If you value your hides, you'll keep moving."

It was the voice he'd have used on board ship. It shocked her, amazed her, took her breath away.

The men scattered like rats.

"Come," he said, speaking once more in the gentle tone reserved for her. "Let's away from here." He took the paper, and tucking her hand in the crook of his elbow, he quoted the old adage, " 'The day has eyes, but the night has ears,' and right now we find ourselves somewhere twixt the two. Best to talk as we walk."

He guided her from the alleyway, his stride confident, but not so swift as to draw attention. She trembled, her nerves still jangling from unspent lust, still shaken from the sudden appearance of the men, and he pulled her closer to steady her.

She knew he was leading her home, and her spirits plummeted. It would mean they'd soon have to part.

With their shared kisses, the dream of one day sharing a home with *Aidan* had come to life in her breast. But today, she and Aidan would say good-bye instead, and she'd have to face her father and the specter of her betrothal to Fraser.

She desperately hoped they'd find solid proof that the old merchant wasn't as reputable as he seemed. Because if they didn't, her father would insist on proceeding with her wedding. And she had no choice but to do as her father made her—it was the way of the world. If they found nothing to damn Fraser, she'd have no choice but to marry the man.

"Let's study this as we walk," she said quietly. "I'm afraid we won't have a chance to read it when I reach home."

With a tight nod, he navigated out from the shadows, and they traveled in silence till the buildings became sparser, gradually replaced by rolling countryside. When nobody but distant cattle were there to overhear, Aidan unfolded the paper she'd stolen from him.

WARRANT OF ENTRY
BRIDGETOWN PORT, BARBADOS
CAPTAIN WM. DERBY-PHIPPS
THE ENDEAVOR (ORIG. LEÓN DE ORO)
TYPE: XEBEC, 160 TONNES BURTHEN, 18 GUNS
CREW: 95
GUARANTOR: DOUGAL FRASER, KING'S QUAY, ABERDEEN

She'd read it a thousand times, but it was just as mean-
ingless to her as it'd been on the first. She mused quietly,
"Whatever could it mean that Fraser is in league with a
British traitor?"

He stopped abruptly, and their arms tugged against
each other. "You know this man?"

"Of course I do," she said, wondering at his intensity.
"Who doesn't?"

"*I* don't." He spoke through gritted teeth, intense focus
in his eyes.

She put a hand to her heart. He'd spent over half his
life out of the country—there was no way he'd have heard
the songs, known the tale. "Oh, Aidan, of course you
don't know. Captain William Derby-Phipps was a famous
traitor." She peered into his eyes. "But why do you care?
What does the connection mean?"

"He's the man who took me. He's my man with the
black pearl."

Her heart hammered with excitement. Might they find
their proof of Fraser's dishonesty *and* Aidan's revenge on
this one sheet of paper? "How can you know?"

"This." He pointed to a single word. "This is my proof."

Xebec. She stared at the strange, foreign word, perplexed. "Is that a man's name?"

"No," he said, and she could hear the anticipation
growing in his voice. "It's a type of ship. A rare Spanish
ship. There's one currently docked in Aberdeen harbor,
and though it sails under a different name"—he pointed
to the names, the *Endeavor*, the *León de Oro*—"I think
it's the same one that took me."

Though loath to interrupt, she had to ask the question
on her tongue. "Is it common to change a ship's name?"

"Hardly," he said, with a baffled shake of his head.
"He'd have been hard-pressed to change the name. Sailors are quite superstitious about such things. He must've
had some good reason—avoiding the authorities, evading

his enemies." He gave a brittle laugh. "I imagine he made quite a number of enemies in his time."

"Like you?"

"Aye, like me. Because I'm going to kill him." A deadly calm stole over his face. "Tell me about this Captain Derby-Phipps."

She pursed her lips, summoning the old tale to mind. "Derby-Phipps captained an English ship, during the Thirty Years War," she began. "Sailing alongside a small Dutch fleet, he encountered a sea of Spanish galleons and certain defeat."

"And, let me guess, our good captain simply turned tail?"

"Precisely. Those of his crew he couldn't convince to turn pirate, he simply killed. But he later stole a Spanish ship and inexplicably delivered the bounty to the British."

"Not inexplicable at all," Aidan said, interrupting her. His eyes danced with an excitement she felt swell in her own breast. "What else to do with so great a prize? The Dutch wouldn't have touched it, and the Spaniards would've killed him. That left bonny old England."

"Indeed," she said. "And bonny old England gave him the Spanish ship and a pardon for his trouble. There's even a song about him," she said, and sang a few bars of the old marching tune.

> *My name is Captain Will, oh Will,*
> *I turned pirate when I killed good men,*
> *Their worthy blood did spill.*
> *Their worthy blood did spill, did spill,*
> *Their worthy blood did spill.*

He laughed, and she felt they were both intoxicated by their discovery. "I said you looked like an owl with your spectacles, but I didn't know you sang like one too."

She gave him a swat. "I don't know that that's a compliment."

"Always, luvvie." He swatted her right back, on her bottom. He shook his head, retreating into his thoughts. "And that's my man with the black pearl."

"How odd," she said, her musing tone a match to his. "A man wearing jewelry."

"Not really. Sailors are a superstitious lot, fearing shipwreck above all things. They think the only way to ensure a Christian burial is to wear the cost of their coffin on their person. Gold, silver, gems . . . all worn in earrings, mostly. I'm sure this man—and much of his crew—is no different. His was a black pearl, though, and I've not seen its like since."

She took the paper from his hand. "This is it," she said somberly. "This will be our proof. We're so close now. We only need evidence of the captain's piracy, and my father will be sure to cancel the engagement."

They crested the final hill on the path to her house. She slowed her pace, until her feet gradually came to a stop. Reaching home meant bidding farewell to Aidan.

She stared down into the glen, looking blindly at the stone fence he'd built for them. She'd never again be able to look at that square of pastureland without thinking of him.

"My fence work is done," he said, as though reading her mind.

Their tutoring work was at an end, as was his work on their farm. Would he be done with her too? Aidan's enemy was within his reach. Would he find and kill the man, only to disappear from her life forever?

Unable to look him in the eye, she stared instead at her flock of dull-eyed beasts, feeding in the distance. "Does that mean I'll no longer see you?"

"I think I might come back," he said casually.

She couldn't bring herself to look at him, and he laughed, and her cheeks broiled with embarrassment.

"Silly woman, look at me." He cupped the side of her face, and when she met his eyes, he told her, "Here's a secret, luvvie. I *despise* milk."

She thought of all the cups she'd brought him, and all the times he'd come to visit, asking for more. She saw her amazed realization reflected in his smile.

"That's right," he said. "Why else do you think I've been coming around? It's because I want to see *you*. Why else find a way to break from Fraser, but to be with you."

It was her turn to give a rueful laugh, and he placed a quick kiss on her smiling lips.

He pulled away, glancing around. "Your father is surely about somewhere. Now, are we of a mind, or do you need me to promise to build you another fence? I don't know that my back can take it."

"No," she answered sheepishly. "We're of a mind."

"Good. Because we've yet to figure why he"—he shook his piece of paper—"is in league with Fraser. I can't simply storm the *Endeavor* and kill this Captain Will. If we discover the nature of their business together, perhaps we'll find *your* evidence and *my* opportunity, in one fell swoop."

She didn't need to think. Only one obvious path unfolded ahead of her.

Heroines stood by their men, and she'd stand by hers. "With this betrothal, I have an entrée into Fraser's inner circle. I can discover the nature of their business, find out when and how you can gain access to the man with the black pearl. Unquestionably, I must proceed with my father's plan."

Aidan looked taken aback. "*Unquestionably*, you'll do nothing of the sort. God's bones, Beth, the sooner we put a stop to *that* nonsense the better."

"No, don't you see?" It was all so clear, coming to her

in a flash. "For now, I must proceed with the engagement. Would you like to hear my plan?"

He took a step backward, as if staggering from a blow. "You can't actually tell me you'll encourage his pursuit of your hand?"

"It's the only way to find out more."

Aidan's expression was stark. "How can you agree to marry him?"

"I won't actually be marrying him."

"Then don't *actually* accept this engagement."

"We need clues as to how to infiltrate Captain Will's network," she said. "This is the best way."

"I admire your courage," he said, his voice tight. "You have an unusual habit of not showing fear. But this is too much."

"I have nothing to fear with you by my side."

"I won't be by your side if Fraser takes you to the marriage bed." He shot her a bitter look, and it was like looking into the face of pain.

"Good heavens, but it won't come to that." It was just like a man not to listen to her plan, focusing instead on a rival for her virtue. "This is merely a ruse," she explained slowly. "One that will end when we discover hard evidence."

She began to walk down the hill toward her cottage. She had a plan to enact, whether Aidan liked it or not.

"This isn't one of your books," he said, catching up to her. "Not every tale has a happy ending. If you agree to this, who's to say you'll find proof of anything beyond what's apparent to the eye—what if Fraser really is just an old merchant, inadvertently caught up in something over his head, and in possession of a fat bank account he'll use to pay your father's debts? What then? Or, who's to say the man won't simply ignore the engagement, and come and steal you away instead?"

She stopped on the hillside. "This may not be one of

my books, but neither is it a page from *your* story. Not everyone is stolen away," she said gently. "I shall be perfectly safe. Steal me away? Really, Aidan. My father would never allow such a thing."

"*I* would never allow it," he grumbled. "I won't allow *any* of it."

Determined, she took a different tack. "This is all idle speculation. My father has set my course. Until we find evidence of any wrongdoing, there is no way he'll break the betrothal."

"Don't I have a say?"

She bristled. He had a say, and more than a say—his thoughts and actions affected her more than he could ever know. But she saw the way of it clearly, and he didn't seem to understand.

She could act as bravely as he, and with as much success. She could solve both their problems at once, if only he'd trust her.

She stuck with the argument that, sadly, was closest to the truth. "My father has made his decision. I'm afraid you don't have a choice. *I* have no choice."

"There's always a choice."

"You, of all men, know that's not true." She sighed, tired of arguing. She knew her plan was their only option. If he disagreed, she'd have to proceed on her own—he'd see the wisdom of her actions later. "I know my father. Whatever your feelings for me, you have no claim. There can *be* no claim."

She turned and was continuing down the hill when she felt him grab her. He spun her, the look on his face dangerous. He held her shoulders in his hands, and she couldn't look away.

"If you think I'll stand idly by while you put yourself in harm's way. Beth . . ." Fury made his words come haltingly. "Dammit, Beth, if you think I can watch as you give yourself . . . to another man—"

"Is everything all right here?"

She recognized Angus's slow baritone. Aidan's grip eased, and though he reluctantly let her go, anger sparked in his eyes.

"Aye," she said, looking up to face the farmer. "I have the situation well in hand."

Aidan gave a bitter laugh. "So you think."

Angus loomed on the hilltop, and though he only held a spade, the burly man somehow managed to make the thing look like the most intimidating of weapons. He pinned Aidan with an unwavering glare. "Is the MacAlpin bothering you? Never before have I heard you shout so."

"He *is* bothering me." She met and held Aidan's eye. "Or rather, his closed mind is."

"I'm not bothering her," Aidan said angrily. "I'm talking sense into her."

She raised her brows. "And you're just about done?"

Aidan reached out to touch her, but after a glance up at the farmer stayed his hand. "This is far from done." He met her eyes, and the expression on his face chilled her. "You're diving into deep waters. Deeper than you know. You must listen to me, listen to sense. Let me keep you safe."

He was being overprotective, but she knew, only she had the power to find the information they needed. "Sense? I'm the most sensible woman I know. You'll see. I'm stronger and cleverer than you take me for. I don't need you or any man to keep me safe, when I am perfectly capable of handling matters on my own."

She hated hurting him, hated arguing, but he'd forgive her the moment he saw her plan triumph. Keeping her face brave, she told him, "Go, Aidan. This is *my* business now."

Elspeth stormed to the bottom of the hill, knowing he hadn't followed. It seemed, where Aidan was concerned, she'd only just found her voice and her confidence, and it broke her heart to have to use both just to squabble. But she would have her way, because she knew, it was in her power to help both of them.

She would prove Dougal an unfit mate. And she'd lead Aidan to his enemy in the bargain.

———

Aidan spent the night tossing on his cruelly tiny cot, the same thoughts running a deep rut in his mind. If he were a better man, *he* could simply claim Elspeth. *He* would be the one marrying her. But he had nothing, was nothing.

He thought of his enemy, and a familiar fury crackled to life in his belly. The *Endeavor*. It was *his* ship—the man with the black pearl. This Captain Will was there for the taking. Aidan could feel him—he just knew he was on board—and lightning crackled through his bones, making him ache for a fight, eager for vengeance. He just needed to find a way. Then he would have peace.

Then he would have Elspeth.

He'd walked down to the sea before dawn, and sat there still, his mind churning, damn it all. But he couldn't stop the negative thoughts from flooding him, cracking the dam that'd held his resentment at bay.

Elspeth wasn't going to fight her engagement. She thought if she insinuated herself into Fraser's circle, she might find hard evidence, might even find a way for him to get to Captain Will. But she was naive, and she was wrong.

Dread was a constant churning in his belly. His enemy was so close, his future with Elspeth within reach. And yet both eluded him. Both, so far away.

Sweet, strange, gentle Elspeth. Finally, he'd found a bit of solace in this world. Finally, he felt a sense of belonging, of home, and with such a simple woman. It was humble, his desire: a modest life with her, she naught but a farmer's daughter, lovely and natural and pure, who, God spare her, had somehow found love for him in her soul.

But he feared that, yet again, what he wanted would be torn from him. He'd forever be denied even the simplest of pleasures.

"Look at you, brooding like an Irishman." His twin stood over him, eclipsing the early-morning sun.

"Cormac." Aidan shaded his eyes to look up at him. "Don't you have fish to catch?"

"Oho." Cormac studied him intently and then chuckled. "I've seen you run wild. I've seen you play the imp. I've seen you nettled, needled, and angry. But I daresay, I've never seen you like this. Aidan MacAlpin, stymied by a lass."

Aidan scowled, casting an angry glance past his brother and toward the horizon.

His brother laughed outright then. "Ah, I see I have the right of it then. Young Miss Elspeth is the cause, I imagine?" He drew in a contemplative breath at Aidan's answering silence. "Well, brother, if it's a woman troubling you, I'm not your man. You'd best seek Gregor's advice."

"*Gregor*. What does Gregor know of someone like Elspeth? She's not like the others." She was different from any woman—any person—he'd ever known. Unsullied and genuine, and he intended to keep her that way. Which meant keeping her away from his damned rake of a brother. "She'd not have patience for a man like him anyhow."

Cormac shrugged. "All I know is that our older brother manages women as easily as a drover his cattle."

"Elspeth's no cow," he grumbled. He'd definitely need to keep her from Gregor. On top of protecting her from Captain Will and his damned black pearl. And Fraser too, certainly.

Cormac laughed. "You're worse off than I'd imagined, Aid."

"You have no idea." He couldn't be any worse off than he was now, his mind churning with thoughts for none but Elspeth. Her eyes. Her mouth. Her gentleness, her innocence.

She was *too* innocent. She'd not be able to protect herself, if it came to that. Just considering all the possible threats to her well-being tightened his chest till his temper felt close to erupting. Elspeth underestimated *real* men, and how jealously they guarded their money and their women. He knew, because *he* was a real man, with the bone-deep need to guard *her*. "How do you keep Marj safe?" he asked suddenly.

Cormac cursed under his breath. "I see I need to put my nets down for this one." He tossed down his fishing gear and plopped by Aidan's side. "Listen, I don't know what's troubling you, or what you and that girl are caught up in . . ." He took a meaningful pause, then added, "And I see you're not going to be forthcoming, are you?"

Aidan gave a tight shake to his head. Vengeance would be his and his alone. The pirate with the black pearl was *his* to kill. Trust was growing once more between himself and his brothers, but this was something he needed to do on his own. "Not yet, no."

"But you think Elspeth might be in danger?"

"I think she's putting herself in danger because she's got the damned fool notion she's helping me." He tasted the familiar rage on his tongue. He savored it, like a fine wine, steeling himself to what might come. Because even if she were ultimately to be denied him, he'd risk all he was to keep her safe. "I'll kill to keep her from harm. Even if it means getting shipped back to the Indies for the crime."

"Then don't let it come to that." Cormac's voice was

grave, and the effect of his words on Aidan was like a bridge across a previously impassable gulf.

Something loosened in Aidan's chest, and his words followed in a rush. "She's such an innocent. She thinks she can control the situation she's in. I told her to let me handle it. But the girl is green, with too many bookish fancies dancing through her head." He remembered how Angus had appeared, neatly putting a stop to their argument. The farmer had glared down at them, making him feel like some dockside brawler. And maybe he *had* been a boor, gripping Elspeth's arm in anger as he had, but her stubbornness was infuriating. "She believes all will work out in the end. Like her stories."

"But you know better?"

"Aye. I know better." He knew better than all of them that not every story had a happy ending.

"What's she up to?"

"Something dangerous she read in a damned book, if I know Elspeth." She'd stormed from him, and there was no way he could've followed. No way for him to win. She would've known what she said about choice, about his claim to her, would've cut him. But if there was one thing he knew about her, it was that she wasn't hurtful by nature. That alone told him she was up to no good. He dared meet his brother's eyes. "Damned lass won't listen to reason."

"They never do," said Cormac.

"I don't see how can I keep her from danger."

"Now, there's something I know a little about," Cormac said ruefully. "I've but one piece of wisdom to offer. These women are willful, and they'll do as they wish, no matter what a man says." He chuckled. "Ree dressed like a man, no matter that I told her it was too dangerous, and damned if the lass didn't stroll down to Aberdeen harbor like she hadn't a care in the world."

Aidan laughed at the image of the elegant, upright Marjorie in men's trews. But he sobered with a sudden realization. "So what you're saying is, I *can't* keep her safe?"

"No, brother. I'm not saying that at all." Cormac clapped him on the back. "I'm saying, don't let Elspeth *know* what it is you're about."

His twin gave him a smile, which he mirrored, every bit as heartfelt. "Thank you."

"Anytime." Cormac stood, gathering his gear. "Now I'd best be off, or I'll be hearing it from *all* the females of the household."

He watched Cormac pick his way across the rocks to the shoreline, thinking back to Elspeth's last words. She'd spoken of choice, and it'd been too much. He'd spent a lifetime without options, and still he had none.

Well, he'd claim his choice now.

He stood and strode back up the hill to Dunnottar Rock. It was up to him to right this wrong. The only sense her father would ever see was that conferred by a five-pound piece. It would be up to Aidan to expose Dougal's villainy before it was too late.

His brother was right—Elspeth wouldn't listen to reason. But there was one way to make sure she didn't get into trouble. He might not have reason to return to her farm, but that didn't mean he had to stay away.

It just meant he couldn't be seen.

Chapter 24

"You'll need something finer than that when you're a merchant's wife." Elspeth's father eyed her threadbare dress with disapproval. "You'll want to polish the brass if you're to curry favor with the man," he added with a wink.

Elspeth clenched her teeth with annoyance. But though her mind reeled with thoughts—*I'll only be Aidan's wife; Fraser's a nasty old sot; I'd have money for a dress if you didn't waste it all*—her mouth stayed shut.

He wandered closer, hovering over her. "What are you writing? Is that how much we produced last month? We should make cheese—we could turn a tidy profit."

We? She wondered at the term, but kept her mouth shut, blatantly focusing on the month's profits.

"The wee beasties are happy," her father said. "They're used to you, and seem to be fattening right up."

She sniffed. "It's only because Aidan taught me how to fix their diet."

He harrumphed. "It's a surprise how much we have, considering all *he* drank."

The milk. Though he hated it, Aidan had guzzled buckets of the stuff, apparently just for an excuse to come calling.

She felt as though she'd swallowed a stone in her belly. Clearing her throat, she forced her voice not to quaver. "We'd have far less profits, and I daresay, a lost sheep or two, had he not built us such fine fences."

"Fences. *Pish*. Hard labor is all the man is good for."

She pressed her pen too hard to the paper, and a splotch of ink bloomed thick and black on the page. She had to get out of this house. She had to enforce her own will. She would be the authoress of her own destiny.

She shot up to standing and dusted her skirts. "I'm off."

"Where've *you* got to go to?"

She tucked the tally book back where she stored it under a loose hearthstone. She needed to get out from under her father's thumb. The man was perfectly capable of managing his own accounts, and it was time he was forced to do so.

That meant she needed to put an end to this foolish business with Fraser. "I've decided to pay a visit to my intended." She fought not to curl her lips into a sneer. "Is it not time to begin *currying favor*?"

Her father seemed to struggle with this a moment, but there was nothing he could say to stop her. "Just don't . . . don't muck it up. Don't say those odd things you do. If you've naught to say, girl, don't say naught at all. And wear the blue dress—that green makes you too pale."

Though she'd hoped a long, brisk walk to the city would've had her legs spent and her anger blunted, Elspeth was as riled as ever when she arrived at Dougal's offices a couple hours later. She *hadn't* changed her dress.

She was through with being underestimated, and was ready to unleash her newly discovered sharp tongue on someone of the male sex. Unfortunately, her intended wasn't there to provide an outlet.

She'd stormed into his offices as though she were already Lady Fraser, but was cut off at once.

"You there!" a young man shouted nervously. He scurried in front of her, but she summoned her inner heroine, sizing him up with as haughty a demeanor as she could muster without feeling silly. Ink-stained fingers and last year's coat proclaimed him to be someone more than hired labor, but less than a partner.

"You are his apprentice?" she asked in a voice of authority.

He nodded, clearly not knowing what to make of a lone woman bursting onto the scene. "I'm afraid you'll need to—"

"I've come to see Lord Fraser."

"You cannot . . . I mean . . . that is, he's away."

She crossed her arms at her chest. Though she wasn't clear about precisely what her plan was, she was eager to get it under way. "What do you mean he's away?"

"Business at the docks. You'll have to return later. And who might I say—"

"I'll wait for him in his office."

They engaged in a silent stare-off, until finally she raised her brows. "Will you show me to his office, or would you be the one to make Dougal's *fiancée* stand waiting?" She dabbed at her damp forehead. "And with me, so weary from my journey."

The man looked stricken. With a quick flurry of bows, he backed up, saying, "Apologies, mum. This way, if you please." He led her down the hall and into a room whose large oak desk and panel of windows told her it was indeed the office of a man in charge of things.

Her dismay at not finding Dougal disappeared. An excuse to sit unwatched in his office was an unexpected coup.

The assistant left her, and she went behind Fraser's desk. She beamed, feeling her chest swell. There were piles and piles of important-looking papers, and her fingers itched to shuffle through them. She'd find her evidence in no time, and then she'd be done with this ridiculous betrothal.

Hadn't she proved in her management of the farm that she didn't need a man's help? She'd be the deftest of spies—courageous, a warrior heroine, like Joan of Arc. Finding hard proof of Fraser's villainy would be easier than even she had imagined.

The beleaguered young man appeared again, his head popping through the doorway, and she snatched her hands to her chest.

"I came to offer you a refreshment, but"—his eyes flicked to the papers, and when they came back to her face, they were suspicious—"might I help you find something?"

"No, no, I was simply . . ." Spinning, she gestured grandly at the bank of windows. They were grimy and looked out onto an alley, but she hoped her enthusiasm was convincing. "I'd walked back here to enjoy *Dougal's tremendous view*. And, well"—she spun back to give a slow and loving sweep of her hands along his desk—"the feel of this desk at my back, I simply had to look at it. What a powerful man is my intended."

Throwing herself into the role, she'd tried to purr that last bit, and had to suppress a satisfied smile. She'd make a most excellent pirate bride.

"Lord Fraser's got his hands in many pots," he said, appearing to breathe more easily. "If that's all, then, I've much work to do."

"Oh, that will more than do it." She rested a hand on the table, knowing the exact stack of papers she'd begin with first.

He left, and she dove right in, cursing that she hadn't brought her spectacles. Aidan had just gotten them for her, but already she'd become accustomed to not having to squint when she read.

The first stack of documents seemed nothing more than invoices and earnings pertaining to his knitted goods business. She knew better than most how to read an account book, and she scanned the different prices for different items. It appeared Fraser dealt mostly in hosiery, but his register reflected a growing number of textiles in the form of plaids and arisaids. There were varying fabrics listed too—wool, cotton, worsted crepe.

"Tedious," she muttered, taking in page after page of tallies. "What a miserably . . . boring . . . business," she said, riffling through the bottom of the stack, clearly more of the same.

This man wasn't nearly so exciting as her swashbuckling Aidan.

She dug deeper, more certain than ever that somewhere in his office some evidence of wrongdoing was sure to be found. She got to the bottom of all his stacks, though, had opened and sifted through drawers, but there was nothing villainous in sight.

Putting her hands on her hips, she turned in a circle, taking in the room. "Where are you?"

She plopped into his desk chair, idly opening and closing each drawer once more for good measure. As she closed the last drawer, her eyes lit on a strange seam along the bottom.

"And what are you?" She dug her fingers along the edge. Fitting her thumb inside the seam, she pried up a small panel. She pulled out a small leather-bound folio and chuckled. "Dougal Fraser, you sneaky old cadger."

She opened it and flipped through, and though she didn't understand exactly what she was looking at, she could tell that it was something out of the ordinary. And one name recurred over and over.

"Virginia Company," she whispered. She scanned

pages of names written on what looked like a passenger manifest. What was an exporter of knit goods doing transporting passengers?

She flipped through some more pages, and the blood froze in her veins. The *Endeavor*—the ship on which young Aidan had been held prisoner. She read on. It appeared as though Fraser had commissioned cargo for the *Endeavor.* Were these the same sort of "passengers" as Aidan had been? She shivered.

If she could just tear out the page, it might be enough to prove that her fiancé was involved in shady dealings. Or enough for her father to postpone the betrothal, at least. She needed to rip it from the seam, and in such a way that Fraser wouldn't notice. She cracked the folio all the way open and ran a finger along the binding.

"Find what you're looking for?"

Her heart exploded in her chest. Dougal Fraser stood in the doorway.

Though he was an older gentleman with thinning, graying hair, he wasn't precisely old. Nor, with a set of well-balanced features and an aquiline nose, was he unattractive. But hovering there, his already pinched eyes narrowed tightly in anger, he struck Elspeth as a very ugly sort indeed. "Making yourself at home, I see."

She was caught elbow-deep in his papers. The only strategy available to her was to lie, and blatantly. "I longed for another visit with you," she said, pasting an amiable smile on her face. "I am to be your bride, after all."

"Indeed. And a lucky man I am." As he strolled toward her, his eyes danced over his belongings as though scanning for anything else that might be amiss. "And how lucky too, that I finished early at the docks. To think I might've missed a visit with my intended."

He loomed over where she sat in his chair. "When my apprentice told me you awaited me in my offices, well, you can imagine I came back here in an instant. To see your lovely face once more, of course." He stroked the backs of his fingers along her cheek, and she tried to conceal her shudder. "Even lovelier than I remembered."

His hand stilled, and he took and cupped her jaw more firmly than was comfortable. "But tell me, is it that you plan to get to know me by reading my private papers?"

More than he knew. Face stiff from her fake smile, she said, "I thought it'd be a good idea to get a better notion of what sort of business yours is. It seems grand indeed."

"You do have an . . . unnatural interest in business." Abruptly, he let go her face and his eyes flicked to his open drawer. "I see I've found myself a thorough bride. You must tell me if you have any questions."

He glanced at the book trembling in her hands. It was still opened to the passenger list. "That, for instance. What do you make of it?"

She closed it, placing it primly in her lap. "It . . . I . . . I can't say I know what it is."

He gave her a patronizing smile. "Surely a clever businesswoman like you has some theory. Tell me," he said more firmly. "What does it look like?"

She was uncertain how to answer. He had a sharp mind, and she could tell he thought hers sharp too. A bald-faced lie would be foolish, so she chose to massage the truth. "It looked as though you're transporting passengers, not knitted goods."

"Did it?" The sound of his falsetto laughter filled the room. "How odd!"

"Yes!" She matched her false laugh to his, her teeth gritted with forced cheer. "Indeed! Imagine that."

Fraser's mood took a sudden turn. He strode to the door, shutting it hard. Shutting them in together.

Her heart thudded in her chest, but she made herself be brave. She'd told Aidan she could handle this herself, and blast it, she would.

He stalked back and sat on the edge of his desk so that she was forced to crane her neck up to look at him. He took his book from her lap, letting his hand graze lustfully along her thigh as he did so. "I don't think I like you snooping about. You must ask me next time. I'd be happy to show you whatever you'd like to see."

Nestling the folio back in its hiding spot, he added, "In fact, I should take you on a tour of the docks."

The prospect gave her a chill. "That sounds . . . delightful."

"But sadly, it's time for me to get back to work. I must make money to buy us a honeymoon you'll never forget." Giving her an oily smile, he stood, taking her hands and pulling her up with him. "But first, a kiss for your husband-to-be."

Her facade cracked, and she instinctively recoiled.

Fraser's grip tightened on her fingers. Eyes narrowed, he said, "Elspeth, dear heart. You don't strike me as the most eager of brides. Is it that you're afraid of me?"

She shook her head. "No, of course not. I simply . . ." *Simply what? I'm simply repulsed?*

His eyes seemed to pierce her. "You are simply . . . overwhelmed, perhaps, at how quickly we are proceeding?"

"Yes," she said, relieved at being given an out. "Perhaps that is it."

"Perhaps you don't want to carry this engagement forward just yet," he suggested gently.

She hesitated. Could it be that Fraser wanted out of the betrothal too? Had it all just been something her father had concocted?

She felt a glimmer of hope. This arrangement might be easier to back out of than she'd thought. "Perhaps you are right, Lord Fraser."

"Ah," he said, taking his hands from hers. He added in a clipped voice, "I had the right of it."

She told herself that his peculiar tone wasn't chilly,

that Fraser was merely acting formally. She gave him a broad smile. "I'm grateful for your understanding."

"Oh, I understand. I understand quite well. You don't think you need to make this marriage."

It sounded like an accusation, and the shift in tone confused her. She shrugged nervously. "I suppose I don't."

"And I tell you that you do," he said sharply.

Her confusion turned to panic. He'd tricked her into confessing her aversion to their marriage. "But I thought you didn't want it either . . . ?"

But instead of responding, he only stared coldly, and so she prattled on. "I'm happy, you see. Our farm is thriving. And I'm very busy—"

"Fool girl. You have *no* idea how deeply in debt your father has fallen."

She bristled. There was nothing that nettled her more than being called foolish. She was smart and clever, yet it seemed the men of the world were blind to it. "On the contrary. I know my father's debts well. And they are not so great as to force me into wedlock."

"Forced, are you?" There was a sneer in his narrow eyes.

She wasn't so impetuous as to take the bait, and took their argument in a different direction. "We've made improvements recently, and have begun to turn a profit."

"A grand success, is it? Your precious wee farm?" His voice and expression were flat, and she didn't know how to read him.

"I believe it will be a success," she replied, sounding more confident than she felt.

"I'd thought you might want a man like me to help. But perhaps not." He stood stiffly at the door, holding it open for her. He'd been difficult to read, but this hint couldn't have been more blatant.

She scurried out. "Good day, then."

He gave her a curt nod. "Good luck to you, Miss Farquharson. *And* to your farm."

===

Fraser shut the door on Elspeth's back. Whatever he'd expected her reaction to their betrothal to be, it hadn't been *that*.

She was a queer little creature, but curious and clever in a way that made him feel awake and alive. It was an unexpected pleasure to encounter such a mind, and in a woman, of all creatures.

He went back to his chair, retrieved his folio, and idly flipped through its pages. What had she been looking for? Had she found it?

Scooting back, he kicked his feet up on his desk. The chit was sneaky and willful. Not unlike himself, he thought with amusement. Though he'd yet to figure out what her game was, he found himself enjoying it very much indeed.

Leaning back, he rested his hands atop his head and smiled. He was enjoying this little game, but not as much as he was going to enjoy watching that pretty porcelain face submit to his will. Never before had he considered taking a wife, but he decided he'd quite like having this one. And he *would* have her.

Because, contrary to her thoughts on the matter, Elspeth would find herself needing him. And he knew exactly what manner of help he could provide.

Chapter 25

Aidan caught up with Elspeth just as she was dashing from Fraser's offices. He ducked into a shadowy doorway, hiding just in time. Damned if the woman wasn't exactly where he feared she'd be.

Had she met with Fraser? And might she actually have discovered something? She was the brightest person he knew—man *or* woman—and nothing she did would surprise him.

She stormed down the alley, turning onto a larger street, and Aidan sprang out, quick to catch up before she got away. She was headed toward the water, without a pause in her step, or even a cowl to conceal her face. Rather, there was purpose in her stride, rushing to the docks as though she were a captain with a ship on fire.

What was the woman up to? She had such fanciful notions, come from reading too many books. She was clearly on some sort of mission, which meant she was bound for some sort of trouble.

Had she no fear? She was utterly dauntless. It was maddening. And, he had to admit, he couldn't help but admire her for it.

They reached the harbor, and as she slowed her pace, he let more space grow between them. Shadowing her was proving fascinating, and he wasn't yet ready to be discovered.

It wasn't until she stopped that he fully realized where they were. He ducked behind a pillar, leaning against it, his heart in his throat, when he saw what it was she was staring at.

The *Endeavor*.

He looked from the ship back to Elspeth, and found he couldn't tear his eyes from her. He knew how to read people—it was what'd helped him survive captivity—and he knew that she was thinking of *him*.

And what she felt was sympathy. It was in the tightness of her shoulders, and the way she didn't seem to breathe. In the tears she suppressed behind pinched lips. But rather than anger him, for once in his life, he found he welcomed the compassion. Rather than making him feel pitied or pathetic, Elspeth's consideration warmed him.

He stepped closer in order to read her more deeply, sensing there was another emotion she held in check. In the way she held a hand to her heart, in the sadness in her eyes, he read something more powerful, more abiding.

He was humbled. Unmanned. Because he realized it was love that he read on her face.

Elspeth was aggravatingly fearless. But she was also clever and kind. Gentle, loving, and tender. And his chest swelled, knowing he couldn't help but love her too.

She spun on her heel and walked on, and he was startled into movement, jogging to catch up. He found that he was smiling. His Elspeth was so many things, but mostly she was utterly, shockingly *unpredictable*.

She marched down the docks, pausing at the head of each quay to peer at the names of all the ships. Noticing that she lingered at the smaller boats, he chuckled, knowledge of her destination dawning on him.

Finally, she came to his boat, and only then did her step become hesitant. He shook his head, marveling at this sweetly shy woman. She appeared to check and double-check the name, *Journeyman*, painted in crimson on the burnished brown timber.

Was she coming to tell him something she'd learned at Fraser's? Had she found evidence, or did she have other news for him?

Or was she simply coming *for him*?

She stood, her hand poised on the rope ladder that dangled down the side of the sloop, and glanced around to see if any would stop her. He'd let go his three crewmen to save some coin, but he'd hired a pair of dock rats to guard the boat. He spotted them, and catching their attention, he silently shooed them away. Nobody would interrupt her.

He bit his cheek not to laugh at the sight of her grabbing both hands to that ladder and stepping on, easy as you please. He waited for her to make her way up and over, giving her an extra few moments for good measure, then followed.

For a while, he stood on the top rungs, peering over, simply watching her. She walked the deck as though in a trance, running her fingers along its varnished surfaces, tracing fingertips along polished bronze cleats and rings.

The sloop had been in fine shape when he'd taken it over, and he took pride that it was in even better shape now. He kept it polished and fine, and the sight of her touching it with such loving appreciation kindled a fierce pleasure to life in his chest.

If he ever took Elspeth for a sail, he'd let her steer.

She wrapped her hands around the wheel, and her lips

parted in a sort of thrall. Another, fiercer heat crackled to life in his veins. Elspeth was such a sensual creature. He wanted to experience her caresses along *his* body. To see her eyes go hazy at the feel of *him* under her fingertips.

A madness overtook him, the only thought in his mind that he must go to her. He made the final climb up and over, landing stealthily on deck.

But she disappeared from sight, reappearing at the head of the companionway steps, where she stood contemplating the deck below. She emanated such grave dignity one would've thought it the gallows and she Mary, Queen of Scots.

A feeling of such great affection swamped him, he stopped still in his tracks. She was as intrepid a woman as those found in any book. Sweeter and more innocent than any he'd ever known. His lust altered, and the raging torrent that'd swept him deepened to a bottomless, hot spring. Him, immersed but not adrift.

She ventured below, and then her head popped up again, looking much like an adorable wee gopher. He burst into a grin, wanting to sneak after her and surprise her. To chase her up and down those steps until he teased from her the laughter he so loved, the sound of Elspeth, joyous and free.

He wanted to catch her, and kiss her senseless.

He wasn't surprised when she ducked back below. His quarters were down there, and he was certain his pretty little spy would find much in the place to entertain her.

Grinning, he pulled in the dock lines, hauled anchor, and got the *Journeyman* under way. As he steered out of Aberdeen harbor, Aidan's smile turned wicked. He'd show his Elspeth what happened to stowaways.

━━━━━

Elspeth looked around at what she deduced was Aidan's cabin. It was tiny, but tidy, with a narrow bunk, lantern, and nautical instruments and maps stowed in neat compartments on a small table.

She pulled out one of the maps, fascinated by this glimpse of a sailor's life. Smoothing it carefully on the table, she thought of her heroic pirate rogue. When he'd sailed from the Indies to Scotland, he hadn't been able to read, and yet he'd navigated his way, in spite of it all. He might not have been able to decipher letters on a page, but he knew how to read the stars in the sky.

Her breath caught, feeling a pang in her heart. Aidan was all alone in the world, and yet, standing in his orderly captain's cabin, she saw how he'd carved a place for himself. He'd endured such pain, rising like a phoenix from the nightmarish ashes of his childhood.

She sat on the hard bunk, and the echoes of him, all around her, were a comfort.

The events at Fraser's office had confused her. Despite her understanding that they'd agreed to end their engagement, at the conclusion of their meeting, the old merchant had gotten a strange, suspicious look in those slitted eyes. But a veil had quickly dropped over them, concealing whatever machinations he might've been entertaining. Wondering what thoughts he hid, she'd left his offices feeling deeply unsettled.

Their ridiculous betrothal *would* be broken—she'd will it thus, if need be. She'd be *Aidan's* wife, or nobody's.

Using thoughts of Aidan to summon strength, she'd gone to the docks, soon finding herself searching for the ship in which he'd been stolen away so long ago. The sight of it had seared her, her heart breaking all over again for the boy he'd been.

She'd always battled self-pity for her own situation—a lone daughter set up as the de facto head of an impoverished household—but her childhood had been the lap of luxury compared to the horrors he'd experienced.

There was a clattering and the boat heaved, and she

gripped the edge of the bunk to steady herself, panic seizing her chest. Were they leaving the dock? Was *she* to find herself indentured to some distant tropical isle?

Forcing her breath to steady, she made her way back up the ladder, her skirts an awkward tangle around her legs. With a calming inhale, she peeked onto the deck.

Aidan. Her pulse leaped at the sight of him, jauntily perched on a rail, one hand resting on the helm. His easy smile met her.

"Afternoon, luvvie. You've always said you wanted a sail."

Chapter 26

"A sail? Truly, Aidan, you're taking me for a sail?" Elspeth spun in a circle on deck, taking it all in. A gray-and-white plume of water trailed them as Aberdeen harbor receded into the distance. It was breathtaking. A sharp gust snapped life into the sails, and she studied them, regretful concern stabbing her. "But don't you need men to help?"

"A sloop this small, one man can handle her." He stood and, tying a rope over the wheel to steady it, stalked toward her. The look in his eyes sent a shiver across her skin. "But *you*." He swept his knuckles along her cheek. "How readily I can handle *you* is another matter entirely."

Her wind-chilled cheeks turned hot. She, an unmanageable sort of woman? Never had she been paid a higher compliment. "Are you saying I require management?" She was proud of the coy lilt she heard in her own voice.

He seemed to give her question honest consideration. "I think that is precisely what I'm saying."

She laughed, but was interrupted by a loud racket as the largest of the three sails began to snap and clang in the wind.

He ran to it, hauling on the winch to tighten the sheet. His shirt strained over his broad back and arms as he spun the handle as easily as she might stir a pot.

"She needed a bit of luffing," he said, cuffing his sleeves as he strode back to her. His hair was a wind-whipped tangle, and he raked it from his face.

Her breath caught. Aidan truly was a rogue, a man alone in the world. Like a hero on a quest, he could go anywhere, be anyone. And with him, she'd finally become the pirate bride she'd always dreamed of being.

"Now where were we?" he asked, studying her.

The smile in his eyes emboldened her, and feeling mischievous, she pointed up the mast to the crow's nest. "I think you were readying to take me up there."

"Was I?" He looked up, shielding his eyes from the glare. "That was a fool thing of me to consider."

"Well?" She raised her brows. If she were to live out one dream, she might as well realize every last one. And she'd always dreamed of climbing the rigging, soaring over the waves like a bird in flight. "Will you?"

"Will I take you up to the lookout?" Widened eyes spoke to his amused disbelief.

She nodded gravely. She'd show him she was *not* an object of amusement.

His eyes grazed up the thin rope ladder to the rickety perch situated high in the air. "It's just a barrel, Beth. Lashed to the mast with a bit of line."

But she was determined to climb as high as any pirate. Sensing that pride might be Aidan's weakness, she asked, "Are you saying your ship isn't secure?"

"You know I'm not," he said, his eyes narrowed.

"Then why not take me?"

"Because it won't fit the two of us."

"Then it's a good thing you don't seem to want to go up there." She smiled, proud of her logic.

"I'm not letting you climb that alone," he said quickly, disbelief in his voice.

"Good, then we'll climb it together." She hiked her skirts. "Shall we?"

He shook his head at her. Gritting his teeth, finally he said, "If you must."

She beamed. "I must."

Instinctively, she knew not to look down and kept her eyes trained on the rungs as she climbed. Before she knew it, she was clambering into the barrel, Aidan holding on to the ladder with one hand and guiding her over with the other.

It truly was just a barrel sawed in half, with alternate slats removed, and she arranged herself as best she could, slipping her legs through the narrow gaps.

She realized Aidan was laughing. "What?" she demanded, summoning as much dignity as one could with one's skirts bunched about one's knees. But he only shook his head, so she pressed: "What is it?"

"It's only that you flew up the rigging like a . . . like a . . ."

"A what?"

"Well, like no overeager cabin boy I've ever seen."

"Are you saying you think of me as a boy?" She'd spoken playfully. But then she caught his eyes devouring her bare legs, and she blushed.

"Certainly not," he said in a husky voice. Clearing his throat, he tore his gaze from her pale skin. His eyes were hooded when they met hers.

He looked so dangerous, clinging to the rigging with that look in his eyes. Shyness struck her, paralyzing her tongue in her mouth.

His expression softened. "Don't be shy on my account," he told her quietly, sensing her discomfort. And of course he sensed it. Aidan seemed always to understand. Even when she'd not been able to string two words together without stuttering, he'd looked past her self-consciousness to see her true self.

He unleashed his most rakish smile. "You have lovely knees—it's only right that you bare them to Neptune himself. And besides, they say a naked woman on board ship brings good luck."

"Aidan!" she shrieked, shocked and delighted in equal parts.

"I speak truly." With an innocence she knew was feigned, he added gravely, "That is why so many ships bear a carved lady as a figurehead."

"Is it indeed?" She didn't know how they'd found themselves discussing such a thing as naked ladies carved upon ships' bows. It made her skin feel taut and uncomfortable, as though it were stretched too tight over her bones.

A sharp gust tore her hair loose, and the wind lashed every which way over her bared calves. She couldn't help but inhale deeply, taking a great gulp of that fresh air. It smelled extraordinary, so brisk and clean, she had to wonder if she were perhaps the first ever even to breathe it. It was so unlike the air of Aberdeen—the oily, fishy rot of its harbor, or the scent of mildew and dung that clung to their small cottage.

Clutching her wind-whipped hair to the side of her head, she eagerly devoured the vast gray swath of noth-ingness yawning before her. The open sea. So much water all around, it was incomprehensible.

For a moment, seated upon her glorious perch, she felt as if time had been suspended. Somewhere people were being born, living their lives, and dying, all in the space of her musings.

The wind gusted again, and she trembled.

"Are you afraid?" Aidan's low, masculine voice cut through the keening sea air.

She looked down at him and shivered again, for an entirely different reason. He clung to the rope ladder, trying his best not to glance at her naked knees, his roguish eyes wrinkling in a smile meant only for her.

"No," she said. "Not afraid."

Shaking his head, he grinned. "No, of course you're not."

"Merely cold." She gave him a rueful smile.

"We'll simply have to amend that." He gripped a broad hand around her knee, tucking warm fingers in the crook of it.

Her breath caught, his hand on her naked skin throwing her back in time, making her as heart-wrenchingly tongue-tied as she'd ever been when they first met.

The boat hit a wave and lurched, and Aidan swayed into her, his hand sliding higher up her skirts. The warmth of his touch turned into a scorching heat, searing up between her legs and inflaming her belly.

She gasped. Uncertain what to say or do, she filled the air with mindless chatter. "It's so wide open out here."

He tore his eyes from her to gaze off into the distance. "Aye, so it is. Open and clean and sure. So much bigger than any plantation, or slave owner, or any of us."

"And perilous too." She followed his gaze, straining to make sense of the horizon. She imagined the hazy line where the earth itself curved out of sight. "There's so much water—it's overwhelming. Almost a little frightening. Do you ever worry about shipwrecks, or drowning?"

"Elspeth, afraid of something? I never thought I'd see the day." He smiled and gave her leg a squeeze, and then, with a shrug, looked back to the horizon. "It's not the sea that scares me. The sea will kill a man, but that's who she is. She casts no judgment, sees no difference between a man with money and one with none. Even the storms have a kind of resolve—as though only nature herself knows what she's truly about. You speak of all this water, but I didn't know peace until I was on the water, headed back to Scotland."

She inhaled deeply, thinking how shocking it must've been, the sea so clean and wide open compared with the oppressive life of an indentured slave. "It must've been so different for you, after you escaped. Did you not simply want to stay on the water, sailing forever?"

"I had to sail back to find you." He'd said it playfully, but the words hung in the air, charged.

She knew in that moment how deeply she loved him.

She'd sensed it before, but this was a revelation that sheared her through, a bone-deep knowledge striking her like a thunderclap. Not only did she love Aidan, she could have no other man but him. She'd be incomplete without him. Unrealized without him.

His hand on her leg burned. She wanted it to move higher, wanted him to move closer. Her body ached with the wanting.

She wanted him to kiss her again, and more than kiss her, she wanted him to take her. She sensed she'd never fully be a woman until he did. She'd be trapped in some eternal limbo between girl and woman until she felt his body over her, in her.

She'd thought him handsome and strong. Dangerous for all but her. But Aidan was so much more than that. He was the other, unrealized part of herself.

"Are you ready?" he asked.

She knew he meant to ask only if she were ready to descend. But when she spoke, she answered quite a different question. "Yes, Aidan," she said steadily. "I'm ready."

Chapter 27

When they'd first met, Aidan thought Elspeth a skittish sort of girl, sheltered and easily frightened. How wrong he'd been. She was simply shy, and he was quickly finding out how large was the gulf that lay between fearful and bashful.

"Before we climb down, you must kiss me," she said, as brazen as any wanton. She leaned down, tangling her fingers in his hair. They were cool, her touch gentle, but rather than soothe him, she inflamed him.

No, she didn't have a scared bone in her body.

He was shocked, and he was grateful. Grateful to be in this woman's life, grateful she found him worthy. And grateful too for all the damned books that'd put the thought into this innocent maiden's head that she might climb a ship's rigging and kiss its captain, despite his being in possession of a soul cursed by the devil.

"I'll kiss you," he said, his words sounding rougher

than he'd intended, and he took control, pulling her down
to him, seizing her in a kiss he'd been saving for years.
His lips met hers, and he gave her the kiss he'd dreamed
of, a kiss worthy of taming such a fanciful woman. Their
tongues twined, and he gave her a kiss to show the world
that he would take what he wanted, that he'd possess as any
other man possessed.

But rather than tame her, his rough taking of her mouth
had only inflamed Elspeth, and she writhed at his touch,
pulling away to gasp for air only to come back down to
him, her hands tangling in his shirt, her legs wrapping
about his body.

The ship hit a wave and jounced. His hand slipped
farther up her thigh, and he realized how close his fingers were to the thatch of hair between her legs that he so
longed to touch.

The muscles of his legs, normally so strong, flinched
with the effort of balancing so precariously high in the
rigging. As much as he wanted to find a way to take
Elspeth then and there, he summoned his resolve. "We
mustn't do this. We need to go back down on deck."

She pulled from him, and she was a glorious sight,
her cheeks red from the wind, her eyes bright with lust.
"Why?"

Joy crackled through his chest at the feel of her in his
hands. She had no idea the danger he posed to her innocence. "You want that I should steal your maidenhead,
here in the crow's nest?"

"No," she said seriously. "We can go back to your
cabin and you can take it there."

A loud laugh burst from him. "Come, Beth. We'll
discuss this on deck, where I'm not in danger of being
unmanned whilst balancing sixty feet in the air."

They made their way back down the ladder, and the
sight of her rump cradled between his arms, nestled just
in front of his face, did nothing for his hardened cock,

now standing at merry attention as though it were a bizarre extension of the rigging.

Reaching the bottom, she leaped into his arms, and he stumbled back a step as he caught her. She was a spitfire in his arms, with unschooled but eager kisses. If she didn't watch herself, he'd take her virginity there on the varnished cedar of his ship's deck.

He kissed her, but fought to keep his head. Elspeth deserved much in this world, and though he could dream of a hundred different things he'd do to her body, taking her virginity before she wed was not one of them.

She pulled away, those beautiful lips parted and gently panting. "Aidan? Is aught the matter? Do you not want me?"

Reminding himself of his resolve, he set her apart to stand before him on the deck. "How could you doubt it?"

She had no idea of the battle that waged inside him. But he'd not take Elspeth's virginity like an unruly ship's hand.

She smoothed her skirts, explaining in a tone a politician might use to present a bill before Parliament, "I don't see the trouble. I want you. Very much. Right now, in fact. There's no better opportunity. And you know what folk say: 'Fools look to tomorrow, wise men use tonight.' "

He laughed. "I don't think *that* was their intent." Some might call Elspeth quirky or strange, but he'd never tire of the unexpected delight that found purchase in his heart whenever she was near. "I can't take your innocence, not like this."

"But if you despoil me, then I'll get to marry *you*, not Fraser."

His jaw dropped—she was too much. She was lovely and artless, and he wanted her more than he'd ever wanted anything in his life. *Very much. Right now, in fact.* "Believe me, as much as I'd enjoy a thorough despoiling, we've the not-so-minor matter of Fraser to sort out, remember? I'll remind you, you're betrothed to the man."

"Not for long," she announced, striding across the deck in the direction of the companionway steps. Hiking her skirts, she began to descend belowdecks.

"Where are you going?"

"To your cabin, of course."

Her words finally hit him. "Wait, Beth. What do you mean 'not for long'?"

She froze, looking over her shoulder at him. She was halfway down the stairs already, visible only from her chest up. He'd yet to understand how it was that a land-loving maiden in full skirts could be so damned fast at moving hither and yon aboard a moving ship.

He caught up to her, looking down from the head of the stairs. "What happened in Fraser's offices?"

"We talked."

He heaved a sigh. "Though I greatly appreciate that there are other pressing goals at the moment"—he shifted the seat of his trews in proof of his point—"I must know, what did you talk about?"

"With Fraser?"

He only narrowed his eyes in answer. She was clearly not going to make this easy.

"Oh, fine." She squared her shoulders. "I told him I felt forced."

"You told Fraser you felt *forced* into marrying him?"

"Something like that, yes."

"Bloody hell, woman. How do you think someone like Fraser would react to that? Those are fighting words to such a man."

"They were neither intended as fighting words, nor do I think they were received thusly." She stood below him on the stairs, but even from that vantage point, he noted her chin lift defensively. "I simply explained how the farm has begun to succeed, and so I no longer require a husband."

She no longer required a husband. Did that apply to him as well? Brooding, he stared down at her. It appeared his Elspeth had found her voice and her confidence.

He forced it from his mind, focusing instead on the issue at hand. "I don't see how that offers a way out of the betrothal." His words came out harshly, the thought of any man laying claim to Elspeth too infuriating to bear.

"It does, if it means my father no longer needs financial assistance." She walked up a step, standing closer on the stairs. "Please, Aidan, can we put this aside for now? Fraser isn't here." She reached one of her delicate hands up, hesitantly touching his leg. "But I am."

No words escaped his clenched jaw. Fraser might not be there, but the specter of him was, a barrier between them.

She climbed up another step, stroking him now. The fabric of his trews was thick, but he felt her touch as keenly as if it'd been on his bare skin. "Please just kiss me. Kiss me like you were kissing me up there."

"You don't understand," he said through gritted teeth. Wealthy men inhabited a far different world from the one she was used to. Wealthy men could simply choose people, and have them. He'd experienced the phenomenon firsthand, for the past thirteen years. He knew if Elspeth was what Fraser wanted, Elspeth was precisely whom he'd have.

"What don't I understand?" She continued to stroke his leg, stepping even closer. "Show me what you need."

She'd misunderstood, and damned if his cock didn't strain for her. He'd show her what he needed: her and only her. What he needed was to grab her questing hands, haul her over his shoulder, and take her and rob her maidenhead on his damned bunk.

She tilted her head, studying him. Was it lust she saw on his face? Did she see his agony too? His dark despair?

"I'm offering myself to you," she said with a tender innocence that shattered his blackened heart. "I'll have you as my husband. And if we consummate our union here, now, nobody can come between us."

Her naïveté gutted him. "I know a whole world that could come between us."

"Don't you want to consummate our union?" Her gaze flicked to his breeches. The question in her eyes was so trusting, curse him but he got harder for it. He saw she'd noticed by the rising blush on her cheeks.

"Want to?" Emotion made his voice ragged. Always there'd been something to come between him and his heart's desire. Never would he get what he wanted, what he needed. Never would he know satisfaction. "Christ, woman, of course I *want to*."

Her hand on his leg stilled. "Is it that you don't want *me*?"

"Of course I want *you*." As if that was all this was about. He wanted her spread naked and writhing on his cot, laid bare for the taking. And the pain of it was, he knew she'd let him. He wanted her in a new wedding dress, with pretty laces and ribbons, and eyes only for him. He wanted her, and wanted the world to recognize her place by his side as right and true. "But I want *all* of you. And some rich pig has decided he'd have you instead, and I know better than to hope for anything of the sort."

Her hands burst into movement again, roving recklessly along his legs. "But I said—"

"What you said tells me you don't understand." He had to get away from her touch. He couldn't have her, and the fury of it was beyond bearing.

Fearing his lust might turn cruel, he stormed down, shouldering past her on the steps. "I can't have you as my own. I can't even lie with you. You're to marry Fraser, and it's a virgin he's paid for."

He heard her sharp intake of breath, but remained staring out the tiny porthole, refusing to look at her. He'd been deceiving himself. He'd lost Elspeth the day Fraser first set eyes on her, and it was only a matter of time before he lost her for good. He didn't know how he was to survive it.

He couldn't bear this pain, but he could make *her* burden easier to shoulder. "You could accept the man," he said, cursing the defeat in his voice. "You'd be wealthy, Beth. He's older—he might leave you a young widow. You'd have money and books, and everything you've ever wanted."

"Do you think I *want* to marry him?" Snapping, she stormed to him, pummeling hard on his back. "*You're* everything I ever wanted. You stupid, stupid man. I don't want wealth. Never have I wanted wealth. I don't want to marry Fraser. I want to be with *you*."

He spun to face her. "*What you want.* You think a person always gets what they want? No, I'll not take what doesn't belong to me. And clearly your father thinks you belong to another."

"But don't you see? I won't go to Fraser." She planted hands on hips. "I cannot. I will not. So we needn't wait because I won't marry anyone. But you. *Ever.*"

It took her shouts, but finally he heard her. Finally he believed her. She wanted him. And not just for one stolen afternoon on a ship. She'd fight to be with him for a lifetime. The prospect amazed and humbled him.

He took her in his arms, but she continued to rave, an overwrought bundle in his embrace. His gentle Beth was hollering up at him, and he marveled at the sound of it, and at the miracle that *he'd* been the one to rouse her.

She clawed her fingers into his shirt. "What do I want with riches? Never would I want that. *You're* all I want."

Her passion matched his own, and it seared the last

doubts from his mind. Dared he hope for what he wanted? Could it be that together they'd find a way?

She went limp against him, whispering, "But it seems you don't want me."

"You're wrong," he said, his voice taut with focus. "I want you, Beth. And I'll have you."

Chapter 28

Elspeth went from despair to delight in one dizzying moment. She'd thought Aidan didn't want her. She'd been wrong.

He scooped her up, and she let loose a delighted yelp. She wrapped her arms around his neck, holding on as he made his way along the narrow corridor to his cabin. "What are you doing?" she asked, even though she had some idea.

Without putting her down, he stood before his bunk, nuzzling at her neck and throat. "I think you proposed."

His kisses were wet and his breath was hot, and a pure, animal lust barreled through her, surging from deep in her womb, shimmering along the surface of her skin in delicious waves, until her breasts pulled taut and a pulse throbbed through her, sounding her want. "Proposed?" she managed, her voice weak. "Yes, I think you're right."

He threw her onto the bed, and the savage possession

in his gaze turned her desire sharp. He shucked off his breeches, not tearing his hooded eyes from hers. "And you said something about consummation."

"I did." She trembled, breathless to see what he'd do, how he'd look. She'd imagined how Aidan's strong body might appear without clothes, but until this moment, her imaginings had been only vague. But now, even though his shirt fell almost to his knees, she spied something ominous straining from the shadows between his legs.

She was about to see all of him. To feel his naked skin touch hers. A fresh bolt of longing speared her, till her body felt wet and hot and needy.

He sat on the bed, and she wasn't sure where to look, so much did she want to see every inch of him, all at once.

He pushed the arisaid from her shoulders, revealing the vest and skirt she wore over her petticoat. "You're mine, Beth." He made quick work of her buttons. "Not Fraser's," he said, tugging at her laces. "The only man who'll tell you who you can and can't marry is me."

Her clothes loosened, freeing her breasts, and the sensation stole her breath. She felt wild and free. "And what if I don't listen?"

Aidan leaned close. The stubble on his jaw scraped against her cheek as he whispered in her ear, "Then I'll make you listen." He claimed a breast in his hand and kneaded it, thumbing her nipple.

Flinching from the shock of pleasure, she gripped his arms, curling her fingers tightly into the muscle of his biceps. "How?"

He moved her hands aside, and she heard the pop of threads as he tugged her clothes down and off her body. "I'll devise some torture."

Her heart was hammering, pounding her blood agonizingly close to the surface of her skin. She felt flushed, barely able to speak. "Indeed?"

"Aye." He took her breast again, quickly replacing his

hand with his mouth, and she cried out. The feel of him suckling her was too much, too exquisite a pleasure to bear. It felt wanton and sinful, and her body quivered, feeling on the verge of some precipice.

He pulled away, leaving her wet skin chilled in his absence. "Because the only man you'll be marrying is me."

She was panting now, an alarming heat thrumming through her body, and she felt as though she were enduring some frightful transformation, like a butterfly emerging from a chrysalis. She looked down at her body. But seeing her meager breast shining damp, hardened to a sharp, aching point, she blushed. She was nude before him, and sudden shyness made her cringe inside.

"You're magnificent," he said.

Clamping her eyes shut, she blindly reached for the blanket to pull it over her body. "I'm thin as a post, pale as a ghost . . ."

Warm fingers gently pinched her chin, and she opened her eyes to his affectionate smile. "And silly as a loon."

He kissed her again, tenderly this time, until her shyness ebbed and she felt herself relax and kiss him back. He laved kisses down her neck, between her breasts, over and below them, murmuring, "Fool woman. Yours is the most beautiful, the finest of bodies."

She looked away, feeling fresh chagrin crumple her brow. "You've seen many, I'm sure."

He was quiet for a moment, and her heart broke with it. But then he tipped her face back to his and said, "Aye, I've seen women, Beth. And all of them pale compared to you. You're the only one. The finest and the loveliest of them all."

His mouth found hers again, and she found herself believing that she *was* glorious and luscious and kissable, and those tender kisses quickly turned hungry and deep. The whole of her responded to him, and she wrapped her hands around his back, roved them eagerly up his arms, frantic to touch him.

The linen of his shirt kept getting in her way, and she bucked her body up to him, tugging at the fabric. She tore her mouth from his. "Get this off."

"Allow me." Aidan pulled away and did the work for her, ripping the shirt up over his head in one violent motion, then dove under the blanket to lie beside her.

Elspeth glimpsed his naked body, and she gasped, her muzzy gaze turning sharp. He was covered in scars.

He froze, uncertainty shuttering his features.

Inching the cover down, she gingerly touched a fingertip to the worst of his marks, the jagged, rippling brand that covered his left forearm. Though she wanted to look away, wanted his marks not to exist, she took in every last one, a map of his pain carved forever on his body. Broad swaths where shackles had rubbed him raw, thin bites of the whip, and the shining *WP* that named him property of some other man. "Oh, Aidan," was all she could manage, her voice tight with unshed tears.

Shifting onto his side, he scooted as far from her as the narrow bunk allowed. "It's who I am, Beth."

There was something foreign in his voice—some vulnerability, some trepidation—and her courage soared. Her dangerous rogue was just a man, and he needed her. She wrapped a steady hand around his forearm. "You're more than this."

She looked at the scars again, facing them full on, her fear gone. She smudged her thumb over the rippling skin of his brand. To mark a man as though he were cattle—it was unthinkable. "How did you ever bear the pain?"

"Pain." He pulled his arm from her, and fisting his hand, studied it. "Some say it lights a fire within."

"And is that what you say?" Though too timid to press her body to his, she was eager to maintain contact, and slid her arm beneath the blanket, idly feathering her fingers up and down his side.

"It certainly fueled my rage. My anger." He inhaled

deeply, as though that alone could clear the memories, then cupped her face in his warm, broad hand. "But no, Beth. You're what's kindled me to life."

She continued to stroke her hand up and down his body, and he grew still. She could tell by the wicked flash in his eyes that he'd become focused on her touch. "And you're kindling more than that, I daresay," he said.

Abruptly, he shifted his hand to her back and pulled her close. It was a shock to feel the naked stretch of him, pressed against her, scorching her with his heat. With a firm and confident touch, he shifted her into a position he liked, and his mastery sent a sensual shiver rippling up from her very toes. Leaning close, he nipped her ear. "You don't know what you're doing to me."

His member was hard, pressing into her thigh. For a moment, for her, it was the only thing in the room, this mysterious evidence of his maleness, of his want for her, and she tried to picture him in her mind. "Nor you to me," she said breathlessly.

"I see I've shocked you." He chuckled, a low, seductive sound. Cupping her bottom, he pulled her closer still, until he was nestled in her cleft.

Her eyes grew wide. How *that* would ever fit inside her, she knew not.

He stilled, his every muscle taut and hard as sun-warmed granite against her. "Are you certain you want this?"

"Quite," she said quickly, and his body eased. But then she hesitated. "It's just that . . ."

He kissed one cheek and then the other. "That?"

"Well, it appears you're quite large and . . ."

"And?" he asked, with a kiss to each temple.

"Well, tumescent."

He pulled from her with a laugh. "Tumescent, am I?"

She grew shy again, uncertain. "I've not offended you, have I?"

"Not in the least. Seeing as I'm the one forced to bear up under it, I'd be the first to agree upon my own . . . tumescence."

"Is it quite heavy, then?" she asked, genuinely curious.

Though he schooled his face to seriousness, she saw the humor in his eyes. "No, not heavy. But a . . . a bit of a burden, nonetheless."

"A burden?"

He considered it. "Aye, one that tends to put all other thoughts from one's mind, you might say."

She glanced down to where he was hidden beneath the covers. "Might I touch it?"

He chuckled again, nuzzling her. "I was hoping you might."

She found him under the covers and wrapped her hand around him. He was thick, and infinitely smoother than she'd have guessed. "Oh, I quite like the feel of you."

"I'm glad," he rasped, tilting his pelvis to her. "Now show me how much."

Unsure of how to proceed, she drew her hand up along his length. The skin dragged in her palm, and it fascinated her, like steel beneath silk, but then she stroked him more and forgot her fascination, the knowledge that she was about to take this most intimate part of him into her body inflaming her beyond reason.

"I want this." She cupped the head of him, rubbing the sticky wetness. "Get closer to me, Aidan."

With a groan, he snatched her wrists and rolled her onto her back. His movements were quick and sure, and the desire simmering in his eyes brought hers to a fever pitch.

Twining their fingers, he pinned her hands over her head, his body hot and hard atop hers. Bearing most of his weight on his elbows, he kissed along the length of her arms, her breasts, he kissed her all over, chafing his cock in her wetness all the while.

She'd lost all sense—no longer a logical being, she'd become pure feeling. Her mind, usually a clamor of thoughts, was reduced only to impulse and sensation. She knew only him, a hard wall of muscle, the rasp of his whiskers, the coarse hairs on his body. The sound of his breathing and his intermittent groans. The scent of salt air and their musk. The ship gently rolling, rocking their bodies closer, grinding his hardness so unbearably close to her, yet not close enough, in a teasing suggestion of what was to come.

She whimpered, her wanting of him become unbearable. "Now, Aidan."

"I don't want to hurt you. We need to—"

She couldn't bear it any longer. Tearing her hands from his, she grabbed his ass. "Now," she cried, pulling him into her.

There was a sharp pain, but his shout of pleasure blacked it from her mind, and he pumped into her until the pain was gone and all that was left was this joining. The feeling of their bodies connected. All she knew was the slide of their sweating bodies, the sweet ache of her breasts, and the acute want growing between her legs, the need for release, to fall spiraling with him into ecstasy.

She became aware that he was whispering in her ear. "Mine," he was telling her. "You're mine."

Her body seized, stilled, and for a breathless moment she floated in blackness, and then the blackness shattered, and she was filled with light. She felt her head rise from the bed, her body curling into his, like a puppet lost to herself, Aidan's body her master.

With a last, hard thrust, he shouted his climax, and collapsed over her. For a while, they simply lay there, panting, she unable to speak, unable even to close her slackened jaw.

And then they laughed. His was deep and unfettered, and she couldn't stop her giggles, so joyful she was, transformed. Her pleasure was too much, it had to bubble from her.

"Sweet heavens above." Aidan rolled off of her, still clutching her close. His laughter faded and he grew serious. "Elspeth Josephina Farquharson, I'd sell my soul to the devil, I'd call myself the devil's own, if only you'd let me do that once more."

"Oh yes," she said, beaming up at him. "More, and more again."

Chapter 29

Aidan couldn't believe his ears. Or his eyes, or his body, for that matter.

"Am I truly to have more of you?" He smoothed the hair from her damp brow. Goose bumps shivered her skin, and he pulled the covers over her shoulders and hugged her closer. She was cool against his body, he like a furnace, on fire with a craving for her he'd only begun to explore. "I dare not believe it."

He molded her breast through the blanket, and her nipple hardened at his touch. He gently pinched her, and her instant reaction had his cock stiffening. She'd feared she was too small for him, but really she was perfect. He'd spent years around women who foisted their lush curves upon the world, propping their goods atop the shelves of velvet bodices, dazzling with silks, feathers, and threads of gold. "You were fashioned just for me, I think."

"I think it so too," she said, giving him a shy smile.

How the woman could be a sexual wanton one moment and a sweetly uncertain miss the next had won him.

She'd given herself so freely. And the honor of lying with her would've been gift enough, but Elspeth contained a fiery ardor that'd staggered him. Her selflessness was humbling, but it was the memory of her consuming ardor that had him fantasizing already about when he might take her again.

He couldn't imagine a woman better suited to him. She was kindness and sweetness, yet with a passion that matched his own, she didn't fear the tempest broiling within him. Fashioned for him, indeed.

"Shall we test the theory?" He tugged the covers down, and her skin pebbled in the cool air. He'd not allow a moment for her shyness to return and took her breast in his mouth, nibbling and sucking, until he felt her body loosen and melt beneath him.

Hoisting himself up onto his hands, he shifted over her to lie propped against the wall on her other side. It was a new angle, and he took a moment to appreciate it. "I could spend the day just staring at you." Tilting his head, he peered closer. "But what's this?"

He lifted her left arm above her head, momentarily transfixed to watch the mound of her breast rise with the motion. Then, cradling her arm in his, he studied a small birthmark at the juncture of her breast and rib. "How could I have missed this beauty?"

"It's a heart," she said proudly.

Squinting, he saw that, surely enough, there was a tan spot shaped like a little heart beneath her breast. "So it is."

"I've always thought it meant I was marked by love." She traced the mark, her fingers knowing where to go without her looking. She watched him, as if she expected he might challenge her assertion. "In Hindustan they read folks' palms. Some people read tea leaves. It seemed reasonable to infer some meaning in such a shape, and on my breast no less."

He, who'd spent over half his life wearing a scowl, couldn't help but smile down at her. The woman was as fanciful as a poet, and he loved her for it. "Destined to find true love, were you?"

"Well, I always knew I'd *feel* love. It's been a surprise that I've actually found it."

His heart soared. "Have you indeed?" He'd not felt loved, not *been* loved, in many long years. He placed his hand over the mark, barely touching her skin. "And this wee spot foretold all that?"

"Yes," she said, looking down to study her body. With a giggle, she tugged the blanket lower, revealing a fresh mark blooming on the uppermost curve of her other breast. "And in case the universe missed it, it looks as though I've been marked elsewhere too."

He brushed the spot with a tentative finger, cursing himself. "Och, I've kissed you too hard."

"You kissed me just right." She snatched his finger in her hand.

The tease in her voice did nothing to ease his worry. She was so delicate, and he so brutish, the thought that his body might be too much for her was appalling. "Did I hurt you?"

"Oh, Aidan"—she cupped his cheek, turning earnest—"not at all. I didn't feel it." A naughty gleam lit her eyes. "Rather, I might have felt it, but I certainly didn't *mind* it."

Relief flooded him, and happiness too. He lay naked in bed with his Elspeth, and for this one stolen moment, the world felt right.

It was heaven, but time marched on, and too soon he'd have to pay the devil his due. With a sigh, he craned his head to glance at the porthole. "I curse that we'll lose the light soon. I must take you home."

"I won't let you." She tucked the blanket up over them with a snap. "I won't go back there. I belong with you now."

He shook his head, marveling at her conviction. He prayed that the force of her will was enough to bring truth to her words. "You do belong with me. And you shall stay with me, and soon. But not tonight."

"You said yourself that you wanted to look at me all day. Here's your opportunity."

It was an opportunity they couldn't risk. It wasn't just that they needed to find her way out of this betrothal. It wasn't just her narrow-minded, tightfisted old father. He'd not allow Elspeth to be ruined.

"Think on it," he said. "Your father will realize you're gone and scour Aberdeen looking for you. There'll be a scandal."

She waved her hand dismissively. "My father won't notice I'm gone till the morning."

What she said couldn't possibly be true. He tried to think of another excuse, daring not to hope. "Then the scandal will come tomorrow morning."

She rolled onto her belly, nestling deeper under the covers, as though putting the issue to rest. "We'll simply have to come up with a plan by then."

Her appeal was undeniable. She was adorable, lying there with her chin cradled in her hands.

"What sort of plan?" he asked, beginning to waver.

"We need something worthy of the greatest of plots." She kicked her feet up in thought, not appearing to notice that the movement yanked the covers down, exposing her back. "Something more clever than the Trojan horse. Something more dastardly than Iago with Desdemona's handkerchief."

She was so precious and lovely and full of life, she sparkled with it. How nobody else noticed, he couldn't figure. Damned Fraser saw it, but Aidan had already decided he'd simply have to blind the man.

The tip of her tongue peeked out from the corner of her mouth as she looked at him, great intent furrowing her brow. "Surely we can think of something original."

Plotting was suddenly the furthest thing from his mind. "I have nothing original in me, excepting original sin," he said with a wink.

"Aidan!" She nudged him with her elbow. "But we need a plan."

"I have a plan." He ran his hand down her elegant back, pushing the blanket down as he went, revealing her pale and perfect bottom.

Might she really stay the night? Would he really get to hold her as she slept in his arms? Would he wake, and she'd still be by his side? All the women he'd been with, and he'd never slept—actually slept—with a one of them. The notion was oddly exhilarating.

"But don't we need to figure out what to tell everyone?"

The vision of her shoulders and back spread before him like supper on the table was more than he could bear. "I have other needs right about now."

They had all night to figure out plots and explanations. He wanted to take her again. And once or twice more after that. Wrapping an arm around her slender waist, he kissed the back of her neck. "And I find you're thinking too much for my tastes."

"I have much on my mind," she said playfully.

But he could see by the growing heat in her eyes that she'd be easy to convince. "Then I'll kiss every last thought from your head." He sidled her into him, kissing and rubbing her shoulders and the back of her neck. When she nestled a hip nearer, he knew she was coming around.

He caressed a hand along that beautiful back, then

down farther to slide his fingers home between her legs. He inched his body closer still, leaning down to nip a shoulder blade. He was hard and ready, and pressed his cock into her, but it was no relief.

"Beth," he whispered. He wanted her under him, over him, wanted her every which way. "I want you again."

She began to roll over, but he clutched her bottom, stopping her. "Not yet. I'm not done looking at your back."

"At my back?" She turned all the way onto her belly, cradling her head in her arms, the pose languorous and sultry. She hitched her hip toward him in question. "What do you propose to do with my back?"

"I could do many things." He shifted, settling closer over her, and wrapped his hand around her hip, his fingers nestled in the soft flesh of her belly. He imagined how easy it'd be to pull her to him, to drive himself into her, and how deep.

"I could do this." He tilted her, reaching around to knead her breast, then slid his hand lower, finding the source of her pleasure in the damp tangle between her legs. "Or this."

She gasped and lifted her hips to him. Catching his cock on her ass, she shifted, and he slipped between her legs. "What else could you do?"

He rolled on top of her, bracing himself on elbows planted on either side of her. "I could take you on your stomach."

"Oh yes," she purred, grinding against him. "That sounds lovely."

Though the lust that clouded his brain was dark, he laughed. Who was this strange and glorious woman beneath him? He should've guessed she'd be eager to try it all. "What did I do to deserve you?"

"The question is"—she took his hand from her breast

to suck his finger into her mouth—"what will you do to keep me?"

"I'll show you," he growled, and they were the last words spoken before he took her, claiming her as he told her he would.

And then they slept, and Aidan held Elspeth the whole night through.

Chapter 30

After enduring fifteen minutes of pounding on his office door, Fraser finally relented and answered, only to find his fiancée's father standing in the doorway. Moonlight backlit the old man, casting his face in darkness and turning his frizzy hair ghostly white. The fellow looked as though he'd just escaped Bedlam.

Fraser wondered if he might be making a mistake marrying into such a peculiar family. "Are you drunk, sirrah?"

"Where is she?" Elspeth's father demanded, standing on his tiptoes to scan the darkened hallway.

Fraser stepped forward to block his view. Not that there was anything to hide—he'd deny the man simply on principle. The dinner hour had come and gone, and what sort of man went banging about Aberdeen at such a time? "What brings you here at this hour?"

Farquharson met his eyes. "Elspeth never came home. Girl said she was coming here."

"Ah." Fraser's mind raced, remembering their earlier meeting. They'd fought, the chit claiming she didn't want their marriage. Could she have run away?

He stepped back to indicate that although the man wasn't entirely welcomed, he'd be allowed inside.

"Well?" The old man stayed his ground, and his challenging tone raised him incrementally in Fraser's estimation. He'd not have figured her father to have spine. "Was she here or wasn't she?"

"She was here," Fraser said, wondering all the while if the girl had found herself another man. What else but an illicit dalliance would send her running into the night? Who else but a man would give her the courage? Rage surged in his gut like acid, but he tempered his words. "We had a bit of a disagreement. And she left."

"A disagreement?"

"Aye, she's a silent thing, but willful," Fraser said tightly. Was she even still a virgin? He refused to be manipulated by an impoverished old man and his whey-faced offspring. "I'll certainly not take credit for her disappearance. She obviously needs a shorter rein."

"Inconstant creature," her father grumbled. "I wanted a son, you know. A *lad* wouldn't go gadding about Aberdeen, going God knows where. A lad would know how to take care of business."

Business. He mustn't forget this all came down to business. Though he had to admit he'd been swept up in the thrill of the chase. She wasn't as timid as he'd first thought, and the challenge was more exhilarating than he'd expected.

Fraser clapped her father's shoulder, adopting an easy attitude. "Come in and we'll discuss this as men. She seems a bit skittish about being wed. No more than that."

Farquharson nodded, seeming to jump to some conclusion. "She's not much experienced with men."

"Clearly." Though he begged to differ on that account.

Elspeth was a clever slip of a thing who clearly understood what their betrothal meant for her family's finances. He'd wager it was an entirely different enticement that gave her cold feet—likely she'd met herself some strapping buck. But he chose to offer her father a different excuse, saying simply, "She's young yet."

He nodded, growing easy. "She is, at that."

Turning his back on the man, Fraser hid a smile as he shut the door. Listening to Farquharson speak, one would think his daughter still bore the first blush of youth. In truth, the girl could've been married off ten years past, if only her father had two merks to rub together for a dowry.

"It was a foolish argument," Fraser assured him. "Nothing to fash yourself over. These young girls can be unpredictable when it comes to men."

"Not my Elspeth. She's a quiet one, as you've seen for yourself. Men have never bothered with her."

Fraser shot him a look. "You can't tell me I'm the first to engage her attentions." She was a meek sort of creature, but not without her appeal. He wondered what the family might be hiding. "Surely she's expressed an interest in marriage before this?"

Unless it'd been money, not a husband, the father had been waiting for. Fraser scowled, thinking the old man had cast a line, and he'd bitten.

Her father shrugged. "She doesn't seem to pay men much mind."

Nor men her, Fraser reckoned. And this was the girl who'd decided *she* didn't need an alliance with *him*? Little did she know he was doing her a great honor.

"She just has an eye for her books and her studies," the old man added.

Fraser grunted his agreement, but his thoughts were elsewhere. She'd fooled her father. He'd wager the girl had her eyes on something—or some*one*—other than books and studies. He'd give her this: the little doxy was sharp. He'd enjoy bringing her to heel.

He endeavored to keep the studied joviality in his tone. "Either way, these girls can be as silly as peahens, thinking a quarrel and a tease will kindle a man's ardor. I'm sure her protests were no more than that."

"Silly . . . aye." Farquharson's head bobbed in a relieved nod. Eyes snapping wide, he quickly added, "But she's clever too."

So the old man saw financial relief on the horizon and wasn't about to let it go. He wanted to sell his daughter to the highest bidder, even though she probably was no longer even a virgin.

Fraser thought of her eerily pale, all-seeing eyes and that lovely mouth, like the bud of a tea rose yet to bloom, and he still accounted her worth the price. Still, although the lass may have struck his fancy, nobody made a fool of him. He would have Elspeth, and fast, before some other man's seed quickened in her belly.

He altered course. "Actually"—he slapped a hand to his brow—"Elspeth *did* say something. About visiting a friend. That's it . . . foolish me . . . I recall it now."

The Farquharsons would learn not to cross him at the bargaining table. So too would they realize just how deeply their need for his assistance ran.

"A friend?"

"Yes," Fraser said. "She was off to visit a friend after she left here. You're certain you didn't see her at home? Might you have missed her?"

"Perhaps," her father said uncertainly.

"She's likely home already, safe abed for the night." Putting an amiable arm about the man's shoulders, Fraser opened the door and steered him out. "And you, all the way here in Aberdeen. Why, while you're on my side of town, I insist you pay a visit to my favorite tavern."

"Do you think so?"

Fraser tugged him down the alley. "I know so. I'm sure your Elspeth is sound asleep, and under the circumstances, I think a dram or two would be perfectly fine. Advisable, even. Seeing as I'm to be your son-in-law, eh? Come now, I'll walk you there myself."

Hours later, Fraser sneaked from the pub, leaving the old man swinging a tankard of ale and singing a lusty tune. He was headed for a farm he knew he'd find empty, a purloined bottle of whiskey in one pocket and a tinderbox in the other.

Chapter 31

Elspeth woke as she had through the night, savoring the feel of Aidan's strong arm wrapped around her, his hand cupping her breast. They lay on their sides, and she nestled her rump more firmly into his lap, even though they were already as close as two people could be.

The boat rocked gently, and she waited to be lulled back to sleep by Aidan's heavy, rhythmic breathing. He seemed at peace, and she could only hope that the last embers of rage she'd seen in his eyes were banked for good.

She'd woken throughout the night to touch him, to inhale deeply the scent of him. Of *them*.

She brushed light fingers over his arm, the tickle of wiry hairs a revelation, a delight. He was warm and sure at her back, his strong arm holding her, and she felt safe and loved.

It was like a dream, and she still couldn't fathom how

it was that *she* was the woman who lay by his side. *She*, no longer merely a dreamer, but one who realized dreams.

She waited to slide back into sleep, but this time it didn't come. Her body was awake, sensing sunrise was imminent, and thoughts clearing from their slumber, she was of a mind to see dawn warm the sky. And besides, her body had begun to register needs apart from Aidan that wanted tending.

She shifted away from him and shivered from the wash of cold air where his body had been. She stilled, grieving over their parting, and though she knew it had to come, she knew too that it would be brief. One day very soon she'd be his bride, and then she'd get to wake every day in Aidan's arms.

She gently shifted his arm to her hip, holding her breath, hoping not to wake him. Before he saw her, she wanted to comb fingers through her hair, wash the sleep from her face, and generally gather herself. Gradually, she edged from beneath the weight of his arm. His breathing changed, became shallower, and she waited until it grew regular again.

She slipped her feet from beneath the covers and began to sit up. An arm grabbed her tight around her belly. "No you don't," he said, his voice hoarse with sleep. "Where are you going?"

Pressing his hand over her belly, she looked over her shoulder at him. It was dark in the cabin, but ambient moonlight shone through the porthole, and she could make out his bare shoulders above the covers. His hair was a dark tangle sprouting over his head, and tenderness swept her at the boyish look of it. "I want to see the sun rise over the sea."

With a nod, he sat up.

She put a hand on his shoulder. "You needn't get up too. It's early yet."

"But I want to watch *you* watch the sun rise," he said, giving her bottom a tweak.

Their banter was easy and affectionate, and she knew a sharp twinge in her chest. It was acute, this feeling, of being seen and being loved. "I'd like that," she told him quietly.

He stood, and she couldn't tear her eyes from his naked form. Blades of silver moonlight shimmered over a body carved from stone. But then he turned, and she bit back a gasp as she saw that same light and shadow play along the marks on his back. Though she'd felt the whip scars with her fingers, seeing them was a shock. Would always be a shock.

Turning, he caught her scrutiny, and she braced to watch shame or anger shutter his features. But instead, he walked to her, and with a gentle kiss on her forehead, said, "It's all right, Beth. It was years ago. I've got you, and it's all all right now."

He extracted their clothes from the tangle of blankets, continuing as though nothing was amiss and the subject was closed. "It's just as well to be awake so early. I'd have you arrive home before the sun gets too high in the sky."

She followed his lead and began to sort out her clothes. "I'll be surprised if my father has even noticed my absence."

He shot her a look that, even in the dim cabin, she could see was doubtful. "I don't want you compromised. There's no better time than first light to dock in Aberdeen harbor. The sailors are still drunk, and it'll be just fishermen roaming about, and they're not the ones who have me worried." Pulling his shirt over his head, he added, "I don't trust Fraser, and I don't think he'll be taking this change in your wedding plans as well as you believe."

"Do you think he'll have men at the docks?"

"I'm certain of it," he said, stepping into his trews. "I'd like us to avoid the lot of them. He'll suspect something is at the root of your decision, and he'll have men sniffing around for some clue about what caused your change of heart. Which means you especially must stay away from him—no more visits to the erstwhile fiancé." He helped her shrug into her vest. "Have I your word?"

"You've my word." She smiled.

Turning her to face him, he finished tying the laces of her bodice. "Now," he said, placing his hands on her shoulders, "I imagine you have needs to attend to."

She darted her eyes down. How mortifying to be discussing one's bodily needs with one's . . . pirate rogue.

Aidan chucked her chin. "I've spent the last hours studying . . . nay, Beth, *tasting* every last inch of you. No need to be shy on account of this."

He led her up the stairs, pointing her to the side of the ship. "Just beyond the sail, luvvie, and over the gunnel you go."

She was to relieve herself over the side of the ship? Dawn had begun to turn the sky gray, and she eyed the monochrome silhouettes of railings and hatches. "Surely you don't mean that I should just . . . hang there?"

"I do, and you shall." With a pat on her rump, he sent her on her way. "You'll need to hold on, mind."

"Obviously." She headed toward the gunwale, considering. He'd set the sails, heaving to for the night, and the water was calm beneath them, the boat bobbing gently. She looked over her shoulder to ask, "And it's safe?"

"'Tis," he said, but his back was already to her, busying himself on deck, and, she imagined, about to take care of his own needs.

She needed to go, and there was nothing for it. Hoisting her skirts, she set about her business, and couldn't help a quick giggle at the exhilarating freedom of it. "What can you do with a drunken sailor," she belted out in her best singing voice, "what can you do with a drunken sailor, errr-lie in the morning?"

"You're a wee daftie," he called out, laughing.

Ducking back from behind the sail, she returned to him, smoothing her skirts in an exaggeratedly ladylike fashion. "I am no daftie. I'm a pirate wench."

"Are you?" He put his arm around her and nestled her close, startling her as he stole a deep kiss. With it came a rush of sensation—his morning beard scraping against her skin, the familiar stab of longing in her belly—her body's response to him immediate.

He finally pulled from her, leaving her breathless. He wiped the damp from her bottom lip with a sensual sweep of his thumb. "Pirate wench, is it? Aye, I think you speak truly."

She beamed, pleased beyond reason.

He opened a hatch to retrieve a woolen blanket then led her to the rear of the ship. "If you're a pirate wench, that would make me a pirate. And you know what pirates are known for."

She watched as he made a cozy nest of the stern. "Ravaging?"

"Aye, ravaging, ravishment. All those." He lay down, patting the space beside him, beckoning.

She joined him on the blanket. "How very treacherous it all sounds."

"A menace, I am. Particularly to fair maidens." He cupped her head, leaning them back to watch as night turned to day. "So, beware. You've requested a sunrise, but I cannot guarantee your subsequent safety."

With a hand on his chest and a leg twined between his, she cuddled close. "I wish we could just stay here, like this."

He sighed, stroking her hair. "Soon, Beth."

They lay in silence for a time, watching as the sky faded from slate to indigo, to blue, and the rising sun cast strangely vivid slashes of light on soft rolling clouds overhead.

He took her hand in his, idly threading their fingers. "It's like we're floating away."

There was such romance in his voice, she fancied her chest might expand with her light heart, and it made her playful. "And you call *me* the daftie?"

Barking out a laugh, he grabbed her and pulled her roughly atop him. "Not a daftie. 'Tis merely the musings of a pirate poet." He settled her more snugly over him, and she felt his hardness through her skirts. Clamping her in place with a firm hand on her buttocks, he warned, "You best not tease, luvvie. I'll make you walk the plank, or worse."

"Worse?" She ducked down to nip at his ear. She wriggled her hips suggestively, able to think of a thousand sweet tortures she'd happily suffer at his hands. "What worse could there be than walking the plank?"

He became suddenly serious. "You could marry me. Be my pirate bride in truth. Forever."

She raised her brows. "Have we not agreed to that already?"

"So we did. But I have a plan. I'll marry you," he said earnestly, "and I'll run your farm for you. With you."

"You'd be a sheep farmer?" Her face fell, thinking of her tiresome existence. "I can't ask you to choose such a life. You've got your boat. You could have such grand adventures."

"Adventure?" He gave a disdainful roll of his eyes. "Don't you understand? I've had my fill of adventure for a lifetime. We can still do this"—he gestured around them—"but we'll sail after the workday is done. We can watch the sun set. We'll watch every sunrise, if that's your fancy. I'll teach our son to sail. Daughters too," he added, smile flashing. "But you and I, we'll manage the farm together. It's been doing better since I began to help, isn't it?"

"Better than ever," she admitted.

"I want roots, Beth. I've been long years without them, and I'm finding I like the feel of being on Scottish soil again. I can contribute something of good. I can build something, *we* can build something, together. We'll make enough, and then set your father up someplace comfortable. In his own cottage, or even in Aberdeen town, if that's what he wishes. He doesn't need coin from some old merchant when you and I will get by just fine."

She stared at him in dazed silence. He didn't want to sail off into the sunset, abandoning her—and her many responsibilities—for grand adventures. He'd leave all that behind, to live with her, tending sheep on a modest slice of land.

"Well?" he asked, sounding uncertain. "What do you think?"

In her eyes, he'd been a hero, but now he was *her* hero. She traced a light finger along his brow, saying simply, "I think it's a grand plan."

He laughed, tangling fingers in her hair, pulling her down for a joyful kiss.

They parted, and her thoughts began to race. Her father would be difficult to convince. With next to no worldly goods to call his own, Aidan brought nothing to this union. But if they tread carefully, she knew she'd find a way.

"You and I will need to part," she told him, her mind working. "But just long enough for me to talk sense to my father. When we dock today, can it be near Dunnottar? If I walk home from there and am seen, I can devise some believable subterfuge as to how I'd been away visiting Anya."

"Subterfuge." A dark shadow flickered on his face. "You mean you'll lie. I hate making you lie."

She propped onto an elbow, speaking in earnest. "You'll make an honest woman of me yet, Aidan MacAlpin. All we need to do is persuade my father."

They locked eyes. She watched as he grew convinced, his gaze transforming from somber to mischievous.

He hiked her skirts up. "That can't be *all* we need to do . . ."

She knelt over him. The air on her legs was brisk, but the feel of the sun warming her naked skin was a revelation. Dangerous and delicious, just like Aidan. And just as with him, there was nothing that felt righter in the world.

Chapter 32

It'd taken Elspeth the entire sail back to convince Aidan
to let her walk home on her own. In the end, it was his
boat that decided it. The coast off Dunnottar Rock offered
good mooring for the likes of Cormac's fishing boat, but
the *Journeyman* was a big enough sloop to require docking in Aberdeen harbor.

She happily meandered along the path, heading home,
her mind skipping hither and yon, thinking about Aidan,
replaying their time together, remembering all he'd done
and said. Might they truly have a son or daughter someday for him to sail with, for her to read to? It was enough
to make her chest expand so that she thought she might
float up to the sky with her happiness.

A plume of smoke drifted faintly on the horizon, and
her mind began to wander further afield, wondering who
was burning what and why. But the smoke grew darker

the closer she got to her cottage, its smell more acrid. Her heart began to hammer in her chest.

As she crested the hill, her world stopped, and she was plunged into a nightmare. Their cottage was a blackened ruin. "Da! Oh God, Da!" Elspeth galloped down the hill, shrieking for her father, trying in vain to scream herself awake. But it was no dream.

She got as close as she could to the cottage before the scorched earth became too unbearably hot through the leather of her shoes, and peered in, making sense through the smoke and shadows. Despite the heat, her skin prickled, cold and clammy. There was not much inside but ashes and charred stone. A few blackened pages from her books were littered across the floor. A cast-iron pot sat on the hearth, looking eerily untouched by the devastation.

Other than that, there was nothing. She had nothing.

The stench, the sight, she took it all in, but her brain couldn't comprehend. Shock made her gasp for air, but she sucked in too much smoke and coughs racked her. Backing away, she scrubbed the tears from her face, breathing into the crook of her elbow.

While she was gone, a fire had raged. While she'd floated away with Aidan, her world had burned. She'd been thinking only of herself while flames blazed with a life of their own, razing everything then petering out, leaving naught but singed stone ringed by a halo of blackened earth.

If she'd been paying mind to her family, to their needs, if she'd only been home, this wouldn't have happened.

But what of her father? Had he been here? "Da!" she screamed again, hoping—praying—he was sleeping off the night somewhere in an Aberdeen tavern.

Fresh dread prickled through her, choking her with nausea, as she realized who had been home. Home, and quite likely helpless. *Achilles.*

"No, God," she cried, wondering how she could have

forgotten her puppy. She bolted from the cottage, scanning all around her. "Achilles!" she called, racing across the glen, shouting over and over for her dog, but she was greeted only by silence.

The silence grew louder. It was unsettling and surreal, and only then did it strike her that the farm had never been silent. Always there'd been sound, always the incessant bleating of sheep that'd driven her mad. But now there was nothing.

Girding her courage, she made her way to the paddock.

A gruesome scene slowly came into focus. She saw the sheep, and her gorge rose. They lay slaughtered, littering their pen. Someone had tried to burn them alive. But wool didn't burn, and their bodies stank of charred fleece and butchered flesh.

She clapped a hand to her mouth, swallowing convulsively, refusing to be sick. She'd bear this. *She'd* been the cause of it, and she'd bear it.

This was no accident. Somebody had done this, somebody had intentionally destroyed their farm.

Forcing herself to cling to reason, she took in the scene, trying to make sense of it. The scorch marks ended several feet from the cottage, then began again near the paddock. And though nothing had burned in the field, the fence had been toppled in places.

Who would do such a thing? Who had they angered? Who did they even know outside their small community?

Fraser. Her blood froze in her veins. The answer was Fraser.

It was her fault. She'd enraged the old merchant, and he'd retaliated by destroying her home.

"You hussy," a familiar voice shouted.

She turned to see her father stumbling toward her. Relief surged through her, seeing him alive. And then dread mingled with her relief, seeing the fury in his eyes.

He stood before her, swaying, and the sour smell of ale

amid the acrid cinders sickened her. The morning light was unforgiving, and he looked like he'd aged twenty years in one night.

"You dare come back here," he said slowly. "This is *your* fault. If you'd been here, I'd have been here. But instead I had to search all over Aberdeen for your fool hide. If we'd been here, the farm would've been fine."

"I . . . I was at Dunnottar."

"Don't lie to me," he spat. "You were with *him*. And now we've nothing left because of it."

She glanced behind her to the cottage, fueled by desperation. "We can rebuild—"

"Can't build nothing from nothing." He shook his head, disgust curling his lip. "He sullied you, didn't he?"

"That's none of your business," she snapped, grateful to feel ire replacing her despair.

He looked incredulous. "Don't you get it, girl? It *is* my business. You'd best hope Fraser will still take you, because if he don't marry you, both of us is off to the poorhouse."

The thought of marrying Fraser was a worse nightmare even than the sight of their smoldering farm. Her father had the right to force her into wedlock, but she was a pirate wench now and she would dig in her heels. "I can't marry him," she cried. "I will not."

"Ye can and will." He stalked toward her, for a moment looking like a younger man again, and it sent a shiver of foreboding up her spine.

She took a step back. "I won't. I'm to marry Aidan. He's strong and able. He'll help us rebuild."

"Can Aidan repay our debts?"

"*Your* debts," she snapped. "Your choices, your vices. These are *your* debts I'm paying for."

"Don't be a fool. They're yours too. That money filled your belly too. Put a roof over *your* head. If you'd been a lad, you could've helped more—"

"*How* could I have helped more?" Sadness swamped her, a dull ache in her chest. Her father was eager to throw her to the wolves in order to save his own hide, sacrificing her for financial gain.

"I'm telling you how you can help," he said, his chin trembling with temper kept barely in check. "You marry that man Fraser, or our debts will see us both sent to the poorhouse."

The horrific truth was dawning. Her father was in debt and they hadn't the money to pay. But he'd been wrong on one count: they'd be *lucky* if they were only sent to the poorhouse. Idle, able-bodied poor were as likely to be shipped off to the Indies or America.

She had no choice. They were destitute. It was marriage for her, or some worse fate for the two of them.

She became frantic. Her world was spinning out of control, and she was powerless to stop it. "Please, Da," she pleaded. "Don't you see? It's Fraser who's behind this. He's the one who destroyed the farm."

"Well, then he did a tidy job of it, because now you have no choice. You just pray he'll still take you. God willing, he'll still keep you even though you're no maiden. Now stop that caterwauling. It's no' like you, and I don't like it." He grabbed her arm and began to drag her up the hill.

"Stop!" She jerked her arm away. "What of the farm? What are you doing?"

"Daft girl, what do you think I'm doing? I'm taking you to him."

It was all happening too fast. Fraser had held the last card, and he'd played it perfectly. She and her father had bills to pay, and no means to pay them. Aidan had no money either, and if he saddled himself with her, he'd be in line for the workhouse, too. She couldn't bear the thought of him being held captive again.

She had no choice but to marry Fraser. Life as she knew it was ending.

She planted her feet, making her father stumble. "Can I at least say good-bye?"

"To that devil MacAlpin? And let the blackguard steal you away? I think not, girl." He tugged her onward. "You're lucky I don't let Fraser's men deal with him."

Another fact dawned, and the shock of it impaled her. If Fraser had done all this simply to have her as a bride, what would he do to Aidan if he were to discover him?

Her heart choked her throat until it was difficult to breathe, impossible to swallow.

Aidan sought the man with the black pearl, a man connected to Fraser, and it was only a matter of time before he found both men. If Fraser realized she loved Aidan, he'd surely kill him. And with a fleet of dockside thugs on his payroll, she didn't doubt his ability.

She thought of those butchered sheep. What tortures might Fraser devise if he discovered Aidan had been the one to deny him the pleasure of her maidenhead? Aidan, who'd already suffered torments enough for one lifetime.

She had to keep him safe. And the only way to do that was to go to Fraser. To marry him.

By sacrificing herself, her very life, she'd keep Aidan free. The image of his scarred wrists and back was seared into her memory—she'd never want to inflict such pain on him again.

———

Fraser heard voices at the door and felt his mouth curl into a smile. Albert and Elspeth Farquharson, he'd wager, and right on time.

The whole fire episode had been so unlike him—it'd taken him a full hour to wash the stink of smoke from his body—but he wasn't one to suffer a plan going awry. He'd gotten it into his head that a bit of sheep pasturage in the guise of a wool farm would be just the thing to explain away his not entirely legal profits in the slave trade.

Besides, he hadn't been about to sit idly by as the girl took it in her head to spurn *him*. Even less would he endure being jilted for some other fool—likely some sodding farmer, or whatever sort of man it was who struck the fancies of young girls.

Though using alcohol as an incendiary had been inspired, torching their farm to the ground had been an ordeal. Yet the moment Elspeth and her father entered his office, he knew at once it'd been worth it.

She was lovely, pale and fragile, with the bloom of exertion on her cheeks. Or perhaps it was anger he saw in her blush, and he thought he might just prefer that even more. He'd want this girl beneath him even if she hadn't come with a strip of land he could claim for profit.

"Well, good day to the both of you." He stood and gestured for them to take a seat. "Please join me."

"Expecting us, were you?" She looked at him with a spark in her eyes. There was anger in her gaze, but something else too. *Fear.*

It sent a bolt of heat to his loins.

He knew the sheep had put the fear there—or rather, what he'd done to them. He could see the horror of his butchery in her eyes. The cursed beasts had as much wool between their ears as they had on their backs, and slaughtering the lot of them had been more chore than challenge. But it'd been the crowning touch, and just the thing to show Elspeth what came to pass when people crossed him.

"On the contrary. After our last conversation, I understood we were to break our engagement." He adjusted the chair as she sat, thinking there was but one thing to be broken, and it was she. He'd break her like a horse, and what a pleasure it would be. "But I see a new light dancing in your eyes. Have I reason to hope?"

She scowled at him, and it took all his control not to smirk. Underneath the shy exterior, this one was a firebrand.

A thousand times smarter than her dimwit father, and a pleasure to spar with. Her pretty lips thinned. "Hope? You'd better hope—"

"That is," her father said, quickly cutting her off, "we're of the hope that you took your last interview with Elspeth to be no more than it was: the silly games of a maiden."

Fraser smirked. *Maiden indeed.*

"I enjoy games." He pinned Elspeth with a look. She squirmed, and he relished the power he had over her. Smart and willful maybe, and not as timid as he'd first thought, but she'd acquiesce to his whims within the year. He'd relish making her yield to him. It was invigorating, like what he imagined a man felt when breaking a wild animal—bringing that spirit to heel, proving that you were its master.

It was exhilarating, better than any hunt. He'd forgotten what it was to feel young, yet here he was, feeling a man of twenty again. Was that how marriage would be? He found himself looking forward to it.

She had a keen mind and sharp, all-seeing eyes, unlike all the other simpering misses he'd ever met. She'd eventually realize he and she were mental matches. She'd grow to appreciate his wisdom.

"I hadn't realized just how staid my life had become," he told her, finding himself gratifyingly moved by his own honesty. He puffed up, believing himself a very great good man. It was indeed time to take a wife—all the brilliant men in powerful circles had them. "Until I met you, my dear. You've added a bit of sauce to the stock."

"Them's welcome words," her father said. "Because we're of a mind to step up the wedding a bit."

"To hasten our nuptials?" He shot her a pointed look—he wanted to hear *her* say the words. Wanted to hear her beg him. "Could that be true, Elspeth? Do you wish to marry me so very badly?"

It gave him great satisfaction to watch the fire kindle in those pale blue-and-yellow eyes.

She gave him a tight nod, and it was all he could do not to laugh outright.

He was a veritable god of planning, he thought, concealing his surge of triumph. First, there'd been his scheme to trade workers for cotton, avoiding the Crown and her taxes. Then came his masterful handling of the Farquharsons. And now he'd be the savior who'd come in and rebuild her idiot father's farm, setting in place a sham enterprise with which to explain away his profits.

And he'd win himself a young wife in the bargain.

What a welcome diversion this was proving. He decided to prolong it a bit more. "What, pray, has brought about such a welcome change of heart?"

Though he'd posed the question to Elspeth, it was her father who answered. "There's been an accident, see. And . . . we were hoping . . ."

He let her father flail for a moment, then broke in. "Oh my. An accident? I hope nothing untoward has come to pass."

"I think you know very well what's come to pass," Elspeth said in a tight voice.

"Mind yourself," her father scolded from the corner of his mouth. The old man shifted in his seat, looking uncomfortable. "There's been an accident at the farm. A fire."

Fraser steepled his fingers, watching Elspeth's reaction. How wrong his first impressions of her had been. Initially, he'd thought her a quiet, plain wisp of a thing, but now such a whirl of emotions animated her face. He decided it was that which turned her pretty.

Would she fight him this much in the marriage bed? Would he feel as much triumph when she finally submitted? She'd be a treat indeed.

"Then you'll need a place to stay," he said, gratified by

his own magnanimous tone. He'd spent many years claw-
ing his way from the gutters—to play the role of wealthy
benefactor was pleasing. "Some coin to get you by."

Her father's eyes brightened. "That's it precisely."

"And we can certainly step up our wedding plans."
He gave his intended a warm look, amused to watch her
bridle in response. "It takes two weeks to proclaim the
banns, but I've a minister in my pocket at my estate in
Arbroath who'll wed us as soon as I say."

Though he doubted she was a virgin, he deemed it just
as well. As long as bastard seed hadn't taken root, he'd
be happy to have young Elspeth come to him a woman
primed. She was a frail thing, looking as though she
might break, and he'd rather not have maiden tears flow-
ing on his wedding night.

And besides, he'd enjoy accustoming her to *his* ways.
He'd make her rue the day she'd allowed some other man
to touch her.

Fraser grew thoughtful. That would be his next
adventure—finding the identity of the man who'd deflow-
ered her. "I'll take you to Arbroath. In fact, we'll leave
today."

A trap, to tempt her wayward suitor from the wood-
works.

Chapter 33

Never before had Aidan known such lightness in his heart. He'd dropped Elspeth at Dunnottar as she'd asked, then turned the *Journeyman* back around to dock at his hired slip in Aberdeen, tasting the salt air in his broad grin all the while.

He was a man transformed, and he had Elspeth to thank for it. Her guileless ways were refreshing, renewing. And when she laughed, she shined warmth and light on the dark corners of his soul, chasing away his rage and leaving joy in its place. Her delight in the little things—in a story well told, in a fresh-picked apple—had reminded him how it was to feel happiness once more.

She still didn't understand just how much she'd changed him. She'd been succor to his tortured body and soul, yet she still didn't seem to see how much he needed her. It was no matter, he thought as he strode from Dunnottar to her farm. He'd be only too pleased to spend the rest of his life proving his devotion.

She'd seemed dumbfounded to hear that he'd marry her and run her farm. Little did she know, the idea of a modest slice of farmland and a run-down crofter's cottage was heaven, particularly if it meant he'd have Elspeth by his side. He was a free man now, but freedom was nothing without pride. Yet with her as his wife, he'd be a man standing tall.

His mind went to her father, and he shoved the thoughts away, not yet willing to address his lingering doubts. He'd never felt this light, this joyful, and he'd savor it just a bit longer before facing the details of reality.

Besides, Elspeth seemed certain she could convince her father, and so he'd be certain too, for her sake. And so, instead of entertaining the dark thoughts that were his wont, his long strides quickly cut the distance to their farm, imagining she'd already explained everything to the man.

Perhaps they'd both be waiting in the fields to greet him. Perhaps Albert Farquharson had agreed already to their union. Surely the man saw what good Aidan had done for the farm, what more he could do.

He crested the hill, and his heart seized in his chest. The stench of ashes choked his lungs. Bodies of sheep baked in the sun. Her farm was a smoldering rubble.

Elspeth.

He wanted to scream her name, to cry out, but couldn't make a sound, could barely breathe. Anguish flooded him. He'd banked it behind a dam, but seeing the devastation, the dam crumbled, and despair swamped him once more, so agonizingly familiar.

He was cursed. He was as charred a ruin as her cottage, and the drifting smoke was his soul dispersing, inconsequential, up to the heavens.

Gritting his teeth, he forced breath in and out of his

lungs. He forced his mind to reason. Forced his legs to work beneath him, taking him to her farm nestled in the glen below.

As he neared, the sight made his blood run cold, but he assured himself that Elspeth was safe. The ashes were cooling, the smoke thinning. It was an old fire. It'd raged when she was aboard the *Journeyman*, safe by his side.

He shouldn't have let her go. He should've kept her close, kept her safe until they were wed.

Safe, he made himself believe. Surely she was safe.

But what if she weren't? A chill crept along his flesh. Because this was no accident.

He went to the paddock, taking in the carnage. This was the work of man's hands, and he knew whose.

But where was his Beth? Perhaps she'd taken shelter with Angus, the neighboring farmer. Even as it occurred to him, his legs were racing there. Perhaps she was at the neighboring farm, even now, waiting for him.

Her blasted puppy bowled him over as he neared Angus's homestead, and damned if Aidan wasn't glad to see the scamp. He bent to pat the dog, praying that when he stood, he'd look up to find Elspeth walking toward him. "Achilles, lad. Where's your mistress?"

"She's not here," he heard a voice call from behind him.

His last thread of hope snapped. He stood and stared Angus down. "Where's Elspeth?" The farmer gave him a slow and considering look, and the man's stoicism infuriated Aidan. "Why do you just stand there? Where is she? What's happened?"

"She came with her father. He said he needed to deliver her to her fiancé in Aberdeen. I lent him my cart."

Her fiancé? Cold dread prickled through his chest. That could only mean one thing: her marriage to Fraser was on. "Why would you do such a thing?"

"Why would I not?" Angus went about his business,

leaning his chaff fork along the side of his barn. "Farqu-harson said it was where she needed to be. She's to be married, and soon."

Aidan felt a body approach and turned to find Cormac standing at his side. The sight stunned him.

"I saw the smoke from my boat," Cormac said, glancing from one man to the other. His body was tensed, with a hand on the dagger at his hip. "What's happened here?"

Cormac looked as though he were ready to throttle Angus first and ask questions later. Aidan wondered briefly, would Cormac truly stand by his side, without question or hesitation? In that instant, he thought his twin just might.

He greeted Cormac with a meaningful bob of his head. "Elspeth's cursed drunk of a father took her. She's to marry some merchant, whom"—he glared pointedly at Angus—"she doesn't want."

Angus shrugged. "That's no concern of mine."

"Couldn't you see the woman was upset?" She'd surely been upset, hadn't she?

He felt Cormac's hand at his shoulder. Could his brother read his thoughts so well, or was it simply that he sensed how dangerously close to violence Aidan was getting?

"I don't ken the lass's mind," Angus said. "She was silent as a mouse. But then she usually is."

He bristled at the comment, but Cormac was quick to switch focus, asking, "Who is this merchant?"

"Damned blackguard is no good," Aidan said. "Elspeth would never marry him of her own choice."

The brothers' eyes met, and Cormac must've seen the truth of the situation in Aidan's expression because he gave a sharp, knowing nod. "Then there's something else afoot."

Angus pondered this as he coiled a stretch of rope and hung it from a nail on the side of his barn. "Her father said the man was going to help them."

The farmer's offhand reporting of events was bringing

Aidan's blood to a boil. "I don't care what her father thinks," he said, his jaw tight. He tossed off a cold, mocking laugh. "*Help them* . . . He's delivering her into the hands of the man who destroyed their farm."

That seemed to get Angus's attention. His attitude went from cool to guarded. "But Farquharson said the man's a pillar of the community, or some such."

"Who comes into his wealth illegally."

Angus rubbed his chin, deep in thought, and Aidan wanted to slug him. While they deliberated, his Elspeth was probably already in Fraser's clutches.

Cormac's hand was once again on his shoulder with a tempering grip, and Aidan wondered if his fury was that obvious. "Do you have proof?" his brother asked.

"I have papers, but they're back at Dunnottar. They raise doubt enough." He gave his brother a weighty look. "He's linked to the pirate who took me."

Cormac tensed. "Does the lass know it?"

"Aye, there's not much that slips by Beth."

"But she went with her father with nary a fuss," Angus said.

Aidan stared, his voice, his heart, a blank. He was grateful when Cormac challenged the farmer, saying, "You're saying she went willingly?"

"Seemed like."

"She'd never willingly agree to marry him." Aidan began to pace, the need for action exploding through him. Elspeth would never have chosen to go, which meant the men had done something to coerce her. He'd kill Fraser. Even if Elspeth *had* gone willingly. He'd kill the man with the black pearl too. He'd kill them all. "I don't believe it."

"Nor I," Cormac said.

Aidan's nod for his twin was brusque, but a powerful wash of relief drove it. He had Cormac's support as much as he ever did.

Though Aidan read suspicion in Angus's eyes, the farmer only shrugged, saying, "That's what happens to women. They get carted away to husbands not of their choosing."

Aidan could bear it no longer—his rage finally erupted. "Good God, man. Maybe that's what happened to *your* woman. Not to mine."

Icy fury stole across Angus's features. He stood, staring at Aidan with dead eyes.

Aidan knew he'd spoken out of turn, and part of him hoped the farmer might fight him because of it. He'd welcome a good bout of fisticuffs—anything was preferable to this inaction. But the man only stared in frozen silence, and so Aidan spun, heading in the direction of Aberdeen.

"I'll take you." Cormac stopped him, his voice demanding.

Aidan looked over his shoulder. "What?"

"I'll take you," Cormac repeated. "Aberdeen is miles from here. It'd be hours on foot." He nodded toward the water. "My fishing boat's docked just yonder. I'll take you to Justice Port."

"And I'll go with you," Angus said in a quiet baritone. The MacAlpin men gaped at the farmer in disbelief, but Angus only dusted off his hands, dismay and irritation settling on his usually stoic features. "I don't ken what's afoot, but I do know Miss Elspeth. She's a good egg, and if her sot of a father has put her in harm's way, then I'd be happy to come to her aid."

If the offer hadn't changed his opinion of Angus, the way the man snatched up his farm tools would have. He grabbed what looked like a reaping hook and a shepherd's crook, wielding one in each hand with as much ardor as another might wield weapons.

Aidan raised a brow in question, and Angus nodded to Aidan's sword. "Better than your blade."

Cormac laughed low. "When you make your mind up about a thing, you really commit, don't you?"

The farmer only shrugged in answer, already headed down the path to the shore.

"It's a quick sail," Cormac said as they caught up to him. "She's slower than your sloop—"

"But all the better to navigate the harbor," Aidan finished, knowing how tight the Aberdeen slips were. "You'll just drop us. Even if you did have warrant to dock, since the trouble you caused—"

"*We* caused," Cormac corrected.

"Aye." Aidan shot him a grin. "Since the trouble *we* caused, I think you'd best make haste away from port before we're recognized."

As they neared their destination, Aidan's heart went to his throat. There was a gaping stretch where the *Endeavor* had been docked. "They're gone."

"You don't know that," Cormac said, rowing to an empty patch of harbor.

Angus scowled. "He's a sailor too? I thought this Fraser was a knit merchant."

"*He* doesn't have a boat." Aidan leaped onto the pier, followed by Angus. "His partner does. A ship."

The ship that'd stolen him away, so many years ago. And now it was out there somewhere, stealing his Elspeth away. He shook off the feeling, thinking he needed to gather himself, battening down emotion as he'd furl a boat's sail.

"Good luck," Cormac told him. "Whoever this pirate is, I couldn't save you from him. But I know you can save Elspeth now."

Aidan reached down to clasp Cormac's hand. "Thank you."

When he turned to Angus, the man was watching him with startlingly sharp eyes. It gave him the unsettling sensation that the farmer could read him like a book. Aidan had completely mistaken him—he was no dullard at all. He gave him a grim smile, eyeing the man's farm tools. "Your weapons?"

Hefting the awkward tools in his hands, Angus headed up the pier, an answering grin spreading slowly across his face. "There are weapons all around. The best are the ones least likely."

Aidan shook his head with a quick laugh. "So it is, farmer."

As Angus's smile faded, it struck Aidan how that'd been the first glimpse of humor he'd ever seen on the man's face. He wondered if it would be the last. Trying to get a bead on him, Aidan watched as he tucked the reaping hook in the belt of his *breacan feile* and strolled on, using the shepherd's crook as a walking stick.

An errant thought struck him, carried on a surge of irrational jealousy. "What's an oat farmer doing with a tool suited for *sheep*?"

"I don't want your woman, MacAlpin." Angus didn't break his stride. "Don't be a fool. She doesn't want me, or my gifts. Never has. I was going to find something to trade her for it."

"Why?" he asked, skeptical. Lately, he was of the mind that all men would surely fall in love with Elspeth, if they'd but open their eyes to her.

"I've seen how Farquharson treats the lass, as I'm sure you have. And, like you, I don't much like it."

Elspeth had told him of Angus and Anya's thwarted affair, and remembering it, he gave the farmer a grudging nod. The man had known Elspeth for years before Aidan had even met her.

Somebody stood at the head of the pier, leaning casually against one of its rotted wooden piles. Though his back was to them, Aidan could tell by his broad shoulders and soiled overcoat that he was the sort of lowlife who knew the goings-on dockside.

"When'd the *Endeavor* cast off?" Too late Aidan recognized him as the yeoman with the shining bald head he'd met in a tavern weeks ago. He was Fraser's man, and the one who'd led Aidan to the merchant in the first place. "I'm looking for the Bishop," he added, hoping the casual use of Fraser's dockside identity would win him the information he wanted.

"The Bishop's off to Arbroath," the yeoman said, turning around. "And what business is it of yours?" He pinned Aidan with a squint. "Do I know you?"

Aidan felt bodies gathering behind him. He was grateful to sense Angus too, coming to stand at his shoulder.

Recognition dawned, and the yeoman's squint turned to a glare. "I *do* know you. We was told to keep an eye out for you."

"For me?" Though Aidan pretended bemused innocence, his hand migrated closer to his sword hilt. How would Fraser know to look out for *him*?

"Aye, we was told a man would come round, chasing after Bishop's ship like a fox on a rabbit's tail. So, chasing the Bishop's rabbit, are ye?"

The men behind him laughed, sidling closer.

There was no more pretending. Standing tall, Aidan wrapped his hand around his sword hilt, wondering what the farmer planned to do with a damned shepherd's crook and hoping it'd be a better weapon than it looked. "Maybe I am. Did he leave with her?"

"Aye, 'twas his bride. And we was told to stop any who tried to interfere." The yeoman popped his knuckles. His fingers were fat, like sausages, to match his thick neck.

Aidan dared not glance back to determine how many stood behind them, but he estimated there were three additional men, at least. He could easily take down two, if nobody carried a musket. He hoped Angus could handle himself, relying on his brawn alone if that's what it took. He had no idea how the man fought, but Angus was a farmer, and Aidan had to assume he'd no experience in a brawl.

But as Aidan was strategizing, damned if Angus didn't shock him by taking action, his face as stoic as ever.

The farmer snagged the yeoman's thick neck in his shepherd's crook and snapped it in, knocking the yeoman to his knees. Angus cracked him over the head, then blindly thrust back, jabbing a man behind him in the belly. He spun and jabbed again, getting the second man in the throat. A flurry of sure and rapid movements, and no more than five seconds later, Angus was standing over two downed men.

Aidan laughed, and the sound of it sent another, younger man running.

He and Angus joined back-to-back to face the other two men. "Where'd you learn to fight like that, farmer?"

"Reaping oats is hard work."

Aidan chuckled. He was going to like having this Angus as a neighbor. "So I see."

Uncertainty was a needle in his heart. *Would* they be neighbors, or was he too late? Was Elspeth bound to another man already? The reminder of what was at stake focused him, and he and Angus easily dispatched the remaining two men.

Aidan's senses were attuned, and movement on the harbor above caught his eye. He strained, making out a familiar figure. The person seemed to want to move both briskly and unnoticed, which only served to make him all the more conspicuous.

"I see him too," Angus said. Both men broke into an easy lope up the harbor, headed for Elspeth's father.

Aidan resheathed his sword. "Curious, no?" The old man looked back, and seeing that they followed, broke into a doddering run. "Almost like he feels guilty about something."

"I'll hear the man out before I jump to any conclusions," Angus said.

Aidan shot him a wry look. "That's right. Just an innocent farmer, you are."

They easily caught up to Farquharson, and Aidan

hopped in front of him, barring his path. "Leave something behind? Your daughter perhaps?"

The old man's lip twitched. "Give it up, boy. She's good as married."

"To a criminal," Aidan said.

"To a man of means." Elspeth's father spotted Angus and glanced nervously from him to Aidan. He took a step back, settling his sneer on Aidan. "My girl went on a grand ship, and without you."

"Your girl was taken, and on the same tub that stole *me* as a child. Tell me, where's the honor in that?"

Farquharson spat. "What do you know of honor, slave boy?"

Aidan felt a half smile curl his lips. The man could fling every insult imaginable, but he was impervious. "I know Elspeth has more honor in her little finger than you ever will in your entire body."

"A lucky thing, that. Seeing as you did your all to sully her virtue. The girl's lucky Fraser took her—"

Aidan punched him. He stopped the man's words with his fist, marking the second time he'd struck Elspeth's father. He'd strike him again, and again if need be, if that was what it took to school him about his daughter's worth.

He shook out his fist. "Don't you realize? You just sent Elspeth off with a pirate, a kidnapper. I know the *Endeavor* well. Pray your daughter isn't shackled as I was on my introductory voyage."

Something flashed in her father's eyes. Aidan hoped it was a flicker of humanity finally dawning.

Aidan offered his hand, pulling Farquharson to standing. Keeping his voice calm and slow, he asked, "Where did he take her?"

The old man didn't answer, and Angus stepped forward, until the two of them loomed tall over him. It seemed Elspeth's father was trying the farmer's patience too.

"Tell me, old man," Aidan demanded. "Where?"

Farquharson shook his head in defeat. "To his estate in Arbroath. They'll be wed by nightfall." Then he pursed his lips, looking away into the distance.

Aidan hoped her father was praying for forgiveness. Because at that moment, forgiveness wasn't something Aidan had in his heart to give. "The man you chose for your daughter could as easily hang from a gibbet as make his fortune." He turned to Angus. "You see this one home, before he does any more damage."

Aidan strode away, headed north up the harbor, to where he'd docked his sloop.

"Where are you going?" Farquharson shouted after him.

"To stop a wedding."

Chapter 34

The reality of Elspeth's situation was upon her. Traveling by boat was a horrid affair, nothing like what she'd experienced with Aidan on his sloop.

At least the mystery of the man with the black pearl was finally solved. She stared at Captain Will. She'd expected the most fearsome of pirates, but he was average. Neither tall nor short. Not particularly hideous, nor was he so very well formed. The only thing that stood out was the black pearl dangling from his right ear.

And somehow it was this lack of exceptionality that was the root of his menace. His eyes were cold but his smile came easy, and she had the disturbing sensation that a horrible secret lay cloaked behind that placid mien. If she found him so unsettling, what must a young boy like Aidan have felt?

A howl echoed from the ship's hold, and she flinched. Even seated in the captain's quarters, she smelled the

Endeavor's stink of pitch and mildew, and the cries of men locked below carried clearly to her ears, making her blood run cold.

Even more chilling was the knowledge that she was traveling on the very ship that'd stolen Aidan away, so many years ago.

Aidan. He'd come for her. She knew it. He'd arrive, greater than any hero from any book. Sailing alongside, he'd toss grappling hooks into their rigging and swoop on deck like the most fearsome of Barbadian raiders. He'd create choices where there were none, revealing some pirate treasure he'd buried away.

Captain Will had been staring at her and apparently saw something in her expression that he found distasteful.

"Damnable situation," the captain muttered. He stood and closed the distance to where Fraser sat. He approached too closely, towering over the merchant, forcing him to crane his neck upward. "You'll pay for this little detour. I'm not in business to take you out for a honeymoon sail." He cast a thoughtful look at Fraser's heavy suitcase, stroking the pearl in his ear all the while. "And I don't like having a woman aboard. The men fear naught but ill fortune can come of it."

Fraser leaned back, affecting amiability. "Not superstitious, are you?"

The captain glared, freezing Fraser's easy laugh in his throat.

Elspeth watched the captain carefully. The way he tightened his jaw ever so slightly, set his shoulders ever so stiffly, showed him in a new light. She'd wager he was superstitious indeed. Very much so.

"No good comes of a woman on board." Again, he absentmindedly rubbed his earring, and she wondered if the strange trinket weren't actually some sort of talisman. His good-luck charm. "*And* it's Friday. One never begins a voyage on a Friday."

"We're almost there, and no evil has come to pass," Fraser assured him. "Your superstitions are for naught. Such are merely the misguided notions of fishwives and aging sailors."

Will's expression cleared, and though he once again made himself unreadable, Elspeth fancied it was only a ruse. He gave a cool nod. "As you say. You are the man with the money, are you not?"

She didn't believe his acquiescence for one moment and studied him, looking for more clues. He was well kempt, but not a dandy, and she imagined that his innocuous mask made it as easy for him to wend his way through the wealthiest drawing rooms as to skulk into the grittiest of dockside pubs.

"You stare," he said, walking toward her.

She startled, caught in the act, and quickly looked away. "Do I?" She had the wild hope that some shipboard emergency might call him back above deck. He might appear utterly average, but she was more afraid of him than of any man she'd ever met. "I apologize."

"No need for apology, I assure you. But I wonder. Is it that I've caught your fancy?" He took her chin in his fingers, tilting her face to the light. It had the effect of illuminating him too, highlighting a clean overcoat of decent fabric and a full head of combed but graying hair. "For I find you've caught mine."

He grew silent, studying her. "How unusual—you've yellow in your eyes. But of course you already knew that." Their eyes connected, and gooseflesh crawled across her skin. He seemed to look deeply into her soul. "Yellow eyes . . . I wonder, what could that augur?"

So he *was* superstitious. She prayed that yellow eyes signaled something lucky, because she didn't want to find herself walking the plank. Her eyes flashed again to the pearl in his ear. She imagined he'd be lost without it.

He smiled, and for an instant, he looked no more

menacing than a benign uncle. But then his eyes went
flat, like a snake's. "Pity you're to be wed to my partner."
He raised a brow. "Unless you'd change your mind?"

She gave a shy shake to her head. Captain Will was
infinitely more frightening than Fraser ever could be.

He chuckled. "Not interested in becoming a pirate
bride?"

Just not your pirate bride. For once, she had the words
ready on her tongue, but chose not to speak them.

But then a wild notion struck her. Her gaze skittered
over that shining pearl, and she gave a coy shrug.

"Could it be? Our maiden is uncertain?" The captain
leaned closer, his eyes locked with hers. "Yellow," he
murmured, the whispered word hot on her mouth. "Perhaps for the blue and yellow of fair skies . . ."

"What is this?" Fraser sputtered. She felt his presence
from across the room, vibrating with anger.

Captain Will smiled. "This is your bride having second thoughts."

Time seemed to stop as she summoned every last shred
of her courage. Holding her breath, she reached a tentative hand out. Her heart thudded so, she thought surely
he'd be able to spy the pulse in her neck. She grazed a
finger along the captain's cheek, and then touched him
again with her whole hand. She stroked his face, keeping
her eyes wide on his so he might not forget their strange
yellow flecks.

Her fingers were close, so close. She *would be* courageous. She'd strike at the very heart of the evil pirate. She
raked her hands through his hair. He chuckled, a husky
sound, so she dared it again. And this time she lingered
over his ears. She stroked some more, and with each pass,
grazed his black pearl. "My da always said sunlight followed in my wake."

She was close to her goal, but needed to push herself
further, to leap from the precipice. She parted her lips on

a sigh, and his mouth closed in. His teeth knocked into hers, and she clamped her eyes shut tight, fighting the urge to shudder with revulsion.

Feigning passion, she made herself return the kiss, writhing in his arms, all the while raking her fingers through his hair, stroking his cheeks.

A commotion on deck distracted him. He pulled away, and she refrained from smearing the back of her hand along her mouth. "You're a peculiar wee minx," he said, cupping her jaw. "They say women aboard ship are bad luck, unless naked. What say you, minx? Are you ready to be naked? Because I think I might like to keep you."

"I think I might not let you." She'd tried to adopt a saucy tone, but her voice trembled, and she hoped he'd take it for excitement, not fear. For in her palm was nestled a single, black pearl.

Barking a laugh, he pushed her chin from his hand.

Men shouted on deck—words sounding like "land, ho!"—and Captain Will went to peer out the porthole.

"You'll excuse me," he said. Giving her a regal bow, he added, "I regret I'll not have more time to convince you. I didn't believe Fraser when he told me. But I see now, it is the still waters which flow the deepest."

As he left, Elspeth's chest shuddered with a quiet sigh of relief.

Fraser glared at her, clearly uncertain what to make of her little scene with the captain, and then he rose to peer out the porthole for himself. "I see by your salacious behavior that you're familiar with a man's touch." He kept his back to her as he spoke, staring out at the water. "I've not asked where you spent last night—I thought I'd spare you the discomfort. For now. Your paramour's identity will be discovered in time."

He stepped aside, pinning her with a flat stare, but all she saw was the hazy silhouette of land in the distance.

They were about to dock in Arbroath, and yet there

was still no sign of Aidan. No grappling hooks, no shots off the starboard bow.

Where was he? She was spinning a wild tale, casting herself as heroine, and needed her hero now more than ever.

What if he thought she wanted this wedding? Even *she'd* convinced herself that marrying Fraser was her only option, that he'd provide financial salvation for her and her father, saving them from the poorhouse.

Even so, Aidan would still come for her. He'd sweep her into his arms, and steal her away, telling her with a kiss that she belonged to none but him.

But they disembarked, and they were whisked into a carriage, and they were taken to Fraser's property, yet there was no Aidan.

"The minister will be here soon," Fraser said. He'd set her up in a dismal salon in his so-called grand Arbroath estate, which was naught but a dank, drafty seaside manor.

She pulled her arisaid tight around her shoulders. "You've never seen reason to take a bride before. Of all women, why *me*?"

He gave her an oily smile. "You've the mind of a man, but the body of a woman."

She recoiled. "You don't seem to think much of the female sex."

"I've never seen the need for a wife before, no. But despite your plain ways, you strike me as brighter than the others. Over time, you'll come to see how like-minded we are." His gaze slithered down her body, then back up again. "I imagine we'll be well matched in other ways too."

She'd agreed to this union to save herself and her father from the poorhouse. But surely there was no worse fate than the one she faced now. "Do you expect me to take your words for a compliment?"

"Aye, and to be grateful for it."

She no longer took pains to hide her disgust. She'd spent a lifetime being grateful for scraps, now she was expected to be thankful for casual indignities as well? This man was a louse, a scoundrel. She'd not marry him, even if it meant she'd have to end her days as a charwoman on a faraway plantation.

She needed Aidan. Surely he'd come to stop this madness, to save her. She only hoped he'd forgive her. What she'd done was dreadful. In thinking this union was the only way to get free of debt, she'd sold Aidan short. Because they could figure anything out, if only they were together.

But her life would end the moment the minister arrived. He would perform the ceremony, even though the banns hadn't been proclaimed. And then she'd be wed for good.

She'd not make a second mistake—she wouldn't let it happen. She'd trust Aidan was coming for her, and she'd hold on until he did. She'd be a worthy pirate bride and help save herself.

Stall him. She racked her brain for an excuse to keep Fraser talking. "What if I've changed my mind? What if I don't want to marry you after all?"

Fraser laughed. Looking bored, he stood to take a turn around the room. "You've no choice."

"What if I do?" As long as Aidan was alive, she had a choice. They could sail away, live off the fruits of the sea, docking in uninhabited isles and charmingly exotic ports.

"Are you thinking of someone else?" He stopped his pacing to give her a pointed look. "I assure you, *I* am the only man with means enough to save your family."

Fraser spoke the truth, and she hated him for it. In destroying her home, he'd taken her options. He stepped closer, putting words to her thoughts. "Only through our marriage will your father be spared the poorhouse."

She shot upright in her seat. "A poorhouse you put him in yourself."

"A man does as he must," he said with a rueful shrug. "But now I am ready to pull you from the ashes, as it were."

"Does as he must?" Her eyes widened. "So you confess it? You set the fire?"

"I am capable of many things. Think of it as a lesson. And I've another one to teach you tonight, after we're wed." Fraser stroked a finger down her cheek.

She shuddered and looked away, unable to bear the sight of him.

He thought she had no choice, but she did, and she would make it. The greatest of heroines endured tragedy and overcame. And so would she.

"Thinking of our wedding night?"

Standing, she strode around him to the window. "You could say that."

Keeping her back to him, she dug her fingers down the front of her bodice, tying a few extra knots into her laces. *And a little insurance never hurt.*

He came to stand at her back, and she gripped the sill, staring blindly out the window. He traced a finger down her spine, making her flesh crawl. "You must relax yourself, settle into the notion. I always get what I want, Elspeth."

Not *everything* he wanted. Not this time.

Her eyes snapped into focus. There was a boat on the horizon. Could it be Aidan? She just needed to hold on.

A bell rang on the floor below, and voices carried up to them.

"The minister," he said with a smile. Fraser proffered his arm. "Are you ready to become the Lady Fraser?"

Her heart thundered in her chest. The moment was upon her. She strained, looking back out the window, but saw nothing but a white-and-gray haze.

What if that *were* Aidan, coming for her on his sloop? She needed to wait for him. Needed to delay, for him.

She sidled away from Fraser. "You won't get *everything* you want, you know."

His expression narrowed. "And what is it I'm to be denied, Elspeth?"

"My maidenhead." She swooped behind an armchair, bracing herself on its back as if it might guard her. "I'm no longer a virgin."

"So I've gathered." He shook his head, looking amused. "I'm no fool."

"Even now, I might carry his child."

Anger hardened his features. He stalked toward her. "Then we'll find a way to slip the babe."

She dashed to the door, leaping for the knob. "I'll escape."

He cut her off, slamming and bolting it shut. "Do I need to teach you your lesson *before* we're wed? I can be quite an unforgiving teacher, ready to school you all the day long."

A gunshot rang out. *Aidan.* It had to be him. He'd arrived. He was coming for her.

She heard voices raised in the hallway. She hadn't been the only one to hear the shot.

"You think *he's* coming, don't you?" Fraser prowled closer, reaching out to grab her arm. "But he can't save you now."

She ran to the hearth, but the only tool at hand was a bellows. She snatched it up, holding it before her like a shield. "I'll fight you."

He laughed. "Little fool. The time has come. There's no avoiding it."

She felt like a caged animal. Her eyes flicked to the locked door. "The moment you open those doors, I'll run."

Slowly, he began to remove his overcoat. "Then I'll simply have to restrain you," he said, his voice gone steely. "I'd feared this, and so borrowed a little something from our good captain."

He picked up the heavy suitcase he'd been carrying and opened it. Dull metal glimmered within.

Shackles? "You wouldn't."

"What I do is up to you. Will you succumb willingly, or must I bind you to make you say the words *I do*?"

There was another gunshot. The voices in the hallway grew louder. Someone jiggled the doorknob. Fraser glanced from his suitcase to the door, weighing his next move.

Her body trembled with desperate energy. There was nothing left to her but extreme measures. It seemed Fraser wanted her to bow to him, so bow she must.

She let the bellows slip from her fingers and fluttered a hand over her brow as she slumped against the back of the sofa. Inhaling deeply, she lent a dramatic quaver to her voice. "You win. I shall yield."

Growing eerily still, Fraser gaped at her, looking as though he didn't trust his ears. "You surrender to me?"

Her face flushed hot. *Never.* But she had a charade to maintain, and so forced herself to speak the words. "Yes, you may begin your . . . lesson, if you must."

Chapter 35

Aidan steered into Arbroath harbor, and though it was far smaller than Aberdeen's, navigating the waterway was simple. Since it was not nearly as thriving a port, dockage was easily had—found just next to a ship he'd recognize better than his own face in the mirror.

The *Endeavor*.

He tied up his sloop, feeling eyes upon him. Rather than glance up, he prolonged the moment, letting the gaze bore into him, steadily going about his work. Because he knew whom he'd find when he looked up.

He'd felt the gaze as a child, and recognized its stillness now. Dead eyes that'd bored into him, raking his soul. But now he was a man, and he knew who he was and what he was about.

Aidan glanced up, finally, his work finished. The man with the black pearl stood at the bow of his ship, docked not twenty feet away, silent as a sphinx and just as unreadable. They stared at each other.

It was his one chance. Captain Will's crew bustled about, readying to cast off. Aidan needed to kill his enemy now—it was what he'd dreamed of doing for most his life. He could lure him away, take him in a sword fight. Aidan had spent the past thirteen years growing bigger, stronger, faster—he knew he'd best the man. Or he could watch him sail away forever, bound for God knew where, never to be seen again.

He could kill his enemy, or he could have Elspeth.

He waited to feel the familiar thirst for vengeance, but found the rage had burned through him. All he wanted now was his Beth.

His choice was clear. Exhilaratingly simple. He'd regret not killing his enemy. But even more would he regret losing her. There was only one thing for him to do. He needed to stop her wedding, before it was too late.

Because he refused to lose her.

Captain Will touched a finger to his head in a mockery of a salute. Only then did their gazes unlock.

Aidan jogged up the harbor, scanning for a likely source of information. He needed to find Fraser's home, and quickly. It was while a dock rat was pointing him in the right direction that he sensed the *Endeavor* get under way at his back.

"I'll just have to avenge you in hell," he murmured, and then raced to find Elspeth.

———

Fraser leaped for her like a starving man spotting a heel of bread.

"So eager you are." She slipped from under his grasp, darting to the window. She stole a peek through the glass, but the ship had sailed past, and though Fraser's house fronted the sea, the view didn't encompass the harbor.

She prayed Aidan was out there. She'd brought this on herself, and regretted it deeply. Why hadn't she waited for him? He'd have helped her find a way clear of her problems without having to marry Fraser.

"If I didn't know better, I'd say you were watching for someone." He approached her from behind, spinning her roughly to face him. "But it's time to attend to *me*."

She sputtered, struggling to formulate yet another excuse. Where was Aidan? In her mind, she urged him to come faster. She was running out of ruses, and didn't know how much longer she could put Fraser off. As it was, her skin crawled and her stomach lurched to be in such close contact. "No . . . I . . ."

"Remember, Elspeth. Will you come to me willingly?" He nodded to his leather satchel, lying open on the floor, revealing the dull metal cuffs. "Or must I make you?"

"I am willing, of course, sir." She held her chin high, as though naught were amiss. "But I find"—once more she slid from his clutches—"you move much too quickly."

He raked an impatient hand through his hair, leaving him looking like an aging madman. "What's the delay?"

"No delay." She watched as his eyes narrowed in suspicion, and quickly added, "It's simply that a woman likes her man . . . to take his time about it." She swallowed hard, feeling revulsion at her own words.

"Take my time?" He snatched her back, his fingers curling painfully into her arms. "You've made me wait long enough."

He dove in to kiss her, but she tipped her chin at the last moment, and his mouth landed on her jaw. Undaunted, he ravaged her neck instead, then, kissing lower, he brought a hand to her breast, cupping her roughly.

He lifted his head to tug at her bodice, and soon discovered the laces were tightly knotted. He pawed and fumbled, demanding, "What have you done? You wretched girl."

She tried to duck away, but this time he wouldn't let her go. Panic consumed her. Never had it dawned on her how weak she really was. He was too strong—she couldn't get away.

Taking both hands to her bodice, he tugged hard, and the front of it began to rip apart. She used the opportunity to wriggle free, and ran to the hearth.

He stalked after her. "You postpone the inevitable, girl."

Her heart was exploding in her chest. She couldn't dash about all night—he'd eventually catch her. And what would happen then?

No, Aidan would come. She knew it. She just needed to keep her wits about her until then. Fight until then.

"Inevitable perhaps." She hopped behind a sofa, putting it between them, and nodded to the window at his back. She forced a coy smile, and it felt like a rictus on her face. "But must we proceed before an open window?"

She could tell by his shifting expression that this mollified him. But there was only so much more stalling she could do before she'd be unable to stop him. He was a man, and just too strong.

"Then I shall take you on the settee," he said.

She pulled her hands from its upholstered back as though they'd been burned. She was light-headed, now, her breath coming in frantic pants.

How would an epic heroine act? What would a heroine do? *Calm.* Her thoughts had grown hysterical, and she forced her mind to calm. Surely, there was a way to overcome. Surely there was a story like this one, a tale of weak triumphing over strong. Like David and Goliath. Or . . .

Her eyes went bright, flicking from settee to side table. And the fat candlestick burning there.

Like David and Goliath. Or Odysseus and Polyphemus. She looked back at the candle, her mind spinning furiously. Odysseus had blinded the giant Cyclops with a flaming stick. She swallowed hard, flexing her hands. She was no Greek hero, but the candle burned brightly, with a thick puddle of hot wax beneath the wick.

Fraser edged around the couch, closing in. But this time, instead of dashing away, she stood her ground.

He jumped for her, and she braced her legs against the back of the sofa, leaning and snatching the candlestick. Molten wax splashed on her thumb, and it burned her, focused her.

She swung for his face. The flame shrank but it didn't go out, making a *whip-whip* sound like a candle in the wind.

She connected, stabbing him in the eye, and he screamed. Hunching into himself, he staggered backward, clutching his face in his hands.

She sprang back, shocked by the contact. Terrified he'd recover, she flung away the candle and grabbed the bellows. She dove for him, swinging it with both hands, slamming the back of his head, a hollow wooden blow that knocked him to the floor.

She stood over his limp body, breathing hard, her heart kicking furiously against her chest. She had overcome him.

There was a loud commotion in the hallway, and her eyes flew to the door. She still gripped the bellows in both hands, as though poised for battle. She heard a man's step, flying up the stairs, and then there was pounding at the door.

"Beth, Beth! Are you in there?"

Aidan.

She raced to unbolt the lock, and Aidan burst into the room. He stood there, sword extended, looking ready to storm the gates of hell. In a split second, his eyes went from her to Fraser's limp body and back again, a broad smile splitting his face. "I told them naught can slip by my Beth."

Relief flooded her, crumpling her legs, and he caught her, snatching her in his arms. He pulled back to kiss her hard, and then clutched her even closer, running his hands along her body, as though to reassure himself that she was safe.

He was there, and she was safe, and suddenly she trembled so violently, feeling cold, like all the blood had drained from her body. She wrapped her arms tightly around him, clinging to his chest. "What took you so long?"

He laughed and tilted her chin up to face him. "*Me?* Could you not have waited for me? Just an hour, Beth?"

It seemed an easy thing, now, to have waited for Aidan. But she'd been so distraught by the scene at her farm, so frightened.

"I'm sorry. I . . . I didn't know what to do. My father had me so confused." Her foolishness had almost ruined everything. She should've trusted that Aidan could take care of things. She should've stood up to her father. "I thought if I didn't marry him, he might come after you."

"You're only allowed to marry one man, and that's me." He shot a disdainful look at Fraser lying in a heap on the floor. "And besides, you thought I couldn't stand up to *that*?"

"He has all the dock men in his pocket, and so much wealth, and, well . . ." She slumped against him. "I just always make such a mess of things."

"Mess? I don't know about any mess." He cupped her chin, sweeping his thumb along her cheek. "I will grant you one thing. You appear to have made a mess of me."

He leaned down for a kiss. It was slow and gentle, spreading warmth in a gentle pulse through her body. With Aidan holding her, no longer was she shaking and cold. She felt instinctively that everything would work out—the farm, her father, all would be sorted to rights. She wrapped her hand around the strong column of his neck, feeling how safe, how right it was to have her pirate rogue by her side.

Her muscles seized. She pulled away on a gasp, remembering. "But what of your pirate with the black pearl? I met him—he was docked *here*. Did you see him, get him?"

He gave a rueful shrug. "It was you or him, Beth. I chose you."

She pushed away, not believing her ears. "But you've always dreamed of besting him, of having your revenge."

He grabbed her, pulling her close with a light thump against his chest. "Don't you see how happy you've made me? No, Captain Will shall live to see another day, and I've made my peace with it. You see, I had a wedding to stop." He kissed her gently on the forehead, and with a wink, added, "And now I've one to attend."

He glanced toward the door, but none of the servants were brave enough to show their faces. With a squeeze he let her go. "I hear there's a minister about. We need to fetch him. There's only going to be one marriage today and it'll be yours and mine."

She grabbed his arm to stop him, and he paused, looking down at her, his brow raised in question.

"I have a wedding gift for you first." She rustled through her skirts, then proffered her open hand, where a luminous black pearl lay nestled in her palm.

He gave her a puzzled look, then touched it with a tentative fingertip. "I don't understand. Is it . . . ?"

"Yes," she said proudly, pursing her lips so as not to smile too widely. "I pried it from his ear."

"You did no such thing!" He laughed and shook his head. "Truly? You just . . . took it? How?"

"I was forced to kiss him, *but it was not*," she interjected quickly, seeing the rage cloud his face, "not so very long a kiss. And it was in front of Fraser."

"Mm-hm." He nodded, seeming unsure what to make of it.

"It was an old thing, you see. And ill made. It slid easily from his ear."

Awe replaced the anger in his eyes. "You clever girl."

She gave a shy shrug, even though his words made her proud beyond reckoning. She held the pearl up to the window to study it. It was shiny and irregularly shaped, with a greenish cast in the light. "He seems a superstitious sort. He kept rubbing it, which led me to think . . . I believe he thought this held off evil spirits. A talisman of sorts."

Aidan laughed hard then, alternately clutching her close and pushing apart to admire the pearl. The noise roused Fraser, who was beginning to stir and moan on the floor.

Aidan wrapped his broad hand around hers, closing it in a fist around the pearl. He nodded to the merchant. "We need to tie up that one."

"I know just the thing," she said brightly, heading straight for Fraser's suitcase and his grim cargo. She pulled out a pair of steel cuffs, dangling them. "Shall we throw away the key?"

He laughed again. "You're full of surprises. I only regret that the *Endeavor* has left port." He knelt to shackle Fraser's hands. "I've half a mind to put this one in the hold so he can spend the rest of his days laboring on some other man's plantation."

She sighed, regretful of one thing. "I'm sorry you couldn't get Captain Will."

"You'll get your chance," a voice announced from the doorway.

She startled, but Aidan only froze, as though turned to stone. Standing in the doorway was the man with the black pearl, and he was seething.

Above that normal body, those normal clothes, his face

was distorted into a mask of rage. Elspeth's eyes were drawn downward, and her flesh crawled to see the weapon dangling from his hand. He held a large ax—a sailor's boarding ax—its flat head tapering into a lethally sharp spike. She knew such a thing was used as both tool and weapon, to hack through rigging, to hook and drag timber across deck, to climb and board another ship. And, of course, to slaughter men.

"So happy you could join us," Aidan said. He rose, unsheathing his sword. "I've been dreaming of this for thirteen long years."

But the captain ignored him, glaring only at Elspeth. "I believe you took something of mine. I'll not leave without it." He strolled toward her, swinging that gruesome weapon. "And I've had second thoughts. I think I might take you with me after all."

"No." Aidan stepped in front of her. "You won't."

The captain peered at him, as though seeing him for the first time. His lips peeled into a slow smile. "I see the little chimney rat has grown up." He scanned up and down Aidan's body, sneering at the sword in his hand. "You overreach, boy."

With a feral growl, Aidan attacked, slashing his sword down hard, but the captain grabbed his ax in both hands—one gripping the base, one the head—stopping the blade with its handle.

Aidan pressed forward, feinting and thrusting. "And you're overmatched," he said, slashing diagonally again and again.

"You won't beat me, chimney boy." The captain bobbed back, blocking the onslaught with the handle of his weapon. "You're naught but chattel to sell at market."

"And you're naught but an aging cur." Aidan had him pinned in the corner, and Elspeth inched as close as possible to watch.

"Well suited, we are. Both men without homes." The

captain edged along the wall, and spun free of the trap. Suddenly it was Aidan who found himself in the corner, his sword useless at so close a range. "The difference is, you're a man without options."

Elspeth gasped then clamped her hand over her mouth. She dared not create a distraction. Her eyes flitted across the room, looking for some weapon, some way to help. Her head buzzed with energy, her body quivering with the need to act.

The captain switched his ax to one hand and hauled back for the kill. "But now it's time for you to die."

Captain Will swung, and though the ax was lethal, it was clumsy, too, and Aidan managed to duck out of its path. The captain swung again, and again Aidan managed to dodge him.

But with no shield for blocking, Aidan would soon tire of hopping to and fro. Soon the blow would come that he'd be unable to evade.

She scanned the room again, and this time her eyes lit on the bellows. Not a shield, but better than nothing. "Here," she called, tossing it to him.

The captain laughed, swatting the ax leisurely in the flat of his palm. "A bellows? Think you to gust and puff me to death?" Face freezing into a grimace, he exploded to action, and this time when he swung, the bellows stopped his blow.

"To death? You misunderstand me." Aidan pried his impromptu shield free and darted around the captain. A quick glance showed that though it was edged in metal, the bellows had been hacked halfway through. "I won't kill you. I'll see you suffer as I have."

Aidan prowled toward the captain, a cold smile on his face, and at the last minute, threw the bellows at him. The pirate was momentarily distracted, and Aidan slashed his sword deeply across the man's torso.

Captain Will looked in disbelieving horror at his belly.

"Gutted like a fish," he said with eerie calm. He raised his ax to strike, but his swing was awkward.

Aidan blocked, then knocked the ax from the pirate's hand. He shoved the man to his knees. "And caught like one."

Aidan glanced at Fraser's suitcase, and Elspeth understood at once. She retrieved a second pair of shackles, this one more elaborate, with four cuffs connected by long lengths of chain suited for hands and feet. "But don't you want to kill him?" she asked quietly.

"And spare others the pleasure of watching him swing from the gallows?" He used the butt of his sword to knock the man onto his haunches. "Nor would I rob him of the many pleasures he has in store. First, I'm going to sell that pretty pearl, and rather than use it to pay for his burial, I've a mind to split the money among the men in his hold."

The captain's head was lolling now, and he looked ready to topple.

Aidan clicked the first metal cuff around the man's wrist. "Extra tight, aye? Don't fret—the bleeding will stop in a few weeks' time, and the skin will toughen nicely. Trust me. Eventually, you won't feel pain through the scars. If you evade the noose for that long."

As Aidan opened the second cuff, Captain Will sprang up.

Elspeth shrieked.

Despite his bloody belly, there was fire in the captain's eyes, and he leaped onto Aidan, winding the metal chain about his neck. "I'll teach you pain."

"You've already taught me." He kneed the pirate in the gut, and his breeches came back bloodied. "It's a lesson I've mastered," he managed to say through gritted teeth.

Aidan kneed again, and again, but the man remained standing, his face flushed crimson with the effort of keeping the chain coiled tightly around Aidan's neck.

Elspeth watched in horror as the captain merely stood there, clinging to the chain, refusing to fall. Aidan's lips were a ghastly shade of blue, his skin mottled white and red. There was something strange about his body, and she realized he wasn't breathing.

Fight. She willed him to fight, and knew she needed to fight too. She ran for the damaged bellows, but Aidan took action before she could.

He butted his head forward, slamming his forehead into the pirate's nose. The man's grip on the chain slackened, and Aidan pounced toward him. He snatched the captain's head at the jaw and forehead, and with a quick yank, snapped his neck. Captain Will's body crashed to the floor, its deadweight making an ungainly, thundering sound, like firewood tumbling from a stack.

Aidan unwound the chain from his throat, coughing and gasping for air. He nudged the man's body with his foot. "I've mastered the lesson, but now it's time for me to move on."

His eyes sought hers, and seeing Elspeth's trauma, he ran to her, cradling her in his arms. He swallowed hard, and it looked painful. "I'm all right. I've suffered far worse."

She chafed freezing hands along his arms. "You must lie down," she insisted, tugging him to the settee.

"I'll do no such thing." His hoarse chuckle turned into another round of coughing. "I told you, luvvie, the only place I'm going is to fetch the minister."

He spun her to face him, his eyes glittering with intensity. "Your father can hunt me, he can challenge me all he dares. But I will claim you, Beth. I've voice enough to speak vows, and I *will* wed you before the sun goes down."

The words were more exhilarating than any she could've imagined from any storybook. His eyes sparked with intent, his desire only for her. All she could do was manage a nod in answer.

He swept her into his arms, pulling her from her feet in a kiss. She tasted salt on his lips, and for a moment, she was his pirate bride, and the sea their kingdom.

Too soon he pulled from her. "I will make you mine. But first, I must go and do one more thing."

She knew instantly what he was about. "You're going to free the slaves." At his nod, she told him, "I'm coming with you. We'll do it together."

"I hoped you'd say that," he said, taking her hand in his. His grip was warm and sure.

She began to speak. "Because from now on—"

"We do everything together," Aidan said, completing her thought as surely as he'd completed her.

Epilogue

Aidan sat with Elspeth, nestled cozily on a bed of hay, in the makeshift barn Angus had helped him build.

Elspeth. *His wife.*

When he returned from the Indies, he thought he'd suffered all a man could suffer. Had lost all there was a man could lose. Until he'd met and almost lost *her.*

She held a baby lamb in her lap, carefully clearing the animal's eyes. "It seems a peculiar flaw to be born with one's eyelashes poking into one's eyes."

The creatures were tiny and helpless, but like many lambs, they'd been born with their lashes in their eyes. And, piteous as it was, Aidan adored watching her care for them.

He brushed a hand along its downy white wool. "They don't seem to suffer for it. And besides, what creature wouldn't want your kindly ministrations?"

Elspeth looked up at him with a smile. She'd donned

her spectacles, and they were slipping down the bridge of her nose. The sight of her rumpled and bookish appearance stabbed his heart through with tenderness.

He gently pushed her glasses up for her and cleared the hair from her brow. "If only we had a real barn for such work."

"The new place will be finished soon enough," she said. "You've been working so hard—too hard. I regret that my father can't find it in his heart to share any of his newfound riches."

"Riches indeed. Who knew the Crown gave such hearty rewards?"

After Aidan left him at the dock, her father had had second thoughts and reported Fraser to the constable. And though the law hadn't given two figs for the safety of some farmer's daughter, they were quite interested in the tale of someone trading men for goods so as to avoid the Crown's taxes.

"Well, he's out of my hair," she said, "and finally managing on his own."

"And in a flat close to his favorite Aberdeen tavern." He saw a shadow cross her brow—guilt? melancholy?—and he chucked her chin. "Don't worry for your father. Nor for us. What we got was reward enough," he said, referring to the bounty both he and Angus had received for their part in stopping Fraser and Captain Will.

Angus had felt guilty about the whole matter—Aidan got the impression the man liked to keep a low profile—and so had given Elspeth a half-dozen sheep, two of which were breeding, in addition to pledging his help with their rebuilding.

"And besides," he added, cupping her cheek, "all this bounty means I can be alone with you. Until a bairn comes."

She laughed, knowing as well as he with what diligence they'd been working on *that* matter. She placed her hand over his. "Oh, husband, how glad I am that you came home, to Scotland, and not some other, more distant shore."

"*You're* my home." He removed the lamb from her lap, pulling Elspeth onto his instead. "And we have so much to start anew."

The lamb cried, standing unsteadily on spindly legs. Elspeth cooed and petted it, a smile in her voice.

But when Aidan eyed the creature, he saw something else, and said with a sniff, "I don't like Angus giving you all these sheep. The man gives you too many gifts."

She shot him a startled look. "Never before has Angus thought to give me a thing in his life!"

"Mm-hm." He grabbed her hand and kissed her wrist. His wife had no idea just how appealing she could be to a man. Especially now with a bloom in her cheeks, and in her fetching new gown. But it was time for her to pay attention to *him*. He began to kiss up her arm.

She gave him a playful squeeze, her mind clearly still on the sheep. "We need to name them all. Aphrodite perhaps," she said, studying the wee lamb, now looking amusingly bereft. Elspeth giggled. "She does have such very long lashes. Very comely."

Nuzzling her neck, he seated her more firmly in his lap. His intentions were unmistakable. "You're the only Aphrodite," he told her, kissing up her throat, along her cheeks.

Their eyes caught, and he saw his intent matched in her gaze. The rest of the world—their farm, their cares—everything fell away, until it was just the two of them. Aidan reached around to untie her spectacles. Pulling them off, he marveled at how lovely her eyes were. How wise, and sweet, and all-seeing. "You're the only goddess here. And you're mine."

Don't miss the *New York Times* bestseller from
MADELINE HUNTER

Provocative in Pearls

Their marriage was arranged, but their desire was not . . .

After two years, the Earl of Hawkeswell has located his
missing bride, heiress Verity Thompson. Coerced into
marrying Hawkeswell by her duplicitous cousin, Verity
fled London for the countryside. Now, the couple must
make the most of an arranged marriage—even if it
means surrendering to their shared desire.

THE NEW VICTORIAN HISTORICAL
ROMANCE NOVEL FROM
USA TODAY BESTSELLING AUTHOR

JENNIFER ASHLEY

Lady Isabella's Scandalous Marriage

Lady Isabella Scranton scandalized London by leaving
her husband, notorious artist Lord Mac Mackenzie, after only three turbulent years of marriage. But Mac has
a few tricks to get the lady back in his life, and more
importantly, back into his bed.

"I adore this novel."

—Eloisa James, *New York Times* bestselling author

penguin.com

M713T0510

Enter the rich world of
historical romance
with Berkley Books . . .

Madeline Hunter

Jennifer Ashley

Joanna Bourne

Lynn Kurland

Jodi Thomas

Anne Gracie

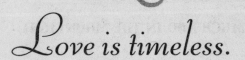

Love is timeless.

berkleyjoveauthors.com